D1714749

Songs in the Year of the Cat

Book 3 of the Tails from the Upper Kingdom

H. Leighton Dickson

To Gwenevere; this is your song!
2016

ISBN-10: 1491032758
ISBN-13: 978-1491032756

DEDICATION

To Graeme and Geoff,
for keeping me in ideas and sushi

ACKNOWLEDGMENTS

Imagination is a funny thing, a contagious thing, a death-defying thing, and perhaps the only true thing that makes us Human.

UNITY

KIRIN

According to the *Book of Truths*, the Year of the Rabbit is a peaceful one. It is elegant and sweet, a gentle breath after the roaring of the Tiger. A year to conduct sensible business, to embrace family, to go on trips. It is also a year to assert the efforts of diplomacy, for a war will never go well in the Year of the Rabbit. There is simply too much peace for that. At least, so says the *Book of Truths.*

The *Book of Truths* is a very old book, translated into all tongues of the Empire -

Hanyin and Shaharabic, Farashish and Hindih. It has also been transcribed for all the reaches of the Empire as well, from Lanladesh to Shiryia, from Hindaya to Aegyp but not in Nam. There is a small and curious problem with Nam. You see, in Nam, there is no word for rabbit.

In Nam, it is simply called the Year of the Cat.

It is a mystery, but cats are, after all, a mysterious people. And so, we begin our story with the birth of a baby, the weeping of a dog and a cup of hot sweet tea, naturally in the Year of the Cat.

***

It was raining on the little pukka house in Nam. The roof was thatched grass, the walls pikes of rattan bound together like a fence. It sat up on stilts, this little house, had no window and only a flap of canvas for a door. Despite its appearance, it did remarkably well at keeping the rainwater off and ground water out on this cold, rainy night. It was a night for candles, lamps and braziers of sizzling coal. And incense. Above all else, it was a night for incense.

Inside, a woman lay on the wooden floor, propped up on spotted elbows, breathing. Two others - a young jaguar and an old leopard - hovered at her knees, linens and oil basins at the ready, while an ocelot sat with her, mopping her forehead with cloths and humming in strange, exotic keys.

"It is a big baby, isn't it, Farit?" asked the young jaguar. She had large eyes and bindhi dots the colour of jade. "A boy, I'm certain of it."

"Oh, it's a boy, Xuan," said the ocelot as she stroked the mother's forehead. "It is obvious by the way she was carrying. All in the front."

"Oh yes. All in the front."

The woman on the floor nodded. She wore only a kimonoh of black silk, perfect for childbirth and her long black hair was damp with sweat, falling wildly about her shoulders. Her pelt was smooth butter cream, spots tiny and well-placed, and a black stripe painted her face like the falling of a tear. Even now, in such a state, she watched everything with great golden eyes rimmed with kohl.

"Yes," she breathed in a voice deep and smoky. "I have prayed for a boy."

"It is the Year of the Cat," the ocelot named Farit smiled. "Your prayers will be answered tonight, Sherhanna. Only good comes in the Year of the Cat."

"Are you really an Alchemist?" asked young Xuan. "Hy'Unh only accepts gold as payment. Are you going to turn something into gold?"

"Of course," said the woman called Sherhanna.

"We don't see many cheetahs here in Nam," said young Xuan. "I think it's too hot. Although I've heard Aegyp is hot. Is Aegyp hot, Sherhanna?"

"Enough talk," said the leopard named Hy'Unh. She was very old with few teeth, multiple hoops through nostril and brow and more rings on her fingers than in the bark of a tree. The midwife. "Push now."

Sherhanna breathed out, clutched her knees and pushed. She did not scream. She did not cry out. Rather, she remained focused and inward, willing some muscles to contract, others to stretch. She had been through this before. Pain, she had learned, was simply a matter of perspective, a means to an end. Tonight, with the birth of this baby, her sins would be forgiven and the world made right. Tonight, everything would change.

"Push!"

"Just a little more," said Farit. "This is good, Sherhanna. Very good."

"Push, now!"

There was a very long moment when all time seemed to stop and the world grew very small. Sherhanna's black claws drew blood in the pelt of her thighs and the breath burned in her chest as everything was thrown into that one final, deliberate act.

"Enough," said the midwife. "The head is out. Breathe now, child. Breathe."

Sherhanna did, letting her head fall back into the jaguar's arms. She closed her eyes, exhausted. She was not done yet but still.

"Much hair," said Hy'Unh. "Very dark. Few spots."

"See?" said Xuan. "This is good, Sherhanna. Very good."

"Just a little more now," said Farit. "For the shoulders."

She did. It was easy. Just a little push and she felt the wobbly mass pass through to the crowing of her midwives.

"A son!" cried the jaguar. "A perfect son."

"A golden boy," said the ocelot. "Spotted, but odd. Not cheetah spots...dapples. Lion."

A few minutes more for the afterbirth but soon, the old leopard was bundling the child in wraps of linen. Lamplight reflected from the many hoops in her old face. She looked up and smiled.

"He has a tuft," she said, passing the cub into the woman's waiting hands. "His father a lion."

"Of course." Sherhanna took the child, drew him to her breast. The baby blinked sleepily, made rooting motions with his mouth.

"You should name him Su'tu." Xuan smiled and rocked proudly on her heels. "I am learning Namyanese. It means Lion."

"No. His name is Kylan."

"Kylan. Yes." The old leopard nodded but the young jaguar shook her head.

"I do not understand. Kylan?"

"Namyanese for unicorn," said Farit as she began to wipe the blood from the bowls, the floor and Sherhanna's legs. "It is good luck."

"U-nee-corn? But I don't speak Imperial. What is Kylan in Hanyin?"

"Such a child..." The midwife shook her head and stomped away, her boots sounding hollow on the rough wooden floor. Sherhanna merely smiled a cryptic smile, her eyes fixed on the cub.

"Kylan," she said softly, stroking the golden head with the tip of a finger. "For his father."

"Oh that's wonderful!" said Xuan. "What is his father's name?"

"Kirin," she said. "His father's name is Kirin."

***

3 months later

Kirin Wynegarde-Grey sighed and looked around the high walls of the Outer Court. He was not sure how long he had been waiting, but there had been a change of guard once already so it had to have been hours. Once again, he studied their faces, those leopards who stood so perfectly still at their posts, swords at their hips, staffs clutched silently in their hands. He didn't know these men. He didn't know them.

He knew he shouldn't be surprised. It had been almost two years, after all. Two years since he had been here last in the rich, beautiful halls of *Pol'Lhasa*. It had only been last night that he'd marched up the One Hundred Steps as if in a dream but had been stopped by the leopards at the doors of the Outer Court. They had not known him either, those leopards and he had marveled at how much could have changed in a world that did not embrace change. There was a time when he knew every guard in the Palace, knew the names and families and stations of every leopard posted in *DharamShallah* and its surrounding district. There was a time when they would have known him as well, but that time had long passed. He was unrecognizable, now.

It was well into morning and people had come and gone. Servants, civilians, ministers, all rushing about with duties and concerns and business in the Heart of the Upper Kingdom. He watched them, his gloved hands folded between his knees, his tail bound in strips of gold, his *keffiyah* falling across his shoulders like a mane. He had seen a few eyes dart to his sash, the tattered sash that had once marked him as noble but now only made him feel old. It was the way of things.

He had asked to see either the Minister of Defense, of Arms, or of Horses or even Chancellor Ho himself. The guards had exchanged glances, they had nodded but that had been hours ago. Perhaps watches, although he couldn't be sure.

What was worse, they had not even brought him tea.

And so he sat in the outer chamber of the Palace, waiting. Another change of guard, signaling yet another watch and he was growing weary, but if the last years had taught him anything, it was patience. Patience and a shattering of that damned glass.

He could still smell the incense.

He closed his eyes and waited some more.

It was entirely possible that he had fallen asleep but at some point he heard a voice.

"Kirin-san? Is that you?"

He opened his eyes. It was Master Yao Tang St. John, Minister of Horses, staring down at him with a strange, worried gaze.

He smiled.

"Yao-san," he said, for the first time in his life using an informal greeting for the man. He could think of no other words.

"Why are you sitting here?" The man was a lion, but a strange, small, thin one, with a high top-knot and a thin, reedy voice. "Does Chancellor Ho know of your arrival?"

Suddenly, everything felt at once like home and wrong.

"I can't say, Yao-san. I have asked."

The small man straightened, smoothed his robes, glanced around at the leopards of the Outer Court.

"Well, yes, well...would you like me to petition on your behalf, Kirin-san?"

Kirin smiled again, marveling at how easily it came to his face now. "That would be acceptable, Yao-san. Thank you."

"Good. Very good." And with a little more smoothing and glancing, Master Yao Tang St. John rushed from the antechamber and into the beating Heart that was *Pol'Lhasa.*

Pol'Lhasa, he breathed. The most beautiful, most glorious place in all the Kingdoms, with her tall ebony beams, winged rooftops and stained cedar walls. She was an explosion of colour, *Pol'Lhasa* was, and every inch of wall, roof and floor boasted more patterns than an AmniShakra Wheel. Monkeys, lions, sea shells and birds all carved into her wood, dragons and cranes brushed like stories into her windows. Every inch of the Palace spoke something - a history, a legend, a prophecy. Sitting high over the city of *DharamShallah,* the Palace was at once the heart, soul and will of the Upper Kingdom.

He did not belong here anymore.

"Captain?"

The voice echoed and immediately all leopards stood a little taller. He turned his head to see the small Sacred figure of Angelino Devine de Fusillia Ho, Chancellor of the Upper Kingdom, at the far Red and Gold Door. He was clad in lush blue robes and it made Kirin smile to see how very tiny the man was to wield such power. He had seen far too much in this past year. Nothing could possibly be strange any more.

And so he rose to his feet, bowed, fist to cupped palm, as the Chancellor moved along the long hallway toward him. His flattened face was round and very white, for he was of Pershan descent, and his yellow eyes had the look of both wonder and suspicion.

The Chancellor did not bow.

"Kirin-san, we..." But he did swallow and that told Kirin more than anything he might have said. "We were not expecting your return...so soon..."

"Ah. I would have thought the kestrels-"

"Only that a small party was returning. You are looking well."

Kirin smiled.

"Please, would you care to join me in my office. I have tea."

It was the kindest thing the Chancellor had ever said to him.

"Of course," he answered, and followed the man into the heart of *Pol'Lhasa.*

***

Jalair Naranbaatar awoke to the sound of weeping.

He sat up far too quickly, threw a quick glance around the outcropping of snow and rock that served as their shelter tonight. They were traveling very lightly, and had no poles for a gar. The night sky had been their tent, their neighbours hares, ruffed grouse and badgers. It took only a moment for his eyes to adjust to the darkness, his pointed ears swiveling for the sound.

Several paces away, his sister sat crosslegged under the stars, tears coursing down her grey face.

"Setse," he whispered as he crawled out from under the skins to her side. He gathered her hands into his. "Setse, I'm here. Tell me."

"Ulaan Baator," she moaned and began to rock back and forth. "Ulaan Baator, I see him…"

"You're not thinking clearly, Setse. Ulaan Baator is a city, the city of the Khan. Do you see the Khan? Is that who you're seeing?"

"No, Rani. I keep telling you. I see Ulaan Baator, the man. Kuren. Kuren Ulaan Bator."

He sighed, squeezed her hands but looked to the north. Ulaan Baator—Red Hero, city of Khans since before the people could remember. Also called Kuren by some of the more northern people. She had been saying the same thing for weeks now. A Red Hero, dragons, eyes and blood.

His sister was rocking more violently now, gripping her knees so that he could see blood beneath her rabbit-skin wraps.

"They are coming for me, Rani," she whispered. "I can feel them."

"We'll keep running. We should be in the Mountains soon."

"The Khan has sent a Legion."

"Two can move where a Legion cannot. We've eluded them all so far."

She took a shuddering breath, and he squeezed her hands again.

"I'll fight a Legion to keep you safe."

"They will kill you if they find us."

"They will kill you if they take you to the Khan."

"No, not at once. Not entirely." She took another breath, turned so he could see her sharp profile under the moon, the tracks made in her pelt by the tears. "They *will* find us, Rani. It is only a matter of time."

"How can they? Do they have an Oracle with them?"

She looked at him, smiled weakly through her tears and he marveled at her face. With sixteen summers, she was a beauty, her hair dark and waving like the dunes, her white and grey pelt soft as doeskin. She was lithe and graceful, a dancer and she would have had many suitors already had it not been for her eyes. One as dark as their Mother the Earth, the other as blue as the sky at midday. She was an Oracle. She would never have a suitor because of those eyes.

"No," she laughed softly. "They do not have an Oracle."

"Well, that's sad for them. I do."

Jalair Naransetseg, daughter of Borjigin Jalair, granddaughter of the Blue Wolf, laughed again. Her voice was like music on the wind.

Her brother, Naranbataar, took a deep breath, sifting the air for the smell of soldiers. What he caught was antelope.

She grinned, for she had caught it too and together, they scrambled to their feet to hunt.

***

He breathed in deeply as the tea flowed over the lip of first the pot, then the cup, causing the patina of the clay to gleam and glow. Chancellor Angelino Devine de Fusillia Ho was taking the very act of Chado to an art and Kirin found himself approving. In fact, he was transfixed in this gleaming wooden room that served as the Chancellor's office. A stick of incense curling in a distant pot, a brazier crackling with warmth, the sound of tea brewed then poured.

He was tired.

"No," the Chancellor was saying. "We have had very little news from your journey. We have had a rather turbulent year ourselves."

"Hmm."

"She is married, our Empress." Not even a glance.

"Yes."

"With a kitten. Prarthana Chiraq Markova Wu." And he smiled this time, but without his teeth. "A daughter. Kalicoh."

The golden liquid steaming in the pot.

"It's unfortunate that you have missed it all. But I am glad that your mission is finished. It did take rather a long time."

Kirin set his jaw. He would not be baited.

"It *is* finished," said the Chancellor and he looked up slightly as he passed Kirin the cup. "You do know that, yes?"

Kirin took it. "Jet barraDunne is dead."

The white hand paused. As good as a splash, Kirin thought.

"Dead? I see. How?"

"Killed by a would-be Khan beyond the borders of Shiryia."

"Would-be?"

Kirin lifted the cup to his lips. "The lion did not die."

The Chancellor held his gaze a long moment before bending back to his tea.

"I understand that benAramis has returned to *Sha'Hadin.*" He sipped slowly, waiting.

"He and Major Laenskaya will be setting things to right there soon enough. With or without the assistance of Yahn Nevye." There was not even a twitch of a whisker. The man was a master. "How did you know?"

"Kestrels."

The Chancellor sat back on his heels, his long blue silk robes splayed out like water on a shore. His eyes were deep, heavy pools of gold. "I'm afraid there is no longer a place for you here at *Pol'Lhasa.* We could not wait on filling a such a position. It was a matter of national importance. You understand."

"Of course." It was amazing how easily it rolled off his tongue. He could hear her voice in every word, the quiet humour, the subtle threat. The crush of her night black hair, the flash of her eyes. "And may I ask who has replaced me?"

"An experienced soldier," said the Chancellor, and he set his cup on the bamboo table. "An older, experienced, married soldier."

Kirin nodded. It was the way of things.

The Chancellor continued. "But I'm quite certain we could find something for you in one of the outer posts. *Sri' Kirtipur,* perhaps. You will want to stay close to your family home, surely. How is your mother?"

Kirin leveled his gaze at the man who had orchestrated all this, these two years of striving and loss. The man who had contracted a ninjah to have him killed so the Empress would be free to marry. The man who had caused the loss of his claws, his tail, his mane. He should have hated him but instead he felt nothing for this little, round, white-faced man. Nothing at all.

"My mother is well."

"Good. Very good."

He should not have come.

"Thank you for the tea."

And he rose to his feet.

"I shall accompany you out, Captain." The Chancellor too began to rise, but paused, his wide face smiling. "I mean *Kirin-san.* Forgive me. Force of habit."

No, he felt nothing whatsoever.

Together they left the large wooden room that served at the Chancellor's office, navigating the many stairs and hallways that made up the Palace of *Pol'Lhasa.* No one watched him this time, although many paused to bow to the Chancellor as they passed, fist to cupped palm. No one bowed to him. No one even noticed him.

Finally, in the Outer Court at the Red and Gold Door, the Chancellor stopped, allowing Kirin to walk the long stretch of hall to the door alone. Leopards watched them both, as even now servants and civilians moved into and out of the Palace. As Kirin walked, he cast his eyes around the chamber, so colourful and high, beginning to shine in the first rays of morning. He drank it in, the blackened cedar beams, the mosaics of glass. Every surface painted with history. The heart, soul and will of the Upper Kingdom.

He did not belong here anymore.

For the first time, he felt a pang of regret that he had not turned, so many hours ago, at the tobacconist's.

Behind him, he could hear the Red and Gold Door open, cast a quick glance to see a party of women sweep in from the Palace proper, clothed in colours found in a wildflower meadow. He turned back to the door and kept walking.

"There you are, Chancellor! Explain yourself."

It was like a strong wind, the way her voice sent people to their knees, palms and foreheads to the floor in reverence, servants and civilians alike. The Leopards stood straighter, their weapons poised and at the ready. All sound in the Outer Court ceased. All breathing stopped.

"There has been a falcon from *Sha'Hadin.* Why was I not informed?"

"Excellency," said the Chancellor. "Forgive me, but..."

"But what, Chancellor? This is unpardonable."

There was a heartbeat of pause. He could hear the rustle of silk.

"Who...?"

His heart thudded in his throat.

"Who is that? Chancellor?"

The door was only steps away but his feet had turned to stone.

"You with the tattered sash," he heard her voice echo like the fall of a baby bird. "Turn. Let me see your face."

His fingers, gloved and clawless, curled into fists of their own accord. He could not breathe. He could not move.

"Turn."

His feet were stones.

"Please..."

He turned.

In the center of the women, at the far end of the great hall, he saw her. Here in a room she had likely visited perhaps twice in her life. She never left *Pol'Lhasa,* never set foot outside its painted walls. She was dressed in purples and blues with a headdress of silver tassels and the women around her were a riot of colour but her golden eyes were the only things in the room.

He did not bow. He could not move.

"Captain?"

Slowly and on slippered feet, she stepped out of the protective circle of women. Chancellor Ho moved but she raised her hand and he fell silent. She continued toward him.

"Captain," she repeated. She had not taken her eyes off him. "You are back."

"Yes," he said weakly.

"*Sha'Hadin* has sent a falcon."

"Good."

"Excellency," hissed the Chancellor. "This is unsafe."

"Enough," she growled back and her black tail lashed once under her skirts. The people held their breaths as Thothloryn Parillaud Markova Wu, Twelfth Empress of the Fangxieng Dynasty, Matriarch of *Pol'Lhasa* and Most Blessed Ruler of the Upper Kingdom, moved across the floor like water, like silk. She stopped directly in front of him.

He could not breathe. Could not think. Could not look anywhere other than the golden spheres that were her eyes.

"You have changed," she said.

"The world has changed, Excellency."

"Indeed."

He felt dizzy, as if the world had suddenly come to a crashing halt on top of him. As if two years had suddenly fallen onto his mane-less head.

And the incense of the tobacconist's shop was instantly forgotten.

"I see," she said. "I would very much like you to tell me about it."

"I—"

"Now. Come with me." She whirled and strode back to the circle of women, and all eyes in the room fell on him now, the strange man summoned by the Empress. He could feel their stares, their questions. He was at a loss.

She paused at the great Red and Gold Door, threw a quick glance back over her shoulder.

"*Now,* Captain. If you please."

He pleased and crossed the floor to follow her, not sparing a glance for Chancellor Ho as he passed.

***

She shook the snow from her boots as she slipped into the Lantern Room of the Monastery and paused, snorting only once. They were still here, the two men sitting cross-legged on the floor facing each other. They had been for days. One was a jaguar, compact and strongly-built, his ringed pelt almost completely hidden under heavy brown robes. The other was of indeterminate breeding and a puma beard circled his mouth to end with a dark point on his chin. She used to hate that beard. Now, it and the infamous scar across his left eye were her entire world.

The two were surrounded by the brothers of *Sha'Hadin* and *Agara'tha*. The crowd had somehow filled the entire room since she'd left last night. Some were sitting, some kneeling in the learning pose. Others were standing, pressed along the carved walls as far as she could see. The room was silent and heavy with the smell of men. They had been here for three days, these silent, sitting ones, and she could tell at a glance how the dynamics were playing out. Half the crowd was dressed in robes of brown, the other clothed in black, each behind or beside one of the two. It was war, she realized grimly. Disciplined and spiritual, but war none-the-less.

She caught the eye of a lynx and he quietly made his way over to her.

"Major." His name was Tiberius and the tips of his ears poked through his silver hair. He smiled at her. She growled at him.

"They are still here."

"Yes," he said.

"They are stupid."

"Simply dedicated. Might I arrange a pot of tea for you? Or some lamb, perhaps?"

"Why?"

"To restore your body and soothe your soul."

"My body is strong and my soul is in no need of soothing," she scowled and pushed past him, striding over to the bearded man. He was dressed in robes of brown leather. She leaned in to his ear.

"End this."

He did not open his eyes.

"Why?" His first words spoken in days.

"You are toying with him."

There was a murmur from those in black, and the tail of the jaguar twitched once.

"So what if I am? It has been a restful three days and I have learned much about the state of our monastery."

"It is boring and my bed is cold. We have work to do."

He opened his eyes. Brown, like earth after a spring rain. Unnatural, but still.

"You are a vision." And he smiled.

"I will kill you. And then all of them."

"And then what will you do?"

She scowled. "Go back to the Army. Resume my commission."

Sireth benAramis took her silver hand and kissed it before looking around the room at the sea of faces. "My wife is quite correct. We all have work to do. Yahn Nevye, you are dismissed from *Sha'Hadin* and from the brotherhood of the Gifts. Leave now and never return."

"What?" The jaguar narrowed his eyes. "You don't have the authority."

"In fact, I do."

"Jet barraDunne—"

"—is dead. *Agara'tha* has no First Mage and I know from all of the thoughts in this room that the Order is directionless and failing."

Nevye snorted. "You can't possibly know all our thoughts. Even you are not that powerful."

"Oh, I can and I have and I am." benAramis smiled. "Tal deHaan over there has stolen bread three nights in a row from the kitchens. He knows it is wrong, but he is big man and hungry and can therefore justify his actions."

Eyes glanced at the man they knew as Tal deHaan. He shifted but did not meet their gaze.

"Willhem Daniel Po wishes he can leave to visit the woman he wants for a wife. He knows *Sha'Hadin* has never allowed women, but thinks it is wrong and is wondering why things cannot change." Again, eyes on the cat known as Willhem Daniel Po, but the bearded Seer simply nodded. "And change they will, Willhem. I promise you that. You may have a wife yet..."

Murmurs anew, nodding as well.

"I have seen a cheetah giving birth in Nam, an Oracle of the Lower Kingdom fleeing for her life and the recent talks of Kaidan in the Land of the *Chi'Chen...*"

"Kaidan?"

The Major glared at him but he kept his gaze fixed on the jaguar kneeling before him.

"But you, Yahn Nevye, you have done a terrible thing..."

A circle of flame erupted around the jaguar and people shrank back or scrambled out of its path. For his part, the man called Yahn Nevye steeled his chin but did not move.

"Your mind is strong but not strong enough," the Seer said. "I have seen Chancellor Ho, Jet barraDunne and you in a winter garden, discussing how to compromise the success of the journey in the Year of the Tiger, and the employment of a *kunoichi* in that regard."

The crowd was silent.

"Your plan did not go quite as you had predicted. I have sent a message to *Pol'Lhasa* petitioning for *Agara'tha, Namroh'Lin and* the entire Order of the Arts to be brought under the control of *Sha'Hadin,* and therefore, as the last surviving Council member," he smiled. *"Me."*

And the flames died as quickly as they had come, leaving a circle of black on the floor. He rose to his feet and looked around the Lantern Room.

"For those of you—Alchemist and Seer alike—who wish to begin to write a new chapter in the history of the Gifts and the Arts, I welcome you to stay. For those who cannot accept this, go in peace, but go. Change is coming swiftly upon us and we must be ready to meet it with all of our strength and heart and will."

He bowed slightly. It was returned by most in the room. Not by Yahn Nevye, the jaguar. And not by most of those in black.

benAramis turned, his robes swirling dramatically and he left the Lantern Room at the Major's side. She was shaking her head.

"Theatrics," she snorted. "You are a politician now."

He slipped a long arm around her waist. "To be honest, I wasn't thinking of anything other than the tragedy of you and a cold bed."

She grinned wickedly and they left the Lantern Room for warmer places.

***

It had never been done. It was scandal. It was blasphemy, but Thothloryn Parillaud Markova Wu, Twelfth Empress of the Fangxieng Dynasty, Matriarch of *Pol'Lhasa,* and Most Blessed Ruler of the Upper Kingdom, brought a man-not-her-husband through the Throne Room, up the winding stairs to the Imperial Residence on the very top floor of the Palace. The most Sacred place in the entire Kingdom.

It was another world here in the rooms of the Empress, for in fact it was her entire world. She had lived her life here on this the very top floor, would leave only on the day they carried her out in a funeral palanquin for burial in the Tombs of the Emperors. The ceiling was very high, with polished beams curved to follow the winged roofline of the Palace, and painted in places to resemble clouds, or stars, or suns. There were trees in ceramic pots, pruned and twisting like large bonsais, and orchids growing from bowls hanging from the beams. Peacocks strutted across carpets from Persha and between statues of gold from Hiraq. There had been a mongoose too, once upon a time.

So long ago. A lifetime.

Servants watched but said nothing as they passed and he was amazed at their lack of response. As one-time Captain of her personal guard, he was appalled at lack of security, but then again, much had changed in these two years. It was beyond him.

She paused at a set of rice paper doors.

"My Prayer Room," she said. "We can discuss your journey inside. We will not be disturbed."

"Excellency," said Kirin, still not believing that he was, in fact, there. He clasped his hands tightly behind his back. "The Chancellor..."

"After two years, you wish to spend your words on the Chancellor?"

"No, but—"

"Well, then?"

She slid the doors open and slipped inside, peering at him with golden eyes. "I will be in here. Come if you will."

And she disappeared.

He cast his eyes around the room, saw a young sandcat polishing a set of ebony candles. She looked up at him, smiled very slightly before bending back to her work. There was no one else in the room. It was entirely empty, other than the maid girl and the peacocks.

He took a deep breath and crossed the threshold into the Most Holy of Holies, the Prayer Room of the Empress, and slid the door closed behind him.

***

There were cushions everywhere—reds, purples, golds and blues, and the walls were silk and paper. She was on her knees, blowing across the tip of a stick of incense before carefully placing it in a bronze bowl. He didn't know what to think, even less what to do, so he stood, hands behind his back, desperately trying to control his breathing. Never in his life had he imagined himself here and he was surprised to find his heart racing as if it would rush right out of his chest.

Finally, after what seemed like hours, she rose to her feet and turned.

She was glorious.

"Excellency," he began. "I regret to inform—"

"Not now," she said.

"But—"

"Ling," she said. "My name is Ling."

He was certain his mouth hung open a moment.

"Say it," she said. "It was your wish. Your one wish."

He dropped his eyes to the floor and fell silent.

"It is my wish as well." She stepped forward again. "Say my name."

His breathing was growing heavy. His chest was pressing in on him from all sides. He shook his head.

"Your husband—"

"He is dead."

It was stronger than the blow from a fist. He couldn't help himself. He looked up.

"Six months ago. The Mal'haria."

"I am sorry."

"No, I am sorry, Kirin-san. I am so sorry for all of this."

And to his utter surprise, she reached out a hand, brushed his jaw with the tips of her jewelled fingers. It was a strangely intimate gesture. He felt light-headed, knowing her eyes were fixed on him but he could give nothing away.

"This...is different."

"It was broken and has set wrongly."

She frowned, moved her fingers to touch the hem of his kheffiyah and he knew what she meant to do. He moved his own hand, stopping her.

"No."

But she took his hand instead, hidden as it was within its glove of thickest leather and he cursed himself, tried to pull away though she held fast, her eyes flashing at him in rebuke. As she began to press his fingers, he felt his cheeks burn with heat.

"Please," he hissed. He wished he had never come. His legs were shaking and he wasn't sure how much longer they would hold him.

Slowly, she slid the glove from his hand, dropped it to the pillows on the floor.

The tips white where the pelt had grown back, closed in over the knubs that once held claws. On each finger, the last segment of bone was missing and the flesh soft and pulpy.

He saw her eyes fill with tears.

"Dogs?" she asked, her voice barely a whisper and he hated himself at that moment. "I did not know."

She reached for the kheffiyah again and he closed his eyes, took a deep shuddering breath as she slid it from his head. He heard her gasp, her sharp intake of breath and he dropped to his knees amid the thick cushions of red and purple.

The only sound in the Prayer Room of the Empress was the sound of his breathing. He lowered his head in shame, did not care enough to stop his own tears. She would see him now for the creature he truly was. He should have let Kerris do it, so many months ago. Kerris had been ready, he had been willing. One sure stroke of the katanah, perhaps two and his disgrace would have been over, his death swift, honour restored. Perhaps they would have even told a story of the man who had made a Khan and lived—a man who had once been a lion.

It was yet to be seen the manner in which she would choose to kill him.

Then, a most unexpected thing. Her lips on the top of his head in a kiss.

Now her fingers running down the last bolt of mane left, smooth as silk in her grasp, her touch like that of a feather on his cheek, his jaw, his chin. Lifting his face with both hands now so that he was forced into the liquid gold of her eyes.

"Ling," she said one last time. "My name is Ling."

"Ling," he breathed and he reached for her and pulled her down into the cushions.

***

It was like a strange but pleasant dream as he walked the stone corridors to his room. For twenty years, he had walked them and the memories were familiar and yet somehow, not. The last time he had walked through these particular halls to pause at this particular door, there had been a snow leopard at his side, her many daggers and swords itching to cut him into pieces on the stone floor. As he gazed down at her long marbled hair, he was thankful that things had improved in that regard. She was a passionate woman. She might still be the end of him.

"What?" she growled, feeling his eyes.

He smiled. "There will only be one mattress."

"I am small."

"You said it was itchy."

"Life is hard."

"I love you."

"Pah. Theatrics." But he noticed the hint of a smile as she laid her hand on the wood of the door to push it open.

yellow eyes falling into white, dragons and arrows and blood

Slowly, he turned.

"That was impressive," said Yahn Nevye from the end of the hall. "Your little trick."

Ursa turned as well, tail lashing. He could hear her growl.

"All my tricks are impressive, brother," he said. "To which are you referring?"

"The ring of fire."

"Oh, you should see what I can do with water. Or, in fact, with stone. I could bring this entire corridor down on your head if it didn't mean someone might be inconvenienced on the floor above."

The jaguar stepped toward them, hands clasped behind his back. "I didn't think you approved of the Arts."

"Life has changed. Can you speak to falcons yet?"

The tawny face was impassive. "The Arts will be welcomed at *Sha'Hadin* under your watch?"

"Men of good conscience and noble character will be welcomed, whatever their calling. That, of course, disqualifies you."

"I have an open mind, *sidi.* A new thing for you, perhaps?"

"I have always had an open mind, brother. Accident of my birth."

"Mongrel *and* Brahmin."

"Exactly."

"Seer and now, Alchemist. Perhaps Jet barraDunne's dream is upon us?"

"Jet barraDunne's dream?"

Ursa made to move upon him but he stopped her with his hand.

"Shall I tell you about Jet barraDunne's dream, brother?"

Nevye steeled his chin but said nothing.

"Jet barraDunne's dream was to set a *ninjah* to compromise an Imperial mission. Jet barraDunne's dream was to see the torture of myself and my wife at the hands of a Legion of dogs. Jet barraDunne's dream was to see a new Khan made in the Lower Kingdom by the death of a Captain of the Imperial Guard. However, both we and the Captain live while Jet barraDunne and our enemies burned to ash in a circle of flame. What then does that tell you about the dreams of Jet barraDunne?"

"Are you threatening me, brother?"

"A man need never revenge himself. The body of his enemy will be brought to his own door."

"I will not leave."

"Well, you *are* already at my door."

The jaguar swallowed.

"Good night, Yahn."

And he pushed open the door and stepped inside. Ursa glared at the man down the hall.

"I will kill you myself," she hissed. "I will break your neck like a chicken and stuff your body in a mattress until you begin to stink. Then I will toss you into the crevice of *Nanchuri Glacier* and no one will ever know what has become of poor Yahn Nevye, the man who could not speak to falcons."

He set his jaw.

She closed the door behind her.

***

Even after these last few years, it is a most unusual thing for me to wake up in a place not my own. I have never been as Kerris is, where inns, monasteries, forests and caves are simply a part of my experience. I have always been a creature of habit, of routine and of preference. But I must admit that waking here, this morning, covered in nothing but red silk and surrounded by cushions, was an exhilarating thing.

I committed blasphemy last night. Happily, freely and passionately.

Chancellor Ho will order my death and I will wholeheartedly kneel under any sword he may choose.

- an excerpt from the journal of Kirin Wynegarde-Grey

"Leave it," said the Empress and he could see her kneeling by a low table, the light from two paper lanterns illuminating her work. She was writing, dipping her brush in small pots of black and red ink, and he marveled at the sight of her, clothed in a simple kimonoh without sash, hands and feet bare and as black as a winter sky.

He had never seen her hair. No one had ever seen her hair. It was always covered by a headdress of some sort, usually gold, frequently with tassels. He had never imagined seeing it, had never allowed his mind to go there, but now, as she sat like a little sparrow in the cushions, her hair was loosed and fell like a curtain of black silk to her waist. It caught and reflected the lantern light, shone blue like a moonlit lake.

He remembered the feel of it under his fingers.

"Leave what?" he asked finally.

"Your kheffiyah." She did not look up, merely continued painting words on paper. "There is no hiding in this room."

He lowered his eyes, convicted.

"Besides," she added. "You have the head of a sham'Rai now. It is entirely worthy."

He could die now and happily.

"The falcon from *Sha'Hadin* is young," she said. "She prefers to sit on my head."

A smile tugged into his cheek. "Mi-Hahn."

Still, she did not look at him.

"Excellency—"

"Ling."

"Ling."

"Say it again, until it finds a home on your tongue."

"Ling."

"Again."

"Ling."

"And again."

"Lyn-ling."

Now she did look up, humour dancing in her golden eyes.

"Perfect. I accept."

He moved to sit up, made certain the red silk spread draped modestly across his hips. He had never been a man to do this. In fact, he had felt certain he would live his entire life without this manner of pleasure but two remarkable women had intervened. First is luck, the saying went, and all in all, he was a very lucky man.

She laid her brush down on the paper.

"Was I your first?"

golden eyes, long strong hands, the smell of incense

"There is no hiding," she reminded him.

"There was another," he said, surprised to find no shame. "Once. I wanted to kill myself. She convinced me otherwise."

The Empress Thothloryn Parillaud Markova Wu now Lyn-ling, was weighing him in her stare. He held it, allowing himself to be weighed. He would likely be dead by sunset regardless.

"Did you love her?"

"I think so. Yes, I did."

"Do you still?"

He thought on this before answering.

"A part of me, yes. Still."

She studied him a while longer before picking up the paper, blowing across it to dry the ink. Even in such a simple act, she was glorious.

"There is a new Captain of the Imperial Guard. Captain Shyam Smith-Honshu."

"He is a good choice."

"Chancellor Ho was insistent."

He nodded.

"Was my Chancellor involved in any of this? In the deaths of my Seers and the devastation of *Sha'Hadin*? In the beating of my Captain at the hands of our enemies?"

His heart thudded once. He still woke in the night because of the dreams.

"Your silence tells me all." She lifted the paper to the lantern light. "What do you know of the history of the sham'Rai, Kirin-san?"

"The sham'Rai." He began slowly. "The highest order of *Shah'tyriah,* warriors bound only to one master until death."

"We do not have this position in our court."

"No longer, no."

"Why not?"

"I don't know."

"In the days of the most Ancient of Ancestors," she blinked slowly. "The sham'Rai served the Empire with loyalty, fealty and honour. A sham'Rai served only one master and would do so until his death, or the death of his master. He would accrue no power for himself, no personal wealth or lands or titles. Service to his master was reward enough and he embraced the Way of the Warrior with his heart, mind, soul and strength."

"Bushido." He nodded.

"This document is a return to the ways of the sham'Rai and the reinstitution of the Shogun amongst the *Shah'tyriah* caste. The sham'Rai are to be chosen by the Empress of the Upper Kingdom and accorded all respect and honour worthy of their calling."

"There will be resistance, Ex—" he caught himself. "Ling."

She laid the paper down, folded her hands in her lap.

"I am an Empress with an infant child and without a husband, with a fine Imperial Captain but a treacherous advisor. I am vulnerable and need the protection of a sham'Rai. My own Shogun-General."

She raised her chin, a gesture of pride.

"You, Kirin-san, have shown honour above and beyond that of a normal warrior. You have beating in you the heart of a sham'Rai and it is my wish that you take on the role of very first Shogun-General of the Empire."

He couldn't believe what she was saying.

"I have sent word for the Imperial armory to begin construction of the yori and kabuto from the Ancient designs, to be fitted to your exact measurements. Also, I have sent the order for both the Blood and Jade Fang to be retrieved from the Archives. They will be your brothers now."

The *Blood and Jade Fangs*. Swords of history, of myth and legend. Always copied, never rivaled.

There was no expression on her face. She was as beautiful as a swan, as sharp as steel.

"You, Kirin-san, shall no longer be referred to as Captain Wynegarde-Grey. Rather, I now and forever more convey upon you the rank of Shogun-General, personal bodyguard to the Empress of the Fangxieng Dynasty for as long as you live and breathe. Will you accept this position?"

Suddenly, the kheffiyah and all notions of his death were forgotten.

"With honour," he said and bowed low to the ground, forehead touching the pillows that covered the floor.

The silk at his hips fell away and she smiled.

THE LAST SEER OF *SHA'HADIN*

It was almost dawn when Mi-Hahn returned and she chirruped and flapped as he fussed over her at the window's ledge. The sun was peering over the peaks of the Great Mountains and the sky was only beginning to streak with purple and red. It was cold, however, and his breath frosted like smoke from his mouth. Snow had fallen overnight, coating the Valley of the Seers like the pelt of a snow leopard and he smiled at the thought.

He could see her down below, leading a group of sixty or so in the Sun Salute of morning. She was a Chai'Chi mistress—her movements slow and graceful, her control unrivaled, her balance unmatched. He could tell from the robes that her compatriots were mostly monks from *Sha'Hadin*. There were a few brothers from the Arts joining the exercise, although significantly more were sitting on the rocks surrounding the valley, making patterns with candle and stone. It was an interesting sight, the Gifts and the Arts together, and he was surprised that it didn't boil his blood. It would have years ago.

He was a changed man.

Mi-Hahn chirruped again from the window and he felt the man before his footsteps announced him. Even still, the steps were quiet and Sireth found himself taking a deep cleansing breath as Yahn Nevye appeared to stand beside him at the window.

They did not look at each other.

"She will have all of them out before long," said the jaguar, peering out at the morning ritual taking place in the valley. "You are a very brave man to have married a woman like that."

"What time are you leaving today?"

Nevye smiled. "I am not leaving, brother. I have told you so."

"Hmm." Sireth smiled now. "My wife is a beautiful woman, yes?"

"Very."

"Skilled, disciplined, strong."

"It seems so."

"She is also deadly. It would take but a word from me—no, a mere arch of a brow to see her slip into a man's room, slit his throat and be back in my bed before the pillow had grown cold."

"I am not leaving."

Sireth stroked the young falcon's breast. She mouthed his hand with her sharp beak.

"You refuse to wear gloves," said Nevye. "Why?"

"Gloves are used to keep the world out. After what I've been through, I realize this is the wrong approach. I can harness the power of the world far better with my hands free and sensing."

"The brothers of *Agara'tha* never wear gloves."

"True indeed. And yet you still wear them, brother. Are you conflicted in your calling?"

"Not at all. I prefer to keep the world out."

"You limit your skills."

"Life has limited my skills."

With that, the jaguar fell silent and Sireth slid an eye to study him. He was an interesting man, he'd come to realize. He had seen perhaps thirty-two summers, was of medium height and strongly built, with a wide nose and deep-set, yellow eyes. His hair was sandy and ringed like his pelt, roached on top and pulled back in a tight knot at the base of his neck. He wore the brown robes of *Sha'Hadin* but had spent two years learning under Jet barraDunne, First Mage of *Agara'tha,* himself.

A very wicked tenure.

Finally, he turned to face Yahn Nevye, leaning his hip against the window and cocking his head like the falcon on the ledge.

"Did you know what the dogs would do to us, Yahn? When you

made your little plans in Chancellor Ho's winter garden? Did you have any idea whatsoever the suffering that would come of it?"

The man clasped his hands behind his back, fixed his eyes on the dawning sky.

"No, I didn't."

Sireth studied him a while longer, before turning his attention back to the falcon. She hopped onto his hand, talon bells jingling.

"Well then," he said. "That is a beginning."

He lifted the bird up to his shoulder and turned, leaving the jaguar alone by the window over the Valley of the Seers.

***

They had run all morning, their pace rough and uneven as their boots sank into drifts of snow. They had been in the mountains for days now, moving steadily south and east as they went. The hunting had been good, but Naranbataar was growing tired of the gamey taste of hare and grouse. His grandmother had made the best soup in all Karan'Uurt, his grandfather the best yak, and he found his mouth watering at the memory.

They had eluded the soldiers but he knew they were near. They had almost been caught outside a small gathering of yurts, when his sister had insisted they trade pelts for a bow and set of arrows. He had approved of the arrows instantly, however. They were fletched with crane and tipped with bone. They whistled when they flew.

It was noon then when a flash of gold appeared behind a strange peak. A wall, high above them, riding the mountain like the crest of a dragon.

He pulled up short at the sight, bending over and dropping his hands to his knees. He shook his head.

"Setse," he panted. "Stop."

She swung back, smiling.

"No, Rani. We're almost there. See?"

"There? We're going there?"

"Yes. There."

She clapped her hands, twirled in the snow. Her reindeer coat flapped like wings.

"Setse," he sighed and stepped through the snow to her side. "Setse, that is the Wall of the Enemy. We're not going there."

She caught his hand in hers, blue eye unnaturally bright in the shadow of the mountains. "Yes, Rani! That is exactly where we need to go. *Ulaan Baator* is there. I know I will find him!"

"Setse, please. We can't go there."

"Kuren *Ulaan Baator*. He will save us. I've seen it."

Cities. It was all she talked about. The Khan of Khans was taking all the Oracles to his fortress-city of *Ulaan Baator*. It was a miracle that they had escaped the gathering, but with the restless way she was talking, perhaps it wasn't a blessing.

"We will keep going east. East, Setse. We can keep moving—"

"Hurry, Rani! He's there!"

"Setse, *no!*"

He snatched his hand away and she blinked in surprise. She took several steps backward, began glancing around like a frightened child.

"Oh, eyes. Eye of the Needle, Eye of the Storm. Ulaan Baatar and an army of blood. Eyes. Dragons. Oh the blood, so much blood…"

He cursed himself for his reaction and immediately moved to gather his sister in his arms. She was pulling at her hair like a mad woman and shaking, eyes focused on something he could not see, could never see. He loved her, but still.

"It's alright, Setse. We'll go a little further. We'll go."

"Oh the Eyes…"

Together, they sank into the snow and still he held her, stroking her hair and speaking to her with soft words. But his eyes were fixed on the wall of gold in the distance and dreading the fall of night.

***

The yori was remarkable.

It had been fashioned out of the thickest of leathers and dyed a deep, ox-blood red. The stitching was elaborate and as he ran his gloved fingers over the seams, he could see patterns woven in silk thread. Dragons. The chest and back pieces were stitched together with entwining black and gold dragons, the symbol of the Fangxieng Dynasty. Clasps of lotus studded the work.

"Exquisite," he breathed and the two leopards straightened at his word. He couldn't tell them apart, these two leopards and he wondered if they were twins. He had taken to calling them Leopard One and Leopard Two. They had not taken their eyes off him as he examined the armour on the bamboo stand, likely because of his appearance. He was wearing the kheffiyah once again and the sight of a lion hiding his mane was unusual and therefore, suspect. He was also wearing only a kimonoh and obi, along with split-toed sandals for lounging. It was a foreign thing for him, but one he was in no hurry to exchange. He had spent two years in the field, so this last week in the Imperial residence of *Pol'Lhasa*—in Ling's company exclusively—was a welcome indulgence. It had given him remarkable insight into her world. She ruled an Empire from a single floor.

The leopards were armourers from the Ministry of Defence Archives. She had commissioned them a week ago after her announcement to the council her plans to reinstate the sham'Rai class of warrior. It had been hotly debated, as many in her council suspected her motives. It was not only Chancellor Ho who hated him now.

Because of this, he was still waiting on the release of both Blood and Jade Fangs from the Armory. As legend had it, the swords had been instrumental in the Battle of Roar'pundih, beating back Legions of Dog Soldiers at the hand of General Li Tam-Mountbatten. Now, they lived under plates of silvered glass in the *Kharta'keia* shrine of the Palace. No one dared touch them.

He studied the *soteh* and *koteh*, the plated sleeves that would support and protect his arms. Gold medallions bolted into the leather, with iron casings that would surely stop the sharpest of swords or the swiftest of arrows. Next, the chestpiece or *doh*, reinforced with steel rings and looking to weigh more than a horse. Shin braces and thigh wraps of smoked leather and shoulder *osodeh* finished the armour. What took his breath away however was the helmet, fashioned from hammered bronze that fell from the face like liquid metal. In fact, the tooling gave it the impression of a lion's mane and he smiled to himself at the irony. It boasted the Imperial crest, along with the crest of the House Wynegarde-Grey. Several tail feathers from a pheasant graced the crown.

He lifted the helmet, testing its weight and finding a small hole in the very top. He frowned, curious.

"For the queue," said one of the leopards. "Ancient sham'Rai would shave their heads, save for a single queue. See here?"

And the other flipped open a massive book that they had brought up from the Archives with them. The pages smelled of dust and shadows, but the images were as bright as the sky—sham'Rai from Ancestral times and the rise of the early feline dynasties. They had been quite correct. Without exception, the feline sham'Rai (lions all) would shave their manes, with only a long bolt of hair left to fall from the crown.

"The helmets are very hot," said leopard one. "Less mane is better for soldiers."

"Hard for lions," added leopard two and they both nodded. "Lions are proud of their manes."

"According to Emperor Felix Augustus Asharbupal Kono, Third Emperor of the Tong Dynasty, a sham'Rai who would not shave his mane for duty could not be trusted."

"Too proud."

"Indeed."

As one, they looked at him.

He studied the helm for a long moment, not really seeing it, before laying it back on its stand. Then, slowly, carefully and with great deliberation, he reached up and slipped the kheffiyah from his head. He held his breath.

As one, they bowed, fist to cupped palm.

"Shogun-sama," said One.

"The yori is perfect," said Two.

He felt an odd rush of exhilaration.

He began to slide the Seer's thick leather gloves from his hands.

"And what," he asked, stretching his fingers wide." Do you think you can do with these?"

***

The day had begun like any other in winter. Dark nights rolled into dark mornings and the clouds stayed low and heavy over the Great Mountains. The days were short and finished early at this time of year. Darkness and wind and snow and darkness. That was the cycle of life at the battle tower above the Gate of Five Hands. The only thing anticipated was the gong for evening meal.

And so, it was with a puzzled frown that Captain Kimball Windsor-Chan heard not a gong this evening, but drums.

He looked up from his desk, out the small narrow window that afforded him a view out over the *Botekoshi Gorge* and the Five Hands Pass. In the blackness thrown by the shadows of the Mountains, he saw lights flickering.

There was a rap at his door, followed by a leopard.

"Captain," said the leopard. They were a quiet lot, his leopards. Efficient, experienced, well-trained.

"Why the drums? Is there someone at the Pass?"

"Forgive me but the Lieutenant has asked to see you at the High Gate, sir."

"Why?"

"He does not know the colour for monkeys, sir."

The Captain blinked slowly. He was an old lion but strong and his golden mane was pulled back into a tight top-knot at the crown of his head.

"The colour for monkeys," he repeated. "I don't understand."

"For the oil, sir." The guard nodded swiftly. "Blue for rats, orange for dogs, yellow for Gowrain. But Lieutenant Yu-Carlyle does not know the colour for monkeys."

The lion was out the door in a heartbeat and the Wall spread out like a stone serpent at his feet. The wind plucked at his uniform, the grey clouds billowing in from the northwest and the mountains shone like dark water under them.

Far, far below, lights rippled like a wave upon the shore.

"White," he growled. "White for monkeys."

Under the red and gold banners of the Eastern sun, an army was moving toward the Gate of Five Hands.

***

The Wall of the Enemy towered above them, built into the mountainside that rose steeply from the ridge. The snow had stopped early but the wind was stinging and he knew it would be a bitter night. He could not believe he was here, could not believe he was so near the Wall of the Enemy, and not for the first time, he wondered how long he could keep his sister safe. Her gift was making her reckless. They would both surely die for it.

Soldiers had been dogging them for hours. It was impossible to hide their tracks through the snow and they were nearing exhaustion. The moon was bright, the laughing moon—goddess of his people—shone down on a ridge of black rock and so they dropped to their bellies and crawled to the top to wait, the Enemy's Wall high above them.

They could hear the grunting of voices and Naranbataar silently drew his bow, nocking the arrow and praying his sister would not moan or sing or do any of the other things she did when in the Sight. He had twenty arrows in his quiver. If this were a full Legion, they would not be enough.

Three men staggered into view, trudging through the snow to stare up at the Wall. Legion soldiers, to be sure. Ears cropped, tails docked, they were wearing thick coats of bearskin and he could smell the sweet scent of pine tar from their pipes. They were laughing and one pulled his sword, shaking it like a fist high over his head.

"Here we are, lazy ones!" he shouted up the mountain to the Wall. "Show us your claws!"

"Ha!" barked another. "They hide their claws like women!"

"I piss on their claws!" shouted the third and they all laughed at that.

"I piss on their Wall!"

"Yes! Piss on their Great Wall!"

Beside him, Setse clapped her hands over her mouth as the soldiers proceeded to do just that. Rani growled at her to be quiet.

Suddenly, the night was awakened by a **whompff** and a blaze of orange fire from a cauldron high above like the sun at midday. Distant shouting in a strange and lilting tongue, and then the rain of arrows from the Wall overhead, pelting the snowbanks and the rocks and the men down below. The soldiers yelped and dropped into the snow. They did not move to get up.

And then there was silence once again.

With hands clasped over her mouth, his sister began to rock.

"No, Setse!" he whispered and he hugged her to him to slow her movements. He could hear the strange tongues shouting once again, pulled her down into a very small huddle as arrows pinged anew off the rock surrounding them. His sister began to whine under his hand, then moan, her slip of a body convulsing now in the Sight. There was a thud in his shoulder and another in his thigh. Pain followed, then heat but he covered her all the more, feeling his hope drain away like the stars at sunrise.

She stilled, lifted her face, her blue eye bright and filling with tears.

"Rani?"

"Hush, Setse. Please. Just once."

"Rani?"

She glanced down at her fingers, the clawed tips dark with his blood. She stroked his cheek.

"Rani, I understand…"

"Please, Setse…"

"No, I do. I understand…"

And she bolted to her feet, her thin arms waving in the moonlight.

"Ulaan Baator! Blue Wolf, Yellow Cat!" Followed by a string of syllables that sounded like the voices so high above, in a tongue previously unknown to her, the words of the Enemy.

"No!" he moaned even as he heard it, the whipping sound of an arrow and the thud of impact and Jalair Naransetseg, granddaughter of the Blue Wolf, fell back into the snow and did not move to get up.

He closed his eyes and surrendered to the bitterness of the night.

And the smell of incense.

***

"Wake, wake now."

Sireth opened his eyes to moonlight and silver glinting through her hair.

"You are dreaming."

"No," he said and rolled to sitting. The mattress was low and stuffed with straw. Still only one mattress, as no one had more than they needed at *Sha'Hadin.* He was breaking many traditions now. "Not a dream."

From behind, Ursa slipped her arms around his ribs, covering him like a cloak.

"What did you see, then?"

"Eyes," he said after a moment. "Eyes and an army of blood. Monkeys. Dragons. And a very young girl..."

She placed her cheek on his shoulder. It was not affection, he knew. It was protection. It was her duty and she lived for duty. She lived for him now. He was her life.

He turned his head slightly in her direction, smiled. "Shall we pick up where we left off, my Empress?"

"Pah. You are old. Again would kill you."

"That is true. I'm not a very good husband, I'm afraid."

"And I am a terrible wife."

She was warm and strong and he loved her very much.

"You forge the steel, my love. I need you more than life."

She snorted, telling him he had said a very good thing. She adjusted her position, slipping her legs round his, sliding her hands through his hair onto either side of his head. Their tails entwined, silver and sand and she brought her mouth to his ear.

"Meditate, now. Find the steel. Become it. I will protect you."

"I know you will."

He closed his eyes and was gone.

***

The servant girl bowed in the fashion of women, with the knees and the eyes, as he slipped past her into the Imperial Residence. He found it remarkable how no one questioned his actions, how easily he could move in and out of the most Sacred place on earth and he made a mental note to ask Ling about it sometime. Perhaps, as women, they simply carried certain agreements, certain understandings, about them. It *was* possible, for he was inexperienced with women and knew little of how they thought or ordered themselves. It was much easier to believe Ling had threatened them with death if they spoke of it. That was how a man would handle it if the roles were reversed.

It was a mystery, but then again, cats are a mysterious people. Women doubly so.

He was being followed. A spy most likely or another *kunoi'chi* commissioned by Chancellor Ho. Perhaps the whole council this time. They would surely be in agreement. He was far too dangerous now.

It was dark, only a few candles flickering as twilight stretched blue fingers into the room, turning statues into shadows, turning chairs into enemies. He strained his ears. Only the sound of wind chimes, sleeping peacocks, fountains.

He saw her standing at a far window, made very small by the height and colour of the panes. She was in deep purple, layers of silk and satin, with a headdress of rich gold. It looked like the sun rising and he thought it fitting. The sun truly did rise and set with Thothloryn Parillaud Markova Wu.

He moved to stand beside her, noticing a peacock chick asleep in her sleeve.

"They have scheduled your debriefing in one week," she said, not looking at him.

He nodded. "I have much to tell them."

"They will not believe you."

"The only glass I can polish is my own."

She smiled slightly, her gaze fixed on the flickering rooftops of the city below. "You sound like a Seer."

"Two years spent in such company." He smiled now at the memory but shook his head. "I cannot convince them, no matter what I say."

"The dangers are real."

"Very. From within and without."

"The council is not united, Kirin-san."

He sighed. "I've heard. I am sorry."

"This has nothing to do with you. And everything."

"I should leave then."

"No. I forbid it."

"Ling—"

"I am a bird in a bamboo cage. They can at least allow me my songs."

His heart broke for her.

"I have done everything they have asked of me. I have ruled well. I have furthered the Wall. I have consolidated the Empire. I have married a man of Sacred blood. I have born a Sacred daughter. I have never set foot outside of these walls and I will very likely die never having done so." She took a deep, cleansing breath. "It is never enough."

"You are Enough."

"Hmm." She smiled again. "I used to dream of the time you'd return."

He smiled too.

"I would dream that I would see you in a hallway, just a glimpse of mane or tail or that tattered golden sash. I dreamed I would run to you and you would take my hand and we would flee together out of the palace and down the One Hundred Steps and disappear forever in the crush of the city. I could live like a common woman, love an uncommon man and never have to pick up the burden of government ever again. That is what I dreamed."

He thought for a moment.

"I myself have dreamed that dream," he said finally. "But it always ends the same."

She turned now and he was surprised to see a single tear making a line of silver down her cheek. "How does it end?"

"With guilt, and shame and a troop of soldiers dragging me to my death while carrying you back to the Palace in a palanquin."

"That's a terrible dream."

"Yes. This is much better."

She laughed. It was the song of sparrows.

"And so I am to accept my cage?"

"For now. But if there is one thing I have learned in these last terrible two years, it is that life is strange. Change is inevitable and not to be feared."

"You have become wise, Kirin-san."

"No. Just older."

She reached up to stroke his face. He took her hand and kissed it, thinking he was the happiest he'd ever been in his life and wondering just how long her songs would last.

***

The drums were loud, stirring the blood and quickening the heart. It was like nothing else in all the world. Captain Yuri Oldsmith-Pak set his jaw and studied the line of soldiers forming a fence along the parapet of the Great Wall. The wind was strong and the night was dark but his archers were skilled. Now they studied the rocks far below for movement.

"Nothing, sir," said the Master of the Bow, shouting to be heard over the drums. "We have killed them all."

"No," said the Captain. "Dogs move like rats. Where there is one, there is a Legion."

An ocelot appeared at his side, a long metallic device in his hands.

Oldsmith-Pak snatched it, drew it up to his eyes. It was a star lens, used primarily for studying the skies at night but as in all things, the army had afforded it a rather different use. The Captain swept the lens along the dark mountains, grateful that even with the heavy clouds, the moon gleamed like a mirror. He paused at the sight of a single fire, almost unnoticeable in the distance had it not been for the lens.

"A Legion," he said. "Not two hours away."

"A Legion has never come this close," said the Master of the Bow. "Villagers, yes, but never a Legion."

"Light the cauldron and dispatch a falcon—"

His words were interrupted by a cry from the watchkeep and suddenly there was light far off to his right. One after another, alarm fires were bursting into life all along the Great Wall. In fact, the line of soldiers was watching them too and the boom of the cauldrons bursting with flame could be heard growing louder over the sound of the drums.

"But that's white," said the Master of the Bow. "Orange is for a Legion, not white."

"White is for monkeys," growled the lion. "It's coming from the East. There must be a movement of the *Chi'Chen.*"

"Two armies in one night?"

"Sir," another soldier jogged up. "The watchkeep is asking for instruction. Carry on the white flame or light the orange?"

Snow clouds were rolling over them as if rushing to the beat of the drums. Blood was boiling now, hearts racing and the Captain grit his teeth once again.

"Tell him to light both."

The Master of the Bow stared at him. "But such a thing has never been done, sir."

"We are under attack. I will not stand on protocol."

He turned to face the soldier.

"Light them both."

***

It was early and the sun had not yet risen in the Valley of the Seers, but in the stone stables of *Sha'Hadin,* there was activity and lantern light and warmth. A young serval, Rodgriego, was slipping into and out of stalls, preparing five horses to set out at dawn. Two mounts and three packhorses and Major Ursa Laenskaya's tail lashed at the sight.

"No uniform, no boots, no Imperial horse. This is bad."

The lynx Tiberius smiled as he strapped the last pack on the sleepy animal. "I have packed much tea, sister. You will be well equipped."

"Pah. I would rather have boots."

"You have boots, my love," said Sireth and he led his horse out of its stall. Mi-Hahn was on his shoulder, hooded, wings outstretched as if for balance. "The ones we bought in The'Rhan."

"The'Rhan is a desert, idiot. How could they possibly make good boots?"

He smiled.

"And these are desert horses. You expect them to plod through snow like it was sand? They will be dead by nightfall."

"Well," said Sireth. "I suppose we could eat them."

She snorted. "Yes. We may have to."

"Is there one for me?"

The voice caused silence to fall in the stables of *Sha'Hadin* and Yahn Nevye stepped into the warmth of the lanterns. Mi-Hahn hissed at him.

Sireth smiled. "Ah. So you are leaving."

"I have had a vision."

Ursa snorted again.

"Indeed," said Sireth and he stroked the nose of his horse. "Tell me."

"Eyes. Eyes and fire and a girl."

"What kind of girl?"

"An Oracle."

"I see." He waited, smiling a long-suffering sort of smile. "What *other* kind of girl?"

Nevye glanced up, steeling his jaw. "She's a dog."

"A dog?" Ursa spat on the ground. "Go back to bed, idiot. We aren't going out in the snow to find a dog."

"As a matter of fact," said Sireth, eyes still locked on those of the jaguar. "We are."

"What?"

The two men stared at each other, while Tiberius discreetly continued his packing. The boy Rodriego said nothing, merely finished the buckles and straps that were the tack.

"We're not going to find a dog. Tell him the truth."

"My love..."

"No. *Never.*" She whirled on him. "You remember what the dogs did. To *both* of us."

"I remember."

"I will kill the first dog I see. And every dog after that. I will kill them before they know they have been killed."

"Then I will not let you see them." He looked at the jaguar. "Why do you want to come? I have no idea what I will find."

"It is a powerful vision."

"Yes."

"The girl is important."

"Agreed."

"That is all." He stiffened, raised his chin. "That is all."

The Seer shook his head, turned back to his horse. "Go back to bed."

"But I need to come."

"Give me a reason."

"I owe you no reason."

"In point of fact, you owe me your life. Either of us could demand reparition for what you have done. Either of us could kill you and be justified under Imperial law."

The jaguar looked down at the sand and straw floor. The only sound was the snorting of the horses, the squeak of soft leather and the occasional chirrup of a young falcon. He cleared his throat.

"Sixteen years ago, when I first experienced the Sight, hers was the face I saw. She was an infant. I have seen her ever since."

"*Dogs.* We should kill them all." Ursa spat again, turned to tug the girth on her blue roan. It had been with her since KhaBull. It was a fine lean horse but could never replace her silver mare.

"That is all." The jaguar shrugged. "Truly all."

Sireth glanced at the boy. "Rodriego, might I trouble you for another horse?"

"Of course, *sidi.* Certainly, *sidi.*" And he disappeared into the stalls once again.

"The pack horses are ready, brother," said Tiberius, his wide hands hidden in his sleeves. "I wish you all journeying mercies."

Sireth smiled. "We will need them. I am sorry for leaving so quickly after we have just returned."

"It is the way of things."

"Indeed. Begin to rebuild, Tiberius. There is a dark day coming and our skills will be sorely needed."

The lynx bowed as Rodriego led a sixth horse into the light, passed it into Nevye's waiting hand.

Ursa leaned into him as she moved her horse past. "We will be coming to *Nanchuri Glacier* sooner than expected…Poor little chicken…"

Sireth benAramis merely smiled as together the three of them led their horses out into the first red streaks of dawn.

***

he is bound by the wrists to the stumps of trees and they have beaten him so he cannot stand, blood running down his face, he can barely see the blades on a flap of deerskin, so many blades and they laugh and he can smell the drink on their breath as they reach for his hand

He opened his eyes.

There was a shape silhouetted outside the rice paper walls.

Ling was asleep, her dark body all but hidden in the shadows of the pillows. Slowly, quietly, he rolled to his knees, reaching for the tanto that he kept strapped to his ankle and moved under the darkness toward the door.

The shape was moving tentatively, bobbing and swaying as if unsure and Kirin frowned. It was impossible to guess the size of the intruder, as the only light was from the candles flickering outside the Prayer Room. He remembered how shockingly easy it was to move in and out of this level of the Palace and reached a hand to the sliding doors, heart thudding only once before growing still and steady inside his chest.

With a swift motion, he rose to his feet and slid the doors apart, bringing the tanto up to the throat of the figure.

It was a servant girl, the young sandcat, and she gasped in surprise and dropped to her knees, forehead touching the floor.

"Forgive, forgive," she cried and he straightened, releasing his breath. Behind him, Ling stirred and sat up.

"Farallah?" she asked and pulled a slip of silk to her chest. "What is the disturbance?"

"Forgive, please forgive!"

Kirin frowned. It was the maid girl from the Residence.

"Why are you here?"

"The Chancellor has called a council, Most Revered Excellency." The girl did not move her forehead from the floor. "There has been a falcon from the Wall. Please forgive."

"Yes," said the Empress. "Of course. Let him know that the Shogun-General and I will both attend immediately. Have Lei-lani set out the Indigo Sunrise."

"Excellency."

"With the Star of Dragons headpiece. Go now."

"A thousand blessings," said the caracal, and she dared lift her eyes for the briefest of moments to the golden figure towering over her.

She very quickly averted her gaze.

"Blast," growled Kirin and he slid the doors shut.

When he turned back, Ling was grinning at him.

"I'm certain she will be discreet, my Kirin-san. Women can be trusted with such intimacies."

He narrowed his eyes at her and reached for his clothing, remembering a silhouette of Kerris and two dancers at the Yellow Scorpion behind a rice paper screen.

"I have spent the last two years in the company of three very remarkable women," he said as he stepped into his boots. "And I have come to believe nothing of the sort."

She smiled.

"And I am not Shogun-General. Not yet."

"You will be."

"We are dancing on the edge of a very sharp blade. It is dangerous."

"Life is dangerous."

"Not like this."

"I will have my songs, Kirin-san."

He shook his head once again and as he began to fasten the clasps of the red shervanah coat, he wondered if the time for singing had finally come to an end.

SHOGUN-GENERAL

Far below them, the fires and lanterns of Ulaan Baator flickered as the city slept at their feet. Here, so high on the mesa top of *Khazien*, Mountain of the Khans, the valley looked as if it stretched on forever. He could see the silver serpent that was the River Thuul, the white flatness that was the Salt Plains, the cresting dunes that were the very edge of Gobay. Here, on *Khazien*, Irh-Khan Swift Sumalbayar was sure he could see the whole world.

He could hear the moaning of the Oracle in the Khargan's tent and decided to spend a little more time out in the cold night air. His breath was smoke as he walked so he tugged the bearskin higher onto his shoulders. He was a tall man, taller than many of his brothers. Taller than the Khargan even and that was saying much. But the Khargan was broader, built more like a bear, his chest the size of two men, his arms the breadth of three. Yes, he was the size and shape of a bear. So in their youth, Swift had called him Bear. Everyone else called him Khan.

Khan Baitsuhkhan, First Khan of Khans, the Khargan. Son of the White Wolf, Father of the Jackal. Ruler of the *Chanyu,* All the Peoples of the Earth.

No one remembered his name, the name he had been given at birth. It had been changed so many times as his kills mounted and his power grew. But Swift Sumalbayar, called Long-Swift by the Khan, had grown up with him. They had killed together. They had found wives together.

They had run many campaigns together. They had been as brothers.

Wives had come and wives had gone. Brothers remained forever.

Still, he missed his wife.

He sighed. There were many tents set up now as he walked around the flat top of *Khazien,* gars and yurts and skins slung from stumps. It had been a year of gathering after the fall of the Star, as the *Chanyu* prepared for war. On the far side of the mountain, the army waited. They were ten thousand and growing and the training fields were flattened like the tundra under their boots. He toured their ranks daily as Irh-Khan, Sekond or High Beta, and he was proud of the spirit of the troops. They would take on the Enemy with relish, bring down their Empire and their unmerited pride. No, he wasn't worried about the troops. It was the killing of the Oracles that disturbed him.

He filled his lungs, feeling the bitter wind bite the back of his throat and the tips of his ears. Not for the first time he wished he had cropped them years ago like the other soldiers. They were bitten with frost now, penance for a lifetime of vanity.

He shook his head, steeling his nerve for his return to the Khargan's tent. It glowed with lantern light from the seams. As he approached, the door flapped open and the Khan himself stepped out, wiping his hands on a bloodied doeskin.

His hair was the colour of iron and fell past his face. Woven into it were strands of lion gold and around his neck, rings of many claws.

"He has nothing," Khan Baitsuhkhan growled, tossing the skin into the snow. "Kill him for me and let the crows pick his bones."

"The crows are growing fat this month."

"Let them." The big man spat on the ground. "They are more useful than a thousand Oracles."

Long-Swift nodded once. "Lord."

"Lord?" The Khargan looked up quickly, small eyes shining. "There was a time when I was Bear to you. Since when do you call me Lord?"

Long-Swift shrugged. "There are many soldiers. Respect is a pearl of great price."

The Khan studied him a moment before nodding. "True enough. You will be Khan soon."

"Only if we find lions."

"Oh, we will find lions. Lions enough to make a hundred Khans."

"That would be problematic," Long-Swift grinned. "Where would we all find wives?"

The Khargan laughed and dropped a hand on his shoulder.

"Kill the Oracle. Like wives, there are always more."

And he pushed past, leaving the Irh-Khan standing before the flap of a doorway.

He peered in.

The Oracle was as old as he had ever seen, perhaps sixty. Almost hairless. His eyes and teeth were gone and his bones stuck out at wrong angles. Killing him would be almost a blessing.

He slipped in to do the Khan's bidding.

***

The sound of raised voices could be heard from a long way down the corridor and Kirin was satisfied to see the Leopard Guard lining the walls, swords at hips, staffs in hand. He himself followed several paces behind the entourage of women and there was the expected hush as the great gold door swung open into the presence of Chancellor Ho and the council of Ministers.

The Ministers dropped to their knees, foreheads to the cool mosaic floor. All save the Chancellor, who merely bowed in his peculiar way, seeming to force his eyes from the sight of the lion in the company of the Empress. In fact, Kirin was acutely aware of the tension in the room and wondered how much was because of him and how much because of the falcon from the Wall.

There was no sound—only the hiss of oil burning in the lamps and the room glowed with warmth but no sunlight. She kept them down longer than usual, perhaps to remind them that even with such a consort, she was still, in fact, Empress.

"Rise," she said finally. "There is a falcon?"

"That is not all, Excellency," said Chancellor Ho. "Orange and white alarm fires have been struck."

Kirin felt the world lurch under his feet. *Orange and white.* Dogs and monkeys. Such a thing had never happened. In his mind, he could hear the sound of drums. It would be a hard night for every man on the Wall tonight.

"The falcon," repeated the Empress. She revealed nothing in her voice. She was as regal as the Mountains and just as strong.

Chancellor Ho swept a hand toward an alcove near a high window and she moved through the room like water, the women slipping back out the way they had come. *Almost as smooth as leopards*, Kirin thought grimly. He wondered if any were trained to kill.

The falcon was rugged, larger than Mi-Hahn and less sleek than Path. It wore the hood and talon leathers of its profession but no bells. It was an Army bird. It would as likely bite a cat as serve one and it stretched wide its wings as the Imperial party drew near. Ling reached out a hand, only the tips of her black fingers visible through the silks, stroked the creature's speckled breast. It hissed but did not strike.

"From the Wall?" she asked and the Minister of the Wall stepped forward.

"From the Gate of Five Hands," he said. He was a tiger, unusual for such a common man to have attained such a rank and therefore impressive. Kirin knew never to underestimate the tenacity of tigers.

"Five Hands? The *Chi'Chen* Gate?"

"The very one, Excellency. It is only two days' ride."

"Do you have the parchment?"

"Excellency," said Chancellor Ho. "These are important matters of state. Perhaps we could ask Kirin-san to wait outside. With the women."

Her golden eyes flashed.

"The Shogun-General is privy to all matters of state."

"Alas," said Ho. "There is no Shogun-General. Not yet."

"It does not require an act of state when the rank is forged in a time of war," she said, keeping her voice even. "Is that not true, Master Soeng?"

A thin pale man of Sacred blood stepped forward and Kirin recognized him as the Minister of Archives. He looked like a slip of paper.

"Most Revered Excellency, may you live forever. You are, of course, quite correct. According to the Archives, the very last Shogun-General of the Upper Kingdom was created to honour General Yasouf Kingston-benMazar under Empress Faisala the Wise. He killed the seventh Khan of the Lower Kingdom in the Battle of the Weikhan Valley and was accorded the title with no opposition from the ruling council."

Ling turned her heavy-lidded eyes on the Chancellor.

"I am not Empress Faisala the Wise and, of course, desire unanimous approval from my council. Captain Wynegarde-Grey has yet to give us his report on his journey in the Year of the Tiger, including the establishment of a new Khan, the death of six of my Seers, not to mention the role of Jet barraDunne and the fall of *Sha'Hadin*. There may be government officials that bear responsibility for crimes against our Kingdom. Surely you will allow him some leniency, Chancellor? Careers could be shattered on one word from his mouth."

Kirin's heart was thudding as if he would surely die. With alarm fires racing across the Kingdom, she was playing a dangerous game with the Chancellor and Ho was a dangerous man. His wide face split wider and he bowed most formally.

"But of course, Excellency. It would be disrespectful of me to presume anything other than righteous motives on behalf of our good Captain and soon-to-be Shogun-General. I withdraw my protest."

She cast her eyes around the Throne Room.

"Are we all in accord? Alarm fires have been struck and I would like to hear the scroll read. When did it arrive?"

"At the commencement of the second watch, Excellency."

Kirin grit his teeth. It seemed all manner of bad things happened in the second watch.

And yet another minister stepped forward. Minister of Falcons, Kirin knew. He was a serval and the tips of his ears rose high above his head. Carefully, he unfolded a very small slip of parchment and began to read.

"Division of *Chi'Chen* army amassed Five Hands Gate. Monkeys number two thousand. Ambassador Bo Fujihara diplomatic envoy requests Imperial counsel. Kaidan with him."

There was silence for barely a heartbeat before the room began to buzz with comments. *Chi'Chen* Army. Five Hands Gate. Two thousand men. Not allowed through. Act of war. But for Kirin, there was only one word that registered, one that shook him to his very bones.

"Kaidan?"

"But why the orange fire," asked the Minister of Arms. "Orange is for dogs."

"Perhaps someone should be reminded?"

"Perhaps someone should be executed."

"Kaidan?" Kirin asked again. "Kaidan is with them?"

"Apparently so," said the serval before turning to the Minister of Diplomatic Affairs.

"But that is impossible."

No one was listening. They were arguing amongst themselves.

"It is impossible."

"The *Chi'Chen* would not dare."

"Ambassador Fujihara grows as bold as his tobacco."

"Kaidan?" he asked again.

The Empress turned to him.

"Kirin-san? What of Kaidan?"

He released a deep, cleansing breath and then another. His head was spinning. *How could this be?*

"Kirin-san," she said again. "I am the only one in the room. Tell me."

He nodded, drawing strength from her great golden eyes. "He went west, west in a ship with Solomon. They were looking for others. There is no way he could now be east with an army."

"That was almost a year ago."

"It makes no sense."

Quietly, she laid a hand on his sleeve.

"Solomon. You told me this. This is the name of the Ancestor, yes?"

"Ancestor?" said Chancellor Ho, and suddenly, all conversation in the room ceased.

"They were all dead in Swisserland," Kirin said. "But he thought there might be more in a place called Kanadah. It sounded like a very far place. A world away, Solomon said."

"Ancestor?" said the Minister of Defense.

"Do you know if they found others?" asked Ling.

He shook his head. "But if they did and Kerris is back with an army, then I can only assume it's a bad thing."

"There are no Ancestors," said the Minister of Archives.

"Oh, most certainly none," said the Minister of the Wall.

"Yes," said Kirin. "There are."

All the ministers were silent now and staring, as talk had suddenly moved quite beyond their experience.

With a gust of cold air, the great red and gold door swung open and a small figure rushed into the room. It was a boy of perhaps fourteen summers, a courier wearing the uniform of the Ministry of Falcons and as such, was allowed free access to all parts of the Palace. He jingled as dropped to his knees and held up a set of talon bells.

"Forgive, please forgive!" he cried. "There is a second falcon!"

"From where?" asked the Chancellor.

"The Wall, Magnificence. North of the foundry of *Shen'foxhindi.*"

"North?" said the Minister of Defense. "The *Chi'Chen* will not be coming from the north."

"No," said the Minister of the Wall. "That would be dogs."

"The orange fire," said the Minister of Diplomatic Affairs.

The Throne Room went silent once again.

The Empress turned and moved to the small wooden chair. It was the only thing in the room that was not carved, painted or layered in gold or jewels. Slowly, she climbed the steps, turned and lowered herself into the Ages Old seat, the symbol of Dynastic Power for longer than anyone could remember.

She sat a moment before responding, her voice as soft as a nest of swallows.

"Ambassador Fujihara and Kaidan will be allowed passage through the Gate of Five Hands."

Chancellor Ho moved to speak, but thought better of it. She continued.

"They and a small party of diplomats will be escorted to *Pol'Lhasa* by a full regiment of the Imperial Guard, where I will grant them Imperial counsel. We will afford them all the honour of a Royal entourage while we discuss matters of peace and war and Ancestors."

Again, silence.

"We will draft a response to be carried back to the Gate of Five Hands, to Ambassador Bo Fujihara and to Kaidan himself. It will be delivered personally by our very own Shogun-General. He has knowledge of such things, knowledge beyond any of us."

The council murmured agreement.

"I order the immediate release of the Blood and Jade Fangs for this express purpose."

"Indeed," said the Minister of Arms. "Our very first Shogun-General should be well appointed."

Again, murmurs of agreement. All except one.

"And the north, Excellency?" said the Chancellor. "The foundry of *Shen'foxhindi* is less than a week's ride from *Sha'Hadin.*"

"You worry for *Sha'Hadin* now, Chancellor?" she asked, eyes flashing. "There was a time when you would have me diverted with fireworks and spectacles."

Oh, such a dangerous game.

The Chancellor bowed low to the ground.

"The security of the Empire is my foremost priority, Excellency."

"I know this, Chancellor. Your loyalty is never in doubt."

She turned to the Ministers of Defense and the Wall.

"All leave is cancelled for the army and forces are to be marshaled along the northeastern front. I sanction conscription notices for all men with more than twelve summers and grant your ministries full discretion in the fortification of the Wall."

With knees and foreheads to the floor, her ministers bowed and Kirin knew beyond a doubt that the only music now was the beat of the drums of war.

***

It was not a normal gar, for the coverings were silks, frost and evergreen boughs. There was a small fire crackling in the center, and as his eyes adjusted to the dim light, he realized it was not a fire but many small fires – candles. At least ten of differing heights, filling the gar with the heady smell of smoke and incense.

Naranbataar tried to sit up but long, strong hands pushed him back down into the warm snow.

"Peace, little brother," said a woman's voice, deep and breathy and accented in very strange and foreign way. She was wrapped in blackness and shadows. "I have stitched your wounds but you will need rest."

"Setse," he said, trying to focus on the woman. There was something very strange in her scent. "My sister—"

"Is resting as well. You both will heal if you only rest."

"Please, help her," he said, and accepted the small lump of snow that she slipped into his mouth. It had a bitter, powdery taste but the water was good on his tongue.

"Of course."

There was a sound, a mewling sound like an infant. He saw her turn toward the candles, saw her profile in the flickering light. Her face was like nothing he had ever seen.

Delusions, he thought to himself. He was likely dying and only imagining what it would be like to be tended by the Enemy. The Enemy would not treat him, would not heal him. Would only skin him and rape his sister. That's what the enemy would do.

"Sleep now," said the woman again. His eyesight blurred and he saw nothing more for some time.

***

The morning stayed gray as the snow clouds settled in over their Mother, the Great Mountains. They were making good time. While the roads to *Sha'Hadin* were not well-travelled, the trail was reasonably clear of drifts and ice. The desert horses did admirably but it became clear very quickly that Yahn Nevye was not comfortable on the back of a horse.

Ursa made sure to mention it every chance she had.

"So where are we going?" she growled. She had taken the fore and did not turn her head to speak. She had found a coat made from the pelt of a white northern bear and her hair swung in straight coarse lines across her back.

"I'm not sure," said Sireth and glanced at the jaguar riding behind him. "Yahn? Do you know where we're going?"

The jaguar swallowed and looked up. His eyes were wide and he appeared to be in considerable discomfort.

"No," he panted. "The Wall somewhere. North, I think."

Sireth looked back to his wife. "North, we think."

She shook her head. "I am riding with idiots."

He smiled. The fur around his mouth and chin had thin wisps of ice coating the tip of each hair. *Marvelous,* he thought to himself. A year ago, he was on the shore of a strange sea, with beaches of white sand and crashing waves and the thoughts of home had been turned upside down. He was home now wherever he was, as long as the snow leopard was by his side. While he loved *Sha'Hadin,* he loved Major Ursa Laenskaya more. She had become his home.

He was a very happy man. Even here, out on the trail to North somewhere, on the back of a horse yet again, for he knew he was riding with a purpose. With a wife and a noble purpose, any man could be truly happy.

He thought of the man riding behind him. It was difficult to get a sense of him, this jaguar. His motivations, his heart. It always had been—even when they had been studying together under Petrus Mercouri, Yahn Nevye had always been a closed book. *"I prefer to keep the world out,"* he had said the other night in the hall outside his door. He could not speak to falcons and yet had found a home in *Agara'tha* with Jet barraDunne and his world of shadows. Now, that home was gone and Sireth wondered how the jaguar truly felt about it.

No, without a wife or a purpose or even a home, it was obvious that Yahn Nevye was not a happy man.

High above them, Mi-Hahn cried, hunting.

"I shall meditate now," he called to the snow leopard. "Perhaps I can find the thread and follow it somewhere."

"If it leads to a dog, I will kill it and then you." She swiveled in her saddle. "Close your eyes and ride. I will watch for you."

"I know you will."

He closed his eyes and was gone.

***

It fit like a glove. An ox-blood glove of strong tanned leather and he moved, twisted, bent and flexed within its confines. The leopards were watching him as he moved, looking for signs of ill-fit or rubbing but there were none. The yori was perfect, as comfortable as his old uniform and it made him feel almost powerful once again. Almost.

"And these," said Leopard One as he stepped forward, a long purple box in his hands. "Tor has had these made for you…"

Tor. So that was his name. Kirin took the box, slid the top to reveal gloves of ox-blood red. They were ribbed and reinforced with steel. Slowly, he slipped his hand in one, made a fist. The leather creaked. It felt strange.

They could tell from his expression and Leopard Two – Tor - stepped forward now.

"I have made them specifically for you, Shogun-sama. They are a strong leather, yes? But soft. Good for gripping the Blood and Jade Fangs. They will hold to the hilts like paste."

"Yes," he said.

"But for you, do this…"

And he flexed his wrist.

Kirin frowned.

"No, no. Do this." And he flexed again.

Kirin flexed his wrist and steel razors sprang from the fingers of each glove.

"Deadly, yes?" nodded Leopard One.

"Better than claws," agreed Two.

Kirin drew his hand closer, studied the five daggers with wonder. He could see the engineering, how the steel ran along the back of the hand mimicking the bones of his fingers. They came out of slits in the fingertips. They were sharp, curved and caught the light like ice.

"Miraculous," he breathed.

"You bend your wrist back to retract them."

He did so and the claws disappeared into the leather with a soft hissing sound. His heart thudded once as he realized what this meant.

The leopards were smiling.

"Both gloves are the same," said Two.

"Ingenious, I'd say," said One. "Simply ingenious."

"We call them the Teeth of the Dragon."

Both leopards beamed at that.

He flexed the wrist again, amazed as the blades popped out, shining in the lamplight. He swung his arm, drew it in close, then glanced up.

"Are they…?"

"Purely ceremonial?" said One. "Not at all."

"The gloves are reinforced with steel," said Two, stepping close and tugging a leather strap. "The same steel used in making katanahs. If you were going in to battle, you would make sure it is tightened on to the koteh like so…"

And he tugged some more, laced the strap into a buckle. "You will need a squire to help, Shogun-sama. There is much armour and many buckles."

Kirin flexed his fingers once again, swirled his hand in the air in patterns of Chai'Chi. The daggers felt remarkably secure.

"And forgive us, Shogun-sama, but…"

"But we could not help but notice…"

As one, they looked down at his tail.

Still wrapped in the leathers made for him by Ursa Laenskaya, his tail was woefully underrepresented.

"I made a Khan," he said softly. They looked at him. "Then unmade him."

Leopard Two produced another box, a blue one this time, wrapped in silver threads. Inside was a series of golden bands and cords of red silk and he held them up in his fingers. The bands were chiseled with the imprints of dragons and he could feel the ridges as sharp as blades.

"Scales of the Dragon," said One. "As deadly as they are beautiful."

"The gold bands snap on to hold it in place," said Two.

"No one will mock your tail now," said One.

His throat was closing.

"When you lash, be mindful of your audience."

"Indeed. You may do them a damage."

He didn't know what to say.

So with fist to cupped palm, he bowed to them.

"You have honoured me," he said. " I am forever in your debt."

"Not at all, Shogun-sama," said One.

"Indeed," said Two. "To work on the yori for the very first Shogun-General of the Fanxieng Dynasty, that is our glory and honour."

"Allow us the honour," said One. "Of fitting the kabuto."

He took a deep breath, cast his eyes to the helmet of hammered bronze. As leopards, they were considerably shorter than he, so he lowered to one knee. The knee twinged as he went down, reminding him of rats and the Battle tower of *Roar'pundih*. It seemed like a lifetime ago.

Slowly, with great deliberation, he pulled the kheffiyah from his head.

Leopard One moved forward, lowered the kabuto over his head. Slipped the pheasant feather from its perch on the crown, dipped it into the hole to hook the bolt of mane that was left. Carefully, he pulled it up and through the hole so that it crested over the sweeping metal. It fell down his back like a ribbon.

He replaced the feather and stood back, admiring.

"Perfect, Shogun-sama."

"You are worthy," said Two. "Remember."

"Yes, remember," said One. "You are worthy."

For some strange reason, his eyes filled with tears.

He rose to his feet and gathered the two leopards into an embrace worthy of a Seer of *Sha'Hadin*.

***

With the advent of winter, the days were short. Too short to continue long into the evening and so they made camp by a new rope bridge that swung across the *Shi'pal* River. They sat around a small fire, wrapped in yak-hide, drinking tea and roasting mice that Mi-Hahn had caught along the way.

"Do you remember this place?" asked Sireth as he poked the sizzling coals with a stick.

Ursa was all but hidden by the thick hide and from behind her curtain of wild hair she narrowed her eyes at him. " You mean the bridge?"

"Yes."

"There *was* no bridge."

"Exactly. We were made to forge the river farther down."

She snorted, spat bones into the snow, drew the hide up on her shoulders. "The Captain almost died that river."

"Yes. We did admirably that night," he said. "All of us."

"This is ridiculous," said Yahn Nevye. Like Ursa, he too was almost hidden by the yak hide. "We can't sleep in the snow like this. We'll be frozen by morning."

"Idiot," growled the Major.

"Why can't we find a cave or something? Make a tree-cover or walls of snow? Something? Anything?" He shivered, flattened his ears into his hair. Like Sireth's beard, they were tipped with frost.

"Do you see any trees, idiot? Did you bring a spade for shoveling?"

Sireth smiled. "Loosen your knot. Let your hair warm you."

The man snorted and looked away. Ursa rolled her eyes and picked at another mouse with her claws. Nevye was right, however. The night was very cold. Even the horses were huddled together, not wanting to expend the heat or energy needed to hunt. It seemed all they could do to keep the fire going tonight. They might very well be frozen by morning.

There was a thump and a rush of wings landed in the snow nearby. *Mi-Hahn,* Sireth thought. The young falcon was not a skilled hunter and frequently caught her prey by force, knocking them out of the sky by speed alone. But he could hear Mi-Hahn's voice high above and he sat up to study the shape in the moonlight.

"It's an owl," said Yahn Nevye. "He's caught a chiwa."

The Seer cocked his head. "How do you know this?"

Nevye shrugged.

"He can't talk to falcons. Maybe he talks to owls," grunted the snow leopard. She was not looking at the owl. Her pale eyes were fixed on the flames as if willing them to warm her more than the hide.

Sireth sat back and studied the jaguar now. Nevye was watching the dark shape as it jabbed with its short, lethal beak.

"What is his name?" he said after a while.

Nevye did not look at him.

"What is his name?" the Seer repeated.

"Hunts in Silence," Nevye said.

"Hunts in Silence," said Sireth. "Fascinating."

"He is young. His mate was killed by an eagle this summer, before their eggs hatched. He is alone. But he hunts well and will find a new mate in the spring."

"He talks to owls," Sireth muttered under his breath. The world was a wondrous strange place. "Can he hear you?"

"What?" Now the jaguar did look back. He seemed preoccupied. "What's that?"

"The owl. Can he understand you when you speak?"

The man snorted again. "I don't speak to owls."

"Have you tried?"

"Of course not. Don't be ridiculous. Seers of *Sha'Hadin* speak to falcons, not owls."

"*You* don't speak to falcons," grumbled the Major.

"Try," said Sireth. "Tell him to look at you."

"This is ridiculous."

"Tell him."

The jaguar tugged the yak hide higher onto his shoulders but in the firelight, Sireth could see his yellow eyes dart to the distant brown shape, now busy tearing at flesh and sinew under its talons. The bird was quite intent and the snow was growing dark with blood.

"Call him by his name."

Nevye's tail whapped under the hide but he said nothing.

"I am going to sleep," said Ursa. "Wake me when the idiot dozes off. I will kill him then, toss his body to the owls."

And she bundled down in the snow. She looked like a small yak sleeping.

"Good night, my love," said the Seer. "I will see you in your dreams."

"We pass *Nanchuri Glacier* tomorrow," she murmured under the hide. He could see the slivers of her eyes, pale like the moon.

"Yes, I believe we do."

"Then my dreams will be sweet and filled with blood."

She closed her eyes, smiling.

He sighed and looked to the jaguar. He could see his profile in the firelight, wondered what could motivate a man like that. Wondered what Dharma had sent his way and if he was running from her as well. Dharma was a cruel mistress. She chased many men.

Suddenly, with ribbons of pink swinging from its beak, the owl looked at them.

It was like a bolt of lightning but then the bird lifted from the snow, the remains of the chiwa in its claws. He was swallowed by the darkness.

"Well, well," said Sireth as Yahn Nevye turned to look at him. "Perhaps many more things will change at *Sha'Hadin* before I'm through…"

With that, he sunk deep into the warm snow, tugging the yak hide over his head.

Yahn Nevye stayed awake for much longer.

***

The Throne Room was filled on all sides with colour.

Ministers from every office in *Pol'Lhasa* were present. Ministers, Under-ministers and clerks as well, everyone eager to see the presentation of the Blood and Jade Fangs to the very first Shogun-General of the Fanxieng Dynasty. It was twilight but the many torches and lanterns in the room filled it with gold and warmth, and while the wind howled outside these walls, inside it was as oppressive as a jungle.

He strode down the length of it, saw Chancellor Ho standing near the Throne, dressed in robes of Imperial Gold. Still, he kept his eyes fixed only on the Empress on the plain wooden seat. His heart was steady, his mind detached, for in truth, he could not believe any of it was happening. This last week had been a dream. None of it real or possible or true. At any time, he would awaken to find himself back in the tent of the dogs, waiting to be cut into pieces by their blades.

The room was silent as he reached the foot of the Throne, the ages-old seat of power for three dynasties. Two ministers were standing at her sides, one of Arms and the other of Defense. They were holding a sword each and he knew them instantly but could not dwell, for he dropped to the floor, elbows and forehead touching the warm stone.

All was silent, save for the hissing of the torches.

"We are entering a time of war," she said, her voice soft as swallows, piercing as the North wind. "With enemies amassing on both Eastern and Northern Borders. The *Chi'Chen* may very well be a peaceful force but they are still a threat to our security. And kestrels are bringing reports of a Legion of Legions gathering in the city of the Enemy. On the outskirts of the Empire, rats are now reported using tools in their swarms. We are beset by enemies within and without."

She paused, letting her golden eyes sweep the room like brooms. No impurity could exist in the corners of this room.

"But more than these, we are faced with another threat, a threat more dangerous than dogs or monkeys or rats."

The entire room was hushed. On the floor, Kirin could barely breathe. He was grateful for the stiff leather of the yori. It gave him support and strength.

"More than these, there is the threat of Ancestors."

He could hear nothing. No one was breathing. No one could believe.

"Ancestors are alive in this world, far far to the West. The star in the Year of the Tiger awakened them and we have sent our dear Kaidan, ambassador of the Upper Kingdom, to verify this. He is back now with an Army of *Chi'Chen* soldiers at the Gate of Five Hands. For this reason, we have commissioned a new Shogun-General. Kirin Wynegarde-Grey, formerly a Captain of the Imperial Guard. He alone has experience with Ancestors."

He wanted to crawl away, hide under a table, a chair, anything.

"The Council has approved this commission and so, without delay, I have ordered the presentation of the Blood and Jade Fangs. Ministers..."

He could hear their feet move, drew in a deep breath.

"Captain Wynegarde-Grey, look at me.

His head was spinning. He couldn't believe.

It seemed someone else was lifting his head.

"Kirin Balthashar Wynegarde-Grey, you are a lion born of a noble house. You were Captain of the Imperial Guard, like your father before you. This is not Enough. The Brotherhood of the Fangs is an historic one, a complex one. The Sword of Blood is violent and thirsty. It has slain over one thousand dogs in its history, twice as many rats. It longs to kill, it lives to sew death. Are you worthy of the Blood, Kirin-san?"

He could see the Minister of Arms holding it out before him. It was a khatanah, its long steel fashioned out of Khamachada iron. It gleamed red in the lantern light.

No, he said with every thought, every sinew, every muscle. *I am not worthy.* Yet his mouth was silent.

"The Sword of Jade is poetry unmatched. It sings when it moves, it dances when drawn. To die by the Jade is a death of music, of beauty, of art. Are you worthy of the Jade, Kirin-san?"

The Minister of Defense stepped forward, holding out the short sword, a khodai'chi of Khamboh'jah iron, oily green in hue.

"Are you worthy of the brothers?"

Are you worthy?

He didn't understand.

"Are you worthy of these blood brothers?"

Her golden eyes pleaded with him to answer, but he didn't understand the question. Was he worthy? Was he?

He was kneeling here before them all, unrecognizable because of the yori and kabuto and suddenly he remembered the leopards One and Two. He smiled to himself. They had been very clever.

Slowly and with great care, he raised his arm and lifted the helmet from his head, allowing the single queue of golden mane to drape down the back of his neck. The pelt of his head, unmaned by dogs, visible for all to see. The pride of lions gone in service to the Empire.

There was a gasp from the Ministers, from the Under-ministers and the clerks. Indeed, from everyone in the Throne Room of the Empress, including Chancellor Ho. Once his shame, now his glory and to his utter surprise, the entire room dropped to their knees now. One by one, elbows and foreheads to the floor, they bowed before him, the very First Shogun-General of the Fanxieng Dynasty.

He met her eyes now, could hear her songs dancing inside his head.

"Yes," she said. "You are worthy."

And she smiled.

THE ENEMY

"Sweetling of days,
Sweetling of days,
The nights have grown colder
And you have grown older,
Sweetling of days,
Remember my song."

It was a scrap of memory from childhood and filled him with warmth and the ache of loss.

"Sweetling of days,
Sweetling of days,
The River has dried up,
Our tears have all cried up,
Sweetling of days,
Remember your home."

It was not his grandmother's voice and when he opened his eyes, he was not surprised to see tree boughs, frost and drapes of dark silk.

Setse was singing.

He flexed his shoulder where he remembered the arrow had struck. It was tight but there was no pain. Vaguely, he remembered a second arrow and he drew his knees, causing the bearskin to bunch and fall.

"Good morning, Rani," sang his sister. Her voice was music on the wind.

Smiling, he propped himself up onto his elbows, mindful not to sit too high. The boughs were low and would likely drop snow all over him if bumped. There were candles still in the centre of the little gar and he could see Setse across the flames. She was rocking something in her arms, beaming like a spring morning.

"How do you feel?" she asked.

"Alive." He remembered the sound of her falling, the crunch of her body in the snow. "And you?"

"Very well. She is a good healer."

"Who, Setse? Who did this?"

"Rah. She'll be back soon. She's gone to collect roots for medicine and pine needles for tea."

He sat up straighter, ran his hand along his neck and shoulder, finding a poultice of moss, tree sap and mustard seeds.

"Who is she, Setse? Where did she come from?"

"Oh, I don't know. Witches come from everywhere," she said and she dropped her eyes down to the blanketed shape in her arms. She resumed her singing.

"Sweetling of days,
Sweetling of days,
The dark days have tarried,
Our dead we have buried,
Sweetling of days,
Remember your clan."

He narrowed his eyes.

"What is that? What are you holding?"

"Ulaan Baator will come now," she said, still smiling.

His heart thudded inside his chest and he rolled to his knees, crawled past the candles to his sister's side.

"He has only a few months," she said. "Perhaps four. I couldn't understand her times. She's speaks the language of the People but her accent is strong…"

From within the folds of the blanket, a tiny golden hand was reaching up, touching his sister's face. He could see the tips of golden claws, sliding in then out of the fingers in a motion that reminded him of his grandmother kneading dough.

"Setse," he growled. "Where did you get that?"

"Rah. She asked me to watch him."

He couldn't believe what she was saying, even less what he was seeing.

"She's brought him all the way from the Southern Sea, where it rains in winter, not snow." Setse looked up at him. "Isn't that strange? Rain in winter?"

"Setse, put it down."

"His name is Kylan."

"Put it down."

She frowned, hugged the child to her chest. Immediately, it began to whimper and flail.

"She asked me to watch him, Rani."

"Kill it."

"No! It's just a baby, Rani!"

"It is a child of the Enemy, Setse. Kill it now."

"Rani, no! Never!"

The child began to wail and he could see tiny pinpricks of red in his sister's chin.

"Put it down, Setse. We can leave now and be back in the mountains before she gets back."

He reached for her but she shrank back, clutching the blankets tightly to her chest.

"No, Rani! She saved us! Both of us!"

"She's a witch, Setse!"

"That's what they said about me, Rani! That I was a witch! Just because I see things, because I know things!" Suddenly, she froze, her blue eye glittering and glassy. She began to speak in the language of the Enemy.

The flap of the tent swung open and a wraith slipped inside.

He scrambled for his quiver, quickly nocked an arrow, drew the string but couldn't loose it. His finger refused to move. For the very first time in his young life, Jalair Naranbataar saw the Enemy standing before him.

She was wearing black leather and a cloak of thick bearskin and her face was hidden in the shadows of her hood. But in those shadows, he could see her eyes, gleaming like the flames of her many candles. She smelled powerfully of incense and magic and when she lifted the hood, he was amazed at what he saw. It was not the face of a monster. Not the face of nightmares or legends told to frighten children. In fact, he thought, as the arrow pointed directly between her large eyes, that she looked less like the night and more like the sun.

"Good morning, little brother," she said and then she smiled.

He swallowed, redressed his grip on the bow.

"What do you want?" he growled. "Why did you bring us here?"

"Your wounds are healing well." Her voice was deep, smokey. "The arrow is not shaking."

"I said, what do you want?"

"I want to feed my baby." She blinked slowly and he felt the strength draining from his muscles. "And then I would like a cup of tea. Do you drink tea, little brother?"

"Green tea?" asked Setse.

"Of course."

"I would love green tea," sang Setse, and she kissed the baby on the forehead. "We don't get green tea at home. Only bone tea. It's good for strength but it tastes very bad."

The witch moved toward his sister and Rani followed her with his arrow.

"Don't touch her," he growled, baffled as the woman folded her long legs and dropped to the snow next to his sister. Setse passed the baby over and with a minimum of tucks and folds, the baby was nursing happily. Setse clapped her hands.

"I knew it," she sang. "Ulaan Baatar is coming, isn't he?"

"He will come," said the woman.

"You see, Rani? I knew it. Blue Wolf, Yellow Cat. Everything will be good now. Everything will be made right."

He had none of the gift himself, but somehow, Naranbataar knew that it nothing would be made right for a long while, and that before it was right, life would become very, very wrong.

***

"This is impossible," said Yahn Nevye as the three of them stared down the long stretch of cord and rattan that made up the rope bridge. Far below, one of the *Shi'pal's* little sisters leapt through the gorge like a team of white stallions, throwing up an icy spray that felt like daggers on their cheeks. "No horse will cross that. We should go father."

"Idiot," growled Ursa. "You know nothing."

She turned to her horse, the blue roan from Khanisthan, cupped his long face in her hands, stared into its large dark eyes.

"You are not a soldier, but you are brave and strong-hearted. You will follow me across this bridge and I will name you Xiao."

"Brave? You would name a horse Brave?" The jaguar peered again over the edge. "You speak to horses as though they understand."

"Pah," she snorted. "I speak to *you* as though you understand."

Nevye looked to benAramis. The Seer merely shrugged.

"The horses will follow," said the Major. "They are all brave. Watch and learn, little chicken."

And with a hand on the reins, she stepped a booted foot out and onto the rattan that crossed the gorge. Snow fell from the canes, disappearing into the white spray as if home. The ropes that formed the rails quivered and squeaked but held.

Two boots now, and she began to cross, the bridge swinging a little at her weight. She did not turn and slowly, the horse stepped a hoof onto the rounded shapes of the canes.

It hesitated, but she did not stop and soon the reins were taut. Behind the men, the horses snorted and shifted in the snow. Mi-Hahn chirruped on Sireth's shoulder as together they watched both snow leopard and desert horse begin to make the narrow crossing. And still she did not turn.

"Xiao," she cried over the roar of the river, not looking back. "Xiao. You are Xiao."

With wild eye, the horse took another step. And another. And another.

The bridge was swaying with each hoof fall, creaking under the weight, and they both grew very small as they crossed the wide gorge over the River. In fact, it seemed like hours but finally, the Major had laid a hand on the pike of the far side and the horse scrambled up behind her. They pushed through the snow drifts and were on solid ground once again.

She stroked its long nose, ran a hand along its blue neck.

"Xiao," she said. "Now and forever, you are Brave."

On the other side, Sireth smiled and turned to his horse. "Well then, what shall we call you, my red desert friend?"

Mi-Hahn cried out and left his shoulder for the great expanse of grey that was the sky. The horse snorted and together, horse and Seer began to cross, the bridge creaking and swaying under their weight. A cane cracked, splintered under a heavy hoof but before long they too were scrambling up the drifts on the other side.

Tan mongrel turned to face red horse.

"Dune," he said. "You move through snow as if it were sand. I shall name you Dune.

One by one, the packhorses followed, the bridge swinging sideways with each crossing. Another cane splintered and disappeared into the spray of the river but none were lost until only a jaguar and one horse were left. Across the gorge, Ursa stared at the horse.

It shook its head, tossed its mane, but soon, it too was following the others. The bridge creaked and a hoof went through, leaving a hole large enough to lose a cat but it crossed. Yahn Nevye was the only creature on the far side of the gorge.

Ursa narrowed her eyes. "Little chicken?"

"That is madness," he called over. "Did you see those canes?"

"The horses weigh far more than you."

The man swallowed, glanced down at the rushing *Shi'pal* far below. He looked up. "How do I know that this isn't a ruse? You might cut the ropes as I cross!"

Sireth smiled.

"If she wanted you dead, brother, we would not be having this conversation."

"I'm not good with heights," called the jaguar.

"We are in the mountains, idiot." And rolling her eyes, Ursa Laenskaya mounted Xiao and headed out, plowing through the drifts as though the horse were a yak.

"I might fall through those canes! Look at that hole!"

"Don't look at the hole," called Sireth. "Don't look at the gorge. Just look at me. Look..."

Nevye stared at him.

"That's right. Just look at me."

For once, the jaguar did as he was asked.

"There is no gorge. There is no river. There is only a path that takes you from the table to the chair."

"I know what you're asking. You think me a novice."

"I think nothing of the sort."

Nevye swallowed but kept the Seer's gaze. "You can do this?"

"Do you trust me?"

"Not in the least."

"It doesn't matter. Just look at me. That's right. The rope is not a rope, it is a chair..."

And Nevye placed a foot onto the canes of the bridge.

"...A chair made of rope and rattan. Reach your hand to grab the back of the chair. Very good. Just ropes and canes that I gathered from the forest. The paths to the rattan fields were not smooth paths. They rose and fell with the forest floor. There are stumps and dips and the roots but the canes were very good and worth the occasional twisted ankle. The ropes are strong, the rattan even stronger and the chairs I made were very fine. I made them all the time in *Shathkira*, a little village in *Lan'ladesh*—"

Sireth hissed as Nevye's foot went through the hole and he dropped like a stone.

"—Feel the chair, Yahn. Hold the back of the chair."

"I *am,*" growled the jaguar. His eyes were glassy, held as they were by the Last Seer of *Sha'Hadin.* He was hanging on to the ropes with both hands as one leg dangled above the gorge. The split-toed sandal sailed down, down, down. "It's a stupid chair."

"Yes," said Sireth, and he raised a hand. The sandal rose with it. "But do remember the forest floor is not smooth. You must lift your feet carefully when you walk."

Nevye pulled his leg up, placed it onto the canes, continued to walk. The Seer released a long breath.

"People paid good money for my chairs. It was a good job and I made a good living. Perhaps, I can convince the Major to give up the army and take up a simpler life, a smoother life of trees and canes and bamboo..."

And with that, Yahn Nevye stepped into the drifts in front of the last Seer of *Sha'Hadin.*

He released a long breath, looked around.

"I was in the jungle," he said after a moment.

"Indeed," said Sireth.

Nevye moved toward his horse but paused, lifted one foot out of the snow.

"Where...where is my other sandal?"

"Your foot went through the gap in the rattan and you lost it. I caught it."

Nevye looked up as the Seer handed him the split-toed sandal.

"You...you caught it?"

"As it fell, yes."

"But you did not move."

"I did not, no."

Nevye swallowed.

"You are powerful."

"You have no idea." And the Seer ducked in time to avoid the snowball that smacked into the jaguar's head.

"Idiots!" cried the Major, now little more than a speck against the snow. "We're losing time!"

"She's a delicate flower," said Sireth as he mounted his horse.

Yahn Nevye brushed the snow from his head, slipped his foot into the sandal and followed.

***

He had been given his choice of stallions from the Imperial stables and he had picked for himself a large blood bay, its black mane roached, its tail bound like a topknot. His name was Shenan. He was not alMassay, however. No horse could ever be alMassay. His chest still ached at the loss and he tried never to think of it. A leopard had been sent to fetch the young aSiffh from the stables of the House Wynegarde-Grey. The colt had not come willingly and for some reason, it warmed him to think of the young desert stallion tossing his head and rolling his large eyes as they dragged him from his home, fighting the entire way along the road to *Pol'Lhasa.*

It reminded him just a little of Quiz.

He had been assigned two divisions of the Imperial Guard, an entourage of more than one hundred men, and they rode out now along the mountains that led to the Wall and the Gate of Five Hands. The road hugged the steep slopes so that only two horses could ride abreast in most places and it reminded him of the road to *Sha'Hadin,* where bandits and avalanches and carts of careening chickens were a constant danger. He could not keep his eyes from darting upwards just to make sure, but all he could see was the expanse of purple shale, white drifts and the occasional solitary farm. There was no sun today—the sky was heavy with snow clouds, but the road was clear and all along the mountains, he could see tigers driving the yaks that plowed through the drifts. Not speedy, but efficient. Yaks could move through anything, he realized. Much labour in the Empire was conducted behind the backside of a yak.

He had also been assigned a Division Captain, a young lion by the name of Haj Li-Hughes. They were likely the same age but for some reason, Li-Hughes seemed so very young. He had overheard the soldiers whenever he would move past, heard the term 'Khanmaker' whispered among them, felt their curious stares. Shogun-General and Khanmaker, wearing the blood-red yori and carrying the Fangs, riding a borrowed horse with another trotting freely at his side. Above them all, the Imperial banner waved high and proud.

What a strange thing his life had become.

Kerris could not be at the Gate of Five Hands.

It was impossible, he kept telling himself, but then again, almost a year had passed since Kerris, Fallon and Solomon had sailed from the shores of *Ana'thalyia* in the bird-like vessel called *Plan B*. He had no idea what had happened, what Kerris had found, or if he in fact found anything at all. He didn't know which disturbed him more but set his mind not to think on it until he had heard the stories for himself. And Kerris so loved his stories.

But Kerris could not be at the Gate of Five Hands.

And so they rode for the better part of the day on the trail that wound through the mountains, past temples, around farms, through villages. Everywhere along their route, both white and orange flames burned in the lanterns and torches and Kirin marveled at the number of people that came to watch them as they passed. He wondered if it was simply the sight of an Imperial force riding under the dual flame or whether the announcement of the first Shogun-General had already reached their ears. He wouldn't be surprised. News moved faster than rushing water.

Soldiers of all Races were on the road. The Empress had ordered all leave cancelled, the entire army recalled and had even begun the process of conscripting young men into service. The roads were filled with warriors, some riding, most walking, others joined together on carts on the way to the Wall. All stopped at the sight of the dual Division and the Shogun-General leading them. Without exception, they bowed. He could not help it. The sight of so many warriors quickened his blood.

They stopped for lunch at the outpost of *Sri'Phan'kai,* ate a simple meal of rice and egg soup before heading out again. It was their aim to make the temple town of *Teken'purana* and if the snow stayed in the clouds, they would succeed. If it fell, their time would be slowed and they might be forced to sleep on the trail. On roads like these, in mountains like these, no one would ride in the dark. It would be suicide, and death without honour was simply death. With orange and white fires racing along the Wall, soldiers deserved better.

And so it was only a brief stop at *Sri'Phan'kai* before heading out onto the road again. The rest of the day was the same as the morning. The snow stayed up, the roads stayed clear, and the torches of *Teken'purana* were lining the way as the skies folded their grey cloaks into the wardrobe of night. Originally a census town, the temple of *Teken'purana* had grown so large as to be considered a city on its own and her winged rooftops shimmered in the shadows of the mountains. In the daylight she was beautiful.

They were met by monks robed in deep blue, led to a hall where they dined on duck, rice, noodles and curried bananas. No one would talk to him without bowing, if in fact they talked to him at all. He wondered if it was because of his new station or whether all monks were the silent type and best left alone. He smiled as he thought of one in particular and was ushered to his bed.

Sleep came swiftly, but in his dreams, he was back in the gar with the knives and the dogs.

***

His grandmother would kill him if she could see this and he shook his head, wondering what the fates had in store to have led them here.

It was night and they were leaving and the witch was filling her bag with the supplies from their strange little tent. He watched her as she packed, her hands long and strong and speckled like a rocky road. The tips of her fingers looked odd with claws hidden and he could not keep his eyes from them, waiting for the secret daggers to catch the candlelight as she moved. She was a predator, it was obvious. He would ensure that he was not easy prey.

But Setse, she confounded him.

She sat cross-legged on the ground, engrossed in the baby in her arms. It was a strange-looking creature, thought Naranbaatar, with it's tufted tail and mop of thick dark hair. But he knew what it was that captivated his sister more than simple girlish instinct, could tell the instant the child had turned its large unnatural eyes on him. He could tell.

One eye was gold, the other blue.

And if cats were anything at all like dogs, then the child was an Oracle, like Setse. Very likely like its mother.

"Now," said the witch, reaching for the child. He did not struggle as she slipped him into a pack over her black-clad shoulders. She drew the bearskin over him now, hiding him completely from view. "We will go now."

Setse rolled to her feet but Naranbataar stopped her.

"The sentries on your Wall will see us," he growled.

"They will not see."

"And it's black as coal out there. These are dangerous mountains. One of us will slip on the ice and the fall will surely kill us."

The witch smiled at him, held out a hand and light began to radiate from her palm. He stepped back, scowled, set his jaw.

"Yes, certainly the sentries will not see *that...* "

She cupped her palm with the other, pressed, released. The light was a glow now, blue in colour. Like his sister's eye. Like the child's.

"Teach me, Rah!" Setse clapped her hands. "Teach me everything!"

The witch fixed her eyes on him before turning and slipping out of the gar.

"Of course."

***

They press the pads of his palms and the claws extend through the tips of his fingers. The dog lifts a blade, turns it in the firelight...

Through the terror of his dreams he heard the sound of horses.

He sat up, allowing his eyes to adjust to the darkness, ears straining to hear the movement of *kunoi'chi* or hassasin. But there was only the sound of the wind and yet again, he sighed. Another room not his own. He would grow accustomed to it one day, but not today. He rose to his feet and moved to the narrow window.

Night over snowy mountains was a beautiful thing. The waning moon painting everything in strokes of silver, the ice giving it all back as an act of worship. The faint stars glittering like water, the elements sleeping under cloud and frost. He could hear the deep tones of chanting as monks from *Teken'purana* carried out their devotions. There was no rest for them, these monks. They lived and prayed and served their Order with their lives. It was a worthy calling and not for the first time, he realized that he could have lived a happy life as a monk.

He smiled to himself, wondering if Ling would approve.

He reached for his tail, shorter now since the night in the gar. The Scales of the Dragon were an impressive piece of armour, but the gold braces rubbed at the pelt, leaving bits raw and blistered. He could not condemn them however. The fitting had been rushed and there had been no time for adjustments. He wondered how long it would be before it felt like home, like the kheffiyah or the gloves.

There again – another squeal from the valley and an answer from the stables far below. Horses, yes. He pulled on a cloak and left the room, making his way through the monastery to the very lowest level where the horses were kept. *Teken'purana* was different than *Sha'Hadin* in many ways – polished wood as opposed to stone, window glass as opposed to none, in the heart of a small town as opposed to isolated—but the stables were remarkably similar. He found himself approving as he pushed the cedar door in on the smell of pine and leather.

Lanterns provided dim light as two men struggled at the stall of a small bay, and Kirin was shocked to see aSiffh rearing and kicking at the boards. His eye was wild, his nostrils flared and the men were trying to catch him with ropes and blankets. Kirin crossed the floor swiftly and they turned at his approach. They were clearly from the monastery, wearing the deep blue robes of service. They bowed, fists to cupped palms.

"Shogun-sama," said one.

"*Sahidi*," said the other.

"What is the problem?"

"There is a wild horse in the mountains," said the one. "It has been calling all night and this little one is disturbed."

"Likely a mare in heat," said the other. "Or an alpha trying to lure an innocent out for an easy kill."

Kirin nodded. He had heard of such tactics. Horses were deadly predators. It was only superior feline intelligence that allowed them to control the creatures at all.

He turned to look at the young stallion, standing on wire-tight legs, flanks heaving. The valley echoed again with the squeal and aSiffh raised his head high, the stables splitting with his answer.

Suddenly, he knew.

"Open the stall," he said.

"*Sahidi?*"

"Let him out."

"But the mountain horse—"

"Pony," he said. "It is a mountain pony. Open the stall."

They did and aSiffh burst out in a blur, racing out the doors of the monastery stables. He disappeared into the shadows cast by the mountains.

Kirin leaned against the doorframe, casting his eyes out as if to follow, his mind spinning with the realization. He smiled to himself.

Kerris was at the Gate of Five Hands.

***

Long-Swift folded his arms across his chest and turned his face to the south. The wind was cold, plucking at the fur of his cheek and he was grateful for the warmth of the gars at night. Only betas slept in gars. The tens of thousands beneath them slept in the pelts of bears, horses, yaks or other lesser peoples. Not cats. Never cats. The skins of cats were far too thin for such wind. They were a frail but persistent enemy.

So very far below at the heel of *Khazien*, the army stretched out almost to the rising sun. The smoke from their fires blackened the sky and the flash of sharpening blades looked like ripples on a winter lake.

He heard the flap of a tent and the Khargan stepped up beside him. He smelled of woodsmoke, wotchka and Tu'ula, his seventh wife.

"What is it?" the Khargan asked, his voice like the rumble of distant thunder.

"A runner," said Long-Swift.

"From?"

The Irh-Khan shrugged. "There is no information yet."

"Perhaps they have found another Oracle."

"Perhaps."

"But you don't think so."

"I do not, no." Long-Swift turned to the Khan of Khans. "This is not protocol for finding an Oracle. The entire Legion would have returned."

"True." The Khargan raised a brow. "Shall I go down with you?"

"The men would be honored."

"Naturally."

Together, the pair turned away from the cliff-face and the sight of tens of thousands gathered at their feet.

***

It was early morning when the ice sheets of *Nanchuri Glacier* came into view. The mountain was very far away, almost obscured by heavy clouds but one side was pure white and traveled away from the cliffs at strange angles.

"Oh look," said Ursa as she pointed a silver finger. "The place where they dump dead chickens."

"Dead chickens?" Sireth frowned, swiveled in his saddle for a better view. "Have you been there before?"

"Once." She turned now. She was smiling wickedly. "Can we go there now?"

"Why?"

"Speaks to Owls wants to see it." She jerked her head at Yahn Nevye, riding behind. "Don't you, Speaks to Owls."

The jaguar steeled his jaw but said nothing.

Sireth frowned again.

"Pah. He is frightened. We can pass it by." She snorted, turned her face to the trail. "We will always come again on our way back."

He didn't need to be a Seer to understand that there was something else being said and knowing his wife, it wasn't pleasant. He could feel the tension from the jaguar but didn't care overmuch. There was a different sense invading his thoughts, a dangerous one and he was beginning to see what they would find at the end of their ride.

Eyes, he saw. Oracles and Eyes, dangers and blood and blackness and eyes. A monster of eyes and dark magic and it had the smell of death about it. He wondered if dogs practiced Necromancy and shuddered at the thought, knowing he would need to be very careful not to be caught in its dark cauldrons. It was like oil, very hard to stay clean of it.

But there was another thought, another mind and he shook his head, feeling *her* dancing at the edges of his soul. Mystery dipped in incense and Alchemy. Protection, magic, vindication, validation. She was with the girl, the Oracle. Arrows, needles, evergreen tea. All scraps of thoughts. She was skilled at keeping him out. A powerful woman, it was obvious and yet for some reason she desired his respect. She was a puzzle, that Alchemist. His wife would kill her. He owed her his life.

What would it take to make a witch love?

Did the Captain love her back?

What would he think, once he discovered there was a child?

He frowned one more time, set his thoughts on the foundry of *Shen'foxhindi* and the Enemy on the Wrong Side of the Wall.

***

Soldiers bolted to their feet, knocking over mugs of khava and dropping their morning rations as Long-Swift and the Khargan marched through the camp. The Irh-Khan was a common sight but the Khargan not so. His fame was legend, his powers almost that of a god. It was a lucky soldier to have lived to see the Khan of Khans. Rations and khava could be replaced. A moment in the presence of the Khargan, never.

The pair slowed as a runner was ushered forward. He was young, perhaps sixteen winters, and as lean as a jackal. He dropped to his knees at the feet of the Khan.

"Lord," he panted.

"Speak."

"I am runner of the 110th Legion. There has been fighting at the Wall of the Enemy, beyond the village of Lon'Gaar. Three have died under their arrows."

"The 110th…" The Khargan frowned, slid his eyes to his Irh-Khan.

"A western unit," said Long-Swift. "From the district near Karan'Uurt."

The Khargan growled. "They were charged with finding an Oracle?"

"Yes, Lord."

"There is no Wall in the west, runner."

"No, Lord. We were pursuing."

"You were pursuing."

"South, Lord. Yes."

"You were pursuing an Oracle."

"Yes, Lord."

There was only the sound of the wind and the crackling of the many campfires. Long-Swift took a deep breath. He knew what was coming.

"You were pursuing an Oracle all the way from Karan'Uurt to the Wall of the Enemy."

The runner did not speak. The soldiers surrounding them shifted in their boots, their rations and morning khava forgotten.

"Answer the Khargan, runner," said Long-Swift.

"Yes, Lord."

"Yes, Lord what?"

"Yes, Lord. We were pursuing an Oracle all the way from Karan'Uurt to the Wall of the Enemy."

"He must be very fast, this Oracle," grumbled the Khargan. "That is a long way."

"Yes, Lord. She is fast. And clever."

"She?"

"Jalair Naransetseg, Granddaughter of the Blue Wolf, Lord."

"Her father served under Rush Gansuk, Lord. Of the 112th." Long-Swift looked at the Khargan. "They were following the star."

"I remember." He turned his small eyes on the runner, still bowed at his feet. "They died at the hands of the Enemy."

"Lord."

"And now, *your* Legion is dying at the hands of the Enemy. Because they cannot find one little girl. What does that tell me about the Legions of Karan'Uurt?"

Only the wind, the crackling of the fires. The runner closed his eyes.

Long-Swift watched as the Khargan dropped his hand on the top of the runner's dark head, allowing it to remain for a long moment, before swinging the other to cup the man's jaw. A simple twist of those powerful arms and the runner slumped to the ground.

The Khargan turned to him.

"Dispatch Tumal Goarnagaar and the 2nd Legion. Burn Karan'Uurt to the ground and kill all who live there."

"Lord."

"We leave for the Wall today."

With that, he strode back through the camp toward the fist that was *Khazien*, soldiers parting before him like wheat in a field. He was gone from view in a heartbeat and the camp resumed their breathing.

Long-Swift glanced at the many faces spread around him.

"You heard the Khargan!" he snapped. "We leave for the Wall today!"

A roar went up from the camp and, as one, each man bolted for their gear, packing up their few possessions, their tin cups and the rations they had remaining.

For his part, Long-Swift looked at the body on the ground and briefly wondered what sort of girl could elude the 110th Legion. He turned and followed the Khan up the mountain.

***

They were following the cliff line far below the Wall and had gone surprisingly far under the strange glowing palm of the witch. It had grown more treacherous with each step, as the path on which she was leading them was not in fact a path at all but rather a ledge running along the ever steepening cliff face. But now, as the sun was turning the sky pink, sweeping the shadows of the night with her golden brooms, they had stopped in a narrow plateau of snow and shale. He could not bring himself to look down. It was dizzying and terrifying and once again he found himself wondering why he had let the woman lead them. This was not the way he wanted to die.

High above, they could hear voices of soldiers echoing down from the Wall, snatches of conversation and laughter carried on the wind. He could see the lights from their lanterns, marveled at the cauldrons burning orange and white. Under the cover of the mountains at night, they could travel, merely dark shapes against the darkness of the cliffs but soon they would lose even that. Arrows would find them easy marks by sunrise.

Mugoh pines were growing into the mountainside. They had been a nuisance during the night, catching clothing and scratching pelt, but now Naranbataar watched as the witch pulled silks from her pack, draping them across the branches and down to the snow. From another pack, a white powder, which she lifted to her lips and blew like a soft north wind. Instantly, the silks were covered in frost.

Another gar.

He shook his head. She was resourceful. He would give her that.

"In," she said, lifting one corner. "We shall sleep now and travel again tonight."

Naranbataar narrowed his eyes. "Why? Why are you doing this?"

"Inside."

"No. No more. My sister and I—"

He stopped, cut off by the quiet whine behind him. Both he and the witch turned to see Setse staring off to the west. She was transfixed.

"Oh, oh Rani…" she moaned.

"Setse?"

"Oh, no, we must go back."

"Setse, you're talking nonsense." He reached for her, to find her shaking but not from the cold.

"Oh no, oh no. Rani, this is bad. We must go back!" And she began to wail.

High above them, the voices turned to shouting and Naranbataar clasped a hand over his sister's mouth.

"Quickly," hissed the witch. "Inside."

He wrapped Setse in his arms and forced her under the silks.

The witch cast her golden eyes upward for only a heartbeat before she too followed.

***

The Wall arched along the Great Mountains, flashes of gold against the dark dark stones. The snow had stayed up yet again and he could hear the faint rush of the *Botekhoshi*, the river that forged a gorge in the mountains and separated Upper and Eastern Kingdom in the Northeast. The Upper Kingdom extended a great deal southeast, but here along the spine of their Good Mother, it was the axis for all three Kingdoms. He wondered if the Lower could truly be called a Kingdom. Dogs were notoriously unruly. Their many Khans proved it.

From the road, Kirin could see the blazing of the alarm fires. Orange and white, burning side by side. He could never have imagined such a thing had he not seen it with his own eyes. Had not two falcons been sent in one night. And while he did not believe in omens, the weight of war was beginning to settle onto his red-clad shoulders. It was a strange sensation, at the same time sinking his heart and stirring his blood. He did not know what to think anymore.

aSiffh had returned, the young desert stallion happily trotting now beside the Imperial warhorse and Kirin wondered if it had indeed been Quiz in the mountains last night. He missed the pony, found himself hoping to catch a glimpse of the wild mane and bramble-filled tail yet again. And yet again, he thought of his brother.

So it was as the sun was beginning to sink into the peaks that the two Divisions came upon the first of the great gates that led to and from the Five Hands Pass. The Wall was redoubled here and for a good way along the river, for the Pass itself was a bridge, a large curving iron and stone bridge that served to cross the *Botekhoshi* into the land of the *Chi'Chen*. Embassies had been built on both sides, flew both the twin dragons of the Fanxieng Dynasty and the red and gold sun of the Eastern Kingdom. It was an uneasy peace, but it was peace. Kirin was thankful for that.

He had been here twice before on diplomatic missions, and the Embassy town of *Kohdari* had not changed overmuch. It was in reality, an army base much like the border city of *Sharan'yurthah* and as they rode through the streets toward the Gate, he could see the state of readiness in the forces here. They were also feeling the tension, he knew it, with the quiet industriousness and intense focus that fell before a battle. Swords were being sharpened, star glasses polished, canons equipped with fresh tinder and dry powder. Horses were being shod with iron and armor fitted with new steel. Even the women and children in the army town were involved, as the dual flame blazed from every lantern on every street corner. It was impossible to feel anything but dread and anticipation in equal measure. It was the way of things.

The Gate of Five Hands towered over the end of the road. It was a massive structure of at least four stories, with ebony pillars, winged rooftops and dancing cranes carved into its double doors. The doors swung open and three men stepped onto the road, two leopards and one old lion in Imperial gold. Kirin felt his heart lurch at the memory. He was not a sentimental man but he still kept the sash hidden under the yori for luck.

He drew Shenan up and felt the Dual Division's one hundred horses fall in behind. The street was filled for a very long way with his troops, quiet and still now save for the clinking of bits and snorting of the horses. From many windows, he could see faces pressed up against the glass. Surely it had to be an impressive sight.

He dismounted, laid a hand on aSiffh's dark neck before turning to the lion dressed in gold. He bowed.

The lion bowed back.

"Shogun-sama," said the lion. "I am Captain Kimball Windsor-Chan. It is an honour to have you in our camp."

"You do me the honour, Captain," said Kirin. "*Kohdari* never fails to impress me with its dedication and service."

Windsor-Chan bowed again. Kirin noticed the man's eyes, green like new bamboo, flick to the swords at his hips. The legend of the Fangs had obviously reached the Gate of Five Hands.

"I have two parchments from *Pol'Lhasa*," Kirin said. "I am to deliver one to Ambassador Han and the other to Ambassador Fujihara. Are they inside the Gate?"

"Both, *sahidi,* in the Friendship Room. I will take you to them presently. Lieutenants Smith and Dharwani will organize meals and barracks for your Division, as well as stabling for the horses."

"You honour us all, Captain. You can never take a fine horse for granted. Even this little one…"

aSiffh tossed his head.

"That is not an Imperial horse, Shogun-sama," the Captain smiled.

"Not yet, no. He is from Khanisthan. Desert stock. Worth their weight in sand."

"I will take you at your word."

"There may also be a mountain pony following as well. Ensure that none of your men shoot him. He is important to me."

"I will, Shogun-sama."

The men turned and stepped through the double red doors. Inside was dark, with very high ceilings, stone floors and large *Chi'Chen* paintings on the walls. They were brightly-coloured and vibrant, not his taste at all but then again, he knew little of art. It was not his world.

The Captain led him to a set of wooden steps.

"Kaidan?" asked Kirin as they began to climb. "The parchment said Kaidan?"

"Ah, Kaidan…" He could hear the smile in the man's voice. "He can drink a monkey under a floor mat."

Kirin could not help it and he found his own face stretching in a smile. His heart was racing like young aSiffh.

"Yes," he said quietly. "He most certainly can."

The Captain swung around. "You have met him, our Kaidan?"

"I have."

"I had never believed he was real until this week. But now, I believe every story. Every one of them."

Kirin said nothing. It was obvious he was being taken to the very top floor.

Finally, the wooden stairs ended and through large windows, Kirin could see the entire *Botekhoshi* gorge, the river and the iron bridge, all growing purple with the coming of night. There were lights from the Embassy on the Eastern side and in his mind's eye, he saw the courtyard and the vases, the pruned trees and the ice sculptures of the *Chi'Chen* compound. His heart thudded at the sight beyond the compound, however – lights from hundreds, if not thousands of campfires. It was an army, he knew.

But why?

Windsor-Chan was waiting patiently, hands clasped behind his back. Kirin nodded and together they left the expanse of glass toward a room with closed doors. It was called the Friendship Room. He had been here twice before, delivering terms to *Chi'Chen* Ambassadors over the years and he remembered it clearly. Inside, it was spacious, peaceful, clean. Walls of rice paper, the floors polished pine, the furniture simple and spare. He had always loved this room. It spoke to his soul.

The Captain paused before sliding open the doors.

"So, you *have* met Kaidan, then, Shogun-sama?"

"Yes, Captain. Believe me when I tell you I have."

"Then, you *know* what to expect?"

Kirin took a deep cleansing breath, tried to calm his heart. "One never knows what to expect with Kaidan."

The lion smiled once more before sliding the rice paper doors open.

In truth, there was no way in the Kingdom he could have expected this.

The once simple room was a shambles, desks upended, carpets covering them, stools upside down or set upon lanterns on the walls. Those walls were ringed by Imperial leopards and Snow Monkey Guards with swords in hands and folded origami hats on their heads. A Sacred man sat on the floor beside a monkey, arranging a tower of brass bells between them. Kirin recognized the Ambassador-Magistrate Theophillus Bertrand Anyang Han of *Kohdari* and *Chi'Chen* Ambassador Bo Fujihara. In their laps sat two kittens, both very grey with exotic stripes around their eyes and against a far wall, a young tigress sat, crosslegged, a large garrison book in her lap.

In the middle of it all, a grey lion lay on his belly, spinning the dice for soldiers and diplomats alike, a bottle of sakeh at his side.

They all looked up at him from the floor.

"Hello Kirin," said Kerris and he smiled.

KAIDAN

Nine Months Earlier

Kerris Wynegarde-Grey had never liked the earth. In point of fact, the earth had never liked him, so he felt quite justified in his singular lack of affection. He always preferred the water and the snow, the clouds and the wind. They were obliging friends but now, after weeks spent rising and falling on the heaving mantle that was the sea under an endless expanse of sky, for the first time in his life he found himself wishing for the feel of something solid under his boots.

He had grown accustomed however, to the deck of the sailing ship, one hand on the wheel, the canvas flapping high above his head. The wind was strong and cold and smelled of salt, the water was happy and grey and bounding with fish, the skies went on forever. On the ship herself, there were dials and screens and ropes and rigging and for the first time in his life, Kerris Wynegarde-Grey felt like home.

But the earth was calling.

He had heard it a full two days before they saw it and when they did see it, it was little more than a low dark slip on the horizon. But it was land and after so many weeks spent searching, the finding had set their hearts racing. They had not weighed anchor, however but had been skirting this land for days with the distant shore always in view. Jeffrey Solomon had insisted they chart more northerly, toward the body of water he had called 'St. Lawrence.' Fallon had been delighted to hear of a sea named after a lion. Cats were very good at names, she had insisted. Apparently, even the Ancestors knew this.

One hand firm on the wheel, he slipped the other into his pocket, pulled out a few smooth stones. They were talking to him, whispering, pleading. They were only small stones, very good at telling him the weather or the lay of the land, but here on the ocean, surrounded by so much water, they were lost and afraid. He flattened his palm and willed them to rise.

Naturally, they did not.

He willed them again, felt the round hard emptiness of them in his mind, felt the laughing of the wind, the mocking of the waves. The stones didn't know what to do, merely rocked along with the boat in his palm. They were only stones. They couldn't move. He growled, whapped his grey tufted tail and shoved the stones back into his pocket.

He turned his eyes to the back of his very young wife, bent over the railing of the ship, emptying the contents of her stomach into the waters. A part of him felt bad for her. Pregnancy and sea-faring apparently did not go hand in hand. She had done well, all things considered, but the mornings always got the better of her. At those times, they were both happiest on opposite sides of the boat.

"Almost done, luv?" he called over the roaring of the wind and the sea.

"Oh yeah, almost," came her voice in return. "I think there's a bit of fish I didn't quite get. Oh wait—" She bent a little lower, made a terrible retching noise, her slim back heaving over the rail. "Nope. Nope. There. Got it."

He smiled.

She straightened and turned, wiped her mouth with her thick cotton sleeve. It was very windy on the open deck and her striped hair whipped all around her face. It used to be orange and black and rather plain, but now, after a good bolt of lightning, it rippled like white caps on water. Fallon Waterford-Grey. Only in her nineteenth summer, already pregnant with twins.

She tried to smile back but he could tell her heart wasn't in it.

"I do love fish, honestly I do. But mother, the thought of an orange

right now, or a pear...Or a pineapple. Oh what I would do right now for a big, juicy pineapple... Oh no...Oh mother..."

Her emerald eyes grew round and suddenly, she whirled, turning back to the railing and heaving once more.

He sighed and looked back at the shore.

Metal

He frowned. There were instruments of metal on the ship but they felt different, precise, useful. He had learned to read a barometer, although his own predictions usually proved far more accurate. He had learned to use a sextant, although the stars sang to him at night. He had learned to use a variety of Ancestral tools but to be honest, his own instincts had proved more than adequate and at times he found himself wondering how the Ancestors had grown so powerful when their tools seemed so clumsy. Still, the ship was a marvelous thing. He could quite happily spend the rest of his life on her wooden decks.

No, the metal was not coming from the ship.

"Hey," he heard a voice and turned his head to see Jeffrey Solomon emerge from the cabin below. It never occurred to him anymore to question the sight of the Ancestor. The three of them had been close company for weeks and Kerris knew more about Ancestors than he had ever dreamed possible. Certainly, more than he had ever wanted to know. They were a strange and curious people and he liked Solomon very much.

The man was a shaggy as a yak, but his browny-pink face was relatively clear of pelt, with only a minimum of nicks and cuts. Shaving, *he called it, and with a katanah no less. Yes, a curious people indeed.*

"You did a fine job this time," said Kerris. "You're getting better."

The man ran a hand along his chin. "Yeah, well, shaving with a long sword is tricky business. I'm constantly surprised that I haven't killed myself somewhere along the way."

Kerris grinned. "We're not in Kanadah yet."

Solomon smiled. "I put the sword back on your bunk."

"In the sheath?"

"Yep. In the sheath as ordered."

"Did you clean off the soap?"

"Yes, I cleaned off the soap."

"Did you polish the tang?"

"You're sounding like your brother."

"Funny how life is," said Kerris.

"Funny indeed."

Solomon turned to study the tigress. She was braced at the railing, rising and falling with the movement of the ship. One hand was gesturing and it looked like she was talking to herself.

"How's our Scholar in the Court of the Empress?"

Kerris followed his gaze and sighed. "Is it supposed to be like this?"

"Every woman is different," said Solomon. "But the rocking of the boat doesn't help. She's a trooper."

"Trooper?"

"Uh, fighter."

"Oh, she is that. I'm terrified for our kittens. I'll have no more peace ever, not one moment."

The Ancestor grinned, knowing it to be quite true.

Kerris frowned. "There's metal in the sky."

"In the sky?"

"Yes. I don't know what it is but it's very strange and sharp."

Solomon looked up, studied the great expanse of clouds over their heads. "It's new?"

"Yes. Just started."

Solomon frowned now.

"Hey," called Fallon. "Good morning, Solomon!"

He waved to her. "And good morning to you too, sweetness."

Fallon Waterford-Grey staggered from the side of the ship across its wooden deck. The wind whipped at her clothing, revealing her tummy and the white bump in her middle. It was fortunate that she wore men's tunics, for her belly had begun to swell out of the confines of her vest. He caught her arms, helped steady her on unsteady feet.

"How you feeling, honey?"

"I'd love some honey," she said. "And a pear but maybe not a pineapple. All this fish is making me sick."

"Sorry to hear it. I'm boiling water in the galley. We'll make some tea, alright?"

"Great. Tea fixes everything." She smiled at him before turning her emerald eyes on her husband. "Have you tried this morning?"

"No," he lied, deliberating turning his gaze back to the wheel.

"You said you'd try."

"They don't do anything."

"They will. You know they will."

"I know nothing of the sort."

"But Sireth said—"

"Just because Sireth benAramis can do things with the water and the fire, doesn't mean I can."

"You are an Elemental, Kerris. That's what he said. I know 'cause I was there."

The grey lion set his jaw but said nothing. Solomon looked from tigress to lion and back again.

"The stones? Is that what you're talking about?"

Fallon nodded. "I know he can do it."

"Well I don't." Kerris rolled his eyes, kept his hands firmly on the wheel. "I am not, nor ever shall be, a monk."

"There's an image," grinned the Ancestor. "What about this 'metal in the sky', then?"

"Metal in the sky?" Fallon cocked her head, her stripes making worried lines across her forehead. "Like Max metal?"

"A bit. Different. Sharp." Kerris looked up, wrinkled his nose. "Hot."

"Wow," said Fallon.

"Hot?" Solomon looked up as well, turned in circles studying the skies, the low grey clouds. "How hot?"

"Like fire?" asked Fallon.

"Yes," said Kerris. "Fire and Metal together. Like Kirin and me. Destructive, really."

"Like that?" And she pointed to the horizon where a speck was gleaming. "That looks very hot."

Together, the three of them moved to the railing.

"Damn," said Solomon. "We have to get off this ship."

"What?" she asked. "Why?"

"Get off now!"

"But—"

She yelped as he grabbed her by the shoulders, shoving her backwards so that she toppled tip over tail into the dark swell that was the ocean. He reached for Kerris but the lion scrambled out of his grip. "Kerris! You too!

"No!"

"Now!"

"But I need—"

"—to get off this ship! C'mon!"

And suddenly Solomon leapt over the railing, hitting the rolling water with a splash.

Kerris peered over the side, spied a bobbing striped head spitting out great mouthfuls of water. He looked up. The speck was a ball now, billowing orange flame and white smoke and so close he could almost feel the heat from it. He turned and bolted for the steps that led to the cabin, sailed down in one go, hit the floor running. The katanah and obi were on his berth, the low narrow bunk he had shared with his wife and he snatched them both before scrambling back up to the deck. He could hear it now, the metal-fire, roaring like Imperial cannons and the air was furious at being pushed out of the way by this strange new element. The light was red hot, blinding him, but he knew these decks well and he raced for the rail, leaping high into the angry air as the metal-fire crashed to the cabin behind him. There was a boom and a roar, yes—very much like Imperial cannons, and he was lifted even higher now by a wall of air. Air, usually his friend, now howling with fury, scorching his back, his tail, his boots, then the water, rushing up to give him a bone-crushing hug, and then nothing for some time afterwards.

***

"Nothing?" Kirin sat forward. "What do you mean, nothing? Kerris? What happened?"

The grey lion smiled and leaned back on his elbows, raised the tiny cup in his hand as in a toast.

"Later, Kirin. It's a long story and we have many nights."

Kirin shook his head. Kerris was famous for his stories and now with this—the most important story of the age—he was bound to play it out, milk it for all its dramatic, theatric glory.

They were reclining now around a low black table in the Friendship Room, Kirin, Kerris, Fallon, Captain Windsor-Chan and the Ambassadors – Theophillus Bertrand Anyang Han and Bo Fujihara. Fujihara was a small man, about the size of Chancellor Ho, with a fair pelt and pink face and small dark eyes, bright and quick. He wore blue-dyed short kimonoh with leather-wrapped legs and a sash that wrapped him round the waist and shoulders. He also sported a ceremonial sword across his back, several large rings on his fingers and like most of his people, beads woven into his braided hair. Kirin had met him twice before, in this very room, and knew that he was an intelligent fellow dedicated to the pursuit of peace between their kingdoms. It was odd to see him here with an army.

There was a tug on his queue and he winced, looked around to see a kitten pulling herself up with tiny claws, batting at his hair. He smiled at her. She flattened her ears and hissed.

"Lada," grinned Kerris. "Leave your uncle alone."

"It looks really good," said Fallon and she leaned forward, eyes curious. She was growing from gangly girl into a woman of exotic beauty, with *Chi'Chen* beads woven into her wild hair. "Your head, I mean. 'Cause last time I saw it, it was pretty bad."

"It has healed," he said.

"May I?"

Kirin grit his teeth as Windsor-Chan and Han exchanged glances. *Cats,* he thought. *Proud and vain, all of us.*

"Of course," and he looked at the smooth wood of the floor as she ran her hands over the top of his bare head.

"Wow, it's really healed well, hasn't it? Almost like you did it on purpose, you know? Like you shaved it or something?"

"Like a regular sham'Rai," grinned Kerris again and he sipped his sakeh. "Shogun-General Wynegarde-Grey. Won't mummie be pleased."

"Are those the Fangs?" asked Fallon. "The Blood and Jade Fangs?"

"Yes."

"I read about them in the University."

"By the Kingdom, Kirin, you've landed on your feet. Yours is the Luck now. First, as always."

"And you've journeyed across the world with a wife and an Ancestor. If that's not Destiny, Kerris—"

"It *is* Destiny, brother. The Tao wheel rejoices in us for a change."

Kirin regarded his brother. It was hard to tell with Kerris whether he was being hurtful or simply truthful. He seemed happy enough. With such a wife and kittens, he should be the happiest man in all the Kingdom.

"It is an honour to meet you once again," said Bo Fujihara with a smile, and Kirin lifted his eyes to study the ambassador. "You have not changed *so* much, Shogun-sama. The Fangs suit you."

"Mine is the honour, *sidi,*" replied Kirin. "Although I never could have imagined you traveling with my brother and his family."

"They are most intriguing, Shogun-sama. Especially this little Lada. *Chi'Chen* children are not like this."

Kirin winced again as the kitten tugged on his hair. "Most feline children are not, either…"

Fallon laughed and swept the little girl up in her arms.

"Soladad is the bad one, isn't she? She reminds me of Ursa. Bad and feisty and tough as a yak."

The kitten snuggled into her mother's arms, threw a look back at her uncle and hissed.

"But our Kirin, on the other hand…"

The second kitten, a little boy with great blue-green eyes, pressed his face into his father's chest, hiding.

"Kirin is the thoughtful one, aren't you my son?" Kerris ran a hand over the boy's head, trying to smooth the unruly grey hair. "He's very smart, like his mother. But quieter."

"Hey!" laughed Fallon. "I am quiet. I'm quiet and thoughtful and peaceful. I'm Wood, remember."

"Oh yes. You are as quiet as a tree, my love."

She sat back, leaning into him and the kittens climbed between them, mewling and batting each other and Kirin felt a rush of emotion, bitter and sweet and sad. He reined it in, took a deep breath.

"So why are you here, Kerris? Like this, with your children and a *Chi'Chen* army? How did you get here and what do you want?"

Kerris and Bo exchanged glances, Kerris drained the sakeh from his flask and sat up, kittens sliding from his chest into his lap, their tiny claws snagging on the fabric as they went.

"There are Ancestors, Kirin," he began. "Many Ancestors and they are dangerous."

"We thought as much."

"No, we didn't think enough." He turned and motioned to one of the Snow Monkey guards. In Diplomatic circles, they were called "the Snow Guard" or simply "the Snow." The man stepped forward, dropped a large satchel wrapped in black cloth and gold cording. Kerris rolled up to his knees, began to unwrap both cloth and cord.

"Oh mother," sighed the tigress. "I hate that thing."

She scooped the kittens into her arms and moved toward the windows, began to rock them, one on each hip.

With a flourish, Kerris folded the cloth away to reveal a strange instrument of tarnished metal. It was long, cylindrical and seemed to have many interlocking parts. Kirin sat forward.

"What is it?" he asked.

"Breath of the MAIDEN," said Kerris. "A weapon, like a cannon. And this is only one of them. They have so many different kinds. We brought back what we could."

Kirin reached for the weapon, picked it up with his gloved hands. Felt the weight of it, the dark chi. It was not even remotely like a sword and he found he didn't know how to hold it.

"Here," said Kerris. "Like this."

And he took it from his brother, hiked it onto his shoulder and aimed the thing toward one of the large panes of flat glass.

"Out of the way, luv," he called and the tigress nodded, tucking her kittens into her chest. She moved to stand behind them all.

There was a strange hum then a flash of light and the guards, Imperial and Snow, leapt back, utterly breaching their training. A circle glowed in the center of the glass for a long moment, before turning smoky, then white, then crumbling away entirely. Left was a large hole open to the night sky and a sharp, blue scent on the wind.

The kittens began to wail and Kirin found his heart thudding wildly in his chest.

"Breath of the MAIDEN," said Kerris again as he laid the weapon back in its cloth, bound it with the gold cord and handed it over to the Snow guard. He looked Ambassador Han.

"Sorry about the glass."

The ambassador was speechless.

Now Kerris turned to his brother.

"We need to be ready, Kirin, for when they come. And not just us. We won't be enough to stop them. All our swords and bows, even our cannons won't be enough to chase them off. They will want what we have and they will take it." He glanced at Fujihara, then back again. "No, the only thing that will stop them will be unity. All the Kingdoms presenting a united front against them."

Fujihara nodded, laid a bound scroll onto the black table. "The Capuchin Council has approved this request, Shogun-sama, as has Emperor Watanabe. We have commissioned all men between the ages of twelve and seventy to join the army for training, and any women that have either the interest or the skill. This is a petition from *Lha'Lhasa* for the Empress, requesting that your people do the same."

Kirin stared at the scroll for some time, before looking to Ambassador Han. "You know of this request?"

The Ambassador bowed so that his forehead touched the table. "I do, Shogun-sama. With orange and white fires burning, it seemed prudent not to waste time on protocol."

Kirin rose to his feet, moved to the windows where snow was beginning to swirl in through the hole in the glass. He could see the dark mountains through it, the lanterns from the Embassy and the lights of the army across the river. Could smell the snow now, and the sharp bite of very cold water. He clasped his hands behind his back.

"But why an army? Surely, this request could have been delivered by Ambassador Fujihara himself, even without our beloved Kaidan." He turned now to face them. "This army is not the might of the Eastern Empire, I know it is not. And it is not a show of force, for that is no way to secure an alliance. What is your plan, Kerris? I am here as the representative of the Empress. Tell me now or I will not consider any of this."

Kerris grinned, rose to his feet as well. He bowed a formal bow to his brother and for some reason it set Kirin's teeth on edge.

"You're right, of course, Kirin. The army is not here as a show of force or a bargaining tool or anything of the sort. As I said, we need all the Kingdoms united." He inclined his head. *"All* of them."

Kirin frowned. His brother was saying something but it was eluding him. He looked first to Fujihara. The man raised his pale brows, nodded grimly. He looked to Ambassador Han, then Captain Windsor-Chan but they had no answer. Finally, he looked to the tigress, both kittens dozing now as she rocked from side to side. She tried to smile and her emerald eyes were singing songs of compassion and understanding and courage and pain.

And he knew.

"No," he said.

"Kirin," Kerris started.

"No," he growled. "Not now. Not ever."

"We need them, Kirin."

He strode to the rice paper door, slid it open past the Imperial guards and the Snow guards, turned his body for barely a moment.

"There will never be peace with the Kingdom of Dogs," he growled. "Not while I am alive."

The rap of his tail left marks in the floor and he turned and left the Friendship Room in silence.

***

Once again, Setse was weeping.

The ceiling of the little gar shone with frost, branches and stars glittering through the frozen silks. He had fallen asleep while holding her but had awoken to her sobs—soft and quiet and heartbreaking. The witch was gone. She had slipped out during the night, left her baby curled in Setse's arms and it was a very strange sensation for him to be this close to one of the Enemy. It was making an odd growling sound in its throat, but it seemed contented and it rose and fell with the baby's breathing. It was a soothing counterpoint to Setse's weeping.

"Oh Rani," Setse moaned. "I should have let them take me. I should have gone with them. I was so weak..."

He hushed her, stroked her hair. He didn't know what she was referring to, didn't know what else to do. She was inconsolable.

"Now everything will be gone because I was afraid. We can go back. We must go back."

"Setse, please. Hush now. There's nothing to be done."

"I'm so sorry, Rani..."

"And what about your Ulaan Baator? Don't you want to meet him?"

She lifted her eyes to his.

"Ulaan Baator?"

"Yes, you said he was coming, didn't you? You said he'd change things, make things right, remember?"

He had no idea what he was saying to her but it just seemed wise to use her own words. She was still such a puzzle and growing worse.

She nodded, sniffed, nodded again. "Yes. Yes he will. People die all the time, isn't that right, Rani?"

"Yes." He lowered his head, exhausted. "Yes they do..."

She nodded once more, sat up and wiped her cheeks. "Death is not a bad thing."

"Only a bad death is a bad thing. That's what grandfather used to say."

"Grandfather." She smiled through her tears. "The Blue Wolf."

"Yes," he said. "He was the Blue Wolf of Karan'Uurt, respected by Khans and kings alike."

"Blue Wolf, Yellow Cat."

"Setse..."

"Blue Wolf, Yellow Cat," she whispered. "Blue Wolf, Yellow Cat.

Blue Wolf, Yellow Cat."

And she began to rock.

He sighed, stroked her hair and waited for the witch to return.

***

Kerris slid the rice paper door closed and sighed. The room was quiet, the light just beginning to break into the single pane of glass that overlooked the gorge. It could easily have been brighter had not the shadows of the mountains blocked everything. Earth was a belligerent ally now. It had been a hard-won truce.

Fallon was standing at the window. He could see her in the dark, a mere silhouette with her back to him, arms wrapped around her ribs. He crossed the floor to stand behind her, slipped his hands around her waist. Even after twins, there was nothing to her. A gust of wind could tip her over.

He kissed her neck and she shuddered. Weeping, he knew, or trying not to.

"Well?" she asked, her voice quiet. The kittens were sleeping, a jumble of arms, legs and tails on a cushion by the wall.

"He won't talk to me," said Kerris. "He won't even open the door."

She nodded. "It's still hard on him. I can tell."

"Well, regardless, he'll need to go back to *Pol'Lhasa*. You'll all go with him. It's not terribly far, two days at most."

"Kerris…" she moaned and turned in his arms, cupped his face in her lightning white hands. "Two thousand *Chi'Chen* soldiers against even a single Legion might have a chance, but against the entire Lower Kingdom?"

"We're not starting a war."

"You won't be coming back."

He smiled. "You don't know that. I might."

She leaned her forehead in to rest against his, said nothing. She didn't need to.

"Remember," he said. "It's a diplomatic mission. If I can speak to the Khan, I might be able to convince him. Especially if I bring the weapon. He'll see. He'll understand."

"You won't make it to the Khan."

"It's the only way. I need to make him understand. I can't believe he won't listen. I can't believe that. Otherwise, well, you know…"

She nodded. He sighed.

"The kittens should do well in the Imperial Nursery."

She smiled now. "Mongrel kittens in the Imperial Nursery."

"Stranger things have happened, luv. Never forget that."

"I won't."

"If they won't allow it, then you go home with Kirin. To our home. If Mummie's still alive, she'll be delighted to meet you."

"And our mongrel babies."

"Honestly, I don't think she'll care at this point. She never had her stars pinned on an advantageous marriage. Not for me." He kissed the tip of her nose. "And look what I got. I still have more than my share of luck, don't I? Because I have you."

She was not so easily placated. As stubborn as a yak.

"What if I can speak to Kirin? Make him understand?"

"Well, that was our deal, wasn't it? If Kirin is in, then we have troops. And if we have both Upper and Eastern Kingdoms represented, we stand a chance at convincing the dogs and avoiding a whole lot of unnecessary bloodshed in the process. So yes, my love. If you can manage to convince my brother to send some feline troops with us, allow us to use the Wall until we reach *Shen'foxhindi,* then you may take your chances along with the rest of us."

"And the kittens will still go to *Pol'Lhasa.*"

"The kittens will still go to *Pol'Lhasa.*"

"Do you have a dagger?"

"What? A dagger?"

"Yep. A dagger. Do you have one? I know you do. It's in your boot."

"Why?"

She kissed the tip of *his* nose now.

"I might need it when I go."

"Go where?"

"To convince your brother." She smiled sweetly. "That was the deal."

"Ah. Hassasin now, are we?"

She grinned. "I prefer to think of myself as a resourceful diplomat."

He reached down a hand to slip it up and out of his yak-hide boots. He passed it, hilt-first, into her waiting hand.

"You are a far better politician than I give you credit for, my love. I am utterly impressed."

She slipped it in her belt.

"Pack our things, Kerris-your-name-was. We're going north."

***

Sireth benAramis opened his eyes. There was an owl watching him.

He pushed himself up on his elbows, looked to the dwindling fire. Ursa was bedded down under her thick yak hide and the jaguar, Yahn Nevye, sat cross-legged and staring into the flames. He had still not loosened his knot and his ears were tipped with frost.

"Is that the same owl?" the Seer asked.

Nevye grunted.

"What does he want?"

"I don't know." The jaguar shrugged, did not look at him. "I don't speak to owls."

"Of course not," said Sireth. "My mistake."

He rolled to his knees, reached for the small pot in which they melted snow and made tea. Ursa grumbled something at him—he could distinctly make out the word 'idiot'—and pulled the hide higher to cover her head. Mi-Hahn was hunting. He could hear her thoughts echoing from the night sky. She had spied a fat rabbit, was planning on bringing it to the fire for breakfast. He smiled to himself. She was nowhere near the hunter Path had been, but still, he could not imagine his life without her now. She was a wild, happy child.

"I had a dream," said Nevye, still looking at the fire. "I think it was a dream. It may have been a vision, but it was unclear."

Sireth paused a moment before dropping the handful of leaves into the pot. Nevye never talked to him like this, like an equal. He would not disrespect the chance.

"What do you recall?"

"A wolf," he said. "A blue wolf. But strange, as if made of painted glass."

"Painted, yes. And a yellow cat?"

"You saw the same?"

"Yes."

"Then it was not a dream."

"No. A vision, most definitely."

Nevye frowned, rubbed his arms, cold. "What does it mean?"

"We will find out tomorrow, I should think. When we reach the Wall. What else have you seen?"

"The girl."

"That is all?"

The man's expression grew guarded and he looked back into the flames. "Many dogs. An archer. A cheetah."

"If the Alchemist is there, I will kill her," grumbled Ursa from the hides. "Then I will kill all the dogs. And then both of you."

Sireth smiled. "Continue."

"Eyes. Dragons, a monster and a warrior covered in blood. A figure with white eyes and white hair. "

"The Yellow Cat. Do you see him clearly?"

"No. Not clearly. Why? Do you?"

"No. He is the same as the Blue Wolf. Not real, a symbol."

"Yes."

No no no bad bird bad no!

There was a rustle and thump as Mi-Hahn dropped onto the snow next to the owl. She began to cry in her shrill voice and beat at the owl with her wings. The owl did likewise and both talons and hooked beaks were brought to bear before he left the snow and disappeared into the breaking skies of dawn. The young falcon watched him go, wings spread, beak open, hissing as feathers drifted down onto the snowy rocks around them. She began to tear at the body of the rabbit, clearly forgetting her intention to share.

"Idiot birds."

As the water bubbled in the little pot, Sireth gazed at the dawning sky.

"Dawnglow red, Stay in bed."

Nevye glanced up. The clouds, their companions for days, were breaking to reveal a sky the colour of blood.

***

In my dreams, I am in the gar. My arms are suspended from poles and my legs are bound together. They have pulled out my mane, fist by fist. I have never felt such pain. It has been a lifetime of pain.

Then, they take my hands, press my palms so the claws extend and with their crude iron blades, they take them. One by one, they take my claws and the bones of my fingers with them. The pain of my head is nothing compared to this.

I do not even feel it when they take my tail.

These are my dreams. Each night. Every night. Only this. Even when falling asleep in Ling's arms, these were my dreams. And Kerris wants me to go back.

I understand what he is saying. In my head, I understand but in my heart, in my bones, I cannot accept it. I try to tell myself he doesn't know what he's asking, but I answer myself that he does. He knows full well and yet he asks anyway. He doesn't think of me. He never has.

Fallon comes to me through the wall. I think she must have a dagger for she cuts open the rice paper and slips through. I wonder if the guard at my door has seen her or if she is a dream herself. If she is, then she is the first dream that doesn't involve dogs.

I am sitting by a candle and she joins me. I think I ask her if Bo Fujihara is expected to pay for both the window and now the wall. She says, yep, or something like that. Tigers. I am still believing she is a dream so I am not really listening.

She tells me that they need troops or Kerris will die. That he, Bo and the Chi'Chen *army are going north with or without cats but that without cats, they will all die. And when the Ancestors come, all the*

Empires will fall and we will serve the Ancestors and bring them tea and be petted and made to fight in arenas to kill each other for sport. I don't want to hear any of it although I know it to be true.

I tell her I will think on this.

She asks me about Ling, about her baby whom I have never seen. She tells me that Kerris is a wonderful father. I'm sure he is, I tell her. He is just a terrible brother. She tells me that he wept for days, those first days on the boat and slept with the katanah clutched in his arms. I call it manipulation. She calls it diplomacy. She kisses me on the cheek and leaves, back through the hole in the wall that she made.

I don't sleep for the rest of the night, but at least there are no dogs.

- an excerpt from the journal of Kirin Wynegarde-Grey

***

For the first time in days, the sun graced them with her presence. She did so infrequently in winter, as the nights were long and the moon was stronger but that morning, she did. The streets of *Kohdari* were once again filled with horses but twenty times more since the Gate of Five Hands had been opened and the *Chi'Chen* army flowed across the bridge and into the city. They had begun the process of preparing the Wall and kestrels had been sent to all battleforts along the route. Hay and water, tea and bread were being stocked for the trek, although no riders would leave the backs of their mounts over the next days. The foundry of *Shen'foxhindi* was a five-day ride along the Wall and nowhere in the history of the Upper Kingdom had anything been seen near the number of horses and men riding as was expected now.

It was an exhilarating thing and Kirin watched it all from the double doors of the Gate. The wind was strong and as he stood, hands on hips, watching the logistics of preparing such a force, the flapping banners of both Upper and Eastern Kingdoms filled him with pride. He was wearing the full yori, his bolt of golden mane flowing from the kabuto like a banner of its own, and once again he heard the term 'Khan-maker' whispered amoung the soldiers gathered before him.

Bo Fujihara was at the head of the *Chi'Chen* force astride a small chestnut with beads braided into its long mane and tail. *Chi'Chen* horses were smaller than Imperial ones, in fact resembling aSiffh more than Shenan, but still, their tack was impressive, their armour colourful and gleaming, and it was all the city could do to hold such a number.

Captain Windsor-Chan stood with him, supervising the riders, the armour, the swords and the rations. *Kohdari* was, after all, his town, these men—his soldiers. Ambassador Han stood next to him, hands clasped, eyes roving, praying that the ceremonious force would leave *Kohdari* without mishap or dishonour. For his part, Kirin was surprised that there had been no incident as yet, for while there was no war between the two Kingdoms, there was no easy peace either. Soldiers were soldiers, no matter what the race.

"Wow, oh, oh wow…"

He turned to see Kerris and Fallon step under the ebony pillars and through the dancing cranes of the doors. Both were dressed for warmth and practicality, wrapped in cloaks of bear and bison. There was little night blue or forest green to be seen and he found himself missing the little identifying dashes of colour that so characterized their journey in the Year of the Tiger. Each had a kitten—Soladad perched on Fallon's hip and little Kirin slung over his father's back. A woman from the village was to accompany the babies on the trek to *Pol'Lhasa,* a tigress of perhaps forty summers, and she waited in the crowds, horseless and smiling.

"Well," said Kerris. "This is impressive. How many are you giving us, then?"

"I will give you ninety of my Dual Division. The remaining ten will be making the journey back to Pol'Lhasa tomorrow."

Kerris nodded. "And we have two thousand and thirty of our own. That's decent enough, I suppose."

Kirin smiled. "Captain Windsor-Chan has just informed me that once the men of *Kohdari* heard of this mission, they were all eager to participate. At last count, we have an additional three hundred and fifty soldiers on top of my ninety."

Kerris raised his brows. "Well, that's something, then. Thank you both. It says much about the men of this town." And he bowed.

Windsor-Chan bowed and Kirin bit back a wry smile. Kerris was indeed a diplomat at heart. He could speak 'military' well enough when needed.

"We will have two hundred feline riders at the fore and two hundred at the rear," said Ambassador Han. "It is a matter of pride and of course, national security."

"Naturally," said Kerris but his attention was fixed on the blood bay Imperial stallion being led onto the street. He wore tack of ox-blood red, with red and gold tassels at his browband, breastplate and flank. Over his haunch flapped the twin dragons of the Fangxieng Dynasty. At his side, young aSiffh danced nervously. He wore no tack, no saddle, bridle nor halter, not even a rope to indicate ownership. His large eye was wild, his head high and tossing.

Kerris studied the horses as they were led directly to the foot of the Five Hands Gate.

"Fine animals, Kirin," he said. "Is that your little desert friend? The one from KhaBull?"

"The very one."

"He's filling out nicely. Why are they being brought out?"

"I am coming with you, Kerris."

Kerris narrowed his eyes. "Why?"

"Oh, oh I'm so happy," squealed the tigress and she swung her daughter high in the air. Kirin was grateful she didn't kiss him again.

"Why?" asked Kerris again.

"Because this is a time of unification, Kerris. I understand that. And there is nothing that unifies our people as the reinstatement of the Shogun caste. Any Shogun-General would do. You just so happen to get me."

Kerris said nothing.

"Besides, if there is war, the Blood and the Jade Fangs have a proven history as dog killers." He nodded at the katanah at his brother's hip. "As do you."

Kerris stared at him for a long moment

"Fair enough," he said and turned back to study the wall of horses assembled before him. "I see Fallon's painted horse but where's mine?

Am I still expected to tack the horses, brother?"

There it was again, the darkness, the challenge. They still lived on this road. Yin and Yang. It seemed the eternal way of things. Their stars would never change.

Kirin sighed.

"Whistle."

"What's that?"

"Whistle, Kerris. Loud and long."

The grey lion frowned, slipped his fingers between his teeth. The sound he produced had been rumored to shatter glass on occasion, and even experienced soldiers winced, covering their ears.

The town square was silent save for the howl of the wind, the jingle of horses, the squeak of leather.

"Again."

Kerris stared at him again before repeating the sound. Again, the entire town was silent, straining to hear something, anything. They had no idea.

And then they heard it, a faint squeal from outside the city gate. aSiffh whinnied a response and behind them, Fallon let out a little gasp. Kerris whistled a third time. This time, the answer was near and growing louder.

"Open the gate," said Kirin.

"Open the gate!" shouted Windsor-Chan and the command was carried down the street until they could see the massive double doors of *Kohdari* groan open and a small, mottled shape burst through.

Kerris seemed to be holding his breath.

The crowd of two thousand horses began to part as if by a knife and finally, Quiz the mountain pony scrambled into view, snorting and snapping at every equine form in his path, except for aSiffh. The young stallion nuzzled the pony, who nipped but did not bite.

Slowly, as if in a trance, Kerris stepped down onto the snowy road.

Quiz rolled his large eye, snorted again, flanks heaving, sides flecked with foam. His tail was tangled with sticks, his mane a mass of ice and the whiskers at his muzzle were white with frost but without reservation Kerris threw his arms around the sturdy little neck and held as if he would never, ever let go.

Kirin stepped down beside him to mount his own horse, a blood red soldier atop a blood bay horse.

And suddenly, there was a charge that rippled through the crowd of soldiers, feline and simian alike. There is an old saying, "Dawnglow red, Stay in bed." The sky at dawn had been blood red. There was a Shogun-General in their midst, wearing a yori of ox-blood red. He carried the Blood Fang, rode a blood bay stallion. He had made a Khan, then unmade him. They were traveling as a united group into a land that despised unity, all because of Ancestors. It was a marvelous, terrible time and they were all fixed to be a part of it.

Kerris looked up at him, his cheeks streaked with his tears.

"Thank you," he whispered and he smiled.

"It is my honour," Kirin said and he realized that, for the first time in months, he meant it.

THE WRONG SIDE OF THE WALL

Ling,

I must speak first as your Shogun-General. Kerris is indeed back, along with his wife and kittens. They have spent time in the company of Ancestors and are now insistent that we, as a Kingdom, prepare for war. This is the reason for the Chi'Chen *army – they wish to present a united front as we approach Khan Baituskhan of the Lower with terms of Alliance. I have promised them my Dual Division and we are currently heading toward the foundry of Shen'foxhindi along the Wall.*

I am also sending with this parchment his two kittens, mongrels both. Please find a home for them in the Imperial nursery – they are blood of my blood. You may tell people they belong to Kaidan and his consort the Lightning, and they will be accepted as royalty.

Now, I speak as Kirin, the man who loves you and will love you until there is no breath in his body, and if the Monks and Priests and Seers are right, perhaps beyond even that. Be careful, Ling. This is a dangerous time. Take nothing for granted. Sleep with a dagger. Be wiser than ever and do not assume with Chancellor Ho or any of the Council. We are all at war now.

I will write once we reach the foundry.

Your Kirin

- an excerpt from the journal of Kirin Wynegarde-Grey

***

It was still dark when the witch came back. Setse had grown quiet and sat now under the cedar branches, eyes dull, the baby in her arms. It was a very quiet baby, he thought, as far as babies went. Most babies fussed and squealed. This one growled. No—*purred,* the witch had called it. Purring. It was an odd sound. He could not fathom it.

She slipped under the silks and he watched her as she unbound the black wraps that covered her face and hair. It could have been for warmth, but he doubted it. She looked like she intended to blend with the shadows of night and he had long since given up trying to understand her. She shook her hair out and stretched her long body, forcing him to avert his eyes. He had heard about women like this. His grandmother had warned him. It was no wonder she had a baby with her.

She produced a pair of skins from the satchel at her hip, passed one into his hand.

"Broth," she said. "From the soldiers of the Wall."

That's what he heard. He didn't believe it at all. She could have been meaning something completely different. She could have been offering him poison. It didn't matter. Days had become nights, nights were now days. He was travelling with cats and they hadn't killed each other. Life had become entirely too strange for him.

She knelt down by his sister, stroked her cheek, kissed her forehead like an older sister. Once again, he felt nothing. If she had wanted to kill them, they would have been dead days ago. His shoulder and leg were hurting, reminders of enemy arrows. He was so very tired.

"Broth," she said again.

He looked at the skin. It was thick and well made with a crest of gold stamped into the leather. Twin dragons. The symbol of the Enemy. They were serpents, all of them. Beautiful and deadly.

"Take it," she said. "It will increase your strength and perhaps… improve your mood?"

He could have sworn she smiled at him.

She unfastened the stopper, lifted the skin to Setse's lips. His sister shook her head and he wondered if she was feeling the ache from the arrows too. They would both be dead by nightfall, he was certain.

"Drink, little sister," she said. "Your people need you strong."

"What do you know about our people?" he growled, lowering the skin. "Who are you to talk to us about them?"

For her part, Setse just blinked up at them, lids heavy and slow.

"And how did you get this broth? Did you climb the wall and steal from your own people?"

"Of course."

"Why would you do that?"

"Your sister needs—"

"Enough," he growled again and he sat forward, feeling strength run through his bones for the first time in days. "Do not talk to me of my sister. We are grandchildren of the Blue Wolf and will let ourselves die unless you give us answers and now. We can do that. You would know if you understood anything at all about our people."

The woman looked down.

"Why? Why are you doing any of this?"

She turned her large powerful eyes on him. They gleamed like suns in the desert sky, like harvest moons over the fields of Karan'Uurt. He didn't know where to look now, was trapped in them like a deep, terrible cauldron of gold.

"Redemption," she said finally.

And she lowered herself to the snow, scooped the baby into her arms to nurse.

The silks above him were turning purple as the night fled the approach of yet another day under a strange and foreign sun. Life would never be the same for him or Setse ever again.

He stared at the skin in his hands for a long moment before lifting it to his lips.

***

They caught the first glimpse of the Wall at noon, the golden crown of the stone dragon that was their mother, the Great Mountains. It rose and fell, skirted and capped and just the sight of it filled them with awe. Even the two who had made the Wall their home for almost two years could not fail to be inspired by its majesty. It represented the Upper Kingdom in a way that was proud and strong, defiant and unyielding. It was an icon among icons and cats are, after all, an iconic people.

Ursa pulled up her horse, lifted her hand to shield her eyes.

"The cauldrons," she growled. "They are burning orange and white."

"What does that mean," asked the jaguar from the back of his horse.

"Orange is for dogs," said Sireth. "But white?"

"Monkeys," said the snow leopard. "White is for monkeys."

She did not look at them and he could tell she was thinking. Alarm fires of any colour would surely set her warrior's blood racing. Not for the first time, he wondered how long she would last as the wife of a priest.

Finally, she turned, her pupils little more than slits in her near-white eyes.

"You saw this?"

"Some, yes."

"Good."

And she urged Xiao forward and they carried down the road.

Soon after, they caught the smell of sulphur.

The foundry of *Shen'foxhindi* was an open wound in the belly of the Mountains, with large pits carved out of the face of the rock that were visible from miles away. Layers of grey and black, purple and blue, like a patchwork of stone, with threads of orange ore running throughout. The sky hung dark over the entire range and they could see smoke from the smelting fires. Heavy wooden beams served as both crane and catwalk to move baskets of ore and iron and men. And there were many many men.

They had passed several huts on the trail in to *Shen'foxhindi* and roads radiated in all directions like the spokes of a wheel. *Shen'foxhindi* was an important place, not only for its iron smelting and smithing, but for its importance as a garrison town. In fact, for years, the debate had raged on as to whether its name warranted a change to *Sri'foxhindi* but the foundry owners had protested, insisting the name change would increase the taxation of the residents and thus, discourage employment. It was a booming town. Tents skirted the edges of the foundry, running up and down the slopes like the spots on a leopard.

Ursa turned in her saddle.

"So we are going there?"

"Yes, I believe we are."

"And we are looking for a dog."

"Yes."

"There."

"Yes."

"In a garrison town full of cats."

"Yes."

"How would it get over the Wall?"

Sireth frowned, looked back at Yahn Nevye. From the back of his horse, the man shrugged.

The Seer turned back to his wife. "I have no idea."

She shook her head and turned away as the horses began the descent down the road into the foundry.

No one took note of them, no one even looked up as the small party passed merchants and diggers, bankers and bakers going about their morning here in the belly of the Mountains. Smells other than sulphur began to wage war in their nostrils. Beer and chicken, sweat and earth, yak and woodsmoke. The road was dark, the snow all but gone as both yaks and oxen pulled carts filled to tipping, and they passed more than one broken wheel in the frozen ruts. Many tongues were heard as well, for while Hanyin was the language of commerce in most of the Empire, Imperial, Farashi and Hindi were close behind. There was laughter, there were orders, there were greetings and there were arguments, every conversation known to cats overheard in the time it took to pass through the heart of the foundry and step upon the road to the garrison.

High above, the Wall towered over the city like a sovereign, protecting it from dogs. Few cities of importance sat this close to the borders of the Lower Kingdom and naturally, the Wall was thick, high and wide. Battle towers were spaced closely and in fact, it resembled a great crown with banners proclaiming ownership and might. It was a terrible, wonderful sight.

There were several stone gates leading up to the garrison and the road had considerably less traffic than those into the foundry. They passed two carts—one filled with breads, the other with firewood. They passed two men leading a small herd of goats and a haggard woman carrying a basket of leather. She had a cap of yak hide tied over her head and a corncob pipe clenched between her teeth.

Sireth pulled up his horse beside her.

"Excuse me, *sidala,*" he said. "What is going on at the garrison?"

She did not pause, nor did she look up, merely chewed on the pipe and kept walking.

"Please, *sidala.* Do you know?"

"*Sidala!* Hah!" she grunted. "Don't no one call me *sidala* round here."

"Highly esteemed *sidala,*" he added.

She smiled behind her pipe. "Don't you see them fires?"

"The orange and the white. Yes of course."

"We prepare for war, we do. All Wall towns prepare."

"War?" The Seer sat back on his horse, glanced at his wife. She scowled at him. Talking to civilians was not her favourite thing.

"An army coming, coming from the east. Biggest army since *Roar'pundih.* Soldiers and monkeys. Damn monkeys. Hate monkeys."

"Is there war with the *Chi'Chen?* Is that why the fires are burning white?"

"Who am I? Shogun-General?"

The woman spat on the ground and trudged off, leaving the three waiting in the road for several long moments.

"Interesting," said Sireth and he sat for a moment longer before urging Dune forward. Nevye moved in beside him.

"Do you believe her?"

"What's that?"

"The woman. Do you believe her story about the war? About the army and the monkeys?"

"Why wouldn't I?"

The jaguar shrugged. "How would she know anything? She's a merchant woman, not a soldier."

Ursa spat on the ground now. It made a hole in the snow beside the road.

"This merchant woman lives in a garrison town, idiot. She makes her living by knowing."

Nevye grunted but said nothing, and together with packhorses in tow, the three of them moved off and under the first of the stone gates that led to the Wall.

***

It was a thing unseen since the beginning of the Fanxieng Dynasty – the Great Wall solid with mounted soldiers. They rode ten abreast at the widest parts, two at the steepest as the Wall rose and fell with the Mountains. From the battle towers along the way, the trotting of the horses looked like an undulating dragon, multi-coloured and fierce with banners flying both crests as it moved along the parapet. This dragon carried on for as far as the eye could see, from one end of the horizon to the other and news of such a sight began to race through the Kingdom, of an army of cats and monkeys and horses all heading north.

At the head of this dragon, the ghost Kaidan accompanied a Shogun-General in blood red. It was an amazing thing, a miraculous thing, but a thing that quickly took root in the collective imagination. It is not surprising. Cats are, after all, an imaginative people.

The plan was to ride for days, not stopping for sleep or rest as the army carried on up and down the many steps that punctuated the Wall. To stop at any point would cause horses down the line to be forced to stop mid-rise or mid-descent, and if any stumbled, tripped or took lame, the entire army would be compromised. Along the Wall, tigers waited at every plateau with skins of soup and tea for the riders, chickens for the horses and all ate as they willed en route. Those tigers also waited with brooms and spades, for any break in the line would be met with cleaning. An army of two thousand horses and as many men produced a huge amount of dung. Normally, it would be collected and reused in the small infertile farms that littered the mountains and fed the battle towers, but now, the sheer volume was literally swept up and tossed over the wrong side of the Wall, hopefully reaching the bottom before it had the chance to freeze.

No matter how noble the cause, death by frozen dung was not an honourable death.

"And so we pulled him up onto the shore of Ancestorland. That's what I call it. Ancestorland. Solomon calls it NorAm but that doesn't make as much sense as Ancestorland. Oh mother, I thought he was dead. It took such a long time to get the breath back into him but Solomon is so good at that kind of thing and finally, he opened his eyes and I was so happy! I was thrilled! Honestly! If you'd've seen him flying through the air like that! That *mis'syle* hit the boat and *bam!* It was just a ball of fire and flying ship bits and of course, Kerris…"

Kirin could not believe how much this woman could talk. He remembered it vaguely in the back corners of his memory, a memory that was tempered by a long year and a mending heart. But now, as they rode side by side across the parapet of the Great Wall, the memory was crystallizing into reality and he found himself getting a headache, a thing that had not happened in a very long time.

"So then, when he wakes up, I think he's gonna kiss me or something but no. He sits up, looks around and you know what he says?"

He opened his mouth to answer, realized his mistake, promptly closed it again.

"He says, *"The katanah? Where is the katanah?"* I could have killed him! Right then and there, with my very fine little black claws. Yep. Strangled the life right back out of him. Oh mother, that was pretty funny."

And she laughed to herself.

He realized that she was grieving.

It was an odd realization for him. He had never been good at reading people, had never boasted of that particular skill, but this young woman, Fallon Waterford-Grey his sister-in-law, he now understood better than he understood almost anyone. Two mornings ago, she had handed her kittens over into the care of a nursemaid and ten Imperial soldiers. She had kissed them tenderly, promised to be reunited soon and finally let them go to take up her position as Scholar in the Court of the Empress on what could arguably be her last journey. She was a complex and fascinating young woman.

She had not wept yet. He admired her but wondered how long it would last.

"And so, do you know what he did? I'll tell you what he did! He jumped to his feet and ran right back into the water! That's what he did! Solomon and I thought he was crazy, that maybe the explosion had knocked his grey head about just a little bit but he just stood there up to his waist in the waves, looking out to the far horizon where there was still smoke from the chunks and bits floating on the sea. He raised his hands and I thought he was going to call the lightning but he didn't. He just stood like that for, I don't know, a few minutes anyway, then we see what looks like a shark racing through the water right toward him. Oh mother, after so long on the ship, I know a thing or two about sharks. Don't talk to me about sharks. I really hate sharks…"

She laughed again, and then sighed.

"It was the katanah. He called it. He called it from the ocean where it was sinking and it came straight to him like an arrow. He reached down and snatched it right out of the water, turned and sloshed back to us on shore. It still was in the obi so he had both and it was impressive and majestic and wonderful and made me so very proud of him. Sireth said he could do it. I always knew he could. *He* just never knew he could and finally, now he did."

She looked at him, her large emerald eyes bright and brimming with tears.

"And that was just the beginning. You should see the things he can do."

He smiled, grateful that her tale was coming to a semblance of a close.

"I look forward to hearing the rest of it very soon," he said.

"Oh sure. We have three more days, don't we, until we get to the foundry? I can tell you lots and lots of stories in three whole days. Oh mother, you're in for a real treat!"

He swallowed and cursed the fact that now, his was the Luck and that Kerris of the Destiny was far, far ahead.

***

They were stopped by the guards at the second gate.

The Major swung off her desert horse and strode up to the leopards, cursing once again at her lack of uniform. The guards stepped in across the heavy black doors, staffs held a little higher in their hands.

"I am Major Ursa Laenskaya, adjutant of Captain Wynegarde-Grey of *Pol'Lhasa*. I need to speak to the lion in charge."

The guards exchanged glances.

Her hands fell to the hilts of her swords. She carried both katanah and kodai'chi, proof of her warrior status, but she was a small woman in yak hide and winter bear, riding a desert horse. She was accompanied by two monks, not soldiers. It was suspicious and strange and they did not know what to think.

"The lion," she growled. "In charge."

And lashed her very long tail just once.

A leopard bowed, disappeared into the gate. The other hiked his bo a little higher, stepped in to cover the entire door by himself. She snorted and shook her head. She could take him down in one blow.

She turned to her husband.

"I told you. This will not do. I need a uniform."

"The Captain did promise one," said Sireth as he swung off his horse. "And very high boots, if I recall."

"Pah. He is probably drinking tea with his mother at the great house, happy to be home and out of uniform."

"I'm sure that is exactly what he is doing."

He smiled at her while Yahn Nevye remained on his horse. It was a very few long minutes before the door opened once again, revealing the guard and a lion in a well-worn military uniform.

The lion bowed, not quite perfectly.

"A Major from *Pol'Lhasa*, I'm told," he said.

"Major Ursa Laenskaya," she repeated but did not bow back.

"Adjutant to Kirin Wynegarde-Grey, Captain of the Empress' personal guard."

"You are a long way from *Pol'Lhasa.*"

"And you are not the lion in charge."

"He's busy, *sidala.*"

"Major."

"Major. We are under battle preparations. The alarm fires—"

"Which is why we are here. This is Sireth benAramis, Seventh Seer of *Sha'Hadin* and Yahn Nevye, also of *Sha'Hadin.*"

"And *Agara'tha,*" added Nevye.

"From *Sha'Hadin?*" The lion paused, ran his eyes over the brown-clad figures. He smiled. "If so, where are your falcons?"

There was a shrill cry from the mountains when, in a feat of perfect timing, young Mi-Hahn settled on Sireth's shoulder, talon bells jingling. She looked at Nevye and hissed and feathers settled onto the snow.

Ursa looked back at the lion.

"The lion in charge?" she asked.

"Yes, Major. This way," and the black gates swung open to let them through.

***

It was a marvel how she could light so many candles and yet not have the little gar fill with smoke. Magic, he knew it. Witches were skilled at that sort of thing. It was late afternoon and he knew that if there were smoke, the Enemy on the Wall high above would spot it in a heartbeat. She was a deceiver. He wondered how many men she had killed.

He looked down at the baby in his arms. How he had let them convince him was also a marvel, a testimony to his sister's large heart and the witch's innate cunning. But here he was, sitting cross-legged under a tent of branches and silk, breathing in incense that did not smoke and holding a baby that did not cry. Life was far too strange for him.

Setse and the witch were also seated cross-legged. They were holding hands, eyes closed and he knew it was some sort of spell that the witch had cast on his sister. They were both whispering in the language of the Enemy—how Setse had learned it was also a mystery. Her Oracle gift was as unnerving as it was exhausting. He was certain it affected him more than her.

The baby yawned and stretched its tiny fists, blinked its bi-coloured eyes slowly at him. He remembered the first time his mother had let him hold Setse, how she had blinked her strange, unnatural eyes at him and he had sworn from that moment on to protect her with his life. He had survived five winters by then. Already a man. And now this.

The baby was purring.

He glanced up, back at his sister and the witch. They were whispering and chanting. They hadn't heard. They didn't know. He looked back down at the thing in his arms.

He studied the hands, so tiny and unnatural, the tips of the claws dark as a winter's night. He wondered what it took to move them. Just a thought? An act of the will? He shifted slightly so that his own hand was free, dabbed at the tiny hand with the blunted tip of his own claw, marveled at the sight as a hook as sharp and curved as a *jamviyeh* slid out through its finger to catch his pelt. No wonder his people were mortified. It was a mystery.

He touched the little hand, felt the pelt so soft as the fingers wrapped around his own. He tugged back but the grip was strong. Just like Setse.

And suddenly, the baby smiled at him.

He tried to look away, to send his eyes to the figures of his sister and the witch but it was pointless. He had been caught now as surely as Setse had caught him so many years ago. He hated the witch with his entire soul for doing this, for giving him this little creature. It was her plan. It had to be.

He would protect it with his life.

He looked up to see the witch smiling at him, Setse smiling at him and he scowled at them both.

His sister laughed, clapped her hands together.

"Now, Rah! Can you feel them? Can you?"

"Yes," said the witch. "Now is the time."

"For what?" growled Naranbataar as he tried to disentangle his finger from the kitten's grip. "More candles? More broth?"

"Singing!" laughed Setse.

"Of course," said the witch. "Now we sing."

And both women closed their eyes and said no more.

The baby in his arms purred contentedly and Naranbataar shook his head, wondering at what could possibly come of songs sung in silence.

***

"Can you hear that?"

"What?"

"The singing?"

Nevye frowned and turned back from the window. "What singing?"

"Listen."

He stared at the man, the last Seer of *Sha'Hadin*, sitting cross-legged on the stone floor, a cup of hot sweet tea at his side. They were in the top of the battle tower and preparing for sleep on mattresses stuffed with straw. They had eaten stew and dumplings, rice bread and curried chicken and his belly was the happiest it had been in days. The woman was gone, off speaking with the captain of the battlefort and being informed on the state of high alert that was sweeping the Empire. Dogs and monkeys, although he could only see dogs, and not for the first time, he cursed the way his life had rolled out. He was glad she was gone. She terrified him.

Through closed eyes, the Seer smiled at him. "Sit, Yahn, and listen."

Slowly, Nevye did as he was asked, bending his knees in the learning pose. *Odd,* he thought to himself. He never sat like this, hadn't since he was a child in *Ban'lahore*. Damn this mongrel for suggesting it. Damn himself for obeying.

"Give me your hands."

"I'm not giving you my hands!" he growled. "You think I'm a novice. It's insulting."

And he lashed his tail, which proved to be painful. He knew it had been bitten severely by the frost, just like his ears. He was glad he was inside.

"Can you hear the singing?"

"What singing? You're mad."

"Your Oracle. She's singing. She has a lovely voice."

His tail lashing stopped, as did his heart.

"*My* Oracle? She-she's not *my* Oracle."

"Oh. I thought she was."

He glanced down at the Seer's hands, ungloved and exposed, long tan fingers and spotted wrists. Mongrels. A scourge on the Kingdom. They should all be killed.

And yet, here he was, searching the stretch of Wall for a dog. *His* Oracle. How much worse could his life grow?

At the window, a rattle and he looked over his shoulder to see a dark shape. An owl, beating at the glass with speckled wings. He frowned again, wondering at the meaning.

"You could let him in," said the Seer. "Mi-Hahn has gone to *Pol'Lhasa*. She won't be back for days."

"It's just an owl," he answered.

"My mistake. Your hands?"

With a deep breath, he looked down at his gloves.

"If you'd rather not—" said Sireth.

"You will close your eyes?"

The Seer did as he was asked. After a long moment, the jaguar removed his gloves, reached out his hands, which the Seer did not see.

But at the touch, his soul rang with the sound of singing.

***

Run, run, run run. Run like a deer, run like the rain, run like the river. Run, run, run, run.

The songs of the army beat in time with their feet. It was good to keep rhythm, keep all their feet moving as one. It kept them strong and fast and focused on their moving. But for Swift Sumalbayar, there was a different song ringing in his head.

He shook his head, ears flattened against his skull. He was careful not to lose balance, however, for he was on point and to stumble might cause him to be trampled by the Ten Thousand running behind.

At his side, the Khargan ran like a bull, steady and strong, his legs churning up the snow like iron, his claw-necklaces rattling against the lion skull he wore on one shoulder. They made the sound of tambours, a perfect accompaniment to the strange new music that had started in his head.

They were the songs of women. He had not known a woman for a long time and he found himself missing their company, their soft bodies and their strong wills. His wife had been his lifemate. He had been lucky to find her, unlucky to have lost her at the birth of his son. Their deaths still saddened him.

The singing was becoming worrisome, but he could not tell the Khargan. The Khargan would think him an Oracle and would likely torture him to death, friendship not withstanding. The Bear was such a man.

And so he shook his head again and ran, concentrating on the sound of the claws against the skull and hoping the songs of soldiers would drown out the songs of women.

***

It was almost night when they moved the basket to the edge of the Wall. It was not a traditional basket as one might imagine a basket, but rather a cage made of wood and ropes and wire cables. It was used to transport firewood, stones and armour from deep in the earth to the foundry. It had taken ten tigers just to get it and it's massive wheeled pulley there. The wind had picked up, bringing with it daggers of snow and it took those same ten tigers—accompanied by a half-division of soldiers and Captain Yuri Oldsmith-Pak, the 'lion in charge'—to set it up at the edge of the Wall.

As Ursa paced and Nevye watched, Sireth benAramis walked along the parapet of the Great Wall, eyes closed, hands extended at his side as if expecting to fly like his falcon. His brown robes and long hair whipped like banners, threatening to lift him from his feet and send him up into the air and over the Wall with the force. They had passed three battle towers as they walked along this section and they had lost most of the sun. Snow clouds were rolling in once again and it looked to be a very bad night.

Finally the last Seer of *Sha'Hadin* slowed, began to circle like a top, hands spread wide. Suddenly, his eyes snapped open and he moved to the cornice, peered over the edge to the very dark and distant crags below.

"Here?" shouted Nevye and he joined him, gripping the stone carapace as he too peered over the edge. The wind was howling and words were snatched like falling leaves. "The music is louder, I agree!"

"Yes!"

"What is that? That language? Is that Dog?"

"The Language of the People, yes!"

"Can you understand it?"

"Not at all!"

"Won't that be problematic?"

"Probably, yes!"

Nevye swallowed and looked again over the side.

"Down there, then? I don't see anything! It's too black! It's all ice and rock and blackness!"

"Believe me," the Seer turned and smiled at him. "There will be a light soon enough!"

Nevye studied the sheer drop. It was a very long way down.

Sireth turned to the Captain and the tigers. "Can we lower the basket over the side, if you please."

The tigers looked at the lion, then back at him. Oldsmith-Pak, frowned.

"I'm afraid you are mistaken, *sahidi,*" he said quite formally. "That side is the Lower Kingdom. Perhaps you mean over here?"

And he gestured with his golden hand.

"No, Captain. This side, if you please."

The lion, tigers and the soldiers all stared at him. Sireth smiled again.

"If you please."

It was not a request.

Against the far side of the parapet, Ursa Laenskaya was scowling. She looked very small in the shadow of the mountain. As the tigers got to work setting up the pulley which would lower the basket over the wrong side of the Wall, he moved over to her.

He did not touch her.

"You have forgotten," she hissed.

"I have not forgotten."

"They only killed you, they did not hurt you." Her pale eyes met his. "They hurt the Captain very much. They hurt me. Is that so easy to forget?"

"My love, you are my life," he said quietly and now he did touch her, reaching out to stroke her cheek. "I would never, could never forget what they did to you."

"I cannot forgive them."

"*They*...are dead."

She set her jaw. "Their people."

"Their people are not responsible."

"You defend them."

"I do not. But tell me..." He stepped close. "How was it any different than what *our* people did when you were small?"

Her eyes flashed at him, furious.

"And yet," he said, undeterred. "You would serve the Empire of the people who did what they did to you. Tell me, my love, how is this any different?"

She looked away, her profile sharp in the setting purple of the sky. Her hair rose and fell with the breeze and he reached to smooth it from her face. She did not fight.

"You forge the steel, my love," he said. "Find it in yourself. For yourself."

Her silver cheek rippled as tiny muscles twitched but swiftly, she turned to him.

"I will not kill them."

He kissed her forehead.

"Thank you. There will be blood soon enough."

He slid his eyes to the jaguar, standing with cloak wrapped tightly around his body near the cornice of the Wall. The wind was strong and his hair was finally breaking free of the knot at his neck. Things would change for them all soon.

There was shouting from the tigers as the basket went over the Wrong Side of the Wall.

***

The devastation of Karan'Uurt was as swift as it was complete as houses, gars and farms were burned to cinders. All villagers were slaughtered in their beds and those who dared flee were set alight and released in fields of snow and dried wheat. The skies above Karan'Urt were black that day and almost without exception, it would be forgotten, erased from the history of the People at the word of the Khargan, Khan Baitsukhan the Bear. Burned from history, gone from memory. The wheat and the bread, the soups and the stews. The songs of childhood, the legends of old men and the wisdom of women, no more than ashes on the wind.

Jalair Naranbataar and Jalair Naransetseg, Grandchildren of the Blue Wolf, would remember Karan'Uurt but they would not weep. There was a basket coming over the Wall and the time for weeping was done.

***

It took more than ten tigers to pull the basket up from the Wrong Side of the Wall. The wind was so strong that the cage was swinging at the end of the pulley and it was a miracle that it had reached the top without shattering entirely. They shouted and strained but maneuvered it closer to the side, managing to snag the slats and draw it to safety on the stone parapet of the Wall.

The distant cauldrons sent orange and white lights dancing across the stone, distorting snow and faces in colour but suddenly, an unnatural light flared to life within the cage, revealing three passengers, shrouded in black.

Sireth benAramis stepped forward to spring the latch for the cage.

"Sidi," purred a familiar voice and like a shadow, the Alchemist came from the basket, her palm glowing like a beacon. Her eyes were golden orbs behind the wrappings of black silk and magic.

"Sidala," he answered and he could sense the shift in the soldiers behind him. This was sorcery, they knew it, and while they were proud of the way the Gifts and the Arts served the Kingdom, they were superstitious to the bone. Cats are, after all, a superstitious people.

The golden eyes slid past him to the small figure dressed in winter bear. Both swords were out and at the ready.

"Major," the Alchemist smiled.

"I have promised not to kill you," growled Ursa.

"That is something, then."

Sireth noticed Yahn Nevye, several paces away, arms still crossed over his chest. The man was a puzzle.

He turned back to the cheetah.

"And your friends?"

"Mmm. Yes. My friends."

She stepped aside but the two stayed in the protection of the basket. The taller had an arm around the smaller, and with the many layers of fabric and night-black silk, their features were almost indistinguishable.

"Perhaps," said the Alchemist. "We might make introductions in the warmth of a battle tower? My friends have been wounded and they need rest."

He met her eyes. It was because of her that both could see.

"Of course," he said archly.

He turned to the Captain, but there was movement as the smaller of the two figures slipped out of the cage.

The soldiers shifted but she moved through them like a dancer, pausing only to stand before Yahn Nevye. He stepped back. She stepped forward.

"You," she whispered, her voice barely audible over the wailing of the wind. She turned her head back toward the other, her profile unmistakable under the moonlight and the stars. "Rani, look…"

"Setse, *ugayi!"* in a language understood by few on the Wall and the second figure stepped forward, not bothering to cover his face. The

Alchemist laid a hand on his chest, holding him back with a strength she should not have.

A current went through the soldiers and they snapped to attention, swords and bos drawn. The Captain stepped forward now but was blocked by a katanah, razor tip poking a small hole in his uniform.

"Do not," growled Ursa, kodai'chi held mantis-like over her head.

Another shift and both sword and spear formed a ring of steel around the Major when suddenly, a wall of flame leapt into life, surrounding all of them in heat and brilliant light. Even the roaring, whipping wind could do little to dissuade it and tongues of fire licked pelt and uniform alike.

"Enough," bellowed the last Seer of *Sha'Hadin.* "Sheathe your weapons! All of you!"

They did not but at least they did not lunge. He turned to watch the figures outside of the flames, the dancer still poised before the jaguar.

"I know you," she said, her voice young and halting as she wrapped her thoughts around a new tongue. "I have seen…"

Nevye stepped back again.

She cocked her head as if hearing a faraway sound.

"Shar Ma'uul. You Shar Ma'uul. I have known for my life…"

He stepped back again.

"Ulaan Baator coming," she said, moving closer. "Is all coming. Blood. Can see it? Can see dragons and eyes and blood? Eye of the Needle, Eye of the Storm. The fall of Ulaan Baator at steel of Ulaan Baator?"

And from the shadows of her reindeer cloak, she reached a hand up to his face.

Suddenly, he whirled and marched off down the parapet, the way they had come. He was silhouetted by the flames of the cauldrons, disappearing in a heartbeat.

Slowly the dancer turned.

"He can't see," she moaned and she pulled the silk from her face. There were tears streaking her strange cheeks, her one blue eye glittering in the moonlight. "Shar Ma'uul can't see. Too terrible. It consume us all…"

And she began to shake.

The other pushed past the hand of the Alchemist and bolted to the dancer's side, catching her as she folded like paper to the ground.

The flames died away as quickly as they had come and the Captain marched up to the last Seer of *Sha'Hadin.*

"What is this?" he demanded. "Tell me or I will toss you all over the Wall, monasteries and palaces be damned."

Sireth sighed.

"Birth pangs," he said softly.

"Birth pangs?" growled the Captain. "Birth pangs of what?"

Sherah al Shiva pulled the black silks from her face, the unnatural flame in her hand dying as well. Her words were directed at the Commander but the great golden eyes were fixed on the Seer.

"Unification," she said.

"Unification?"

"Unification." Sireth nodded slowly, and turned his attention to the pair huddled on the snowy parapet. Surrounded by terrified, sword-wielding soldiers and cauldrons of oil burning orange and white, he hoped they would all live to see the morning.

And for the first time in hours, he realized that the singing had stopped.

KHANMAKER

They had seen no Ancestors since the destruction of the Plan B, so they made it a point to start walking. There seemed no other reasonable alternative. It was spring in Ancestorland and the seacoast was cool and windy. Kerris had managed to catch and dry several lines of fish and but they needed fresh water so reluctantly, they left the shore and headed inland, hoping for signs of human life, all the while dreading what they might find.

The land was a deciduous forest, filled with ash, beech and serviceberry and they found a creek almost immediately upon leaving the shoreline. Like the road to Ana'thalyia, *there were Ancestral ruins as well - saplings grew through rusted carts and foundations of stone were covered in moss and ferns. Also, like in* Ana'thalyia, *birds were everywhere and once again, Kerris had proven to be an able hunter. Food would not be an issue in this new world, which Fallon had taken to calling Ancestorland. Solomon insisted they were in either Virginianna or Maryland of the Eastern Sea Board, but somehow, Ancestorland stuck.*

After four days, they came upon a fence. It was tall and made of wire but it had buckled in places under the weight of time. Thin trees had grown up through it as well, branches pushing the wire into awkward shapes and there were great gaping holes where it had completely deteriorated. But stranger still were the bodies of the animals at its base. Some were skeletons, others dried as if they had perished in a desert. There were even bones of birds that seemed to have died as they perched on remaining fence posts. It was a strange macabre sight.

"They look dessicated," said Solomon.

"Dessicated?" asked Fallon.

"Dried. Freeze-dried, actually." He rubbed a hand along his neck. "That's weird."

"Can you hear that?"

"What?" said Solomon. "I don't hear anything."

"Exactly," said Fallon, rocking back on her heels. "No birds."

She was right. No birds, no crickets. The only sound was the rustle of the breeze through the trees.

Solomon turned around, hands on hips.

"Yeah," he said. "With all these dead critters, there should be flies too."

"No flies," said Fallon.

"No flies," Solomon repeated.

"I don't like this," said Kerris. "It smells white."

"White?" The Ancestor blinked at him. "It smells white?"

"And hot. And angry. The air is angry."

Tigress and human exchanged glances.

"Another missile?" asked Solomon.

"No, but I think we should leave."

Solomon studied the fence, the dry forest beyond.

"Well, a fence is a construct. That implies constructors."

"Ancestors?" said Fallon.

"Yeah. It may be a couple of hundred years old but there may be a city inside. Tech we could use."

"We need to leave," repeated Kerris.

"And where are we going, Kerris?" said Solomon and he shrugged. "I mean, without the boat, we're kinda stuck here and it's quite a long walk to the Canadian Shield."

Fallon sighed.

"Maybe we could find another Humlander?"

"That's what I'm hoping. Or a Griffen."

"Griffen?" said Fallon.

"Yeah, a GyroRotar--"

She was staring at him.

"Never mind. It's simply astounding the things that are rattling around inside my head."

She grinned. "Oh look! A bird."

Sure enough, a tiny songbird flitted in through the trees, landed on a thin arc of fence wire, bobbed up and down with quick little motions.

"Please, we need to leave now," said Kerris and he began to back away. "The air is very angry."

"Kerris?"

He clapped his hands over his ears, backed away some more.

"Can't you hear it?" he moaned. "Why can't you hear it?"

Suddenly there was a sound unlike anything they had ever heard and a pulse of light from beyond the fence. All three of them were forced to look away, hands over ears, eyes clenched tight. It seemed like a lifetime wrapped in a blanket of intense light and when it ended, it was a sudden as when it had come. Slowly, carefully, they straightened, looked back at the fence.

The bird was dead on the wire, dried like a leaf in autumn.

"Damn," said Solomon. "Maiden."

"Maiden?" asked Fallon.

"Yeah, MAIDEN. Microwave-Assisted Ion Desorption ENergy. Old tech. Kills living things but leaves structures intact. It was banned when I went under." He began to back away. "Kerris is right. We better—"

He didn't have time to finish his sentence before they noticed white shapes moving beyond the fence.

"Bones," said Kerris.

And the grey lion grabbed his wife's hand as the MAIDEN fence began to hum once again.

They ran.

Back the way they had come, leaping over the rocks and roots of the young forest, but they didn't get far when the white light pulsed a second time. Without even a cry, Solomon hit the ground hard, rolling and tumbling and finally coming to a stop in a heap on the forest floor. Fallon swung back, releasing Kerris' hand but the pulse struck her next, causing her slim body to arc violently in midair. She too fell to the ground.

"No!" Kerris cried and he scrambled back to his wife, dropping to his knees and cradling her in his arms. "No, no, no, no, no..."

The forest cracked with sound as three figures thundered through the trees, tall and white and entirely unnatural. They slowed when they reached the trio and Kerris looked up at them with wide eyes. He could feel the angry white from within their chests and inside plates of dark glass, he saw the faces of Ancestors.

"Bones," he said, rising to his feet. "An Army of Bones."

He slid the katanah from the obi, heard the light gather, felt the air breathe deep and recoil into the bones. He knew what was coming but he snarled and swung, the steel slicing a clean line into the white fiber of the thigh. The face behind the glass howled, its voice like the scraping of tin cups when the chest burst with light, cold and white, and then nothing more for some time.

***

Kirin looked down at his brother from the back of his horse.

"Seriously, Kerris?" he said. "This is sounding worse and worse."

Kerris grinned up at him. "And that's not even the half of it. Head down."

As one, the brothers leaned low as their horses scrambled up the set of steps in the starlight, reaching plateau at the count of twenty.

It was dark now, the moon illuminating the Wall and painting the mountains in strokes of silver. Snow was floating from the skies and even with the roar of a hundred cauldrons burning along the Wall and the stomp and snort of over two thousand horses, it seemed as if the night were holding its breath. Tomorrow, they would make *Shen'foxhindi* and everything would change.

In the moonlight, Kerris reached down to run his hand along the thick, tangled mane. Quiz snorted, tossed his head

"Thank you," he said, looking up at his brother. "I never thought I'd see him again."

Kirin grinned a sleepy grin. "It was entirely his own idea. He is a very headstrong creature."

"I love him so much. And Fallon and the kittens. Honestly, Kirin, sometimes I think my chest will burst."

Kirin looked over his shoulder at the figure of his brother's young wife, eyes closed, head bobbing as she dozed on the back of her painted horse. After a year on the trail, all of them could function perfectly from the saddle and it was serving her well. They had been riding for four days now and had made good time considering the ice and snow and wind on the Wall.

"Head down," said Kirin and together they leaned forward over the necks of their mounts as hooves scrambled up the stone steps toward the next plateau. In the Great Mountains, the Wall rose and fell with the peaks, skirting some, wrapping others and steps were almost as common as battle towers. It made Kirin grateful for the cauldrons of orange and white, for even with the bright cold moon as a guide, the steps were dark under so many horses. A slip or a stumble could mean a break of a leg and a horse that would not live to finish the journey. He marveled it had not happened yet.

"Have you been counting the cats?" panted Kerris as they reached the next plateau.

"Counting the cats?" he answered. "What do you mean?"

"We pick up a few more at each battle tower. About seventy or eighty have joined the front but it's impossible to count the ones that have joined at the rear. I honestly can't see that far back. I was wondering if anyone was keeping track?"

Kirin sat back in his saddle, cast his eyes around at the mass of horses moving together, now merely glinting, jingling scales of a huge lumbering dragon. It hadn't occurred to him that others would be joining. He hadn't noticed their number increase, but it made perfect sense. This was a mission of nationalistic pride, and cats were, after all, a nationalistic people.

"No," he said finally. "But I'm certain we'll find out once we reach the foundry."

Kerris grunted. "I pulled the sticks this morning."

"And?"

"Five."

"Five sticks?"

"No," he grinned. "The number five."

"And that means?"

"Death," the Geomancer lifted a flask of sakeh to his lips. "Five is the number of death. Sakeh?"

He held the flask out to his brother. Their horses were very close. Kirin could have taken it easily.

"No, but thank you Kerris. You know how I am with drink. I don't wish to fall asleep just yet."

"I remember. You were mortified with all the snakes." Kerris pocketed the flask. "Do you think they'll be at *Pol'Lhasa* yet?"

"They?"

"The kittens."

Kirin studied his brother's profile, wondered if he too was grieving the loss of his children in the same manner as his wife. *He's a wonderful father,* Fallon had insisted. Kirin wondered if it could possibly be true.

"Most likely," he answered. "I sent a parchment with their nursemaid for Ling's eyes only. She will see they are cared for, I promise you."

"Ling?" Kerris turned to grin at his brother. "You call her Ling?"

"Aaah..."

"Kirin? Do you?"

He steeled his jaw, not certain how to proceed.

"Well??"

"I do."

"I thought she was married?"

"He died. Mal'haria."

"So sad. Really. Really terribly sad. So, ah..." Kerris' grin widened. "Was she... *happy* to see you?"

He felt the heat in his cheeks but he smiled all the same.

"Quite."

Kerris threw back his head and laughed so that horses startled and soldiers snapped to attention and the entire Wall and surrounding mountains echoed with the sound of his laughter. Fallon opened sleepy eyes and smiled unawares.

"Oh my dear brother," Kerris panted, finally wiping tears from his eyes. "Well done, I say. Well done indeed."

"Kerris, hush!"

"They'll be writing odes in no time!"

"Kerris, please—"

"From Imperial gold to Shogun red, he finds himself in a royal bed."

"Kerris!"

"I'll say no more, brother. But I am glad for you. Really. Truly." And Kerris turned away from him, the smile becoming a knife on his face. "She's a better match than your Alchemist."

There was an edge to his voice and Kirin understood. Sherah al Shiva had almost destroyed the group with her devices and schemes. Of them all, Kerris had been the most affected.

"We'll never be allowed to marry," Kirin said, eager to avoid the subject of Alchemy. "And I don't know how long I'll even be allowed to live. Head down."

And they scrambled up yet another twenty steps.

"They won't touch you," said Kerris, once they reached the plateau. They were very high up now and the silver mountains in moonlight were breathtaking. "Not after such a public reinstatement of the Shogun-General."

"I'm certain I was being followed in the Palace."

"You probably were. And now? On the road to the Gate of Five Hands?"

He shook his head. "I can't say. I don't know."

"Hm. Did you see Mummie?"

And now it seemed Kerris was holding his breath. Their mother was old and he loved her very much.

"Yes," he said. "She was happy you were with tigers."

"Hmm."

"Fallon says you called the katanah out of the sea."

"I suppose I did."

"She says you can call many things."

"Well, our Seer was right on that account." He released a deep breath, frosting like a snowdrift in front of his face. "The earth is sick, Kirin."

"Sick?"

"Yes. And I think it's angry."

"About what?"

"The foundry, I expect. It's a very large mine, yes?"

"I believe so."

"Hmm. Understandable, really. No cat would be particularly happy with creatures digging around inside, taking bits out of you and not saying sorry. Cats are rude that way. No, I can understand completely why the earth is sick and angry."

Kirin studied his brother for a long moment before a set of down steps demanded his attention. But he thought on his words for a long while after that, even as the night began to break into the colours of morning.

***

There is more to the making of tea than simply adding leaves to boiling water. *Chado* is a skill, an art form, a way of life. Not one was master of the art of tea like the Alchemists of *Agara'tha* and none of them more so than Sherah al Shiva. Now, as the sun sent her golden brooms through the narrow window into the main battle tower of *Shen'foxhindi,* she knelt by the brazier, pouring from an iron pot, allowing the tea to spill over the sides of the cups and deepen the patina of the clay. She had also slipped a few incense sticks into the coals and the cold stone room was transformed into a lair of warmth and peace.

On a blanket of yak-hide, her baby, Kylan stretched and rolled in a loose garment of golden wool. He seemed delighted with being free, out of arms and packs and slings for the first time in weeks. While too young to crawl, he had pushed up on hands and knees and was content to watch his mother as she brewed. His tufted tail whipped under the woolens and he took in the entire room with large, bi-coloured eyes.

For her part, Ursa had not taken her eyes of him the entire time.

They were in the upper most level of the battle tower and the doors were barred by leopards. No one was allowed out, although fresh stew had been brought in and Setse had finished three servings, now licking the bowl with her long pink tongue.

"I am filled," she said and sagged against the stone of the wall. "More stew would burst my skins."

"I'm glad you liked it, little one." Sireth smiled as he wiped his bowl with the naan. "Any more gravy and you might turn that blue eye brown."

She gasped, smiled brightly and rolled over onto her hands and knees, just like Kylan. She crawled over to study the Seer, her tail waving in the air behind her.

"Setse," Naranbataar growled. He had not touched the stew and was leaning against a far wall, arms folded across his chest. *"Zogsoogooroi!"*

"Your eyes," she said, ignoring her brother and staring at the man sitting before her. They were almost nose to nose. "They are colour of Rani's. Colour of my people's. I did not know this be possible."

Ursa growled, her hands falling to the hilts of her swords.

Noticing the motion, Naranbataar's hand moved to the bow at his shoulder.

The Alchemist continued to pour tea into five small cups.

"You part dog?"

Sireth grinned "Not to my knowledge."

The young Oracle raised a hand, passed it over the scar on his brow. She frowned. "This, this bad..."

"Yes."

"But...*Oh.* Oh Rah..."

She paused, turned to look over her shoulder at the cheetah. Sherah sat back on her heels, raised a cup to her lips, blinked slowly.

"Hm," said the Oracle before shaking her head and curling her dancer's legs beneath her. "You see?"

He laid the bowl aside. "I don't understand."

"See?" She waved a hand in front of her eyes, then touched her head. "See."

"Ah." He sat back and smiled. "Yes. Yes, I do."

"Shar Ma'uul see?"

"Shar Ma'uul?"

"Yes."

She nodded and he looked at the Alchemist.

"It means yellow cat," said Sherah.

"Yellow cat," said Setse. "Shar Ma'uul."

"Yellow cat," he muttered. "Blue wolf."

Setse gasped. "Blue Wolf, Yellow Cat! Yes! Yes!"

"Shar Ma'uul means Yellow Cat?"

She nodded.

"Amazing," said the Seer. "Yahn Nevye is Shar Ma'uul. The Yellow Cat."

Behind him, Ursa snorted. Yahn Nevye was nowhere to be found, had not been since the middle of the night when the cage came over the Wall.

"Ulaan Baator," Setse said now. "Red… oh red what, Rah?"

"Hero," added the Alchemist and she rose to pass Naranbataar a cup of tea. He shook his head, eyes locked on the figure of his sister. She smiled and turned back to Setse, lifted his tea to her own lips. "Ulaan Baator means Red Hero."

"Blue Wolf. Yellow Cat. Red Hero," said Sireth. "Isn't Dharma a colourful mistress?"

And with a smile, he offered her his hands.

"No," growled Ursa.

"Uguyai," growled Naranbataar.

But she took his hands and closed her eyes to colours bleeding into morning.

***

He was so cold that he could barely feel his feet. He was a jungle cat, hated life in these miserable mountains. Even with skins and furs and a pelt like his, he was sure he was going to lose his ears or the tip of his tail and he cursed the morning he left his bed for the company in the stables of *Sha'Hadin.* He should have stayed in his room, would have been rid of the arrogant Seer and his fearsome wife. Could have spared himself the discomfort of the last few days. Could have spared himself the ridicule.

And so he sat with his back against the cornice of the Wall, rubbing his gloved hands and watching the sun rise over the Great Mountains. He had to admit it was a beautiful sight. Despite the cold, the Mountains were a very good mother to cats. Despite the cold and the heights. Tigers were shouting now, calling to each other from the great cauldrons of orange and white flame and he shook his head. Despite the cold and the heights and the tigers.

Oh yes. And the owls.

It sat now on the snowy cornice of the Wall, staring at him. It had been there for hours since he dropped to sit where he was sitting, after the damned tigers had pulled the dogs over the Wall and the Oracle had tried to touch him. He shook his head as if trying to rid himself of the memory, her tiny slip of a body, her long face, the blue eye that danced like moonlight on an icy lake. She was more beautiful than in his visions and he cursed her for it, ensnaring him in the unnatural, otherworldly grace of her. He cursed himself and his belligerence and his life-altering fall and the owls.

It was still watching him.

"What do you want?" he growled and it twisted its head, almost upside down at his words.

He reached down, pulled the stone smooth of snow, packed a ball in his hands. It was still watching him as he threw, watched the ball sail over its harmlessly head.

"You know," he said to it. "There was a time I could have hit you even if you were on that tower over there. You know that? You could have been two towers away and I still would have hit you."

It ruffled its feathers, twisted its head the opposite way.

"You look like Chancellor Ho."

It blinked one eye.

"Yes, you do, with your flat face and bulging eyes."

It blinked the other.

"Silence," he said now. "Hunts in Silence."

The owl hopped, lifted its wings, settled again.

"I don't talk to owls. I won't."

The owl lit from the Wall and suddenly, he could hear singing.

Her singing, her voice. She was in the tower, the main tower of *Shen'foxhindi* with the arrogant Seer and his terrifying wife and she was *calling him*. She had been calling him *all his life. He could not help but come.*

There was a Yellow Cat, there was a Blue Wolf, there was a Red Hero and there were dragons, flying dragons that soared like arrows through the sky. And dogs, so many dogs, and Eyes and swords and death and the world filling with blood. Eye of the Needle, Eye of the Storm. A deadly barter, a trade of lives, of love and death, of steel and bone and Eyes and white, the world was turning white of the moon—

"Come, *sidi.* Now!"

He gasped as he was yanked him to his feet and dragged away from his little perch on the Wall. It was a soldier and there was shouting, much shouting, louder now and commanding. Down the long road that was the Wall, there was movement, there were banners and he shook the arms off, staggered to stand on his own. It was a massive army of horses and cats and some other creatures and it looked like a dragon with armored plates and scales and spines moving toward him, churning up snow on the Wall as they came. A figure in blood red and a grey ghost at his side.

"What is that?" he gasped again and the soldier, a leopard in battle dress, grabbed his sleeve.

"The Khanmaker!" the leopard cried. "The Khanmaker and the Army of Blood! Quickly, *sidi,* or they will trample you under their hooves!"

And he was gone, leaving Yahn Nevye backpeddaling as the wall of horses closed in. He turned to run but the horses were upon him, the ring of metal, the smell of leather, the heat of their bodies, when a red-gloved hand grabbed his collar and his cold feet left the stone.

***

It was a thing unseen in the history of *Shen'foxhindi* as almost three thousand horses and riders poured through the tower and out through the gates. In fact, it would take the better part of the day for the last horses to leave the stone of the Wall for the earth of the town and more than one soldier dropped to sleep at the feet of his horse once there. Blankets were brought for both horse and rider and homes were opened to all. For once, sakeh flowed freely amongst the troops, as cat, horse and monkey would rest for three days to prepare for the journey to come.

In the battle tower of *Shen'foxhindi,* Kirin dismounted, passing the reins into the hands of a leopard. He watched as his passenger slid from the back of the saddle to the floor. It was a jaguar, a monk most likely, for he was dressed in very familiar brown robes. The horses had almost run him down and it had been fortuitous that Kirin had been able to snag his hood and swing him up behind before he had been trampled. The four of them—Kerris, Fallon, Bo Fujihara and himself—had stayed on the Wall as Li-Hughes led the army out and down the steep road to the foundry but now, as his own feet hit solid ground for the first time in days, he found himself wishing to hold on to his horse for just a moment longer.

"Are we there yet?"

He looked over at Kerris as he helped Fallon off her mount. Her arms wrapped around his neck and she sagged into him, looking ready for bed.

"Yes, luv. We're there."

She smiled sleepily.

"'Cause I've been thinking about how we're gonna get two thousand monkeys, five hundred cats and almost three thousand horses over the Wall."

"Have you now?"

"MmHm. I have an idea. A really good one. Do you think there's cocoa?"

Next to them, Bo Fujihara sprang from the back of his horse, slipped a handful of sweets from his pocket and up to its mouth. The horse chewed happily as it was led to the stables downstairs. Both Fallon and Kerris showered Quiz with hugs and kisses before he too was led to the stair, disappearing into the darkness and the smell of hay and sweet grass. Shenan and young aSiffh were led off and soon, the room was left to cats and one small, fair, pink-faced monkey.

The lion of the garrison bowed to him.

"Captain Yuri Oldsmith-Pak," he said. "It is an honour to have you in our tower, Shogun-sama." His eyes flicked to the monkey. *"All* of you."

"And you lit your white cauldrons just for us," sang the ambassador. "To make us feel welcomed, of course."

Oldsmith-Pak had no answer for him and Fujihara smiled like the sun.

"The honour is ours," said Kirin as he pulled the helm from his head, tucked it under his arm. He did not bow in return. "This will be a difficult few days for the town with this number of soldiers and horses. I am certain you will not disappoint your Empress."

Oldsmith-Pak bowed again.

"I have never been so far inside your Empire," said Fujihara. "Only and ever Kohdari."

"Pol'Lhasa then, when we return," said Kirin and he turned to the monk who was leaning against a wall, eyes wide, a furrow between his spotted brows.

"I hope we did not spoil your meditations, *sidi,"* he said. "Once moving, a force like this cannot be easily stopped."

"Who are you?"

"Right to the point," Kerris laughed. "How very like a monk."

Kirin ignored him. "My name is Kirin Wynegarde-Grey, Shogun-General of House of Thothloryn Parilaud Markova Wu."

"That sounds so wonderful," murmured Fallon. She was leaning on her husband's chest, eyes half closed and smiling like a sleepy child. "Shogun-General Wynegarde-Grey ..."

"Oh..." But the jaguar swallowed, eyes widening. "Of course..."

"And you, *sidi?* You wear the robes of *Sha'Hadin."*

"Yahn Nevye," said the monk. "We've never met. Ever."

"Oh!" exclaimed Fallon, suddenly awake. "Yahn Nevye? Council candidate Yahn Nevye? Yahn-the-man-who-cannot-speak-to-falcons-Nevye? That Yahn Nevye?"

"Um…"

"You assumed control of *Sha'Hadin,*" she said, smiling brightly. "I know 'cause I was there. Not at *Sha'Hadin*. On the Wall. But I was at *Sha'Hadin*, just not when you were there. We were on the Wall. Sireth told us. Remember, Kerris?"

"Is the Seer here, then? Sireth benAramis?" Kerris cocked his head. "Because I could have sworn I saw that damned falcon, the one who likes to sit on heads."

"Mi-Hahn," grumbled Fallon. "I hate that bird."

"Upstairs." Nevye swallowed again. "In the keep."

Fallon squealed, clapped her hands. "And Ursa? Is Ursa here too?"

Nevye nodded, swallowed again.

Kirin turned to Captain Oldsmith-Pak. "These people are dear friends of ours. I would like to see them before we make any plans for the rest of the army. Is that acceptable, Captain?"

"They are under guard, Shogun-sama." The lion looked worried.

"Under guard?" Kirin frowned. "The man is a member of the Council of Seven. The woman serves with me in *Pol'Lhasa.* Why should they be under guard?"

Captain Oldsmith-Pak exchanged glances with Nevye.

"I'll take them," suggested the jaguar. "I, I should take them."

"Yes, please," said the lion. "Take them."

Kirin frowned again. This behaviour was very strange.

"Then take us, *sidi,*" he said.

"Right," said the jaguar and he pushed himself off the wall. "This way."

Kerris grinned. "Brilliant."

And they all trotted up the many stairs that led to the keep of the Battle Tower of *Shen'foxhindi.*

***

It is an amazing thing to note that for brothers so different, there are times when they were remarkably the same. They were, after all, sun and moon, Yin and Yang, opposite spokes of the same wheel. The four of them followed the jaguar up the winding staircase that led to the keep and there were leopards, fully armed, at the door. They stood aside as the Shogun-General pushed open the door and strode in.

The room smelled of incense and five pair of eyes looked up.

What would have been smiles and greeting quickly dissolved into the song of steel when, in one smooth motion, two lions pulled katanahs on three of the guests.

Quickly, Sherah al Shiva dropped to one knee as Kerris' blade froze inches above her neck.

Likewise, Setse shrank under the Blood Fang, her brother pulling the bow from his back, an arrow aimed directly between the blue eyes of the lion.

"No!" Sireth benAramis rose to his feet. "Captain, no!"

There was silence in the keep, save the breathing of lions.

"I should kill you now," snarled Kerris. "What you did to him, to me, to all of us. I should take your head off right here, right now!"

Sherah did not look up.

"Kerris," said Fallon quietly, taking his arm.

"Tell me why I shouldn't kill you."

The woman said nothing.

For his part, Kirin was transfixed. The Fang was silent, its red blade gleaming in the sunlight from the window, yearning to spill canine blood. The Fang was silent but the lion was not, and his growl was deep, almost visceral. The Scales of the Dragon whipped from side to side and the archer leaned back, pulling the string taut on the bow.

"Captain," warned the Seer. "They are not your enemies."

"This is wrong," Kirin growled. "This should not be."

"Why is she here?" snarled Kerris again, his blade hovering ever so close to the cheetah's spotted neck.

"They are not your enemies," repeated the Seer.

At his side, Ursa did not move. Yahn Nevye could not, for he was caught in the drama of the sight, knowing that it could quite easily be his neck on the line, and that at some point, if this was same lion—Jet barraDunne's lion—it would be.

Bo Fujihara watched it all with small, quick eyes. He was a smart man. There was far more going on here than simply the presence of Dogs.

Slowly, like a dancer, the girl with one blue eye lifted to her feet.

"Ulaan Baator," she whispered.

Her brother growled something but still she moved forward. She moved like a breeze, quiet and soft, forward again until she stood directly in front of the golden lion in blood red armour. She took the point of the Fang in her palm, pressed it until it raised a drop of blood between the pads. She moved it then to the layers that covered her heart. All the while, she kept her eyes fixed on the lion, did not look away.

"Kuren Ulaan Baator," she said again. "I knew. I saw."

All eyes were on the lions and the women at the points of their swords. No one dared speak, no one even dared breathe until a very strange thing happened.

A baby cried.

No one moved. It was a most unexpected thing. It did not belong in the room, this night.

"A baby?" asked Fallon.

There was a second cry and a tiny figure flailed from under the hides.

"A baby? Who has a baby?"

"I do, little sister," said the Alchemist. She did not move, her eyes were fixed on the floor, Kerris' blade still a breath away from the arch of her neck. "It is my baby."

"You have a baby?"

"Yes," she said. "His name is Kylan."

"Kylan?"

The baby wailed and thrashed and a tiny fist could be seen from the blankets. Kerris gripped and regripped the katanah, uncertain and unsure.

She finally looked up, golden eyes pleading.

"Please, *sidi,*" she said. "My baby."

"Her baby," said Fallon and she squeezed his arm. "Kerris, please."

With a lash of his grey tail, Kerris sheathed the long sword and stepped back, allowing the cheetah to turn and gather the infant into her arms.

"Captain?" urged Sireth but Kirin's gaze was fixed now on the cheetah. She held the child to her chest and could not bring herself to look at him.

"Sherah?" Fallon moved over to the woman who had once been a friend, lowered herself next to her to get a better view. "Did you say his name was Kylan?"

"Of course," said the Alchemist.

"That's Namyanese," she said. "I learned it in the University."

Sherah said nothing.

"It means unicorn, doesn't it?"

In fact, no one said anything. No one said a word. No one dared.

Fallon looked up at the warrior in red.

"It means Kirin."

There was not even a breath in the room.

It was a very long moment before the golden lion lowered the Fang and slipped it into its sheath. He turned and exited the room.

The breathing returned some time after.

A COUNCIL OF TEN

I have loved Ling from the moment I met her. It was in the Imperial nursery—I had perhaps four summers, she perhaps two. The first thing I did was to stop my lessons, lower my brush and stare, not because she was the daughter of the Empress, not because she was accompanied by peacocks, but because of her eyes. I had never seen anything like them. Her face was ebony, her cheeks dotted with red paint, there was even a bead of jade on her forehead, but all I saw were her eyes. Large, deep and brilliant gold. I was lost from that moment on.

The first thing ***she*** *did was push me down and pull my tail. I suppose she was my Empress even then.*

This *woman has golden eyes.*

She sits on the snowy parapet surrounded by candles that flicker with unnatural light. They are Alchemy candles. They are not dampened by the snow or put out by the wind. Her hair is loosed and rises and falls around her face, calling like come hither fingers. I remember the feel of it under my hands, which is surprising because my hands were bleeding and raw at that time. Or perhaps it is a trick of the mind. She is good at that.

It is dawn and I have spent the night alone, wrestling with my fear. I never used to wrestle with things. Life was understandable, my path straight. But then again, I never used to have fear. Fear changes things. That is one thing I do understand.

I could have killed the dogs last night. I think I would have had it not been for the baby.

I don't know what to make of that.

Kylan is Namyanese for Kirin. Can this be possible? It was one night and I was almost dead. At least, I think so. I barely remember. What does that say about me? What does that say about her?

She is a liar and a deceiver. Kunoi'chi. Untrustable, a shadow. What is she doing with the dogs? Why did she bring them and here, of all places? What does she know that no one else does? I should ask her but she would answer in riddles. The Jade Fang could take off her head. Bushido would demand it. It would be a clean kill, an honourable death. It would be poetry.

I think about asking her but I see movement in the snow at her knees. It is the baby, the one with the bi-coloured eyes. I will not look on him for I may be forced by Bushido to kill him too. I have never killed a baby. I can't imagine it would be difficult, not even if he is my son.

She turns her head, sees me watching from the shadows of the battle tower. There is a strange tightening in my chest and I wonder at that. We hold the look for a very long time before she turns back to the candles and the baby.

I linger a moment longer before returning to the tower and my fear.

--an excerpt from the journal of Kirin Wynegarde-Grey

***

The space beside him was cold and he opened his eyes. In the light of the high window, Ursa was dressing, slipping into the many layers of undyed fabrics that were her clothing. A linen shift and woolen yukata tied off at her narrow waist. Wide silk trousers wrapped to the knees with strips of leather. A sable coat rolled at the neck, her cloak of winter bear, long and white and almost as glorious as her own pelt. He watched her tuck the knives, daggers and throwing stars into every slip and fold, watched her cinch her leather obi and slide the dual swords home.

"Where are you going?" he asked from the floor. Their presence at the battle tower of *Shen'foxhindi* had been unexpected. No arrangements had been made for sleeping but blankets and bedrolls had been provided. A private corner was a precious thing.

She turned her pale eyes on him as she bound her hair high over her head.

"Captain Oldsmith-Pak has agreed to have me fitted."

"Fitted?"

"For a uniform. There's a commissary outside the gates with a seamstress on duty."

"For a uniform. I see." He pushed up to sitting, pulled the blankets up on his shoulders. She had been angry last night and his body was still aching from the bruising. Her lovemaking was rarely tender. Lately, her temper made it violent. "Perhaps I could accompany you?"

"No," she said. "It is a military thing. You are not military."

"Yes, of course."

"I will get you a bo."

"I don't want a bo."

"You are Kenshi. You should have a sword."

"I don't want a sword."

"A dagger, then. I will get you a dagger."

"*You* are my steel."

"I will get you a dagger."

He sighed as she paused at the door.

"Did you see him?"

"Him?"

"The Captain—" She shook her head and her tail lashed behind her. "The Shogun-General. Did you see that he would be here?"

"Yes."

"And you said nothing."

"It always remains as to how things play out. I never saw it in detail, just that we would meet when we found the dogs."

"You should have told me."

"Perhaps."

He could see the muscles in her jaw ripple and twitch.

"He wanted to kill them."

"Yes."

"He should have."

"Perhaps." He cocked his head like a falcon. "What would you have done?"

She stared at him a long moment.

"Helped him."

She whirled and was gone and he sighed. The stone was cold behind his back. He could hear Mi-Hahn's thoughts as she swept in to the aerie at the highest point of the tower. There were many falcons and kestrels in the keep – army birds all—and they did not mind sharing. He could hear the songs of the Oracle inside his head, felt her young but strong heart beating like a drum. Not a war drum, however. A dancer's drum, a beat of timing and rhythm. He could feel the elements swirl and dance around the grey coat, Kerris Wynegarde-Grey, could feel them waiting for his commands and he wondered if the lion had finally accepted his gifting, if he could master them the way he was born to. He could feel the touches of Yahn Nevye's mind as the man struggled with his privacy, wanting to understand and yet terrified of being understood. He could feel the magic of the Alchemist as she too danced around the edges of his mind, defiant and proud and so very dangerous.

In his mind's eye, he could see the Captain—*no,* Shogun-General. His wife had been quite correct. Could see him standing by a tall window, watching the sun rise over the Lower Kingdom, could see the bolt of mane fall like molten gold down his armoured back. The lion wore much armour now, more so than before and he wondered at that. *"I prefer to keep the world out,"* Yahn Nevye had said so long ago. He wondered if Kirin might now say the same.

Ten thousand enemies were coming from the north. A world of enemies were waking in the west. There were only nine of them here, ten including the *Chi'Chen* ambassador and he could not see the end of it. Eye of the Needle, Eye of the Storm. Death and fire, bones and eyes.

And that would only be the beginning.

He closed his eyes and was gone.

***

Her eyes were gold.

Gold like a field of western wheat.

Gold like the sun gleaming over the wasteland of Gobay.

Gold like the manes of lions braided into the Khargan's hair.

Her eyes were not the eyes of the People and she pushed him down with long, strong hands.

The first pink streaks of moondown in the sky, slashes of blood in the cold flesh of the night. Long-Swift sat up quickly, glancing around at the sea of sleepers stretched out beyond the horizon. Their backs were rounded and dark and covered with a dusting of fine snow. Some were waking but most were still asleep, sentries stood and breathed the wind for scents of yak or goat or cat. He threw a quick glance at the tent where the Khargan slept alone for once, no wives or Oracles to keep him entertained.

He shook his head and swallowed.

He had dreamed of the woman last night, the singer of the songs that had been in his head for days now. She was a witch, a wraith, a spirit dancer, slipping through his mind like memory but one he did not, could not, remember for she was also the Enemy and while he had killed his share of the spotted and striped men who guarded the borders, he had never in all his years killed a feline woman. Indeed, he had never even seen one.

Her hands had been strong, her magic stronger. He had been captivated first by her singing, then by her eyes, more powerful than the army, more intoxicating than their wotchka. She was hypnotic and therefore dangerous.

But he didn't dare tell the Khargan. Not this. He could tell no one this. The Bear would wring out his life with his massive hands for dreaming of the Enemy in this way.

It had been a very good dream.

He grinned, shook his head one last time and rolled to his feet.

***

When Jeffery Solomon awoke, he knew he was dreaming.

He opened his eyes, waited as his pupils sought to focus. The lights were dim, the white noise a comforting drone and the air was warm and smelled of ozone. His limbs were still heavy from the pulse, fingers and toes tingling and he was surprised to see the hairs on his chest standing up with static charge. He wondered if it had been a Dazzler that had taken him down. Consistent, he thought, with the MAIDEN technology of the fence and he wondered if the 'bones' that had chased them were in fact people in carbon-fiber armor.

As his unfocused eyes drifted upwards to the ceiling, he realized two things. Firstly, that the ceiling was a mirror and he could see himself reflected in its concave surface and secondly, the fact that he was laying on a cot, naked.

He couldn't help himself. He started to laugh.

It was understandable, really. He had survived a privileged childhood in an underprivileged world and then survived the mercenary institutions of higher learning that had led to his many degrees and doctorates; he had survived the many plagues that that stricken the populace before he went under as Supervisor 7 of SleepLab 1 in Kandersteg Switzerland; had survived hundreds of years (if not thousands) in a state of disambiguation and had survived the subsequent waking that had killed six others; he had survived on vitamin squares and protein powder and ice and had survived the raising of the Humlander and swarming of the rats and the crossing of an entire continent; had survived several months living in forests with cat people and on seashores with cat people and on the ocean with cat people, had even survived a ship-to-shore missile that had blown his ship out of the water and here he was after all that miraculous survival, laying on a bed, naked.

It was - he had to admit - obscenely funny.

When he could move, he waved at the ceiling. It was an Arc en Ciel *or ArcEye, a surveillance system that had been 'state-of-the-art' when he went under. ArcEyes had thousands of tiny mirrored sensor-screens that would transmit images to and from the concave surface, recording the activities in the room while projecting blue skies or gently-moving clouds or stars at twilight. This ArcEye was old – only the mirror remained, and from this angle, he could see the bronzing of the screens. He wondered if he was actually being observed or if this were now merely a ceiling, nothing more than a distorted relic of a distant age.*

Slowly, carefully, he swung his bare legs over the side of the bed and sat, waiting for the vertigo to end.

"Hello," he called out to the empty room. "Hey, can I get some clothes, please? I'm not modest, but honestly, folks. We haven't even met."

There was a sound, a faint ping from behind the wall and soon, a door swung open. Ramshackle, he thought. With an ArcEye system, doors should slide to form a seamless part of the wall but this gave him a world of information about the level of technology about to walk through that swinging door.

Two figures came in, soldiers obvious by their black uniforms and face shields. They had very large, imposing weapons and flanked the door as a team of others came through, wheeling a cart with them. It was carrying a variety of instruments, some he recognized, others he didn't, and his eyes flicked from the cart to the people moving it. They paused as a woman in black fatigues and goggled cap pushed past to stand in front of them, folded her hands behind her back.

To a man who had not seen another living example of his species in five thousand years, she was the most beautiful thing he had ever seen.

"Shi Main nin," she said. "Por qué the hell shi nin zhe monstruos?"

"What?" he said.

"Zhe Monstruos. Estaban tamen de yaoming shesi'er?"

"Chinese and Spanish?" Solomon frowned. "What the hell?"

"Zhegin hell."

He blinked slowly. It was a dream. It had to be.

The people with the cart moved forward, began to poke at his arms, his throat, his chest. Drawing blood, scraping skin, plucking hair. An older man with a shaved head and filthy white jumpsuit tugged on the wire at the back of his skull.

"Hey," Solomon growled. "Paws off the wire."

"Wire?" said the woman. "Ni, Feed."

"Yah, the Feed into Satcom. Hey, can I get some clothes? Anything. Just not one of those ugly jumpsuits."

The woman jerked her head and a bolt of grimy fabric was presented. He grinned.

"A jumpsuit. Whaddayou know..."

"¿quién the hell shi shui?"

"Ah, one sec..." He stepped one foot then the other into the suit, pulled it up over his shoulders, then ran his finger over the tabs. They did not close easily and he could see how they had fabricated clasps with twine and bits of metal. Fascinating. He stood up tall, thrust out his hand. "Doctor Jeffery Solomon, Supervisor Seven, SleepLab 1."

There was silence for a moment in the room.

"Slabwun?"

"SleepLab 1, yeah."

"Slabwun es SleepLab 1, Doctor."

She turned to the bald man – "Jiǎnchá the archivos por Supervisor Solomon, Jeffery, Slabwun hé dédào jìyì memoria, Version san"— but took the hand he offered her. She did not seem to know what to do but for his part, Jeffery Solomon held it for a long moment, surprised at the tightening in his throat.

She arched an eyebrow. She had nice eyebrows. He had never seen such nice eyebrows. Not in five thousand years.

"Do you have any idea how long I've waited to do this, just to touch another human being? Just like this?" He swallowed back the tears that had sprung into his eyes. "It's a miracle."

She cocked her head at him, made a puzzled but slightly amused face. He took a deep breath.

"Kay, yeah, sorry. And you? What is your name? Where am I, how many people are left and what have you done with my friends? You know, all the typical questions a guy in my position would ask."

"Wǒ de míngzì es Damaris Ward, Jiān d'Area CeeDee."

"Damaris Ward."

"Si."

"Jiān? Uh..." He searched his memory, trying to find the word. "Hah! Supervisor! Like me! Uh, CeeDee..."

"Si, Area CeeDee."

"Columbia District. Got it. Makes sense. East Coast. Maryland."

"Mai-land," she corrected and looked down. He was still holding her hand. He let go just as the bald man returned. He spoke too quickly for Solomon to understand but he passed something to her. Damaris Ward held it up to the light.

"Damn," said Solomon. "A Plug."

"Bug, si. Por nin de Feed." She passed it into his hand. "Zuò down first."

He studied the Plug. It was a receptor designed to fit on the end of the wire, giving him access to selected programs or archives. He was hoping it was a translation program. Of all things, that would be the most helpful.

He reached around to slide it onto the wire at the base of his skull.

"So, Damaris, where are my friends? Mis amigos? Wǒ d péngyǒu?"

"Guàiwù?" she said. "Los matamos. Tāmen dōu sǐle. Zuò down."

He was not prepared for the sensations as wave upon wave of information poured directly into his brain and his knees buckled beneath him.

"The monsters?" the Plug translated inside his head as he went down. "We have killed them. They are dead. Sit down."

It was the last thing he remembered and they caught him as he hit the floor.

***

He could understand why people loved the Sun Salute of Chai'Yogath. Dawn over the mountains was a beautiful thing. He never did it himself, the Sun Salute. It seemed a perfectly good waste of time. The sun wasn't alive. She didn't have golden brooms or a sister the moon or any of the things people ascribed to her. No the sun was a welcomed thing, a good thing, an enjoyable thing but she was not alive. Kerris knew this because she never spoke to him. Not the way everything else did.

The earth was very angry here. It told him of the indignities of being robbed, of having its flesh rent by greedy cats for ore and gold and bits of metals. The snow told him of its plans to stay long this year, past the New Year's festival while the Year of the Rabbit prepared to leap off the Celestial stage as the Dragon roared in. The trees dreamed under blankets of snow, their blood cold and hard inside their branches. The wind was strong this morning, chasing the clouds until they grew heavy and wept their contents to the ground somewhere else for a change. The skies would stay clear for days now, they told him. The skies would be clear, the sun would be out and the cold would descend like a hammer.

Even the Wall was more alive than the sun. Each stone had a story and if he had the inkling, he could discover every one. Where they came from, how they had been taken from the earth and brought here by cats. The Wall was a community now, of slate and rock, gravel and clay, very much like a town or a city, only without the barter.

He sighed. He could move any or all of it if he tried.

"Kaidan," came a voice from behind and he turned to see Bo Fujihara walking towards him along the Wall. The man had a pipe in his mouth and he was smiling. He was always smiling, but then again, monkeys had smiles built into their faces. Their eyes were always bright, their steps always springy. Their tails were a marvel and he found himself envious. He wished he had a tail like that.

"Morning, Bo," he called back. "Are you up to perform your *ki?"*

"Not this morning, Kaidan. Although after last night, my *chi* could use a little *ki* I think."

"It was dramatic, I'll grant you," Kerris said, grinning. "But cats are, after all, a dramatic people."

"I have learned this. That woman, the cheetah—is that the one you told me about?"

"Yes, and what she's doing here, *now,* has me very nervous."

"I can understand." He puffed a few times and the smell of the tobacco was strong and sharp. "Your brother reacted strangely to her."

"He always did."

They stood for a while, side by side, watching the sun rise over the peaks, turning them from purple to blue. All around them, soldiers moved about the Wall and at the top of all the battle towers, cauldrons still burned with orange and white flame.

"Do we have enough cats?"

Kerris sighed and looked down at the man. "Nowhere near enough, Bo. I don't know if I can ask anyone to do this with me."

"Kaidan…"

"I've never had an army. It's always been just me and I've always landed on my feet. But this, this doesn't feel easy or clear to me. None of it does. Not any more."

"Was it ever easy or clear?"

Kerris grinned. "No, you're right. Never. Never ever. I suppose I'm just not used to it, then?"

"Most likely not. Have you pulled the sticks?"

"Was about to when you showed up."

And the grey lion reached deep into his pocket, pulled out a tangle of carved sticks, wrapped with red thread. He frowned, tried to separate them but the threads were fully entwined.

Fujihara narrowed his eyes. "Do they usually stick together like that?"

"Never," and he carefully pried them apart to read the words painted along their narrow surfaces.

"Red, Yellow and Blue." He looked up at the ambassador. "That's very strange. The odds of pulling only colours…"

"Red," said Bo. "Could that be your brother?"

"Perhaps."

"But the yellow and the blue?"

"No clue."

He shoved the sticks back into his pocket and together the pair turned back to watch the sun climb over the crest of their mother, the Great Mountains.

***

The door creaked open and emerald eyes peered in.

"Hi," said Fallon Waterford-Grey as she poked her head into the room where the dogs were being kept. "Can I come in?"

Setse rolled out from under her reindeer coat and sprang to her feet, light as a leaf on the breeze. For his part, her brother slid up the stone wall to stand, hands falling to the bow and quiver almost of their own accord. He growled, flattened his ears but did not show his teeth.

The tigress pushed open the door and entered. She was carrying three mugs in her hands. She bumped the door closed with her boot and golden liquid splashed onto the floor.

"I brought tea. I don't know if you like tea, or if you can understand me or anything, but I thought, well, I won't know unless I try and you won't know if you like tea unless *you* try, so well, here I am with tea. And well, naturally, me. Trying."

She smiled brightly and held out the mugs.

Setse stepped over and took one.

"Tea," she said. "I understand. Tea good."

She turned and held it out to her brother.

"Tsai," she said. *"Rani, guij baina!"*

He scowled at her.

"See?" said Fallon and she took a long gulp, made a smacking sound with her lips. "Good. Good tea."

"Good tea," said Setse and she too took a long gulp, made a smacking sound with her lips.

Fallon laughed. "I'm Fallon." Pointed to her chest. "Fallon."

"Fall-on," said Setse.

"*Fa*-llon."

"*Fa*-llon."

Fallon laughed again. "Yep. Fallon Waterford-Grey. You?"

"Jalair Naransetseg." But the girl smiled. "Setse."

"Set-say."

"Yes, yes." And she turned to her brother. "Jalair Naranbataar."

Fallon studied him.

"Jalair Naranbataar," she said. Her dialect was perfect and it was Setse's turn to laugh now.

"Yes, yes! Jalair Naranbataar. Rani."

"Rani," and Fallon smiled at him.

He snorted and walked away to stand at the window, looking out over the mountains.

"Husband?" asked Fallon.

"Worse." Setse rolled her eyes. "Brother."

"You understand Imperial," said Fallon, grinning. "But not him. Why?"

Setse gulped down the rest of her mug, tapped her head with her hand. "I see. Rani not see."

"I see," said Fallon.

"You see?!" The Oracle's eyes went wide. "You see too?"

"No, no, sorry. I see, but not that way. It's a saying, a phrase. I understand. Don't bother with me. I talk a lot, not all of it makes sense."

"I like you," said Setse.

"And I like you," said Fallon. "Can you teach me your language?"

"The Language of the People?"

"Yes. That."

Setse cleared her throat. *"Sain uu.* It mean hello. Greetings. "

Fallon cleared her throat. *"Sain uu."*

"Uguyai," growled Naranbataar.

"He say no."

"Uguyai," said Fallon.

"Zogsoogooroi," growled Naranbataar.

"Uguyai," said Fallon.

Setse laughed.

And her brother turned and began to speak very quickly to her. Fallon didn't need to understand much to know he was angry. The girl was adamant however and she wondered if in the Lower Kingdom, all women were strong and fearless and bold. It would be a fascinating thing and would explain much.

Suddenly, the girl gasped and turned toward the door. Her mouth was open, eyes glassy and far away.

"Shar Ma'uul," she said. "Shar Ma'uul come."

There was a rap on the door and a jaguar in brown robes peered in.

"Hey," said Fallon. *"Sain uu."*

"Oh, I'm sorry. I'll, ah…"

"That means 'hello' in the Language of the People."

"Oh."

"Shar Ma'uul, come, come!" And Setse danced toward him, catching his gloved hand and dragging him into the keep.

The leopards at the door looked in, swords and staffs ready but Fallon slipped over, smiled and quickly closed the door in their faces.

"Hey, about last night. We, um, didn't really get introduced or anything. I mean, you know lions. When they get angry, everything gets a little scary. And then throw in some dogs and a back-stabbing magical assassin, and well, it's bound to get crazy, if you know what I mean!" And she laughed to herself. "So are you really Yahn-the-man-who-can't-speak-to-falcons-Nevye?"

"Yes?" He blinked at her.

"Did you really study under Jet barraDunne at *Agara'tha?* 'Cause if you did, you better be careful 'cause Kirin—that's my brother-in-law, Kirin, the big golden lion Kirin, brand new Shogun-General Kirin—he'll kill you if he finds out. He'll take your head off with the Blood Fang. Or the Jade Fang, but I'm betting on the Blood. The Jade is far too pretty. I'm Fallon Waterford-Grey, by the way. Enchanted to meet you."

And she bowed, fist to cupped palm.

Setse gasped, released the man's hand and bowed, fist to cupped palm.

From the wall, Naranbataar glared at him and growled, laying back his ears. This time, he showed teeth.

Nevye swallowed. "I, I should go..."

"No, Shar," said Setse, grabbing his hand again. "Stay."

Fallon grinned. "She likes you."

"But *he* doesn't."

"Oh he's fine, just a little protective. I think." She strolled over to where the young man was standing, smiled and bowed to him. *"Sain uu, Jalair Naranbataar."*

He bared his teeth at her.

For her part, Setse seemed fascinated by Yahn Nevye's hands, held his one in both of hers, squeezing his fingers, pressing his palms. He seemed quite discomforted and didn't know where to look.

"My name is—Hey, Setse! How do you say 'my name is?'"

"Mini neriig ... gedeg." She did not look up, continued her study of the jaguar's hand. "But you put name in middle. For you, you say "*"Mini neriig* Fallon *gedeg."* And then say, '*Tan neriig hen gedeg vei?"*

Her brother snarled at her again, this time they sounded like curses.

Fallon took a deep breath. "*"Mini neriig* Fallon *gedeg. Tan neriig hen gedeg vei?"*

"Uguyai," growled Naranbataar.

"C'mon," said Fallon. "It'll be good. We need to understand—"

"No!" snapped Nevye and he snatched his hand away. She had begun to tug at the glove.

Naranbataar lunged forward and grabbed his sister by the arm, pulled her away and into the protection of his side.

"But I just... but Shar hands..."

"Leave me alone!" It was Nevye's turn to growl and he turned to leave when Setse began to moan.

"Falling."

"What?" He turned back. "What did you say?"

"Falling, falling, *falling,"* she wailed and suddenly, her slim body was wracked with convulsions. Naranbataar held her tight as the Oracle's moan rose in pitch until it was a scream. The door swung open and leopards poured in, swords drawn, staffs aimed but Nevye spun on them, clapped his hands together and they were flung from the room with the force of a tsunami, the door slamming shut behind them. Naranbataar hugged her tightly to stop the flailing of her arms but it was impossible to stop her legs and the pair of them sank to the floor.

"What is it?" yelped Fallon. "How can I help?"

Nevye dropped to the floor beside her, pulled his gloves from his hands and reached for the girl. A backhanded blow from Naranbataar sent him reeling but he scrambled to his knees and to her side in a heartbeat. Without waiting, he placed his hands on the sides of her face and closed his eyes.

Setse gasped and opened hers and the room became oddly still.

Her thrashing ceased, her screams silenced and it was only then that Fallon noticed his hands.

The fingers were twisted, deformed as if hammered by mallets, claws struck out at wrong angles, the yellow pelt gone from the knuckles and blackened as all bad injuries go. Fallon was amazed that he could use his hands at all, given their appearance. Soon, as their breathing became one and he opened his eyes, Setse looked up at him.

"Owls?" she whispered. "And *me?* You bleed…"

She reached her own hand up to touch his chin. There was blood from where Naranbataar's fist had struck.

He snatched his gloves and scrambled to his feet, throwing a look at the tigress before leaving the room.

***

It was quiet in the office of the Captain of *Shen'foxhindi.*

The Shogun-General stood by the window, waiting for his people, and those not his people, to arrive. He had taken most of the day to think and plan and think some more and finally he had summoned all to inform them of their course of action. It was strange, this new power, and yet not so strange. His whole life had been built around the concept of unquestioning obedience, of *Bushido*, the Way of the Warrior. It had only been these last two years, and the awareness of his damned darkened glass, that had changed things. But he was a different man now, wiser and more resilient. He desired the input of others. Most especially these.

He had requested the office be prepared for a council and he looked over the fittings in the room. There were ten cushions circled around a small brazier of coals, and in the brazier, a pot for tea and ten cups. Ten hearts and minds and wills about to chart the course of the Empire. He shook his head. It was madness.

A push of the door and a very tall figure strode in. Kirin smiled.

"Has it been even a month?"

"Almost," the Seer grinned, walked over to his side and they embraced like old friends. "You have been busy."

"Indeed. And you were right."

"Aren't I always? About what?"

"My reception at *Pol'Lhasa* was entirely different than what I expected."

"I'm glad. She was happy to see you, then?"

He shook his head. *Had he been such an open book?*

"Quite."

"And Shogun-General now? You see? What you have endured has only served to make you stronger than you were before."

"I still have dreams."

"You will always have dreams. Let them shape you, not control you."

"Hm." He nodded. "And you? How was *Sha'Hadin?* Tiberius?"

"Well. Changed. Strange. Not entirely home anymore."

"But not bad?"

"No," and he grinned again. "Not bad. But not prepared. Not for this."

"Hm," Kirin said again. "Ursa? Where is she?"

"Fitting a uniform or something like that."

"Ah, blast. I did promise, didn't I?"

"And she's not one to forget."

Kirin smiled. The woman had been his right hand for years. The Seer went on.

"There is a man that has been travelling with us…"

"A man or a dog?"

"Well," said Sireth slowly. "There are two men actually, a dog man and a cat man. I was referring to the cat man. But the dog man is still a man. Yes?"

Kirin said nothing.

"At any rate," the Seer continued. "This man is a Seer and a man I may have sworn to kill at some point or another…"

Kirin raised his brows. "But you haven't."

"No, not yet. *You* might but I don't want you to. Not yet."

"Indeed?" Kirin thought a moment. "The jaguar? He was meditating on the Wall. I almost trampled him with my horse. Who is he, this man whom you have sworn to kill but haven't?"

"Yahn Nevye."

"I remember you speaking of him on the Wall at Lahore."

"Yes."

"And on the way home."

"Again yes."

"Why would *I* want to kill him, exactly?"

Before benAramis had the chance to answer, the door swung open and a small figure appeared. Kirin smiled to himself as Ambassador Bo Fujihara entered the room. He was smoking a pipe and the sharp scent carried before him like a banner. He crossed the room to stand in front of them and bowed most formally, fist to cupped palm. Kirin bowed back, as did the Seer at his side.

"Ambassador Fujihara," Kirin began. "Sireth benAramis, Seer of *Sha'Hadin.*"

"I have heard much of you, *sidi,*" said Bo. "It is an honour to meet you finally."

"And I you," said the Seer.

"Our Seer is a painter," said Kirin.

"How wonderful," said Bo. "Have you seen any of the pieces in the Yellow Sun Room of the Palace? They are by Kai Yamakazi, one of our most celebrated painters."

"I have yet to set foot in *Pol'Lhasa,* but I will make a point of it should I go."

The Ambassador bowed again and his marvelous tail waved like a flag.

The door swung open again and Captain Oldsmith-Pak entered with a small troop of leopards. Between them, very much like prisoners, were the dogs. Male and female, for it was hard for Kirin to think of them as man and woman, as people. To his utter surprise, the tigress was with them, arms filled with parchments and he shook his head. Naturally, she would have no problem with her companions. Pure Gold could just as easily have been a dog in her eyes.

Fallon lit up when she spied him.

"Captain!" Her emerald eyes grew wide. "No wait! I mean, Shogun-General. Oh dear! I don't think I'll ever get used to that. It's far too long. And well, 'brother' just seems too familiar. Can I call you Kirin? Would that be okay? Kiri? Kirinni? Kirin-tin-tin?"

He had not taken his eyes off the dogs, their awkward movements, their rough clothing, their unnatural eyes, their teeth.

"Kirin it is, then," she said quickly. "This is Jalair Naranbataar and his sister Jalair Naransetseg. We can call them Rani and Setse."

The female danced over as if on the tips of her toes and stared at him with her strange eyes. She released a long, deep breath.

"Ulaan Baator," she said. "Kuren Ulaan Baator. You save all our people."

And then she bowed, fist to cupped palm. He stiffened, feeling the cold rush down from his ears. She should not bow, not like that. It was dishonourable and he wished with all his heart that he could kill her for the affront. Bushido might not allow it but no soldier on the Wall would think less of him. His tail lashed once, the Scales of the Dragon causing sparks to rain onto the floor and the male dog growled. Kirin turned to study him. Young, it was obvious, perhaps twenty summers. Full of pride and confidence and savagery. He could beat that out of him with one fist.

"Oh, Ulaan Baator," the girl moaned. "Not my people…"

And before he knew it, she was raising her stub clawed hand to his chest. He stepped back, hand instinctively reaching for his sword, which caused the male to growl again and suddenly, the Scholar in the Court of the Empress slipped in between them all.

"Now, Setse," said Fallon. "Let me show you our Tea Ceremony. Oh look! Pillows! Come with me, let's sit over here. I can put these crazy parchments down and we can have another cup of tea…"

"Brother," said the Seer as he put a hand on Kirin's arm, leaned in to his shoulder. "You've come very far, but the glass is never fully clear."

Kirin grit his teeth and released a long, cleansing breath. There was only a hint of a growl.

The dog, Jalair Naranbataar, had not taken his eyes off him for one moment.

"The others?" asked Kirin, fixing the dog with a stare of his own. "Kerris? Ursa? The Alchemist?"

"I am here," said Sherah and suddenly she was, separating from the shadows, the baby asleep in a sling on her back.

Kirin shook his head, baffled at how some things never changed.

He threw one last look at the dog before moving toward the fire and the tea.

***

"Right Quiz, I think I got them all." Kerris rubbed the brushes together, causing a cloud of dust to hover above the stone floor of the battle tower. He had spent a good part of the afternoon pulling the sticks, burrs and brambles out of the pony's tail and there was a sizable pile on the ground. The pony had tolerated it, largely due to the occasional marzipan from Kerris' pocket. *Chi'Chen* marzipan was known in all the Empires. It was the best marizipan in the world.

There was the sound of boots on stair and Kerris looked up to see the jaguar, the monk from *Sha'Hadin,* come trotting down. The late sun was strong through the small high windows and dust could be seen moving in the beams.

"Hello," said Kerris as the man peered around through the haze. "You looking for something?"

"That's none of your concern."

"Right." And he slipped out of Quiz's stall, dropped the brushes into a bucket by the wall. "The horses from *Sha'Hadin* are over there."

The man moved past him into one of the stalls. The horse made a grumbling sound as it rose to its feet. Straw fell from its sides and it yawned loud and long. Kerris watched the man snatch a bridle from the post, glance around at the walls of the stable.

"What are you looking for?"

"His saddle. Where are the saddles?"

"You don't need a saddle, you know. Horses like it quite fine without them."

The man grumbled, began to look into every corner, over every stall. Quiz laid back his ears and snapped, almost catching the spotted tail in his teeth. Finally, he moved back to the stall and the horse lifted its head and nickered.

"Please just tell me where the saddles are," he said, stroking its long nose.

"You going into town?"

"Saddles?"

"Well, yes," said Kerris grinning. "There are saddles in town. Out the big gate, through the little gate, down the road and to your left."

The jaguar sighed.

"That was a joke," said Kerris.

The man grew quiet, stood for a long while by the sleepy horse, stroking its face and simply breathing.

"Say," said Kerris. "Are you alright?"

"Have you ever," the jaguar began. "Have you ever wanted to just leave?"

"Just leave?"

"Yes. Just get on a horse and go somewhere, anywhere. A place where no one knows, no one lives, no one sees."

"Never done anything like that in my life," Kerris lied and he leaned against the stall door. "Why? Do you feel like that now?"

The gloved hands stroked the horse's face, just stroked.

"You *can* leave, you know. You're not a soldier. No man is your master."

"Ah, right. That's right..." The yellow eyes looked up at him. "What's your name?"

"Kerris Wynegarde-Grey. Yours?"

"Of course. The brother." The man shook his head. "Yahn Nevye."

"Oh yes. The man who cannot speak to falcons. Why of course?"

Nevye opened his mouth as if to say something but the words never came. He shook his head again, turned and continued to stroke the horse's face.

"Right," said Kerris. "Forget I asked."

"Are you afraid of anything?"

"Me? Afraid?"

"Yes. Are you?"

Kerris grinned, glanced around the stables. They were alone and the golden haze was disappearing into twilight. "How long have you got?"

For the first time in a very long time, Yahn Nevye smiled.

"I am afraid of a great many things," Kerris sighed. "I am afraid of losing my wife and my kittens. I am afraid of seeing my home again, and at the same time, of never seeing my home again. I am afraid of not being loved, of growing bored, of growing old. And I am afraid of the earth."

"The earth?"

"Yes, of being crushed by the earth. Of being wrapped in her arms until the breath in my body grows so hot that I crumble inwards and disappear in a puff of grey fur. We have an uneasy truce, the earth and I. She terrifies me still." His quick blue eyes glanced at the jaguar. "You?"

Nevye sighed, made a face. "Falling."

"You're afraid of falling?"

"All of life is falling. You fall in love, you fall out of love. You fall out of grace, you fall into luck, you fall out of favour. You fall out of one life and into another. You fall on your knees, you fall on your face and when you hit the ground, all your bones shatter and you wish you didn't have to get up again. Yes, I am very afraid of falling."

"Hm," said Kerris. "Do you drink much?"

The jaguar smiled.

A sound on the stairs brought him back years in his memory, the sound of sharp angry clacking and Kerris smiled. A woman was leading her horse down the steps to the stables, clad in a uniform of thickest leather, dyed to match the silver of her pelt. Pewter shoulder plates stamped with the visage of a snarling lion, arm vambraces studded with steel and a multiple of straps along one thigh, holding her daggers and throwing stars in place. And of course, her boots, high, laced and white, with heels that looked like they alone could kill.

Ursa Laenskaya scowled at them as she led her horse into the stall, began removing its tack.

"Is the insignificant excuse for a lion going to teach the little chicken how to clean dung?"

"As sweet as a summer rainfall," said Kerris. "I've missed you, my love."

"Pah. I thought you drowned in the ocean."

"If wishes were horses…"

Yahn Nevye glanced from grey coat to silver, eyes wide in disbelief. Kerris went on, unmindful.

"Nice uniform. Is it new?"

She snorted, pulled the saddle from the blue roan's back. "Your brother promised to send me a new one but he did not."

"Ah, the life of a Shogun-General."

With the saddle in her arms, she swung around to the jaguar.

"*Him* I understand. But you? What are you doing with the horses?"

Nevye's mouth hung open a moment.

"Are you deserting?"

"I..."

"You are! I will kill you now—" And she moved a hand to the hilt of her sword.

"He's helping me, Ursa," said Kerris. "With the horses."

"Helping you."

"Yes. He's a very friendly, talkative fellow and I'm grateful for his company."

She scowled at the jaguar now.

"Yes," Nevye swallowed. "He's teaching me where things go and, and about the earth."

There was silence in the stable for a very long moment until she shoved the saddle into Yahn Nevye's arms.

"Good. The Captain—" She cursed in Hanyin, stamped her foot. "The Shogun-General wants us upstairs by dusk. He has a plan to get the army over the Wall."

"Actually, my wife has a plan," said Kerris. "Kirin has asked her to share."

"Then don't be late."

She snorted and left the stables echoing with the sounds of sharp, angry clacking.

Yahn Nevye released his breath and sagged against the stable wall.

"Falling...and her. I'm terrified of her."

"Me too. But you get used to it." The grey lion grinned and pushed himself upright. "Look. You have a saddle now. Still want to leave?"

Nevye sighed, shook his head.

“Good choice. She’d kill you before you left the Wall.” Kerris took the saddle from the man’s arms. “Well, let’s head up for more fun with lions.”

The jaguar laughed, something he hadn’t done in years, and followed the lion out of the stall.

***

It was late now and lanterns cast light around the office of the Captain. Across his desk, the Scholar in the Court of the Empress had rolled out her parchments for all to see.

“Now, our main problem right here, right now, is how to get 3,946 troops over the Wall and into the Lower Kingdom.”

Kirin looked at her. “3,946?”

“Actually,” said Captain Oldsmith-Pak. “It’s closer to 4500 now. Enlistment is doubling almost every hour. We are taking only those who come with horses.”

Standing behind her husband, Ursa Laenskaya snorted.

“Well, well,” said Kerris and he looked up from the cushions. “I told you I couldn’t count the rear joiners. Bo?”

The ambassador puffed a few good puffs on his pipe. “Feline soldiers have more than doubled *Chi’Chen* ones. I am impressed, Shogun-sama. Truly impressed.”

Kirin nodded. “Go on, *sidala.*”

“Anyway, we need a way to bring out troops over the Wall that doesn’t involve lowering everyone in baskets, which would take half a year or more and if there is indeed a Legion still waiting on the other side—

“There is,” said Oldsmith-Pak.

“Then they could make short work out of us with their arrows. So this plan can’t involve doing that, nor can it involve riding north to *Roar’pundih*. That would be a very long way and with our numbers increasing daily, we simply couldn’t manage it. We couldn’t stop to eat, to sleep, to have a leisurely scrub. Nothing. And at no point in our history has a force such as this carried on along the Wall for such a stretch. We are, in fact, making history."

She looked up at them, her emerald eyes serious.

"So I asked the Captain to fetch the Mayor of *Shen'foxhindi* and to get some parchments of their digs. Everyone, say hi to Musaf Summerdale, Mayor of *Shen'foxhindi.*"

Musaf Summerdale was a tiger, round of face and soft of middle. But his eyes were sharp and he bowed in almost perfect fashion.

"What I learned here..." And the tigress bent low to move some papers over others. "Was that the mines go deep into the Great Mountains here..." She moved them again. "And here..."

"Which is why they are angry," said Kerris.

"But it serves us well." She straightened. "Why go over the Mountains when we can go through them?"

There was silence in the Captain's office.

"Go through them?" said Kirin.

"Yes," she said and she nodded. "Setse says--"

"Setse?" said Kirin. "Setse the dog, Setse?"

"Um, yes?"

More silence.

"You are consulting a dog on the movement of Imperial troops?"

"Uh...well, actually..."

"That is treason, *sidala.*"

"Kirin," Kerris growled a warning.

"Sister," she corrected. "Or Fallon. I'm not fussy. And no, I asked Setse because she's been there and I couldn't find Sherah."

The cheetah raised her tea to her lips.

Sireth cleared his throat. "What did you ask Setse, *Khalilah?*"

She beamed at him. "I asked her about the terrain on the other side of the Wall. If it was all sheer and steep and cliffy like here and she remembered there was a plateau and valley about a day's journey north."

"Where we were hurt. Arrows," added Setse. She was looking around with quick, eager eyes. Her brother, on the other hand, was leaning against a window, arms folded across his chest. "Rah heal us."

Fallon bent back over her parchments. "I studied the maps of all the mine shafts in *Shen'foxhindi*. Oh mother, are there mine shafts! Like a regular rabbit warren! But I found something very interesting. There is an old shaft also about one day's journey north from here that seems to bore right through the mountainside. Almost. They stopped because to continue would open a tunnel to the Lower Kingdom and that," she looked up again. "That would be bad."

There was the sound of people shuffling as they processed her words.

"Are you suggesting, *sidal*…sister," Kirin said, frowning. "That we finish what they started, bore through the mountain and open a doorway to our Enemies?"

"Yep," she said and she smiled.

Oldsmith-Pak shook his head. "Do you have any idea how dangerous that is? What a weakness we would be presenting?"

"And how would we do this?" asked Musaf Summerdale. "I mean, we could open it surely, but close it? It would be impossible to perfect a seal from the outside that the dogs could not breach."

"Kerris could."

And she looked at her husband.

In fact, all eyes looked to her husband now, the grey lion laying on his stomach, a flask of sakeh in his hand.

"Ah, I see now," he said, blue eyes gleaming. "You clever girl, you."

She smiled.

"Could you?" asked the Seer. He was smiling almost as much as the tigress. "It would require a complete and profound control of the elements. Something I am sure you are able to do, if only you were willing."

"Ah, well, I can move rocks…" he rolled to sitting. "Quite big rocks, actually. But this…"

"We would have you too, wouldn't we, Sireth?" and Fallon gazed at him, biting her bottom lip and holding her breath. "You are still the most powerful Seer in the land, right?"

The Seer nodded, thinking.

"And *sidalord* jaguar over there," added the Scholar. "I saw him practically fling a dozen guards out the door with a wave of his hands."

Oldsmith-Pak growled.

Seated on a cushion, happy to be a spectator, Yahn Nevye swallowed.

"And not to mention Sherah."

"Ah yes, the Alchemist," said Sireth and he turned to her. "A woman whose powers have no equal in all the Kingdoms."

All eyes fell on her. She was sitting, dangling a long black braid for her infant to swat, humming in strange, exotic keys.

Kirin put his hands on his hips, the armour creaking with the movement.

"So, sister, you are suggesting we take almost five thousand soldiers and horses into an old tunnel, have these four civilians move the mountain, let the soldiers and horses out onto some proposed plateau, a plateau that is known by the Enemy, and then have that tunnel blocked up as new by those same four civilians before the Legion stationed there has a chance to attack? That is what you are proposing, sister?"

She thought a moment, her mouth twisting into many different shapes.

"Yep," she said finally. "That's about right."

"Kerris? What do you say to this?"

The grey lion shrugged. "I can try, Kirin. That's all I can say."

"*Sidalord* Seer?"

"I would love the challenge, Captain—forgive me. Shogun-sama."

"*Sidalord* jaguar?"

"Uh, yes. Fine. I think."

"*Sidalady* cheetah?"

And he held his breath, waiting for it.

"Of course."

He released it and glanced up at both Oldsmith-Pak and Musaf Summerdale. They looked at each other, shrugged, nodded.

"Well then," he said. "We will bed down for the night. In the morning, we will take a small party and ride north. There we will commence our tunnel to the Wrong Side of the Wall."

There was little more to say after that.

THE MAGIC AND THE MINE

It was a thing unseen in the history of the Khans—ten thousand soldiers moving as one, running across foothill and plain, through forest and frozen tundra, churning up everything under their boots and turning snowfields black as they moved toward the Wall of the Enemy. From *Ulaan Baator* they ran, rising from their blankets before the sun and bedding down again with the singing of the stars. It was the time of the *Saran'temur*, the Iron Moon and the days were very short. They lost men in the crevices of the mountains of KhunLun. They lost men in the thin ice along the rivers and lakes. They lost men in the avalanches caused by the pounding of their feet on the earth. They lost none to sickness, none to fatigue, none to temperatures of extreme cold. These were the Legions of the Khan. Nothing in all the known world could stop them.

It was dawning as Irh-khan Swift Sumalbayar yawned and stretched his arms to the skies. While he was lean, he was very strong and the days already spent running only made him sharp, not weary. They had khava. They had wotchka. They ran down and caught reindeer and antelope and partridge and hare, which they ate while on the move. Even through the bleak wasteland of Gobay, where the steel frames of Ancestral towers stood like fists of bone, they had all they needed.

It was almost dawn now and he cast his eyes across the vista of bodies. They spanned from one horizon to the other, as far as he could see. Some were still sleeping, others sitting around small fires, talking or drinking or both, and he could see the breath from their mouths frosting above them in the cold night air. The smoke from the fires caused silver to dance against the stars and he wondered how long it would take to make the village of Lon'Gaar. They were moving well but Lon'Gaar seemed a world away.

There was a wail from the Khargan's tent. It was the *only* tent actually and it was silhouetted against the purple sky by torchlight. He took a deep breath. Another Oracle. The Khargan was desperate for visions and was convinced he could beat them out of an Oracle if necessary. Pain was a useful tool but with Oracles, Long-Swift was not sure of anything. Oracles were chosen by the Moon—their eyes proved it. They were sacred in their giftings. It was a foolish thing, he thought, to harm the Oracles. A very foolish thing. Naturally, the Bear had thought otherwise.

And to believe there was still one who had outrun them. A girl. A little girl. It was a miracle.

He grinned to himself.

He hoped she lived long enough for him to meet her.

He wondered if she knew what the Khargan was doing to the Oracles.

He wondered why she was moving towards the Wall of the Enemy.

He wondered if in fact, there would be any war with the Cats that they could ever win because such a thing had never happened.

He wondered why there were still songs in his head, songs in a language not his own and he wondered why he was dreaming of the Enemy or if anything had ever come from such fantastical dreaming.

He wondered a great many things. He was such a man. But soon he would be called in to clean up the bones of this last Oracle before the men had a chance to see. It would not serve his Khan well to have the men see the desecration of Oracles.

And so he set out for another mug of khava. It would steady his nerve until the job was done.

***

It looked like a great wide mouth, frowning and ready to swallow them all in one go. Kerris shivered and looked around. There were at least twenty of them here, and as many horses, so one gulp might not be possible. But with the anger he was feeling from these rocks, the Great Mountains might indeed take a nip or two out of them before the day was done.

"It looks big enough," said Kirin as he stood in the snow, hands on hips, surveying the opening to the mine. "Does it continue this wide all the way through?"

Fallon looked down at the parchments. "Yep. Pretty much. It's more like a cave, really, rather than a mine…"

"Oh it's a mine to be sure," said Musaf Summerdale. "Quite profitable in its day."

"And why did you close it?"

"The overhead strata became unstable. We lost two dozen men during the fall."

"And look," said Kerris. "We have almost two dozen now."

"Kerris," said Fallon, emerald eyes flashing. "It won't happen. You and Sireth will make sure, won't you, Sireth?"

The Seer smiled. "We will do our best, *Khalilah*."

Fallon looked at Nevye, standing next to his horse, stroking its long nose. "And you too, *sidi?* You don't like people to think you're powerful but you are. I know you are."

The jaguar looked at her, swallowed.

"Shar Ma'uul powerful," said Setse and she leaned down to hug the neck of her horse. "Horse beautiful. I love Horse."

Kerris grunted. Dogs *ate* horses, not rode them and it was a testament to the will of Imperial stallions for the creature to have allowed the girl on its back. She had laughed and sang most of the day as their small team rode out along the Wall to the mine but her brother had refused a mount and had run at her side. Kerris was impressed. The fellow didn't look remotely winded and he stood now, angry and guarded. Dogs were formidable enemies.

"What *about* the horses?" asked Kirin. "Will we need to walk them in? That would be problematic, *sidi.*"

"Not at all, Shogun-sama," said Summerdale. "The mine is as high as it is wide for the most part, and well braced. Except, of course, at the end."

"Where the earth fell in," said Kerris.

"Exactly. Horses and riders should fit very well, perhaps six abreast. For the most part." The tiger turned to the tigress. "Will we need yaks, *sidala?* Or diggers or carts? There will be much stone to move if we wish five thousand horses to go through."

"Nah," said Fallon. "Our people can handle it."

Kerris laughed nervously.

"And what about light?" asked Kirin. "That mine will become very dark very quickly."

"There are oil lamps," said Summerdale. "And torches, although we will need to light them as we go."

"Not a problem," said Sireth and he turned his brown eyes to the mouth of the mine. One by one, the torches along the walls began whoosh into life and glow, causing shadow to retreat farther and farther down the throat of the cavern.

He smiled proudly and his wife swatted him from behind.

A sound began to echo, growing louder and louder and a mass of blackness rushed toward them like a fist. The cavern roared with the thunder of wings and suddenly, an entire host of bats was upon them, spooking the horses and forcing them all to duck to avoid being struck but even so, the beating of their wings and the screeching of their voices left them as bruised as a night in a hailstorm.

After a long moment, they were left with only the stomping of the horses and the sound of their own breathing and the wind.

Mi-Hahn swept into the cavern, settled on the Seer's shoulder, the remains of a bat in her talons.

"That was disgusting," moaned Bo Fujihara.

"Idiot," growled Ursa.

"Sorry," said Sireth.

"I told you the earth was sick," muttered Kerris. "It just vomited bats."

"Well," said Fallon. "At least, they're all gone."

"If there is nothing else, shall we go?" said Kirin. "Now, Kerris, please?"

For some reason, all eyes fell onto the grey lion.

He swallowed, cast his eyes around the dark, grinning mouth.

The earth was laughing.

"Right," he said, springing onto Quiz's back like a hare. "Let's go."

***

Kerris Wynegarde-Grey woke to find himself once again in a jail cell.

It was not altogether an uncommon sensation, for it was not altogether an uncommon occurrence. He had often found himself waking in various locations, from Chi'Chen *palaces to watery ocean caverns. And yes, on the odd occasion, jail cells. It always involved tigers, these penitentiary occasions, and this time, he could distinctly remember stripes. A woman's stripes to be honest. At least he was waking. The how's and why's of it were never particularly important to him. With a deep breath, he pushed himself up to his elbows to look for the stripes.*

He was naked.

He blinked slowly, then grinned. A woman, most definitely. He tried to remember but every hair on his body was tingling and he wondered if his lover, the lightning, had paid a visit last night. Lightning was a jealous mistress. There had only been one woman who had survived the lightning and that had been the skinny little tigress he called his wife.

His wife.

He bolted to his feet, staggered as they failed to hold him, flung a hand to the wall for support.

Metal metal earth** and **metal

He snatched his hand away and dropped to his knees, feeling the wrath come in waves from the surface of the walls. Underground. Under the ground. He fought for control as the fear sent his heart racing but he needed his wife, he needed his wife and the thought of her became an anchor against the waves. The floor was filthy sand and it smelled of oil but he could feel it sharp and cold under his fingers so he stayed down for a long moment, simply breathing and trying to negotiate with the earth. It wouldn't hear him over the roar of the metal and at some point, he realized he was not alone in the cell.

He looked up.

The center of it was bright as if from skylight but around the edges the ceilings were low and rusted and cast shadows as black as night. He could see yellow and green pinpricks of light moving through the shadows in pairs. Eyes, he knew, and he took another deep breath. Prisoners were generally the same, all hardened but all wronged. All easily bent to a friendly smile and listening ear. That knowledge had saved him on more occasions than he could remember, so he breathed again and again, then smiled like the sun.

"Hello," he said. "My name's Kerris. Anyone seen my wife?"

A hiss ran through the shadows and he watched the eyes bob and dart.

"So," he said. "What are we here for? Did we all get drunk or something?"

A rock sailed at his head and he managed to duck in time to avoid being hit.

There was laughter from above and he looked up, shading his eyes against the light. Sunshine, and he realized that the cell was open to a grimy sky. They were underground however, and the walls here were metal and went very high up and he could see shapes peering down on him, silhouetted in the sun.

"Hello!" he called. "Do you think someone could find me my clothes? And my sword? Oh yes, and my wife?"

There was a scrabbling sound from the left and a shape barreled toward him from the shadows, leaping into the air and taking him down onto the sand. Kerris rolled out from underneath, surprised to find a bright red line spring up across his chest, a perfect counterpoint to the long white scar given him by his brother. Cheers echoed down from the silhouettes. High up, a plate slid aside and something pink and gelatinous dropped out, hitting the sand with a thup.

His attacker glared at him, and Kerris realized it was a monkey, but not like any Chi'Chen he had ever seen. Its eyes were wild, its face disfigured and it grabbed the little missile and bit into it, sand and all, before slinking off into the shadows. Shiny eyes closed upon the attacker and the snarls rose as prisoners fought over the scrap of food. A second figure rushed him, but he was ready and this one was met with grey claws and a spray of blood across the sand.

More cheering from above and another gelatinous blob, but this time, his attacker was dragged off and finished by the eyes in the shadows.

Kerris looked up, shielded his gaze once again and willing his pupils to become slits as they focused on the silhouettes high above.

The figures stayed for only a moment longer before disappearing into the sunshine and Kerris knew that he was not in a prison because of any crime he had committed. He was here deep in the belly of the earth because the Ancestors had put him here.

***

They had ridden for almost five hours before the mountain blocked their way. The end was not smooth like the floor nor braced like the walls. Rather it looked as if the mountain had merely fallen in on itself, with rocks of many sizes piled up for a long way until they were met with utter blackness.

"Okay, Kerris-your-name-was," said Fallon. "Get to work."

He glanced at her before sliding from the back of his pony.

He studied the rocks and beams of the ceiling, black and flickering in the torch light. Ran his fingertips along the rocky barrier, their cold hard faces, the sheer weight of the stones. They were rough and heavy and smelled of bat droppings.

"Pah," grunted Ursa. "He's a kitten. He can't move a thing."

"Hush," said her husband and he dismounted his horse. "May I help?"

"Well, it's not a matter of helping, really," said Kerris. "It's a lot of rock. I have to ask it to move."

The Seer cocked his head, fascinated.

"It may take some time." He turned to his young wife. "Is there tea, luv? I would dearly love a cup of tea."

"There's always tea." She smiled and slid from the back of her horse. "Sireth, you can still light the fire just by thinking, right?"

"As long as we have wood, *Khalilah*," the Seer said. "We will have fire."

"I have fire powder, *sidi,"* breathed Rah, slipping off her dark horse like a shadow in the night. "Do you need firepowder?"

He stared at her for a long moment, before releasing a long cleansing breath.

"Yes," he said. "We can use firepowder."

She smiled and set to work pouring circles on the ground.

"This is ridiculous," grumbled Ursa. "There is no battle. There is no war. We are camping in a cave."

Kerris merely stood, arms folded over his chest, eyes fixed on the wall of rock and Kirin turned to the twenty behind him on horseback.

"We will break for now," he called out, his voice echoing through the dark depths of the mine. "Tea for cats, water for the horses."

"And for the monkeys?" grinned Bo Fujihara as he slid off his mount.

Kirin did not stop the smile. In the twenty that rode out that morning, there was only one monkey.

"For the monkeys, anything at all."

Fujihara reached into his pocket and pulled out a sticky pink lump. He broke it in two.

"Marzipan," he said and he popped one half in his wide mouth. The other he held up to his horse, who eagerly accepted. "And then maybe a pipe or two."

"And for dogs?" laughed Setse and she too slid from the back of her horse. She gave it a big hug and kissed its flat cheek. "Tea for dogs, please Fa-*llon?"*

"Yep," sang the tigress. "Tea for dogs."

Kirin glanced at the male, standing near his sister, tense and wary. He wondered if they could drink tea with their strange faces. Cats had flatter faces, very much like Ancestors that way. No, dogs had faces like horses, bears or other animals. They were barely even people. The brother he understood. He would fight and kill in a heartbeat but the girl, she confounded him.

"Shar Ma'uul drink tea?" she sang as she danced over to where the jaguar was slowly sliding from his saddle. "Shar Ma'uul sit with Setse. We drink tea together, like always."

The jaguar threw a look at Naranbataar, who laid back his ears and growled. He swallowed.

The Oracle took his hand and dragged him over to the circles.

The Alchemist looked up.

"It is ready," she purred.

The Seer smiled and immediately, the circles of firepowder burst into flame, casting golden light up the sides and curved roof of the mine.

Setse clapped her hands and laughed as Fallon dropped a handful of leaves into the pot for tea.

***

This was madness, thought Naranbataar. He was sitting with cats deep in the belly of a mountain. The Magic was around the circles of flame, the yellow cat with hands of bark and the tall cat with the eyes of a dog, the grey cat and the witch. And of course, Setse, as though she belonged with this party, as if she had been with them for her entire life. He didn't trust any of them, not even the striped woman who babbled in their strange tongue and offered him tea, or the monkey with his pipe of foul odors and his strange hairless face, but here he was, in their company deep inside a mountain, holding a baby.

The witch had given him the baby without even asking. She assumed, this woman. Assumed that he would carry it, protect it, tend it and not tear its tiny arms from its tiny body or eat it whole. That's what he should have done. Still, he found he was growing accustomed to the weight of it in his arms, feeling its tiny claws batting at his hair or it's teeth gnawing on the pads of his fingers, feeling the rumble of its purring against his chest. It was a better weight than many arrows.

These horses smelled terrible. He knew he should eat them too. The little one at the front kept trying to bite him and he wondered if it was true that horses could kill a dog with one stomp of their iron feet. He would never get on one. His sister was foolish for doing so. She would be the death of him.

They were deep inside the mountain and it looked very old. The floor was smooth, the walls braced with teak and reeking of bats. The ceiling was braced as well but he could see it buckling as the wood strained to hold back the weight of the stone. He hoped they wouldn't all be crushed. That would be worse than slipping off the side of the mountain. Inglorious death was just death. It changed nothing.

The big lion wanted to kill him. It was obvious, even without a common language. He didn't care. His life had been dedicated to preserving the life of his sister and he had managed to be successful for sixteen winters. He wondered if he killed the lion, could he be made a Khan and thus protect her all the more? Not while they were in Enemy lands, of course, but if what Setse was saying was true, they were headed back into the Land of the People. He would wait for his opportunity and then, put an arrow into his throat.

The baby was cooing in his ear now and he could not help but smile. It was experimenting with its voice. Little laughs, little grunts. No words, not for a long time he knew but still, the cooing was sweet. Setse had cooed and sung as a baby. It had been his music, along with his grandmother's lullabies. It had been a good childhood, all things considered.

No, he would wait, kill the lion, take his sister and run all the way back to Karan Uurt where he would eat stew and yak and live in the gar of his father's father for the rest of his life. It was a good plan. There was only one problem.

He'd never actually killed anyone before. He knew it was likely harder than he thought, so he stayed deep into the belly of the mountain, listening to the strange language of the cats and holding a baby in his lap.

***

It was an amazing sight, one I would never for the rest of my life forget. We had been sitting for over two hours, me on my knees in the Learning Pose. It was easy to sit this way, less strain on the one knee that had been wounded almost a year ago in Roar'pundih. *The yori itself was bulky and getting up from sitting frequently proved difficult. The Learning Pose was efficient, graceful and allowed me to keep both dignity and a watchful eye on the twenty waiting by the fires.*

From this angle, I could see my son.

The dog had it, a thought that should have boiled my very blood. The child batted and swatted and the dog was surprisingly gentle with such a youngling. In fact, he seemed to be playing with it and it set my teeth on edge. I would just as soon see the Blood Fang take off the creature's head but there it sat, playing with my son.

My son.

I did not know what to think anymore.

Despite the fires, the air was cold and smelled of horses, pipesmoke and alchemy. I watched Bo Fujihara play dice with the Seer. Physically, the two were as different as night from day but they had struck up an easy friendship and I knew it was the matter of Race. Fujihara would never care that the Seer was a mongrel, not the way a cat would, and it seemed that once again, the way of things was set upon its ear in favour of a new and different way.

A stranger sight was that of the Oracle and the jaguar. She sat facing him, trying to learn the language and she was still holding one of his hands in both of hers. It was clear she was taken with him but for what reason, I could only guess. He was both Seer and Alchemist, but seemed to exhibit the traits of neither. While he was undoubtedly powerful, he seemed driven along the lines of fear rather than aggression or pride. It was a mystery and Alchemists were fond of their mysteries. I wondered if the man had ever known Jet barraDunne. Something in my memory made me think that he did and I made a note to ask at some later date.

Along the walls of the mine, two tigers were examining veins of ore running through the rock. Fallon Waterford-Grey could befriend a bear if she had the opportunity, and she was an eager learner. For his part, Musaf Summerdale seemed keen to share his knowledge of ores, minerals and the business of rocks with such a pupil. My new sister had a large collection in her many pockets and it was causing her trousers to sag at the waist. A strong wind could still blow her over.

Ursa stood along the wall as well, watching everyone and everything with her ice blue eyes.

For his part, Kerris merely sat, legs crossed, staring at the pile of rocks.

At one point, a feathered shaped swept in from the throat of the mine and I thought it looked rather like an owl. Soon, the cave echoed with the shrill sharp cries and young Mi-Hahn streaked in after it, beating it with her wings and chasing it around above our heads until finally, she chased it back out the way they had come. Feathers rained down on us like snow.

"Idiots," grunted the Major.

"What?" moaned Nevye. "It's not my owl."

Time was creeping by and people were growing weary and I was beginning to despair of this plan when suddenly Kerris rose to his feet and began to walk toward the crumbled end of the mine.

Just walk.

It started like a low rumble and all the horses began to snort. The sound grew quickly into a roar, the sound of grinding gears and falling trees and the very ground beneath our feet began to tremble. It looked as though Kerris would walk right into the rock wall but the stones moved out of his way.

Pulled themselves up, around, away from him as he walked deeper and deeper into the mine, arms spread out at his sides as if pushing with his palms. Soon he disappeared entirely as the mountain opened its mouth wider to suit him and all the horses that would be coming after him, wider even than the rest of the mine that lay behind us. Dumbfounded, I watched as they continued to move, climbing onto each other like brick and mortar, crushing some under the weight, forming dust and sand and fine, fine powder. The thunder of the rocks was deafening and I realized that everyone had clapped hands over their ears and the horses were dancing nervously in the darkness until finally, after what seemed like ages, there were beams of light slicing through the choking dust and then silence.

We were all on our feet now, coughing and gagging and watching the ceiling, waiting for the first of the rocks to slide back down to kill us all. There was nothing but pebbles settling to the floor and soon not even that.

The high pitch of a whistle pierced the silence and the mountain pony bolted down the long black corridor, his hoofs staccato and fading on the bedrock of the mine.

My brother was an Elemental. I couldn't believe it. The Seer had said it, so long ago, my sister had repeated it on so many occasions. I must have known it, growing up the way we did but had never truly believed it.

Fallon stretched her arms over her head and yawned so that her tongue curled inside her mouth.

"See?" she said sleepily. "He makes great pancakes too."

And she bent to pack up the tea and the pot. I shook my head and moved toward my horse.

- *an excerpt from the journal of Kirin Wynegarde-Grey*

***

The snow beneath their feet trembled and as one, the 110th Legion looked to the mountain and the Wall towering above them like an overlord. Black clouds billowed up and into the late afternoon sky and as one, they rose to their feet.

The beta, a stocky black and tan mastiff, turned to the alpha.

"Lord," he said. "Is it their cannons?"

"No, not cannons." The alpha shook his head, his breath like smoke. "But it is an act of war, do not doubt. Take a third of the men, fully armed with stealth and arrows. Go."

The beta nodded and barked a command. Twenty men fell in at his heels.

The alpha motioned to a footman, who dropped to one knee, head down.

"Take a third of the men, go to the village of Lon'Gaar. Tell them to prepare for the slaughter of their Enemies. Bring weapons and any man with the heart of a wolf."

"Lord," said the footman.

"Tell the women to prepare food and drink and blades for killing the wounded. As for the children…" He looked up at the mountainside, still billowing dust into the thick cold sky. "Tell the children to watch and learn. We will show them how to skin a cat."

"Lord," said the footman, smiling.

***

"Three days," said Kerris as they stood, looking out over the sweeping landscape that was the Lower Kingdom. "That's all we were given. The rocks will fall back and close off the pass in three days. Your army had better hurry."

Kirin shook his head.

"It's not enough time," he grumbled. "Not nearly enough."

"It's all I could get."

"Do you think you and the Seer could hold it if it chooses to fall?"

"And make the mountain angrier?" Kerris shrugged. "It's a fair bit bigger than us, Kirin. It will do what it will do. I'm surprised it gave me anything."

Kirin sighed. The falcon had been sent back to the battle tower of *Shen'foxhindi* to set the army into motion but still, there was no way they could be guaranteed of getting all their troops through the crossing in time. It would take a day to make preparations, then another day for the almost five thousand troops to ride to the mouth of the mine. A third day to allow for them to move through the new tunnel and exit out on the other side, the Wrong Side of the Wall.

It was twilight and he could hear voices carried down from the battle tower high above them. They had also been informed of their plan, those soldiers, and he knew they were covering the party with arrows, spears and cannons if needed. His eyes swept the plateau, a valley of rocky blue against the deepening blue of the mountains. It was wide but steep and he knew they could not make headway in the dark. In the distance, he could see pinpricks of light like the twinkling of stars, wondered if they were from the village or the Legion stationed outside.

"Legion," said the girl and he wondered if she could read his thoughts. "From Karan Uurt, my home."

He looked down at her, her long face hidden by dark hair and the layers of reindeer cloak moving with the wind. She pointed to a small mound, now covered in snow.

"Three dead. Arrows. There."

"Where is the village?"

From behind them, he could hear her brother growl, wondered if he understood anything at all of their conversation or whether he merely objected to his sister speaking with the Enemy.

"Lon'Gaar," she said. "Not far. If we leave at moondown, we be there at high sun."

"Moondown?"

She looked up at him, her odd bi-coloured eyes reminding him of both earth and sky and his son. "When sun chases moon to gar for day."

He stared at her for a long moment, his mind working to understand her imagery. Abrupt, yet poetic at the same time.

"Sunrise," he corrected her. "Not moondown."

"My people do this?" she asked.

"Do what?"

"Make you hate."

He held her gaze for only a moment longer before turning to the twenty gathered along the new mouth of the mine.

"We will bed down for the night in the mouth of the mine," he called to his people. "Keep the horses close. Major…"

"Sir."

"Divide the watches. We have cover from the soldiers above but we are still vulnerable and the Legion is close."

"Yes, sir." She was an arrow, released by his command.

The Seer blinked slowly, watching her go before turning to his horse.

As his brother set about making arrangements, Kerris slipped back into the mine, looking for and finding his wife with Musaf Summerdale.

The tiger had a large collection of stones and mineral samples and it was clear he was revisiting his decision to close the mine. Profit was profit, no matter how many lives paid for its pursuit.

"Hey," said Fallon, her voice echoing slightly as it bounced off the stone walls. "Musaf is showing me this fantastic vein of ore. It's amazing really, how they get the ore out of the mountainside, then how they smelt it down to make all kinds of useful—*oh!"*

Kerris grabbed her hand, swung her around and pulled her close.

"Have I told you how much I love you today?"

"Um, well," she grinned. "This morning, I think you said something like that, yes."

"Well, I do."

"I know."

And he kissed her.

She kissed him back, curled her tail around his leg.

"You're trembling," she said.

He grinned, laid his forehead against hers, but his hands were moving along her back. "Yes, well, I moved a mountain today, didn't I?"

"Aah." Her grin widened. "I told you you could."

"You did indeed."

And he kissed her again, began fumbling at the wraps of her bison-skin cloak. But he paused, threw a glance over his shoulder.

"Excuse me, *sidi,* but I am about to make mad, passionate love to my wife," he called. "I think I'll ask to you leave before I bring a very large stone on top of your very orange head."

Summerdale's eyes grew wide before he turned and fled, rocks jingling in his pockets.

"Oh, that was subtle, very subtle." Fallon wrapped her hands around the back of his neck. "Tell me again how you charmed the palace courts?"

"Well, it went something like this…"

And her bison cloak dropped to the floor.

***

With the sun gone, there was nothing to provide warmth. They would not chance a fire, not with a Legion so close and the wind bit at their faces and ears and tails like a very sharp blade. He was grateful now for the bulk of the yori for it cut the wind but the pelt around his mouth and nose were white with frost. Not for the first time, he wondered why the Ancestors had chosen a place such as *Pol'Lhasa* as the seat of the Upper Kingdom. He loved the mountains but winter was hard on everything.

Sireth, Nevye and the Oracle were seated very close to each other on the slope of the mountainside. They were in a circle and he noticed they had joined hands in the ritural of *Amnishakra*. He remembered the very strange sensation of being in someone else's mind, of someone else's heart beating in his chest, someone else's breath filling his lungs. It was a disturbing sensation for him but, as he studied the trio, he realized it was a good thing. Here, as they took the first steps into a dangerous land, they would need the skills sharp and the Magic strong.

Bo Fujihara sat watching them, almost hidden by the heavy cloak he wore. The odor from his pipe was heady and little puffs escaped his pink lips as he smoked.

The male dog stood behind his sister, arms folded, defiant and proud. Kirin shook his head. To his knowledge, the dog had eaten nothing since being delivered up the Wall, neither had he slept. He wouldn't last long like this but perhaps that was his aim. Kirin didn't mind. One less dog in the world was a worthy goal.

He wondered where his own brother was.

"Sidi," came a voice from behind, and he did not need turn. He could smell the incense well enough.

"Sidala."

"I was wondering…"

He would not look.

"…if you would like to meet your son."

He did not bring himself to look. His heart was racing like a young stallion.

"No," he said.

"He looks like you but with dark hair," she went on, unmindful. She always did what she wanted. "Oh yes, and one golden eye."

"What are you doing here?" he asked.

"Hmm. Working."

He did turn now, steeled himself against those marvelous eyes, wicked and wise and painted in black.

"Working how? For whom? Jet barraDunne is dead."

She pulled the baby up to her chest, stroked the thick woolen blankets that wrapped him. He remembered the feel of her hands on him so very long ago, waking senses that had never been awake before her.

"For Dharma, *sidi,*" she purred. "For destiny."

"Riddles," he growled.

"Of course," and she smiled and turned, slipping away towards the circle, throwing him once last glance over her shoulder, eyes gleaming like beacons in the night.

There was movement in the circle. It was the girl, the Oracle. She was moaning, rocking back and forth when suddenly, Sireth benAramis bolted to his feet.

"Captain," he cried. "Archers! We—"

They heard the whistle of the arrow only moments before the Seer was sent backwards onto the rocks.

***

The arrows were tipped with horn or bone, drilled in places so that the sound of the wind would cause a shrill, wraith-like shriek. One would set teeth on edge, many would terrify. There were many flying towards them that night.

The second took down Musaf Summerdale as he emerged from the new mouth of the mine. The arrow struck him in the throat and he went down.

The third struck Captain Li-Hughes as he ordered the rotations of the soldiers that had accompanied them from *Shen'foxhindi.* The arrow struck him in the back and he went down.

The fourth and fifth struck Kirin himself, in the shoulder and the chest, but the *osedeh* sent it ringing off into the snow and the *doh* absorbed the tip in deepest leather. He staggered at the impact but did not go down.

From high above, the drums started and guards from the Wall sent down a rain of arrows in response, but it was dark so the volley was sent wide as a precaution. With a snarl, Major Ursa Laenskaya pulled both swords from her hips and rushed down the steep incline, three soldiers at her heels.

"Cover the civilians!" Kirin called to the remaining soldiers, as he pulled the kabuto down onto his forehead. "Back, into the mine!"

The whistles were deafening now, preventing thought and filling even the hardest of hearts with dread. Arrows shattered off stone, thudded into horses and snowdrifts as soldiers scrambled to obey. Two more men went down and a cannon boomed from the Wall, lighting the night sky with fire and causing the distant drifts to erupt with snow and ash. Howls followed, but the whistling did not stop.

Horses squealed and bolted and as his soldiers rushed towards the circle with swords drawn, he could hear the cry of the baby.

Kirin marched to the circle, hoping to protect them with the sheer bulk of the yori when he spied the dog with its sister in his arms. She was wailing and thrashing like a madwoman.

"The mine," he said, and gestured with his arm for emphasis. "Take her up to the mine! Go!"

The dog whirled and disappeared and Kirin was grateful for the obedience. He turned to see the Alchemist, baby clutched to her chest, kneeling beside the monkey and jaguar who were helping the Seer to his knees. Arrows were thudding into the snow all around them and there was a shaft protruding from the mongrel's chest.

"Be still," said the Alchemist.

"No," the Seer gasped. "Hands! Give me your hands! Both of you!" And he held up his.

Yahn Nevye hesitated.

"Do it!" Kirin snarled and they obeyed, Sherah taking one and Nevye quickly pulling his gloves and dropping them into the snow to take the other.

"We stop the arrows…*as* they fly," Sireth panted, closing his eyes.

"This, like this…"

He could almost feel it, the power that flowed out from them strong like a river current and suddenly, the whistling changed as the hail of arrows seemed to strike a wall above them. Wave after wave shattered, raining bits of bone and splintered shaft onto the rock and snow all around them. A second boom of the cannon and a third and the earth erupted far below but the sound seemed to go on and on and on. It was thunder, he realized, clouds blacker and heavier than the mountains themselves and lightning flashed across the sky. Kirin shook his head. There was never thunder in winter. Never lightning. He looked up to the mouth of the mine, where sparks were gathering.

Kerris.

Sparks were swirling and a roar of cloud upon cloud as the sky erupted with light, forking and splitting and reaching to the distant lights of the Legion's camp. Forking again, down to the rocks and scrub trees at the base of the plateau where screams were heard then silenced. Again and again, crack and flash, boom and flash until there were no screams, there was no whistling and the only lights were the flames of lightning fire that burned the scrub until it too died in the snow and cold and the wind.

Kirin looked back over his shoulder as Kerris dropped to his knees, greyer than the rocks around him.

The clouds stayed, low and grumbling overhead and he could hear the Major's voice echoing from valley below.

"Ensure they are dead. We take the fight to their camp."

There was a rustle of wings and a shape settled onto the snow at his feet. It was an owl. In its talons were arrows, at least twelve, likely snatched out of the sky the way a falcon might catch pigeons. It looked past him to the others and cocked its head almost upside down.

Kirin turned, forgetting it in a heartbeat.

"Go up, *sidala,*" he growled to the Alchemist. "Take your baby and get to the mine. Your skills will be needed tonight."

"Of course," and she disappeared into the shadows of the mountain.

"You too, Ambassador."

Fujihara shook his head. "I will gather the horses."

"No, the horses are soldiers. They can look after themselves." Kirin laid a hand on the small shoulders. "You are more valuable than a thousand horses."

"Don't let the horses hear you say that," the monkey said but he put the pipe in his teeth and turned, trudging up the short distance to the mouth of the mine.

Kirin bent to slip an arm under the Seer's.

"Sidalord jaguar…"

"Sorry, yes of course."

Together they helped the Seer to stand.

"I'm fine, Captain," Sireth said but his face was strained in the darkness. "I'm quite familiar with arrows. Besides, pain…"

"Is simply a matter of perspective. Yes I know."

"My gloves!" Nevye turned his head but Kirin cut him off.

"Your owl can get them, *sidi.* Please concentrate."

"But he's not…" Nevye looked at him, swallowed. "Yes. Yes he can."

They shouldered the Seer under their arms and together, staggered up the hillside. They were accompanied by an owl, carrying gloves.

***

The trees were black against the snowy ground as Major Ursa Laenskaya slunk toward the Legion camp, moonlight glinting off her blades. Three soldiers were behind her and she motioned for them to fan out, circling the remnants of the Legion camp between them. The few gars were burning, scorch marks rending the snow like the claws of a dragon. There were weapons scattered on the ground, and the night air smelled of burnt flesh and fur. A few were moaning.

There was movement behind and she whirled, bringing the long sword up in time to stop the blow from a halah'bard that would have split her in two. The strength of it sent her to one knee and a rough hand swung up to catch her throat, stopping her breath and forcing her neck back. The dog stepped closer, the odor of him striking like a fist and she could see him grinning in the moonlight as he pushed the halah'bard down onto her steel. She fought to keep the katanah steady, fought to keep her chin up and defiant. She was a warrior, trained and tested and the bane of dogs for she fought with two swords. In her left hand, the kodai'chi swung like the strike of a serpent, taking his leg out from under him and sending him falling backwards into the snow. She sprang on top of him, bringing the katanah down onto his forehead with a thuk. He twitched beneath her and lay still.

Swiftly, she rose to her feet, not bothering to wipe her blades. She could hear the tang of steel and knew her soldiers were dispatching the remnants of the Legion. She moved into the heart of the camp, let her eyes sweep over their few personal effects, the bedrolls and weapons, the crackling tents and tin cups. There was a man on hands and knees, his torso blackened by lightning, attempting to crawl to his sword. Valour, she thought to herself. Valour and duty. Traits she could appreciate.

Because of that, she took off his head in one blow.

Her blood was racing with the passion of battle, her heart as sharp as the sharpest steel. As she moved through the camp, taking off all the heads that remained attached to bodies, she knew that she had made the wrong decision at the path to *Sha'Hadin*. She had likely made the wrong decision at the beach in Ana'thalyia or in the gypsy camp or in the mountains of *Hiraq*. She was a warrior, only at home with a blade in her hand. She should not now nor ever be the wife of a priest.

She cast her eyes up to the mountain where fires were burning on the Wall. She had not stopped to help him. She had seen him hit by the arrow and still, she had not stopped. Her chest tightened and she prayed he was still alive. She was a very bad wife.

Find the steel in yourself, he had said. *For yourself.*

She was steel. That was all she had ever been.

It was *he* that was changing her, trying to make her soft, vulnerable, useless.

It was *he* who needed a lesson in steel.

She snarled, hiked her swords and pushed deeper into the camp.

***

The mouth of the mine was a crowded bloody mess.

Horses and cats, a monkey and two dogs and the smell of blood was heavy and hot. The Alchemist had given the baby to the Scholar, who was sitting with Musaf Summerdale as he gurgled life out through the arrow in his throat. It was surprising how long it took the man to die, but after a long while he sputtered, clawing the air with his fingers, and then he stopped, eyes wide and terrified still. Fallon wept bitterly at his side, clutching the baby to her chest.

The young captain who had ridden with Kirin since *Pol'Lhasa,* Haj Li-Hughes, was dead, an arrow piercing his heart through the uniform. Two other soldiers were dead along with three horses. The dogs huddled together, the sister shaking and moaning, the brother holding her, stroking her brow with his hand. Kirin remembered all the times he would care for Kerris after a night of lightning or drink.

The last Seer of *Sha'Hadin* sat with his back against the rough stone wall as the Alchemist slowly, carefully peeled the many layers of brown leather and linen away from the pelt of his chest. There was little blood – if they did not shatter on impact, arrows of this sort would not bleed until after removing. She had opened an ominous dark roll she had been carrying and Kirin saw needles, tubes, sticks and vials. It all reeked of incense. She smeared a thick line of salve around the shaft.

"We've covered this ground before, haven't we?" asked the Seer, a weary grin tugging one corner of his mouth.

"Of course."

"I never had the chance to say thank you."

Golden eyes met brown.

"Wait, *sidi.* If you live, you may then thank me twice."

"Agreed."

Sherah glanced up at Kirin. "You may help, *sidi."*

"Any way I can," he said. "How?"

"Removing the arrow will bring pain and blood. Brace him against the wall so I may work."

He nodded and knelt down, grasping the Seer's hand and using his shoulder to pin him to the wall. The Alchemist did not wait, did not spare a moment for a deep breath or a dramatic pause, but swiftly yanked the bolt from the flesh causing blood to spray across the plates of the *osedeh*. The Seer hissed but Kirin pushed and the Alchemist set to work.

It was strange and quiet then, as Yahn Nevye slid down the wall next to Kerris and the Ambassador, both with backs against the stone. The grey lion looked exhausted, his eyes barely open, hands draped limply across his knees. Nevye studied him for a moment before the lion turned his head.

"Yes, *sidalord* jaguar? Is there something you want? You're a-looking at me strange."

"Sorry. It's just," he sighed. "Well I can't see you being afraid of anything, *sidi,* especially not earth. Not when you can do the things you do."

"Hm." Kerris leaned his head back against the stone. "It devours me."

"What does?"

"The power. The elements. They all devour me, my mind, my strength, my *chi*. I don't want any of it. Not at all."

The jaguar grunted, understanding. Bo Fujihara slipped a pipe between his teeth, pulled a match.

"You should have seen your owl tonight," he said.

Nevye looked. The bird was sitting at the mouth of the mine, not willing to fly in lest a falcon chase him out.

"What do you mean?"

"He was catching arrows."

"Catching arrows?"

"Yes," said the monkey, puffing to light the tobacco inside the pipe. "He was swooping around, snatching arrows out of the sky

"Why would he do that?"

"Protecting you, I think."

"Protecting me? Why?"

The bird opened its wings, hopped in place.

"You Seers," said Kerris, eyes closed once again. "You don't understand anything, do you?"

"Nothing," said Nevye. "We understand less of the world than the average cat."

"That's the truth."

Fujihara grinned. "He has your gloves."

"I know."

"What happened to your hands?"

"It's a sad story."

"My favourite kind."

Kerris grinned. "But another night, please. I'm far too tired for stories. I was just about to make love to my wife, too. It's a bugger, life."

The jaguar continued to study the owl, which turned its head almost upside down watching him back.

"Give me my gloves."

The owl blinked one eye.

"My gloves. Give them back."

The other eye.

Nevye held up his arm, hand hidden in the folds of his robe. "Please give me my gloves, Hunts in Silence."

The bird lifted into the air, swept forward and dropped the gloves between the jaguar's feet. He circled once before landing on Nevye's arm, wings folding across his back.

"Well, look at that," said Kerris.

"What a beautiful bird," said Bo.

For his part, Yahn Nevye didn't dare breathe.

At that moment, Ursa Laenskaya blew into the mouth of the mine, bringing the cold north wind with her.

"Oh joy," the grey lion groaned. "Keep your head low, *sidalord* jaguar. Looks like our Major didn't get her fill of blood tonight."

The jaguar swallowed and tried to make himself disappear into the wall, but the Major moved past him to stand over her husband, arms folded across her chest, as the Alchemist worked and hummed to herself in strange, exotic keys.

The moon is bright, the wind is quiet,
The tree leaves hang over the window,
My little baby, go to sleep quickly,
Sleep, dreaming sweet dreams.

Kerris looked up. His wife was sitting cross-legged on the stone, rocking the baby in her arms and singing a *cuīmián qǔ,* a sweet sleeping song for babies. He rose to his feet, made his way over. Someone had wrapped the body of Musaf Summerdale in his cloak but his blood was still fresh on the mine floor. The tears had dried on Fallon's cheeks and she seemed very sad.

The moon is bright, the wind is quiet,
The cradle moving softly,
My little one, close your eyes,
Sleep, sleep, dreaming sweet dreams.

He knelt down beside her, stroked her lightning hair.

"I want you to go home," he said quietly. "I want you to take our nephew and a few of Kirin's soldiers and I want you to go home. Please, will you do this for me?"

"It took him so long to die," she sniffed. "I would never have thought an arrow could take so long."

He sighed. She had not been there in the camp of the dogs a year ago. She had not seen, she had not heard. She had not witnessed the devastation the dogs had caused, the horrors they had wrought. She had been in the Humlander with Solomon, safe and burning the dead and singing.

"Will you go? Please, luv? I could do this much easier if I didn't think for every moment that the next arrow could be yours."

"It won't be."

"Fallon, please."

She looked at him and broke his heart. She did that often. He was surprised at how it always grew back, however, just a little bit stronger.

"It won't be," she said again. "Sireth saw six kittens. Six grey striped kittens."

"We only have two."

"See?" She tried to smile. "Sireth benAramais is never wrong."

"I hope so." He leaned forward, kissed her forehead. "I couldn't live without you. You know that."

"I know."

Kerris looked around at the men and women in the mine, all wounded and hurting in some way or another. He looked down at the baby, his nephew, child of his brother and the woman he hated more than anyone in the Kingdom. He should have killed her the other night, he realized. He should have taken her head off as she knelt but her blood would have spilled over her baby and that would have been wrong. Besides, it would not have been good to start a journey of peace with the spilling of blood.

"Sing," he said to his wife. "Sing the *cuīmián qu* again. I think we all could use a little soothing."

She smiled at him and her tears started anew, but she did sing and it was sweet, soft and healing.

The moon is bright, the wind is quiet,
The night is cloaked in starlight,
My little one, dream of morning,
Sleep, sleep, sleep, dreaming sweet dreams.

And so they passed a very quiet, sad night in the mouth of the mine, their first night in a new and foreign land. The moon was bright, the wind was quiet, but no one was dreaming sweet dreams. In fact, no one slept at all.

***

The falcon returned the next day with news of the army. They had headed out from Shen'foxhindi *and we were to be expecting them very soon. Captain Windsor-Chan was also estimating that our numbers had swelled to almost six thousand soldiers and a thousand extra horses. I was unbelievably proud.*

The falcon also relayed a letter from the Empress that had been waiting for me at Shen'foxhindi, *sealed in wax and the scent of lotus. I have yet to read it, although every hair on my body is telling me to do so.*

Kerris buried the dead by calling on sheets of rock to slide down the mountain over top the three horses, two leopards, the one tiger and the young lion. It was fitting, for while a basket from the Wall was an adequate means to bring our small team provisions from above, it was not so adequate for the transportation up of the dead. I still am a firm believer in honour, no matter what the last years have taught me.

The Seer himself spent most of the next days in meditation. The Alchemist's remedies proved powerful yet again and I wondered at the breadth of her skills. Salves, potions and competent stitchery could in no wise work the healing magic that she does. My chest aches every time I look at her and I am glad I have a letter from Ling. It will help me remember my choices and the reasons for them.

Major Laenskaya has been in a foul mood these days, more foul than I can remember in some time. I wonder how long she will remain content as the wife of a Seer when the heart of a warrior beats within her. She and the remaining soldiers forayed out to secure the plateau, counting eighteen dead from the night's brief but bloody battle. They also sought out and found the remains of the Legion camp. The cannon had done some damage but the lightning had killed most and she counted twenty-three charred bodies twisted on the ground there.

With now the death count at four cats to forty-one dogs, I wonder how long it will be before our canine company betrays us.

The Seer, the Oracle, the Monk, the Alchemist and the Elemental (the Magic as the soldiers were now calling them) were sitting together in a circle. Kerris had refused to sit next to Sherah. They were made to join hands and he refused to acknowledge her in any way. It was a sentiment I understood well, although perhaps did not share. The Oracle had made a point of sitting with Yahn Nevye and I wondered at her strange fascination with him. He seemed uncomfortable with her attentions and with the constant growls of her brother. This may prove to be an awkward situation very soon and I will tell him to put a stop to it at once.

They are working on what benAramis has called a Shield, much the same as what they created the other night only larger. Protecting six thousand troops would require more power than I can even imagine, but anything that can serve to halt even a fraction of those deadly whistling arrows would be a welcomed thing.

I wonder at so many things but above all, I wonder if Kerris' path to Unification is the right one. I can't see any way out of this that doesn't involve massacre and blood on all fronts. But it seems we have started something that cannot be stopped. Once the mountain comes down, we are committed. For good or ill, for war or peace, we are committed, and I have never been less committed to anything in my entire life.

- *an excerpt from the journal of Kirin Wynegarde-Grey*

***

The army began to come through at dawn.

In fact, it sounded like the rumble of distant thunder, and their horses began snorting and pawing inside the mine. It gave them time to rouse from their bedrolls and ready the horses, for the plan was to ride out down the plateau and into the valley. Thousands of mounted cats and monkeys would quickly overfill the mouth of the mine and surrounding area. It remained to be seen how they would handle any conflict with the local people once they came across a village. Kirin desperately hoped there would be no more bloodshed but his heart was heavy inside him.

And so, as the army came like a great undulating dragon, with spears and banners and plumes and swords, the team went ahead of them led by Kaidan, the Shogun-General, the Ambassador, the Major and the Magic. They were the head of this dragon now, its eyes, its ears, its teeth, its breath of flame. First one hundred, then five hundred, then one, three, five thousand. In fact, he couldn't see the end of it if he turned in his saddle, so he did not, merely kept his face forward watching for signs of life or dogs, the army flanking him and following like a wave. The plateau stretched out and down to a valley and the mountains rose up on both sides. They were still the Great Mountains, that was obvious, but here in the Lower Kingdom, it seemed her teeth were yellow, almost brittle, and her peaks were streaked with snow. In fact, the wind bit like fangs as they rode and he hoped the way would remain as level as it was now. Higher altitudes meant a narrow line, and that was not a safe strategy for such a force. Wide, like a wall, they could meet everything in their path with force.

There were wagons as well travelling in the rear carrying supplies for such an army. Hunger, not cold, would be the determining factor as food would be scarce during the harsh winter. A thousand free horses could not be counted on to bring down enough game to feed six thousand horses let alone their riders, and each man carried a basket of barley, rice or millet, a portion to be mixed with snow overnight. By morning, porridge would be filling, if not tasty. Kirin was hopeful the journey would be a short one – they had eaten better for the entirity of the Year of the Tiger, even in the Dry Provinces.

The free horses would also be used to relieve others who would grow weary forging through drifts and over rough terrain. Access to fresh horses meant better time but just arranging the rotation of mounts would become complicated very soon. The complexities of such a force were boggling. Winter was a bad time for many reasons.

Like him, the Magic was at the fore, spread out with ten horses in between. Each one of them was fixed forward in concentration, eyes glassy, faces like stone. None of them was 'riding', merely passengers and Kirin was grateful for the dependability of the horses. Young aSiffh was trotting freely at his side, tossing his head and snorting and he remembered the first time he had ridden out into battle with alMassay. They had both been so young.

There was the boom of an Imperial cannon from the Wall so far behind them now, signaling the last of the troops to pass through the mine. Kirin shook his head. Four hours from start to finish. These were logistics he simply could not fathom and he needed to speak at length with the Major. Stopping, starting, sleeping, even something as simple as watering the horses when all the water was frozen. A small force was practical and easy to lead. This force in this terrain, this was impossible.

He raised his fist over his head and turned Shenan to face the sea of horses spread out all the way to the Wall. All forward motion ceased but still, he needed to wait a lifetime before the army came to a complete halt. He glanced at Bo Fujihara, and the small man pulled his horse alongside. He took a deep breath and turned his eyes to the Oracle, the girl sitting like a child on the back of an Imperial horse. He nodded and she urged her mount forward until she too stood before the army and he could feel tension roll like thunder from the sight of them, cat, monkey and dog, united under the banners of both Upper and Eastern Kingdoms. He wondered if the dogs had a banner of their own. He doubted it, doubted any of them could even read.

He let his eyes sweep over the sea of bodies before opening his mouth to speak.

"This is an historic time," he shouted, carefully and slowly, his voice echoing over the wind, words translated by first Fujihara then Jalair Naransetseg, carrying on up the mountain by lieutenants in both Imperial, Hanyin and *Chi'Chen*. There was no one else to translate Dog. "A proud, turbulent and terrible time, a time never before seen in the history of our Kingdoms. We have been called "The Army of Blood" and that may be so, but men of the Kingdoms, we do not go to blood. We do not go to war with the Lower Kingdom. We go to Peace."

He paused, letting his words carry forth before continuing. "We may be men of war but now, right now, we go to Peace. We go to Unity. We go to Strength. If we fail in this, we will go to Death. We go to Death and Diminishing and the Destruction of our way of life, and not from the Dogs but from a people much older and more savage than they."

There was no sound but the wind.

"The Ancestors are rising. The Star announced it, the Magic has seen it, Kaidan has confirmed it. The Ancestors, with their bloody weapons and their Ancient ways, will seek to rule our peoples as they did in the beginning. There are those that might suggest that this is acceptable, a Natural Order, the Way of Things…" He paused, took a deep breath. "But I am not one of them."

There was a murmur from the army and the wind.

"We are a People. We are, in fact, many people, and we have the right to govern ourselves, in our ways, by ourselves and for ourselves. This journey is the first step in that pursuit, as we must present a united front to ensure that even the least of us will remain free to do so. This force, this 'Army of Blood,' is nothing if it is not firstly an Army of Peace."

He looked for and found the face of the dog. He was standing on the ground near the Alchemist, unnatural brown eyes locked with his own and he felt his heart lurch within him. They had always been enemies. There had always been war. This was madness.

He looked away.

"Take a look to your left. Take a look to your right. You might see the face of a cat. You might see the face of a monkey. You may even be seeing the face of a dog. Whatever face you see, it is the face of your brother, your sister, your friend. No one is better, no one is less, and we need to believe it in our very bones. There will be quarrels, there will be misunderstandings but we cannot allow them to rule us. We will be sorely tested in these next weeks as the Rabbit leaps off the stage and the Dragon shakes his head and gnashes his teeth. We need to be ready for anything, for if we fail, we consign our children to servitude and slavery. I, for one, do not wish that for our children."

He felt golden eyes weighing upon him. He did not look at them.

"Soon, the mountain will come down and our way back will be barred. If any of you wish to return to your old life, go in peace, *for* peace but go. Go and prepare your village for a new way but go. If you stay, you will be charting that new way and a new Kingdom where cat, monkey and dog are equal partners in its building. Equal in every way to the Ancestors who will seek to rule us. I don't know if this will happen in my lifetime, in any of our lifetimes, but I do know that I, the very first Shogun-General of the Fanxieng Dynasty, can do no less than try."

Once again, there was no the sound but the wind. His heart felt heavy. It was possible, probable even, that most of these soldiers were here for war. Even their name – the Army of Blood – promised it. To leave homes, families and commissions for the vague and untenable notion of peace was unexpected at best, disappointing at worst. There was no way to convince them.

Finally, there was the sound of slow, deliberate clapping. Kirin looked and was not surprised to see Sireth benAramis from the back of his horse, smiling in the all-knowing way of his. The tigress joined him and then Bo Fujihara, but in the way of monkeys, with raised arms and snapping fingers and shouting. Very quickly, all the *Chi'Chen* army joined in until the valley echoed like a nightmare, hooting and snapping and whistling, but it was the *Chi'Chen* army, not the cats. On this matter, the army of the Upper Kingdom was strangely silent.

He looked at his brother, grey ghost and miracle worker, on the back of the little mountain pony. If there was anyone who embodied this very dream, it was Kaidan.

"They won't leave," said Kerris. "No matter what they think of this plan, they won't leave."

"It won't be enough."

"It will have to be, Kirin. The rocks are going home."

And Kerris turned his face to the mountain. With a roar that sent clouds into the sky, the mouth of the mine closed on itself like an earthstorm, sealing their fate and setting them on their path. Three days they had been given. Now, they were committed. For good or for ill, he thought grimly, they were committed.

He turned his horse and headed out.

THE EYE OF THE NEEDLE

"I did tell you to sit down," said Damaris Ward.

Jeffery Solomon glared at her as the Maglar rolled through the underground. The Plug had done an efficient job at translating their language but the frequency had been unexpected and he was still struggling with nausea.

"So they're not dead?" he said. "You're sure about that."

"The Jiānkeeper said the male was in the Compound and the female was in the lab." She eyed him from across the car. "Why the hell are you traveling with monsters, Super 7?"

"It's Jeffery and they're not monsters. I keep telling you."

"It's been a long time since you went down, Jeffery 7. The world has changed."

"Not so much, I think."

Solomon, Ward and two guards were travelling in a Maglar from the medical wing of the DC compound to a communications wing. It had the look of an underground system but he couldn't be sure. Windows were dark, revealing again the bronzing of an old ArcEye and he remembered traveling through Brussels before he went under, how the ArcEyes varied from green hills, blue skies and vineyards to seasides, forests and mountains. Those were much better, he thought. Dark windows looked like empty eyes, made him feel lost and sad.

"I'm using up valuable comm time for you," she said. "I had to trade it for something and your monsters are it."

"So they're on display?"

"Only the grey.

His stomach lurched as the Mag took a bump in the track and he shook his head.

"Why?"

"Why what?"

"Why did you treat them differently than me? They're people. Okay, cat people, true enough, but still..."

She leaned forward, clasped her hands between her knees. Her eyes were dark and shone with intelligence.

"Everything, every living thing in this world will try to kill you, Jeffery 7. We are no longer the dominant species on this planet. The contagions that have developed can turn a normal man or woman into a cannibalistic monster within weeks. You do not go outside without a C-FAS and even then, you do not go beyond the fence. It's madness."

"You really believe that?"

"I do."

"Damaris, I've been outside in Europe for almost a year and I'm still alive. I've been walking your seaboard for days since you blew up my ship, hunting the quail and the turkeys and the rabbits. I'm still alive and after tasting that turkey roasted over an open fire, nowhere near as cannibalistic as I may look."

He could have sworn she smiled but she had looked away so he couldn't tell. It was hard to guess her age, whether she was older than him or life in this new world had conspired to make her strong and hard. Wrinkles at the corners of her eyes said laughter, lines at the corner of her mouth said resolve.

She turned back to him.

"Maybe you're immune."

"And maybe you're wrong."

"It's bad for a Security Chief to be wrong. People die."

"It's bad for scientists to be wrong too, but you know what? The world goes on."

Again, he thought she smiled. She was a smart cookie, no doubt.

He sat back, sighed.

"So who are we going to talk to, then?"

"I've asked CommWing to patch us into the Shield."

"The Shield?"

"Slabtu," she said. "CanShield North."

"Slabtu." It took a moment. "Sleep Lab Two?"

His heart thudded inside his chest.

"Si, Jeffery 7."

"Just Jeffery, or Jeff."

She leaned back and folded her arms across her chest, raised a tattooed brow.

"Jeff 7."

He tried to smile but couldn't and wondered what kind of world those ArcEyes were hiding behind their sad, bronzed glass.

***

It was late when they came to the village of Lon'Gaar.

Earlier, a cry had gone up and they had seen the shape of a boy sprint along a path that might have been a rocky stream in summer. The boy quickly disappeared but the tracks he left in the snow were easily followed and it was clear that he had not been alone. Still, they saw no others for the rest of the day. The stream had narrowed and grown steep with mountains and they were forced to ride no more than ten abreast along some areas. Traveling six thousand deep would become dangerous soon enough.

Finally, as they were losing the light of the winter sun, they came upon another plateau and a circle of the low round tents called gars. On the edge of the village, other tents with the hides of yak and goat hanging from poles. But there was no woodsmoke, there were no people. The entire village of Lon'Gaar was abandoned.

The army split like a river into three forks, two to flow around and one to flow through. Kirin led the center fork, making sure he had Bo Fujihara on one side of him and the dogs on the other. When he reached the center of the village, he raised his gloved hand, bringing the army to a slow, rippling stop. As the horses circled the village one hundred then one thousand fold, they waited, eyes sharp, ears straining. They heard nothing, no shouting, no drums, no deadly whistling arrows. Kirin glanced down at the male dog, tried to remember his name.

"Rani," said the Oracle. "His name Rani."

The dog growled but, to his credit, looked up.

"Where would they go?" asked Kirin and the girl translated. The dog growled again, flattened his ears to his skull but answered in his guttural language. The girl translated once more.

"Into mountains," she said. "Or to next village. North."

"Can you guess how many soldiers were in the Legion following you?"

She bit her lip. "Six tens? Maybe?"

"We counted forty-one bodies," said the Major from her horse. "That leaves almost twenty unaccounted for."

"They are with the villagers," said Bo and he puffed on his pipe. "It makes sense."

"It makes them dangerous," said the Major. "I can take a party and hunt them down."

"No," said Kirin. "Let them run. They will find the Khan's army and tell him of our strength. It may make him think twice before committing his army to a war they cannot win."

He could feel his people move their horses toward him, his brother and the tigress, the Seer and the jaguar. And, of course, the Alchemist. He still could not bring himself to look at her.

"We will camp here for the night," he said and raised his voice to be heard by every man in the Army of Blood. "There are blankets and skins here, perhaps some food. Take what you need. Leave nothing of value. Use everything."

"Hardly an act of peace, Captain," said the Seer.

"Shogun-General," growled his wife.

"My mistake."

Kirin shook his head.

"These people are gone. They will not miss what they have left behind."

"An army is only as strong as its stomach," said Fujihara. "Beyond all things, it will be hunger that will make or break our journey."

"It's true," said Yahn Nevye from the back of his horse. "And a soldier can chew on a scrap of hide for hours, dulling his hunger and filling his belly. For a very short time but still."

They all looked at him.

"I…I, I heard that somewhere."

"Idiot," growled the Major."

"There are many hides," said Kirin. "We will take what we need."

He looked at Ursa. "Have the wagons distribute rations to the soldiers. Release the free horses, have them hunt and bring back what they can."

"They can hunt the dogs," she grinned.

"No!" gasped Setse.

Kirin shook his head. "By morning, we will have taken everything. Then we will move on."

"Sir." Ursa wheeled on her horse and was gone.

"No hunt dogs!" moaned Setse and she glanced at the cats surrounding her.

"No hunt dogs, little sister," purred Sherah al Shiva. "I will make tea."

And they began dismounting their horses in the village of Lon'Gaar.

***

It had taken them many days and cost them many soldiers, but finally, they had passed through the cliffs of KhunLun and entered the vast high plateau region known as Tevd. Tevd, the Cradle of the Moon. Wide, rocky and surrounded on all sides by mountains, Tevd was dry, cold and surprisingly free of snow. Perhaps the wind was too strong, perhaps the air too dry, for it seemed only in crevasses the snow stayed. The Plateau of Tevd was a sacred place, a holy place, where the world was born and old men came to die.

They had made the village of Jia'Khan, more than half of the moon-long run to Lon'Gaar and the Wall of the Enemy. The village was overjoyed to be witness to the Khargan's Ten Thousand, even more to be host. The Khan had decreed a rest and yaks, reindeer and goats were slaughtered for a feast that would last three days. Children sang songs of victory and women were demonstrative with their pride. To bed a soldier in the Khargan's army would be advantageous for any woman and any child conceived during such a feast would be honoured in the village for a lifetime.

They sat in the gar for the night was bitterly cold, the Bear running a stone along the massive blade known as *ala'Asalan*, or Killer of Lions. It was as long as the Bear was tall, made of black iron and hooked on one end. Long-Swift had seen that blade tear out the insides of many a man, some lions. Most men couldn't lift it without strain. When he wasn't using it, the Khargan wore it strapped across his back like a bow. It made his back very strong.

"Why don't you go take a woman?" asked the Bear, not looking up from his sharpening. "You are Irh-Khan. You can choose from any woman in the village. It would be her glory and your pleasure."

Long-Swift stared into the flames and smiled. It was a small fire, just a few coals and some sticks. Not enough to keep warm – the packed snow did that well enough but it did cause light to dance around the inside of the gar. Even for the Khargan, there was little extravagance. A hide for sleeping that wrapped *ala'Asalan* during the run, a horn of wotchka, a pipe. His armour lay to the side – the skulls and claws, the one-armed leather coat and mail cuirass, the braces and hide-bound boots next to the *kushagamak,* the lethal dual hook-and-chain weapon of the Khans. Sitting, disarmed like this in a simple woolen undershirt and trousers, the Bear almost looked like a common man. If one did not look at his size. If one did not look at the scars.

"What?" the Khargan grunted and now he did look up. "You don't need a woman? Long-Swift the *Sekond* is now Long-Swift the Celibate?"

"I am hearing talk in the ranks," the Irh-Khan said. "About the strength and power of the Army of Blood."

"Tell me."

"It is said that they have assembled a force of over five thousand cats and monkeys."

The Bear spat on the ground. "Pah. We have twice that."

"They have horses."

A growl now. It was a well-known fact that not even the Khargan's Legions could stand against a rush of Imperial horses.

"That is not all," Long-Swift continued. "They have magic."

"Magic?"

"More than Oracles, Lord. Alchemists and Elementals. A runner from Lon'Gaar even witnessed the lightning bending in the sky to destroy the camp."

"Big stories," grunted the Bear. "From little townspeople."

"Still," said Long-Swift. "Is it not worth sifting the bag of sand for a single grain of wheat?"

The Bear grunted again, bent back to his sword. "You are not helping me, Long-Swift."

"Well," the Irh-Khan reached for the horn, breathed in the wotchka's rich, sweet smell. "I hear many things with my ears uncropped, Lord."

"Hah. Tell me."

"The villagers talk of an Oracle on the Plains of Tevd."

"An Oracle?"

"Yes. The Eyes of Jia'Khan, called *Edinae Tebchech.*"

The stone paused on the blade and the Bear stared at him. "Eye of the Needle?"

"And *Edinae Buran.*"

"Eye of the Storm? Which is it?"

"Both."

"This Oracle has two names?"

"Yes."

"Strange."

"It is stranger still, Lord. This oracle prophesizes for the villagers and they must pay him in eyes."

"Eyes?" The Bear blinked slowly. "He accepts payment from these villagers…in eyes?"

"In eyes." The Irh-Khan arched his brow, raised the wotchka to his lips. "And he is bigger than you."

The fire crackled. The wind outside the gar howled. There were the sounds of people in the village, the singing of the children, the crowing of women, the drinking of the Ten Thousand but all sounds were drowned as suddenly the Khargan threw back his head and laughed. He laughed so that he was made to lay *ala'Asalan* down into the snow. He laughed until tears sprang from his lashes and made rivers down his cheeks.

"He is bigger than me?"

"Much bigger."

More laughing and Long-Swift could well imagine the ten thousand soldiers outside the gar, glancing about at the sound of the Khan of Khans laughing. There had been a time when it had been a common thing but not any more. Life had hardened them all.

"Ah, what a wonderful thought," said the Bear as his laughter died and he wiped the tears from his eyes. "I think I very much like this Oracle. I will enjoy killing him."

And as he bent back to the Killer of Lions, Long-Swift released one breath and then another. He was playing a dangerous game, distracting the Khargan from the Singer of Songs in his head. He didn't want to take a woman from the village, not when the Singer was slipping through his mind. He was becoming obsessed with the thought of her, couldn't wait to lay his head down in the snow at night for her to visit in his dreams.

He wondered if it could be called treason, and if it were, what that might mean. Dreams and reality rarely mixed well. If she were riding with the Army of Blood and if he met her in battle, he might be forced to kill her after all and that, he realized, would be a very tragic thing. She had captivated him, body and soul.

Perhaps, that was her intent. She was the Enemy, after all.

With that thought, he emptied the wotchka and rose to his feet.

"Where are you going?" asked the Khan.

"To find a woman," he said.

The Khargan grunted and Long-Swift left the tent for the bitterness and the cold.

***

The CommWing was heavily guarded and they walked along a narrow corridor that used to be a moving sidewalk that no longer moved. All the windows were old ArcEyes as well and he wondered what time of day it was. He wondered what the compound itself looked like from the outside, what sort of buildings they were, whether the grounds were landscaped, whether there were farms. So far, all he had seen was interiors. Stairwells, undergrounds, labs, ozone lights, metal floors, plastic chairs.

There was not one potted plant in the place and he doubted that anyone knew how beautiful the world was outside the fence.

There was music everywhere, however. It sounded like a small chamber orchestra and he wondered if it was from archives. It had an organic, echoing sound to it and it was growing louder as the four of them trotted up a long wide set of stairs to a crowded mezzanine. He smiled as he spied a quartet was playing Haydn in the center of a breezeway. Two violins, a viola and a cello singing the song of strings, as people in colourful jumpsuits moved past. Everyone stared at him as he went by, gave him a very wide berth and he realized it was because of his hair. Everyone else was bald.

Shaved, he realized, for he could see the shadows above the hairlines. Even the women. It made sense in a way. If they believed that every living thing existed to kill, then it would be important to remove any safe harbor for bacteria, mites and parasites. The human head was a gold mine for critters.

Beneath her goggled cap and tattooed eyebrows, Damaris Ward was likely as bald as a billiard ball.

"How many people in DC?" he asked.

"CD?" she corrected. "Seven thousand seven hundred and thirty-six."

"More or less," he grinned.

"Exactly. We have sixteen women pregnant."

"Seventeen if you count the Scholar in the Court of the Empress."

"Scholar? What Scholar?"

"I don't think you've met her. She's a skinny girl with orange and black stripes. Smart as a whip for a monster."

She raised a tattooed brow but said nothing and they passed through the colourful breezeway into yet another corridor.

Finally up a spiral staircase and into a building with huge screens on the walls and armed guards flanking the doors. Ward was waved through and Solomon watched as the door swung open on pulleys in the ceiling. Ramshackle, he thought again. He wondered what their power source was.

In to another room, smaller and dark with floor-to-ceiling bronzed ArcEyes. A waiting area and he was surprised to see books on a table. Books. He hadn't seen a book in ages. He couldn't help it. He picked one up, opened the cover, breathed in the woodsy smell of very old paper, fading ink and time.

"We wait," said Ward. He smiled at her and she didn't seem to know what to do with her eyes.

After several long minutes, a door swung open and a woman stepped out. She was short and stocky, had eyes like little stones and her buzzed head revealed a shadow of silver hair.

"Cece?"

"Jeffery Solomon, you old dog..."

And he swept her up into the air, spun her around and around, utterly ignoring the look of horror on the face of Damaris Ward.

"Put me down, you idiot," grumbled Celine Carr in her clipped English accent. "You'll bust my other hip."

But she was smiling and did not let go of him when her feet touched the floor.

He held her out at arm's length.

"You look..."

"Old," she said. "It's alright. You can say it. It has been a millennium or two, after all..."

"When the hell did you wake up? And how? Max—"

"One moment, Jeffery." And she glared at the other woman in the

room. "Thank you, Jiān Ward but I am completely safe with Dr. Solomon."

"Si," said Damaris but Solomon cut her off.

"Could you please check on my friends?" he asked. "Just make sure they are alive, unharmed and together. I'll sort this out asap. Would you do that for me please, Damaris?"

"Si," she said again. "I'll do this for you."

"And please let me know once you know they're safe." He glanced at the woman he knew as Cece. "How would she let me know?"

"Transfer," ordered Celine.

Ward reached up to the wire at the base of her skull, pulled the tiny plug from its tip, reached over to affix it to Solomon's. He gasped as the current buzzed directly into his brain, but then grinned.

"You just gave me your number. I feel like a seventeen year-old kid."

She rolled her eyes and took back the plug but she was smiling before withdrawing from the room.

"In here," said Celine and she led him into another room. It was completely black with six large screens and a set of rolling chairs.

Celine wheeled a chair towards him, lowered herself down.

"Sit, Jeffery. The titanium is wearing out of these old legs."

She had been right earlier on. She looked perhaps seventy-five but he knew she had to be older. Her face was hard, weathered and sharp as steel, but truth be told, she had looked the same even before they went under.

"Would you like some tea?" she asked and he grinned. Cats, Brits. Funny how both loved their tea.

"Nah, but thanks," he said, reaching over to take her hands and she raised a brow at him.

"Ah, yes. You still need to touch. I remember."

"It's a weird thing, coming back like that."

"Yes, it is."

"So? SleepLab Two was obviously a success."

"Moderately," she agreed. "Six of us survived. We woke about forty-five years ago. From what I understand, there was a meteor storm

and that damned satellite was sent into a very high orbit. On every anniversary of the wake date, it would repeat the signal. I don't know how long it was doing that, centuries I think, but somehow, it started the process. We lost Khofi Mamadou."

He nodded. He hadn't known Khofi well, but still.

"It took years, Jeffery. Years to make the preparations to wake everyone else. The Canadian Shield is a very harsh place in winter. It was such a damned struggle..."

Her eyes grew distant as she remembered.

"But we did it. After six and half years, we began waking the others. We had decided on five outposts, with Marathon as the central base, but five new outposts to begin civilization here in NorAm. Each base got five hundred residents. We tried to distribute the occupations, arts and skills as evenly as we could. Yellowstone is Portillo's, Banff is Jorgenson's, Washington took Cimarron and Claire has Rocky Mountain."

And she smiled wearily. "Shenandoah is mine."

"Paolini stayed in Marathon?"

"He seems to have the toughest skin."

He nodded, looked down at her hands.

"Celine, everyone else at Sandman One is dead."

Her face became stone.

"We were afraid of that."

"Have you heard from 3?"

"Nothing."

He sighed.

"The IAR succeeded, Cece. They made people, living, breathing people with thriving civilizations."

"With their experiments."

"Yes, with their experiments. The people I came over with are not animals. They're friends. They saved my life. I owe them."

She sat back. "You'll never convince them of that here."

"Maybe I can't, but you can."

"They're probably dead by now, anyway. The creatures they keep in the compounds are horrific. Gruesome caricatures of animals. Monkeys, bears, sloths, snakes." She shuddered. "Have you ever seen a deer with

fangs?"

"I've seen a few horses with 'em."

"And the rats—"

"Don't talk to me about rats," he grumbled. "But remember, that was Tuur Oewehand's work, his monkey/rat hybrids. That has nothing to do with my friends."

She studied him, her eyes small and sharp.

"This is a different world, Jeffery."

"More different than you know, Cece. That woman, Damaris Ward, she believes that the air has been poisoned somehow, that people can't leave this compound without turning into beasts. You know that's not true. You know it's just the success of the IAR. It's engineering, Cece, not epidemic."

"Modification, not mutation."

"Exactly. Out there, the air is sweet, the land is bountiful. It's a very good place to be."

"Perhaps so, but we're still starting out. It takes time. People need time."

"But start it right, not with lies."

"Well, I suppose we'll never know how you would have handled Europe then, since your entire compound was lost."

She turned and moved her hands across a console and five screens began to hiss and flicker.

"We're using up all the comm time for this, Jeffery. There are only three working towers on the entire continent. We only get an hour a week. It's been bloody hard..."

As one by one, the human faces of his colleagues from centuries past appeared on the screens, he couldn't help but think about his feline colleagues. He missed them more than he'd expected and prayed that Damaris Ward would find them not only quickly, but alive.

***

Kirin shook his head. This tale of Ancestorland was growing worse with the telling. Perhaps his brother was right. Perhaps this journey was worth the danger. Perhaps there was only one way to stop this threat to their way of life. Perhaps the dogs would listen.

He cast his eyes across the fire to where the young dog was staring at him, brown eyes hostile still.

Kirin sighed. Perhaps they would all die in the Year of the Cat.

It was late and the Alchemist had started a fire. She was humming and the baby was cooing happily on a skin while tea was steeping. Bo Fujihara's aromatic pipe carried over even the woodsmoke, rich and heady in the cold night air. Soldiers had finished stripping the village of the last of the tents and the resources had been distributed amongst the few wagons that accompanied them. It was a strange and quiet moment, the hush before the rumble of a storm.

The night was filled with the sounds of restless horses and wind and two thousand *Chi'Chen* practicing hand-to-hand combat by the lights of many fires. The fighting was fascinating, he thought as he watched—hands and feet, arms and legs and even tails all moved like striking serpents. They fought with grace and honour, for when a match was won or lost, a very respectful bow was given and received. There was a crowd gathering around one pair, both members of the elite force known as the Snow, and he shook his head. Their blows were lightning, so swift that he could barely follow their movements and he realized it was an art form. Like *Jujutsuh* or *Kenjutsuh* or even his own Bushido. They were skilled beyond skill, trained beyond discipline and he found himself approving. He was certain his own troops could not fight like that.

He looked back to the fire and the teller of stories.

After this last installment, Kerris had curled up, head in Fallon's lap. She was stroking his hair and whispering to him. Kirin watched them with a growing ache in his chest. He wondered if it were fear or jealousy. Neither one would be a welcomed companion on this journey. Perhaps he was simply missing Ling. He had not read her letter and he wondered at that. Perhaps he did not know what to think of the fact that Sherah al Shiva had borne him a son and they both were here, around this very fire. It was a strange and surreal thing.

It was a strange and surreal night, he realized, this night in a ransacked foreign village. Strange and surreal and sad, so he rose to his feet and left the fire, contenting himself to watch the monkeys.

The other half of the Magic were sitting together around another fire under the flaps of one of the gars. The Seer, the Monk and the Oracle were not holding hands for a change, all equally exhausted from their morning spent working on the Shield. The wound in Sireth's chest had begun to ooze once again from the exertion of the trail, but Ursa was preoccupied with the army so he sat cross-legged in the tent, eyes closed in meditation and healing. Nevye and Setse were watching the *Chi'Chen* exercises just outside the flap, their eyes fixed on the poetry of motion and martial art.

Another match came to an end and the pair bowed, fists to cupped palm. Setse clapped her hands fiercely and another round with different pair began.

"It's marvelous, isn't it?" said the jaguar. "How they move like that. Like a mongoose and a cobra. So fast. So sure."

"Indeed," said Sireth, eyes still closed. "They are a miraculous people."

"It's a blessing," the man went on. "When your body responds as quickly as your mind. Quicker even than your thoughts."

"You speak like you know this," said Sireth. "Alchemist, Seer *and* Soldier?"

"Oh no," said Nevye. "No, not me. Not for a very long time. Forget I said anything."

There was the crunch of very high boots on snow.

"Bah," the Major snorted as she approached from behind. "This little chicken cannot fight."

"Ursa," said her husband but she pushed past the jaguar and ducked under the gar.

"Here," she said. "I want you to take this."

And she handed him a dagger. It had a silver blade and a phoenix carved into the hilt.

He did not take it.

"I told you I didn't want a dagger," he said.

"I may not always be here to protect you," she snorted. "And you need protection."

"This dagger would not have stopped the arrow."

"I want you to take it."

He looked at her for a long time.

"Take it," she repeated.

"Ursa…"

"We are in a hostile land and the dogs have killed you once already."

"That is not the steel I need from you."

"That is all that I can give." And she pushed it into his palm with such force that a thin line of red sprang up along his thumb. It fell from his hand and into the snow.

"Don't take it, then," she growled. "You are being a fool, not a leader."

There was silence for a brief moment, only the crackling of the fire and the weight of thoughts and the cold night sky. He sighed, bent forward, picked up the dagger.

"It's beautiful," he said.

"I found it in the Armoury at *Shen'foxhindi.*"

His eyes studied the carving. A phoenix, symbol of life from death, flame from ashes, rebirth, renewal, the wheel of life. *Fitting,* he thought to himself. He had died and now he lived.

"Thank you," he said.

"It is a military blade. You are not military, but still."

She was not looking at him, her pale eyes evasive and he knew she had something weighing on her mind. It would have been simple to learn it, a mere drifting of a thought but he would never, not with her. She had not been tamed with their marriage, merely joined.

"Are you done for the night?" he asked.

"No. In the army, you are never done."

"I see."

"Even a small party of dogs can be dangerous. Look what they did to you."

"I should have seen it. I was distracted. I was searching for something else."

"*They* should have seen it, then," she said and gestured toward the jaguar and the Oracle sitting outside around the fire, watching the matches. *"They* are weak."

"They are learning. Not all of life is as orderly as the army."

"You defend them again."

"Never in this world can hatred be stilled by hatred; it will be stilled only by love and peace — this is the law of eternal."

"Brahmin," she growled and her tail lashed. "The law of eternal will still die at the blade of a dog."

"Have you not had enough of blood?"

"There is never enough blood."

"Stay with me tonight."

"I am working."

And she turned to leave, ducked under the flap of the gar. Outside, the Oracle clapped her hands as yet another match came to an end.

"Amazing," said Nevye. "I can watch them all night."

"Shar Ma'uul fight," said Setse and she sprang to her feet, onto the tips of her toes like a dancer. "Fight me, Shar! Teach me!"

"Yes, little chicken," snarled the Major and she swatted him as she walked past. "Stand up and fight the little girl."

"Ursa," snapped her husband from the gar. "That's enough."

She whirled back to the fire.

"He needs to know what it is like to fight a dog. *He* needs to know what it is like to be beaten by one. Maybe *then* he'll pay attention to the arrows of dogs." She grabbed him by the back of his robes, hauled him to his feet. "Fight the dog, traitor."

"No," moaned Setse. "No hurt Shar."

"It's alright," said Nevye as he scrambled to get his feet underneath him. "I understand her anger, I do."

"I don't think you do," hissed the Major.

"No, I do. Really."

"Then prove it, little chicken. Fight me instead."

"Ursa," the Seer rolled to his knees. "That's enough."

"Pretend you're a monkey and not a coward and a traitor. Fight me."

And she hit him.

It was a little hit, just a cuff to the side of his head. Sireth slipped out from the gar, moved toward his wife but Nevye held up his hand.

"No, no," he said, rubbing his head. "She's angry. It's alright. Really."

She hit him again, this time a sharp jab to the chest.

"Aiya," he grunted.

"Ursa, stop this. Now."

"Stop, bad cat," wailed Setse and her brother appeared at her side. "Bad cat, Rani."

"This is how we do it in the Army," said Ursa. "But of course, you wouldn't know. You're not a soldier. Only an Alchemist and a traitor."

And her hands struck again and again and again. Nevye staggered under her blows. Sireth looked to the sky. The owl, Hunts in Silence, landed on his shoulder, wings wide, beak open.

The silver fist flew one more time. The jaguar blocked it with his wrist.

"What?" he said, as they all stared at the sight.

She struck again and again he blocked.

"I'm sorry," he said. "I don't… I don't know how—"

Again she struck, again he blocked until they were moving like the Snow, like a cobra and a mongoose and soon, Yahn Nevye was smiling.

Setse clapped even more fiercely. "Shar Ma'uul brave fighter!"

Mi-Hahn dropped from the sky onto the Seer's opposite shoulder. He closed his eyes as his wife's high boot heel sliced upwards. The jaguar caught it easily.

Incredulous, Nevye looked at the boot in his hand.

He laughed.

The Major was lethal, however, and using Nevye's grip as an anchor, she flipped her body into the air, the second boot heel connecting with the man's jaw, sending him backwards and into the snow. The Oracle was at his side in a heartbeat, her brother targeting them all with arrows. The Major landed on her feet, one hand dipped into the snow for balance.

"What is going on?" growled the Shogun-General as he stepped into the firelight.

Both falcon and owl left the Seer's shoulders, Mi-Hahn shrieking and chasing the other with furious wings.

"Merely practice," said Sireth, opening his brown eyes. "My wife and my friend decided to try to spar like the *Chi'Chen*. Ursa is a little more skilled, I'm afraid."

"Bad cat," groaned Setse at her place beside the Monk. For his part, Nevye remained on his knees, kept his eyes fixed on the ground.

The Major pushed herself to standing. Her hair was wild and her eyes barely slits in the darkness.

"The Snow are brilliant at hand-to-hand," said Kirin. "I am not surprised none of you can compete."

There was silence from the company, only the sound of restless horses and the wind and the two thousand *Chi'Chen* bowing to each other.

"Go to sleep, all," said Kirin. "We have a long and difficult road tomorrow."

And he turned to head back to the fire, where the others lay bedded down for the night.

"He betrayed you," said Ursa.

"Ursa!" snapped the Seer.

"He betrayed all of us! He sold us to Jet barraDunne in Chancellor Ho's winter garden! You saw it yourself, husband!" And she flung an arm in the direction of the fire where the Alchemist sat, eyes golden and gleaming. "Sold us to *kunoi'chi* for a seat in the monastery!"

Kirin paused.

There was no sound now, no restless horses, no wind, the *Chi'Chen* had ceased their art, begun preparation for the long night ahead.

Kirin turned his face to where the jaguar still knelt, head bowed, in the snow.

"Is this true?"

There was no answer. He looked at the Seer, who sighed but said nothing.

"Oh, I see. Yes, I see." Slowly Kirin turned, took a step toward the bowed cat with the dog at his side. "The man whom you wished to kill but did not."

"Captain..."

"The man whom *I* may wish to kill but shouldn't. A Seer of *Sha'Hadin* on sabbatical in *Agara'tha.*"

The lion towered over the jaguar and the fire sent their shadows dancing across the mountains. Setse looked up at him, eyes wide. A cold fire settled into Kirin chest.

"Sidalord jaguar, did you know Jet barraDunne?"

Nevye swallowed, nodded quickly, still looking at the snow.

"Did you do what my Major suggests? Did you have a part in betraying us to Chancellor Ho?"

"No," said Setse. "Shar Ma'uul not betray. Shar Ma'uul good. Shar Ma'uul kind."

"Yes," said Shar Ma'uul.

It seemed like a very long time as the lion stood and the jaguar waited but suddenly, the Shogun-General reached down with his gloved hand and grabbed the Monk by the throat, lifting him off his knees and into the air. The Oracle lunged after them, but Kirin swung the man around, drawing him close, face-to-face, blue eyes to yellow.

"Do you know what they did to us, *sidalord* jaguar? Do you have any idea?"

Nevye said nothing. He could not, with the Teeth of the Dragon around his throat.

"Was it worth it, the torture of a Captain of the Queen's Guard, the rape and torture of a valiant woman, the torture and murder of the Last Seer of *Sha'Hadin?* Was all that worth the price of a monastery you no longer run?

"What's going on?" asked a sleepy Kerris, now standing with his wife near the others. "Kirin?"

Kirin turned and dropped the jaguar to the ground, slowly slid the Blood Fang from its sheath.

"No!" shouted the Oracle.

Yahn Nevye bowed his head.

"Kirin?"

Assumed the two-fisted stance.

"Captain?" asked Fallon.

Raised the Fang high into the air. It's Khamachada steel gleamed like fresh blood in the firelight.

Yahn Nevye closed his eyes.

The Fang came slicing down, stopping only inches above the Oracle as she threw herself across the yellow cat.

There was no sound, not even the wind. No one dared breathe, not even Jalair Naranbataar, grandson of the Blue Wolf, whose bow was drawn tight, fixed on the lion with the blood-red sword.

The Oracle looked up at him, her odd eye shining.

"Kuren Ulaan Baator," she pleaded. "You will save our People."

All eyes now, cat and monkey both, were upon that sight, as the Fang of the Red Hero held the lives of the Blue Wolf and the Yellow Cat on the sliver of its blade.

With a long, cleansing breath, the Shogun-General straightened, returned the Fang to its home.

"Leave," he said to the jaguar. "I spare your life this once. If we meet again, I will kill you."

The jaguar looked up now. There were stripes alongside the spots on his cheeks.

"Captain," said Sireth, stepping forward but Kirin snarled again, cut him off with a palm.

"Leave, jaguar, before I remove your head." He repeated, whirling and leaving the group for the distant fire, where the Alchemist was waiting.

Nevye stayed on the ground for a long time, trying vainly to restart his breathing. Naranbaatar dropped into the snow, pulled his sister from the back of the Monk. He wrapped his arms around her as she began to rock. Her eyes were dull, glazed and her lips were moving, though no sound came.

Finally, the jaguar struggled to his feet and looked at the Seer, the Last Seer of *Sha'Hadin.*

"I'm sorry," he said and he tried to smile. Somehow, it did not find a home on his face. "I'll—I'll go. May I take my horse?"

"No," said Ursa. "It belongs to the Upper Kingdom. *You* do not."

"Take the horse," said the Seer, stepping toward him, laying a hand on the brown-robed shoulder. "We *will* meet again, Yahn. Do not despair."

"My life is despair," said the jaguar. "It is nothing new for me."

The Seer leaned in close, his voice barely a whisper. "You *know* what we are going to. You need to go ahead."

Nevye blinked. "But the Shogun-General—"

"Is a good man but a warrior. He needs us. He needs you, but he cannot see what we see. His glass is still dark."

Nevye stared at hin.

"Trust your owl. It will hunt for you, it will see for you. Protect yourself from the Eye of the Needle. This may yet be redeemed."

Nevye nodded, looked over at Kerris.

"I should have taken than saddle in *Shen'foxhindi,"* he said.

With that, he turned and left the firelight to find the horses.

Kerris shook his head. "Anyone care to tell me what in the Kingdom just happened?"

Naranbataar looked up at him as he held his sister and laid back his ears.

"Good," he said in heavily-accented Imperial. "Shar Ma'uul bad for Setse."

Jalair Naransetseg said nothing, merely stared past the snow at her feet, rocking.

Sireth benAramis looked at them, the young girl trapped in a terrifying world of vision and farsight, the young man who had never uttered a word outside his own tongue. Then he turned to the snow leopard, heart of a warrior, wife of a priest. The first woman he had loved in twenty years.

She raised her chin, defiant.

He tossed the dagger, point down, into the snow.

"You are a stranger to me," he said before returning to the gar.

For her part, Ursa Laenskaya held her ground for a very long time before she too disappeared into the shadows of the night.

Kerris turned to look at the tigress, still clutching his arm.

"You're not leaving, are you? Please tell me you'll never leave."

She shook her head, emerald eyes brimming with tears. He gathered her into his arms and kissed them away.

And snow began to fall over the village of Lon'Gaar.

***

Beyond the village of Jia'Khan on the wide bleak holy Plateau of Tevd, there was a field of stone and in the center of the field, was a temple.

It was a small temple made of the Ancestors' square gray stone and it rose from the field like a gar. The peak was gold, pure gold that gleamed in the dawn's dim light and drew the eye as if it were the only thing on the plain. Around the temple, driftwood mounds were assembled like altars, rising from the ground almost to the peak of the temple itself. Far, far behind them, they could see the early morning smoke of Jia'Khan and the army of ten thousand, looking like a black sea under a heavy sky. There was no sound but the wind, no smell but the scent of incense and decay.

Long-Swift looked at the Bear. The man stood with his hands on his hips, *kushagamak* looped at his side, his iron hair waving in the cold wind. There was frost on his chin and it made him look old. Long-Swift couldn't imagine the Khargan old. Khans never lasted long. Rivals took them down, wore *their* skulls as armor in much the same way Khans wore lions. But then again, the Bear was no ordinary Khan.

"The Temple of Eyes," the Bear growled as he studied the strange building and its surrounding area. "That is a small home for such a large man."

"You go down," said Long-Swift. "The villagers say his home is underground."

"I cannot wait to meet this Oracle." The Bear grinned, his teeth sharp and white. "Perhaps I will take *his* eyes as payment to me."

Long-Swift shrugged. The thought of the Bear torturing yet another Oracle was unpleasant. It would not go well if the man continued this way. Perhaps the Eye of the Needle was Fate's answer for such treatment. Both roads were dangerous.

"You are afraid," said the Bear.

"The villagers are afraid of him."

"The villagers are afraid of many things. A long winter, a raven at moondown, an army of cats. An Oracle is a god to them."

"What if he *is* bigger than you?"

"Then I look forward to beating him."

They looked back at the temple. There was a raven sitting on one of the altars, pecking with its sharp beak. It was a sickening thought as they realized the mounds were not made of wood.

"A raven at moondown," said Long-Swift. "It is a bad omen."

"I am not afraid of a bird, at *any* time. We have a volunteer?"

"Yes."

Long-Swift looked back to the group of men standing behind them. Three soldiers, ears cropped, tails docked, and a villager – a thin man with wiry pelt and bound hands.

"What did he do?"

"Took his brother's young daughter who was not yet a woman. He was being starved to death as punishment. Losing an eye in the service of his Khan will restore his standing in the community." The Irh-Khan looked back. "Of course, the shock might very well kill him."

"Then we'll have two eyes," said the Khargan. "Good plan."

"I thought so."

The Bear smiled again and together, they crossed the field of stones toward the temple.

***

It was dawn when Kirin awoke to the sounds of shouting. He was on his feet in a heartbeat, hand on the hilt of the Blood Fang as natural as breathing.

The young dog was shouting, cursing in his guttural language, pointing and snapping and making wild gestures. Several soldiers had weapons drawn, Ursa included and her steel glinted in the early morning light. As he approached, he could make out the Seer, his brother and the Scholar all trying to calm the creature down but with the tension brought by the mere presence of dogs, he knew it wouldn't take much for an arrow to be loosed or a blade sent flying, ending their very first attempts at diplomacy in blood.

"What is it?" he asked, mindful to keep the Fangs in their beds.

Five heads turned at his approach.

"Setse," growled the dog and he pointed to an impression in the snow. "*Setse alag bulokh.*"

"She's gone," said the Scholar and she wrapped her thin arms around her ribs. "Setse is gone."

"Good riddance," said Ursa.

"Setse *ali Shar Ma'uul,*" the dog growled. "Know this true. Shar Ma'uul bad for Setse."

"That's two fifths of the Magic, Captain," said the Seer, not bothering to correct his rank. "We will not be able to create or maintain a Shield now and the entire army will be vulnerable. Sad, isn't it?"

"Can you find her?"

"I suppose I can."

Kirin grit his teeth. He knew how this would play out. It had happened time and time and time again.

"Will you?"

The Seer arched a brow, the one with the scar cutting through.

"She will not return without Yahn Nevye. She loves him."

At the name, Naranbataar laid back his ears and growled again.

"And you have sworn to kill him when you see him next. It's a dilemma, I'll give you that. All because you couldn't lay it down. All because you couldn't see beyond your own bloody glass."

Kirin stared at him.

"I can find her," said Ursa.

"No," said Kirin and Sireth in unison, and she glowered at them both.

"I'll go," said Kerris. "I can track better than any of you."

"No, Kerris," said Kirin. "Kaidan is our Ambassador and this is your mission. If anyone goes, it will be me."

"But you can't track. And after what you did last night, why would either of them want to return?"

The Shogun-General sighed, turned to the dog.

"Will you help me?"

The dog stared at him.

"Will. You. Help. Me?" he repeated, speaking slowly and loudly, as if translation could be overcome by speed and volume.

"Bi oilgokhgui baina," said the dog.

"I don't understand," growled Kirin.

"Ba nadad tuslahgui yu," came a throaty voice from behind and the Alchemist slipped into the conversation, her baby perched on her hip. "I can come with you, *sidi*. To translate, of course."

"Her?" Kerris snorted. "Better to travel with a snake."

"Kerris, that's enough."

"And who will lead the Army, Kirin? That *is* why we're here. The girl is sweet and it's a bonus to have dogs travelling with us, but honestly, we're here with an army, *as* an army. You are the Shogun-General of that army. Who will lead if you're not here?"

Kirin took a long deep breath, looked around at all the faces awaiting his words, needing him to say something that would reinstate their faith in this mission. Truth be told, he needed it as much for himself.

"You, Kerris. You will lead the Army. You and Bo Fujihara and Fallon Waterford-Grey and Major Laenskaya and the last Seer of *Sha'Hadin*. You will all lead the Army of Blood until I return with the Oracle."

"And Yahn Nevye?" asked the Seer.

"And Yahn Nevye," said Kirin, gritting his teeth.

"Well then," said Kerris. "You should go now, while the trail's fresh."

Kirin turned to the dog, Naranbataar. "We go now."

"Garakh ba," said the Alchemist, and the dog nodded, bent to grab his bedroll from the snow. The cheetah turned to the tigress.

"Will you tend my baby, little sister?" she purred. "It will not be good for him on this trail."

And she held Kylan out, wrapped in hides and wool blankets. Tentatively, the Scholar took him, spared only a glance for her husband as she fell into the baby's large, bi-coloured eyes.

"Oh, Sherah," she whispered. "It would be an honour."

And she clutched the baby to her chest.

"No," said Sherah. "It is my honour."

The cheetah slipped a pack from her back, passed it into the Seer's hands.

"Medicines for your wound. It still presents a danger, *sidi.* The Eyes will see. Do not neglect it."

"I will, *sidala.* Thank you again."

"Of course."

And finally, the Seer turned to the Shogun-General.

"There is an old proverb, Captain, in the Book of Truths. 'It is easier for a khamel to go through the eye of a needle than a proud man to enter the gates of NirVannah'."

Kirin sighed. "At the rate I'm going, *sidi,* I may never reach the gates of NirVannah."

"Well, we do need you alive a little longer."

"I will do my best."

"I would expect nothing less."

Kirin shook his head, glanced at the snow leopard, her steel still bare, hair wild in the cold morning breeze.

"Major, this is not a mission of blood. You need to remember that."

"Sir."

"Can you carry out this mission without the shedding of it? I trust you can, and more than that, I trust you *will.*"

"Sir."

"You will listen to Kerris for here, he is not Kerris but Kaidan, Ambassador of the Upper Kingdom. You will listen to Bo Fujihara and Fallon Waterford-Grey and to your husband and you will use your skills to serve the Empire, not your desire for retribution or revenge. I believe we will see more of that than either of us have ever needed or wanted. Is this something you can do, Major? Are you willing to lay down your glass, even as I struggle to lay down mine? Can you take this journey through the eye of the needle?"

Her lip curled.

"I will try, sir."

"Well then..." He looked up at benAramis, his gaze defiant. "That is all anyone can ask."

"Belen," said the dog, standing at the ready.

Kirin nodded and turned to the Alchemist. She smiled and he could not remember a time when she had looked more beautiful. His heart twisted in his chest.

He looked down. There was a dagger sticking out of the snow.

"Ah, there it is," said the Seer and he reached down, tugged it from the drift. "I must have dropped it last night."

He slipped it into one of the folds in his leather robe.

Major Ursa Laenskaya said nothing.

"Hopefully, we will meet you by sunset," said the Shogun-General. "If not sooner."

He bowed to them all, fist to cupped palm before turning and heading for his horse, the Alchemist and the dog at his heels.

***

The Temple of Eyes was empty, save for two candles, the skull of a yak and a circle of rusted metal in the center of the room.

The Bear swung around, grabbing the throat of the villager and lifting him high into the air.

"Where is the Oracle?" he growled. *"Where is the Oracle?"*

"The circle," gasped the man, his feet swinging above the floor. "A gift from the Ancestors. Stand on the circle, Lord. Stand on the circle."

"What is your name?"

"Tsakhiagiin Yisu, Lord."

Long-Swift and the Bear exchanged glances before the Khargan swung the villager around, releasing his grip.

"*You* stand on the circle, Yisu."

Long-Swift could almost hear the man's teeth chattering as he stepped first one boot, then the second onto the rusted metal plate. Immediately, a railing began to rise from the floor and both Khan and Irh-Khan stepped back. Yisu wrapped his hands around the railing and the temple was filled with an unnatural hum. There was a jerk, then a start and suddenly, both circle and villager began to descend through the floor into darkness.

Long-Swift swallowed, peered down through the hole. There was candlelight and the odor that wafted up was an assault on his nose. The Bear growled where he stood.

They waited for several long minutes until sounds began to echo up from the depths, along with the rising of the circle. Sounds of bootfall, frantic and fast. Sounds of mountains moving underground, sounds of snakes slithering and slapping, and voices. Three voices, one sharp as a crow, one low as thunder, one whose pleas grew progressively louder until they became a scream, silenced as the metal circle slid back into place.

The Bear turned to the three behind him.

"Give us the count of one thousand. Then follow."

The men nodded as their leader reached over his shoulder, drew *ala'Asalan* from his back and stepped onto the circle. Pulling his curved sword, Long-Swift did the same and stood back to back, weapons at the ready. Together, they began their descent into darkness.

For several long moments, the platform shook and groaned until finally came to a lurching end. They remained on the circle for several moments while their eyes adjusted to the darkness. The air assaulted them. It was old and smelled of blood and excrement and oil. The room was vast—one chamber opening onto another in the distance and moss grew down the walls in black slicks. There were flames dancing in trenches along the floor and cables swinging from the ceiling and the Irh-Khan could tell in an instant that this was no natural place. It was a cave of the Ancestors.

There were eyes everywhere. Old, decayed and shriveled, eyes lined the oily floor. Eyes sat in nooks in the pocked walls, sat on urns, sat on rocks. Eyes dangled from the cables, attached by the veins and tendons and hooks. Symbols of eyes were carved into the stone of the walls, the floors, the posts and beams of this crumbling Ancient cavern. It was almost impossible to walk without having to step over them.

Long-Swift shuddered. This was a nightmare.

To their left, there was a shape moaning on the ground. It was Yisu, curled up on himself in the shadows. Long-Swift crossed carefully to where the villager lay, writhing on the floor. He rolled him over with the toe of his boot and immediately, Yisu's hands sprang up to cover what was left of his face. It was a caricature of horror, mouth frozen wide, tongue stiffly protruding to one side. Breath was coming in short, shallow gasps and there were bloody holes where his eyes had been.

Long-Swift swung his sword downward, pressed the tip onto Yisu's chest.

"You should never bed a girl without her father's consent," he said. "Not even your eyes will absolve you of that."

And he drove the razor-sharp point down, ending the man's flailings.

"I see you," hissed a voice inside his head and he swung around, gripping the sword with both hands. There was no one but the Bear.

"I am Khan Baitsuhkhan," called the Bear into the darkness. "First Khan of All Khans, Son of the White Wolf, Father of the Jackal. Ruler of all Peoples of the Earth. You may call me Bear."

"Bear cub," hissed the voice inside their heads. *"Rat-ling."*

"I am here for an Oracle, if one exists in this pathetic excuse for a hovel." The Khargan turned in a slow circle, his Lion Killer gleaming deadly in the oil light. "Show yourself, Little Needle."

"Little Needle..."

Laughter now like the rumble of distant thunder and they could see a shape rise in the darkness. Long-Swift swallowed as a creature twice the size of the Bear began to move. From another corner he saw a second shape, this one small and distorted and shining in the oil light. It dragged itself toward the bigger, the palms echoing as they slapped along the floor. It reached the mountain shape and began to climb, heaving its skeletal body up and up, before sliding under the skin of the massive shoulders, home. The mountain turned and trudged toward a pit made of bones. Slowly, he waved a large hand and fire erupted in the hearth.

Long-Swift and the Khargan exchanged glances before moving cautiously around the fire. They were astounded at what they saw.

It was the biggest dog Long-Swift had ever seen. Easily the size of two Khargans, with pelt the colour of ink and arms the size of men's torsos. His ears were cropped to tiny points, his muzzle blunt with many layers of folding, swinging jowls and his long rotting tail dragged on the floor as he moved. He wore little clothing and watched the fire with one small, drooping eye.

Over his right shoulder, the hideous pale face of a hairless dog whispered in his ear. It also had only one eye, large and bulbous, and an appalling lack of teeth. The lower half of its body was gone, sewn into the back of his companion.

The Eye of the Needle and the Eye of the Storm. Two oracles. One body.

Long-Swift glanced at the Khargan. There was no way even a man like the Bear could stand against such a mountain.

"We know why you are here," came the voices together, almost as one. The Storm was a half-beat behind the Needle and it created a disparate, echoing effect as they spoke.

"Why are we here?" asked the Khargan.

"You fear the Khanmaker and his Army of Blood."

"I fear no one, Needle and Storm. Not even you."

"You need Magic. We have Magic."

"You will serve your Khan with all your skill. It is your duty."

"We have no duty, only pleasure and pain. How will you pay us?"

"You have already been given two eyes," growled the Khan. "I will give you none of mine. I do not need you that much."

"You need us more." The hairless dog shifted in its cradle of flesh, held out his bony hand. Two eyes swung from his fingers by a measure of tendon and vein.

"We will accept these, then, as down payment on your debt. Two prophecies for the Khan of Khans of Ulaan Baator, Son of the White Wolf, Father of the Jackal. Ruler of all Peoples of the Earth." It cackled like a crow. *"Muunokhoi Gansorigar of Gobay."*

The Bear's birth name, known only by Long-Swift and the Bear himself.

With a flick of a bony wrist, one eyeball was tossed into the fire. The flames hissed and the Eye of the Needle began to convulse.

"The fall of Ulaan Baator," he moaned and the Storm swayed slowly with him. *"The fall of Ulaan Baator at the steel of Ulaan Baator.*

The girl has seen it. The eyes have seen it. The head of the Head of Ulaan Baator falling at the feet of Ulaan Baator on the Deer Stones of Tevd."

The cavern echoed with the groan and hiss and then silence for a very long time. Finally, the creature called the Needle wheezed and pushed the second eye into its empty socket. It squealed and howled, the Storm a heartbeat behind.

"And you, Swift Sumalbayar, son of Swift Sumalnagar, also of Gobay. What would you give to see your Khan victorious?"

"My life, Oracle," said Long-Swift. "But not my eyes."

"Swift as swift, but one is swifter. Singer of Songs caught by the Lover of the Lover of Lions. On the Field of One Hundred Stones, a Khan rises, a Khan falls and an Abomination sleeps in the gar of the Khanil! It is Abomination! Aaaaah!!!"

The Eye of the Needle shrieked, clapped a hand over the new eye and slowly, as if in a trance, the Eye of the Storm did likewise.

"No eyes, the Magic will betray us all. Ancestors and bones rise from the ashes. A trio of dragons race through the skies. The world ends in ash and flame at the feet of Ulaan Baator and Blasphemy will rule the day. The Khanmaker and the Magic and the Army of Blood! The girl has seen it. The eyes have seen it. The Kingdoms of the World will fall on the Deer Stones of Tevd."

It was several long moments before the Oracle grew still and took a deep breath, and then another. It sounded like the breaking of ice. It sounded like an avalanche.

The Needle pulled the second eye from its socket. This too was tossed into the flames to the smell of burnt hair.

"We accept," they said as they raised their ghastly faces to the Khan. Black tears were running down the cheeks of the Needle. *"We will help the Khan of Khans defeat the Magic of the Enemy. For a very small price."*

"And what would that be?" asked the Khan.

"The eyes," they said. *"Of the Khanmaker."*

SHAR MA'UUL

There was a small crowd gathering around the screens as all the duty staff of the lab had gathered to see. Even a few from the Compound and Medicore had shown up, although the fetus wasn't due to be harvested for days yet. They were waiting on Persis Sengupta, the linguist, to decide whether the writing was in fact, a form of Chinese or merely the anxious scratchings of a terrified animal. Stranger things had happened in forty-five years since they had been awake.

The animal herself had finished her writing and was sitting cross-legged on the floor. She had dumped all the pink jellied food pellets in order to use the tray and had placed them all back after sniffing each one and making a face. Her mouth was moving now, eyes closed, and it seemed she was singing to herself. The small crowd was enthralled and for some reason, Dell felt a wave of relief. If the staff liked this new addition, it might mean better treatment for her, perhaps a reprieve from display in the Compound. Animals never did well when they were on display.

"May I see?" came a voice and the staff parted as a tall elegant woman came through the lab. Persis Sengupta paused to study the screens and she smiled at Dell. He could not bring himself to smile back. She was so very elegant and he was only a junior keeper.

"Is there a way for me to speak into that cell?"

"Yuh," said 6 and everyone in the lab held their breath as he raised

the volume.

The sweet sounds of singing floated up from the screens and now Dell allowed himself to smile. Only birds sang so sweetly, birds and human sopranos, and this animal was no bird.

"Zǎo ān," *said the linguist into the speaker and the animal looked all around.*

"Hello?" she said. "Zǎo ān! Ni shi shui?"

"This changes everything," the linguist said softly and Dell nodded. "Wǒ de míngzì shì bǎo sheng. Nǐ jiào shénme míngzì?"

"Wǒ de míngzì shì *Fallon Waterford-Grey,* Huánghòu fǎyuàn xuézhě."

"Empress?" Persis shook her head. "I must be translating wrong..."

The animal rose to her feet, stared up toward the speaker in the ceiling.

"Wǒ yǒu wǒ de yīfú?"

"She wants her clothes..."

"Wǒ de zhàngfū?"

"Her husband..."

"Hé yī dà bēi de chá?"

"And a big cup of tea." Persis Sengupta turned to look at 6. "I need to speak to someone in security. This is not an animal. It is a weapon of war."

***

The jaguar slid off his horse to stare at the most unnatural sunrise he had ever seen.

He had traveled all night in the darkness and with very little moonlight, he had trusted only the goodwill of his horse to keep from falling. They were very high up and normally, his heart would be in his throat but for some reason, he felt nothing at all. Even the thought of plummeting to his death down the mountainside wasn't so bad. He had fallen before and survived. Perhaps a fall from these peaks would do the trick. There would certainly be no Alchemists or physicians to pick up the pieces of his shattered life. No one to stitch him together or bind his broken bones or feed him broth through a waterlily reed.

He sighed and looked out over the gorge, eastward where the strange sun was rising. The sky was yellow, as yellow as his mother's eyes and the sun hung like a brilliant white lantern suspended from a golden ceiling. Behind him, the Great Mountains shone purple—mighty and regal and very, very cruel but here, as the Lower Kingdom lay before him, he was surprised to see it flatten into hills and valleys and rocky plains. It didn't seem possible but there it was, almost friendly and certainly easier for horses. The gateway to the Lower Kingdom lay across this one last gorge.

There was another bridge.

Wide, flat and Ancestral, it spanned the gorge on iron legs and he wondered how long it had been there. It looked much safer than the rope bridge across the *Shi'pal* but then again, he could see places where the railings had rusted through and others where the square grey stone had crumbled away. He didn't care. It could fall out from under him and he would be dead from either the fall or the vast crushing weight of the stones on top of him. But his horse would die too and that would be a loss. It was a good horse.

He could hear the owl swooping from above and he reached out a hand, catching a chiwa that dropped from the sky.

"Thank you," he called and the owl arced a wing and soared over the gorge and for the first time in his life, Yahn Nevye wondered what it would be like to be a bird.

He turned to the horse.

"Do you want this? I don't like chiwa. It's too stringy."

The horse snatched the rodent out of his hand, tossed its head several times to break the bones, and dropped it to the ground. Holding it down with a hoof, it began to tear the furry body with its fangs.

Nevye sighed again and looked back over the strange yellow plateau of the Lower Kingdom.

"Shar."

"Yes," he said to the horse. "Yes, that's right. That's the word for yellow. Shar."

"I find you, Shar."

Now, his heart did leap into his throat and slowly, he turned to see the Oracle appear from the trail behind him. Everything he had ever believed in the world was changed in that instant.

He caught her as she ran into his arms.

***

They left the village of Lon'Gaar before the sun's brooms had swept the sky but it was easy to follow the trail. While the night's snowfall had covered Nevye's tracks, it recorded the Oracle's perfectly and Kirin was hopeful they would meet up before long. The girl was at most three hours ahead of them, the jaguar perhaps six. Kirin shook his head. Her brother, Naranbataar, was on foot once again, still refusing a horse even after one was offered. He seemed tireless and Kirin wondered if it was the stamina of dogs that made them such fearsome enemies. But they were brutal as well and he vowed that, no matter what he had promised the Seer, he would never forget that simple fact.

The morning grew bright very quickly, the sky as clear as a summer's day in *Pol'Lhasa* and the sun was warm on their backs as they followed the mountainside north. In fact, Kirin was surprised at the sunshine. He wondered how high they were, higher likely even than *Sha'Hadin* or the Inn at the Roof of the World. The air was thin and it required many breaths to fill his chest, and he wondered if that was why dogs had longer noses, to breathe more air.

The terrain was far less harsh than he had expected. It seemed the mountains were flattening, as if their Good Mother were stretching her arms thin over this land. Peaks of purple could be seen in the distance but for the most part, the land was gray and gold and rolling. Sandstone, he knew and he wondered if the dogs mined these mountains for ore. He couldn't imagine it, not dogs and not with these roads. They were little more than goat paths for it was well known that in the Lower Kingdom, there were no true cities, only tribal villages, trading posts and Ancestral ruins. Nothing that could be truly called civilization, not like the Upper or Eastern Kingdoms. *Indeed,* thought Kirin to himself, he wondered if there was little more than wilderness, shale and snow.

He shook his head, knowing it was his pride talking. The road through the eye of the needle would be a long one for him.

The Alchemist was riding at his side and he tried not to look at her. It would be his undoing. She still held a power over him and he would be hard pressed to resist. He prayed they would return to the Army before nightfall. He still had Ling's letter tucked in under the yori. He hadn't read it yet and he wondered why that was.

Sherah looked over at him as if reading his thoughts and smiled.

"Thank you for letting me accompany you," she said.

"I needed a translator. Nothing more."

"Of course."

Naranbataar had paused on an outcropping of rock and Kirin watched him as he breathed the thin air, sifting the scents. They reined their horses in to wait. Finally, he left the rock and joined them. Travelling freely alongside, young aSiffh tossed his head and snapped. The dog laid his ears back but Sherah said something to him and he grunted. Kirin thought it sounded like a laugh.

He shook his head again. *Easier for a khamel*, the Seer had said. He would never understand his life.

"Ask him if all of his land is like this?"

"Like this?" said Sherah.

"Yes. Flat, hilly, rocky." He swept his hand toward the terrain before them. "Bleak."

She spoke and the dog answered.

"Vast," she corrected. "And wide. He says much room for people and many yaks. He calls it the Plateau of Tevd. The Cradle of the Moon."

"Plateau of Tved," he repeated, rolling the words on his tongue as if they might find a home somewhere.

"Tevd," said the dog. It sounded natural, earthy. "Holy Place. Cold."

Kirin studied him, the Imperial words sounding as odd on a canine tongue as canine words did on his.

"We call it Shibeth," said Sherah.

"Shibeth?" he frowned. "This is Shibeth?"

"Of course."

He couldn't believe they were in Shibeth. He had never been to Shibeth. It was taboo, forbidden, lost to them. It was an Ancient province, indeed a holy one. The Ancestors had divided the three Kingdoms from Shibeth according to history, given its capital, *Lha'Lhasa*, to the cats. Many dynasties of war with the dogs and treaties with the *Chi'Chen* had cost them most of Shibeth including *Lha'Lhasa.* It was still a matter of bitter political debate but cats are, after all, a political people.

"No war *Chanyu,"* said Naranbataar.

"Chanyu?"

"It is their word for their people," said Sherah. "People of the Wolf."

"Tell him this is not a mission of war, *sidala.* But we will fight if we must."

"He knows this," she said. "But still."

The dog—Kirin found it hard to think of him by his name—began to speak to the Alchemist and by the tone of his voice, he was angry.

"What is he saying?"

"He is worried for his sister," she said. "He fears she is being led down dangerous roads by Shar Ma'uul."

"Nevye," Kirin growled. That was one sentiment he shared with the dog. Perhaps the dog would throw the jaguar over a cliff, sparing Kirin the trouble. Perhaps he would shoot him with an arrow. He chased the thought from his mind.

"Asalan kill Shar Ma'uul?"

"Asalan?"

The Alchemist smiled, her golden eyes gleaming.

"Lion."

Kirin grunted now.

"Asalan kill Shar Ma'uul." The dog grinned wickedly. "Naranbataar *bayartai."*

Somehow, Kirin didn't need a translation for that.

Together, the three of them turned back onto the road to Tevd.

***

"So you not see this?" she asked and he shook his head.

"No," he said. "No, I don't see many things."

"You are not Oracle."

He looked up at her. She was so very young.

"I am nothing," he said. "I was a soldier, but now, I am really nothing at all. Or maybe…"

He shrugged, looked down at the ground. It was stone, earth and some snow. "Maybe I'm a little bit of everything. I don't know."

"I think that is best way."

He smiled to himself. Her accent was adorable.

"Tell me story of Shar," she said and she knelt beside him in the learning pose, open and trusting like a child. "Come please. Tell me."

"It's not very interesting."

"I am judge, Shar."

They were alone, sitting high above the bridge with only mountains and pines, a horse and an owl for company. Hunts in Silence sat on an outcropping of rock, watching them with huge yellow eyes.

"Stand up," he said. "Back against that rock."

Eagerly, she did and he grabbed a stone, drew a very tight half-circle around her feet in the snow.

"Don't move now," he said, looking up at her. "You are standing on a ledge over a very steep drop and if you move, you will fall. Do you understand?"

She clapped her hands and laughed and he realized that she was very beautiful. He swallowed and took her hand, pulling her back to the ground. "Now you may sit, but don't move from this ledge. Your legs may dangle over but don't move your body. Do you understand still?"

She nodded, lowered her body to the ground. She was lithe and graceful. A dancer.

He sat back on his haunches.

"I used to be a soldier," he said. "From the beginning of my life, I was a soldier. I ran the fastest in my entire village. I shot the farthest arrows. I could throw a dagger through the heart of a bushbuk from across a clearing. I was the very best soldier in all of *Keralah.* That's a very big province in *Hindaya* and because I was the best, I was promoted very quickly to the Governor's personal guard."

"Impressive," she said and her tail moved from side to side in the snow. He thought it odd. His tail would lash when angry or irritated, hers when happy. They were so very different.

"Since I was the best soldier but still a very young soldier, they made me the personal guard over Tilka Ragnar-Poole, the Governor's only son."

"Oh, very good!"

"No, very bad. Tilka was very bad. He was a horrible boy. Brought much dishonour on his house to his father's shame. But still, it was an important position and I did it very well."

"I know you did."

"When I was in my sixteenth summer, the Governor chose to make a tour of all the cities and landmarks of *Keralah,* and I was chosen to go along. To protect Tilka, naturally. To make sure he stayed out of trouble."

"Naturally."

Now he adjusted position so that he was sitting cross-legged on the ground.

"There is this amazing place in *Keralah* called *Edukkalah* in the Nambukuthri Mountains. It takes an entire day to climb up, up, up but once up, there is a cave, and you squeeze inside and then go down, down, down into the very heart of the earth. It's called the Mouth of God. It is a very holy place, but cats are, after all, a very holy people."

"Dogs not holy," she said.

"Well, some cats are not very holy either. The Governor and his party were having a tour of the cavern when my dear little Tilka slips through a crack in the wall and is gone! I follow him but before I can catch him, he is outside on the very top of the rock! It is so very high up and you can see the entire province from up there!"

"Like your Wall."

He tried to smile. "Yes, like our Wall. But strange. Round. The rock is so smooth that it's almost a dome. Two sides are sheer and smooth, and the others are very craggy. Of course, Tilka is balanced on the very smooth side. So, I move carefully to where he is. I can tell he doesn't want me there and he screams very loudly. He tells me to go away, that I never let him have any fun, that he wishes I were dead and that he will kill me when he gets the chance. And then he falls."

"Falls?" She sat forward.

"Yes. He is wearing silk slippers and they have no grip. He slides down the dome toward the cliff face. There are roots and scraggly bushes and I can see him trying to grab them but he is an awkward boy and dresses inappropriately and he keeps on sliding. I run after him, throw myself on the rock just as he is about to go over the edge and I catch him but barely. We both go over but I have a hold of a dry root that is somehow growing out of the rock and we swing there for a moment and I am very grateful to the god from whose mouth we are hanging, until the root begins to pull out of the rock and we begin to fall. And we do fall, but not terribly far, because I am strong and there is a ledge."

She gasped, looked down. "This big?"

"Just that big. No bigger. I bounce off it first on the way down but then my hand catches hold and we swing a little bit more—"

"You have bad boy still?"

Her expression was so eager. He had forgotten what it was like to be in the company of a woman, even one so strange. He looked down again.

"Yes. So one hand on the bad boy, one hand on the ledge. I manage to pull myself and then him up to sitting but it is so narrow there is room for only one and he must sit on my lap. He hates this and he is kicking and scratching and hitting me to try to push me off and I am forced to use a soldier hold on him to make him stop."

"I would let him go," she said quietly.

"Believe me, that thought crossed my mind. But I was a soldier and he was my charge and I couldn't. Not honourably. I would die before I let him die."

She nodded.

"I called and called but there was no one to hear. Everyone was deep inside the Mouth of God. We were very high up and the sun was hot – it gets very hot in *Keralah* so I knew we couldn't stay on that ledge for long. So I made him hold on to my back and I began to climb."

"Climb up smooth round rock?"

"Exactly. It was difficult and we slid back many times. He was holding on with his claws and I could feel the blood running inside my uniform making everything sticky but I needed to keep going. The roots and bushes were not very helpful. I would grab them and they would hold for a moment then let loose and we would slide back yet again. It was sunset when I heard them calling. We were almost at the top and Tilka started to scream."

He paused, stared at the ground. Silence blinked one eye.

"He began to climb up my back using his claws. He had kicked off his slippers and was using his feet and my uniform was almost gone from his tearing, but he is screaming and climbing and I was desperately trying to get to the top and suddenly we are there! I get one hand and then the other and he scrambles up and over my head onto the round top of *Edukkalah...* "

He took a deep breath.

"Then, he found a large rock, picked it up in his hands and began to strike my fingers. One by one, Tilka struck my fingers until they were all broken and I could not hold any longer and I fell."

She was silent.

"I fell for a very long time. It seemed like years. I was falling and falling and falling and as I fell, I saw owls and dragons and Empires and you."

He looked up now and smiled. It was not a pleasant smile and he quickly looked away. "And then I hit the ground. The physicians say I broke every bone in my body. I don't know. I don't remember. But I was not a very good soldier after that."

They sat like that for a long while before she leaned forward and kissed him on the cheek. He thought that there were tears in her eyes, but he couldn't be sure. She rose, pulled him to his feet and led him to the horse.

***

The feasting came to an abrupt end as Eye of the Needle and the Eye of the Storm lumbered into the village, dragging the carcass of Tsakhiagiin Yisu behind them. Their footfall was the sound of thunder and without exception, all who saw them stopped to stare. Soon, a path was opened through the Khargan's Ten Thousand to the heart of Jia'Khan where the feast fire was raging.

With a savage twist, the Eye of the Storm ripped one arm from the body of the dead villager the same way Long-Swift might tear the wing off a roasted quail. The rest he tossed into flames alongside yak, goat and boar, and the pelt sizzled with smoke. Holding the arm by the long bone, he dipped the hand into the flames until the flesh burned away and the tendons and fingers began to curl. One finger remained outstretched and the Storm stood for a long moment as if thinking, turned his body once, twice, three times before settling on his haunches like a mountain. He began to draw in the earth with the arm like a stick.

The Needle had been hidden under a tattered cloak and now, his hairless skull could be seen peering out beneath the hood. Long-Swift could see the wires, threads and pins that held the scrawny creature in its pocket of flesh and he shuddered. Of all the Oracles the Bear had tortured and killed, none had been as unnatural as these.

The Needle began to whisper into the Storm's ear.

"Tsgaan," they hissed in their syncopated voices, one like a crow, the other like thunder. *"Give us tsgaan ari..."*

The Bear reached out as the Ten Thousand pressed in, grabbed a horn from the closest soldier. He passed it to the Storm, who turned it and emptied the contents into his gaping mouth. Wotchka spilled over his lips and down his jowls and the Needle crawled over his shoulder to lap at the overflow. When finished, the Needle snatched the horn and disappeared under the fold of skin. The Storm continued to draw with the fingerstick, seemingly undmindful of the creature in his back and Long-Swift wondered how life could have conspired to create something as dark and disturbing as these.

Soon, the Needle reappeared, holding eyes in his bony fingers. Five eyeballs still attached to tendons, and one by one he dropped them onto the ground. The Storm began moving the orbs with the fingerstick, one north, one south, one west and two east.

"The Magic," rumbled the Eyes. *"Five souls serve the Khanmaker with power."*

"The Khanmaker?" asked the Bear.

"Kuren Ulaan Baator. Khanmaker, Khan ***Un****-maker. Lion Lord of the Army of Blood."*

There was a murmur in the ranks and Long-Swift snarled at them all. They could not fear lions. Not now.

"We can break the Magic," the Eyes hissed and groaned. *"We break the Magic and we break the Blood. One by one, we break them all."*

And with the tip of the finger of the stick of bone, the Storm pushed at one of the eyes. He poked it until it swelled and burst, spilling jelly onto the rocks. He lifted it with the fingerstick and dropped it into the fire. The soldiers murmured anew and this time, the Irh-Khan did not stop them.

He approached the Khargan, leaned into his ear.

"Lord," he said quietly, not wishing the men to hear. "There is a saying."

The Bear arched a brow.

"Choniin amnaas garaad, bariin amand orokh," he said. "From the fangs of a wolf into the jaws of a tiger."

"And your meaning?"

"This is Necromancy, Lord. Dark magic. It is dangerous to use dark magic to fight a war."

"There is also a saying, Long-Swift. '*Be* fire, *with* fire.'"

"This is no way to win a war."

"I use any way to win a war, Long-Swift. Perhaps that is why I am Khan and you are not."

And he turned back to the feast fire and the Oracle of Jia'Khan.

Long-Swift tightened his jaw. His plan to distract the Khargan had failed and worse, he had the sinking feeling that he would be the one falling into the jaws of the tiger.

***

"You *see* them, Shar?"

"Yes, I see them."

"They will try kill you."

"Just because I'm a cat?"

"Especially because."

Yahn Nevye released a breath, steadied his breathing, fixed his eyes on the end of the bridge. Remnants of the Legion were waiting in ambush, along with the rest of the village of Lon'Gaar. Their heartbeats were loud, their thoughts all but deafening, but with Setse's arms wrapped around his waist, he feared nothing. In fact with her, he felt strong, something he hadn't felt in a very long time.

The horse had carried them both easily, for the Oracle weighed less than a chiwa. They had first felt the Legion as they navigated the winding road down to the bridge and Silence had confirmed it as he swept over the rocks. It was a new thing for him to be seeing through the eyes of a bird and he understood why it was so important for the Seers of *Sha'Hadin.* Now, as they approached the wide expanse of the bridge and he counted their numbers—nineteen Legion soldiers and more than forty villagers—it occurred to him that they might need a plan.

He turned his head in the saddle. "Do you think we can make a Shield? You and I?"

"We try. If not, we fight."

"I don't fight. I can't. Not any more."

"You fight last night. You beat bad cat."

"That was the Seer, the one with the eyes like a dog. He was moving my hands and my feet." He shook his head. "It wasn't me."

"No, not Sakal. *Shar.*"

"Sakal?"

She grinned, touched her chin. "Sakal."

He laughed softly. He felt so light in her company, as if the word 'despair' had never existed in his lifetime.

"Make horse run," she said. "Dogs fear horses."

"Yes, that's a good plan. A Shield and a running horse." He looked at the far end of the bridge, blew out a long deep cleansing breath. "Blue Wolf, Yellow Cat."

She smiled, leaned her head on his back and closed her eyes, turning her mind to the formation of the Shield.

"Blue Wolf, Yellow Cat," he repeated. "Blue Wolf, Yellow Cat."

He drove his heels into the horse's side and they leapt onto the bridge.

They were halfway across when they heard the whistling. The wind on the bridge was strong and rushing in his face, making his eyes sting. The horse increased its speed and the hard stone rattled with the sound of hoofs. He could see the arrows like a swarm of bees closing in and he clenched his eyes tightly, not wanting to know whether or not the Shield would hold. He could feel the power from her tiny body, joined it with his own, pushing the air out in front of them, making it grow hard like steel. He heard the crackling as the wave of arrows shattered against it, felt the Shield advance and the arrows ricochet in all directions, felt the Legion fear and turn and run.

Sudden, unexpected and cold like a dagger, a thought pierced the sight, echoing through his mind. He felt Setse scream even before he heard it, felt her head snap back and her arms fall away and he knew that she was falling, falling backwards and he twisted in the saddle, managing to snag her reindeer cloak as she collapsed from the back of the horse. The movement cost him his balance and he went with her, hitting the stone hard and tumbling, rolling and skidding toward the rail-less edge of the bridge. He lost his grip on her for a heartbeat, watched in horror as her body slid to the edge before slowly, ever so slowly, tipping over the side.

He lunged, catching the cloak and almost pulling his arm from its socket. He prayed she didn't snap her neck but he held even as her weight dragged him to the very edge of the bridge.

His claws ached and he flattened his body, peering over the side and knowing it was a mistake. The wind howled as she swung by the cloak high above the gorge. Mountains rose up on either side, steep and fierce, a last reminder of their Good Mother. Far far below, a valley of rocks, snow and shale, almost black in the shadows of the cliffs. Small scrub cedars, twisted pines, brokenness and pain and death. He knew these things well.

Eye of the Needle, Eye of the Storm.

There was a mind, a dagger-mind, tearing her apart, crushing her soul to death and he pleaded with it to spare her and crush him instead.

Above the wind, he heard the whistling arrows, heard the squeal of the horse as they thudded into its body, realized that with Setse's fall, they had dropped the Shield and the horse was paying the cost. His heart broke for in that instant he realized that he had never, unlike the Major or the Seer, named his horse.

Spare her, he prayed to the Eyes. *Crush me.*

He swung his other hand to grip the reindeer cloak, forced his claws through the thick leather, began to drag her – hand over fist – up to the edge of the bridge. The uneven weight of her pulled him closer and he braced with his feet, cursing the split-toed sandals that were standard fare for brothers in *Sha'Hadin* and he willed his claws to push through for grip.

There was a snarl from his left. He could feel their thoughts, knew an arrow was being leveled at his head. He didn't care. If this girl, this Oracle, this little slip of a dog, died, he would as well. He knew that in his bones and so he hung on as more and more arrows were being leveled at his head.

"Guij baina!" he said, not knowing their tongue but speaking anyway. "*Tuslaarai Jalair Naranseteg!"*

Hand over fist, he continued to pull until he could see her over the stone of the bridge, but he could also see the clasp that held the cloak begin to twist and pull.

"*Guij baina, ahtai!"* he pleaded.

"Jalair Naranseteg?" he heard a voice growl. *"Be Karan Uurt?"*

Suddenly, there was shouting, shoving and several stub-clawed hands reached over the edge, grabbing hold of the cloak, her arms and finally dragging the unmoving form of Jalair Naransetseg onto Ancestral stone.

The dagger-mind moved, releasing her from its iron grip. He felt the weight of it fall across him like a stone.

Many dogs grabbed him, pulled him to his feet and off the bridge but they brought the Oracle as well and for that he was grateful. She had been spared. He would be crushed. It was a good bargain.

He didn't fight as they beat him into the snow.

***

A wail went up from behind him and Kirin turned to see the Alchemist, doubled over in her saddle. They were very high up in the mountains, still following the Oracle's trail and the dog was far in the front. Kirin reined Shenan back.

"Sidala?"

She was breathing heavily, one arm around her waist, one hand at her forehead.

"*Sidala,* can I help?"

"An attack, *sidi.*" She looked up at him, golden eyes wide. "Of the mind."

"On you?"

"On all of us. The Khargan is using a Necromancer."

Kirin shuddered at the thought. Darkest of the dark. He was certain Sherah al Shiva knew this well.

She turned her eyes to the dog ahead of them on the road.

"But Setse has fallen."

"The Oracle?" Kirin frowned. "Are you certain?"

"I am not a Seer, *sidi.* But I felt this as surely as I felt the birth of our baby."

"And the others? benAramis, Yahn Nevye, my brother?"

"I cannot see, *sidi.* My soul reels still."

He sighed, cast his eyes out over the mountains, the glimpses of *Tevd* between the peaks. There appeared to be a gorge separating them and he wondered if there was a bridge somewhere. This would be futile without a bridge.

The dog had paused on the road, turned back to watch them and wait.

He spurred his horse toward the gorge.

***

"Well well," said the Seer out loud. "They've made a Shield."

"Oh? What?" Fallon looked over at him from the back of her painted horse. She was riding without reins, holding the baby in her arms. "Who's made a Shield?"

"Yahn Nevye and Setse. Do you feel that, Grey Coat?"

Kerris and Quiz were in the lead and he turned only his head. "Nope, don't feel a thing. I'm not a Seer, remember? My problems are entirely more pleasant."

"Don't mind him," Fallon grinned. "He's just being a kitten. Speaking of kittens..."

And she buried her face into the baby's belly, made happy mommy noises and Kylan cooed with delight.

Next to them, Ursa scowled and lashed her tail.

Bo Fujihara laughed at them all and put his pipe between his teeth.

Like an ocean of dragons, the Army of Blood was spread out behind them, growing narrower and tighter as the road rose one last time into the mountains. The falcon had returned with the promise of a flatter land, a vast plateau of high hills and yellow rocks. They would make better time with such a land.

Sireth sighed, sat deep in the saddle.

"I wonder why they've made a Shield?"

"Well, think about it," said Fallon, her attention completely focused on the baby. "Why do *we* make the Shield?"

"For dogs, stupid girl," snorted the Major. "To stop their arrows."

"So that's probably what they're doing then—*Oh.*" Fallon clutched the baby to her chest as she realized what she was saying. "Oh mother..."

"Oh mother, indeed," said Bo. "They must be close to the Legion."

And the Last Seer of *Sha'Hadin* closed his eyes.

"This is useless," growled the Major. "We should take the entire Army and run straight down their throats.

"In these mountains?" said Bo. "Once this army begins a charge, there is no stopping it. We would kill more horses than dogs with that tactic.

Her marbled tail lashed once again.

"There is a bridge," muttered Sireth, eyes closed. "They are together and there is a Legion and they are on a bridge—*Aiya!*"

He hissed and doubled-over in the saddle.

"What?" and the snow leopard reached across horses to push his thigh. "What is it? Is the jaguar dead? Is the dog?"

"Kerris," called Fallon.

"An attack," growled Sireth through clenched teeth. "A very powerful mind…"

"Yahn Nevye?" asked Fallon.

"The Alchemist?" growled Ursa.

"A monster…"

"Fight back," said Ursa. "You are steel. Kill it."

"I can't…It is Necromancy. Dark, dark magic." He raised his head, eyes still closed. "Grey Coat, come here."

"What?" said Kerris. "Me?"

"Over here, idiot," snarled the Major.

Kerris eased back on the little mountain pony and soon was beside Dune the red desert horse and the mongrel on his back.

"The Khan of Khans," said Sireth. "On the plains of *Shibeth*, ten thousand gathered and dark, dark magic…"

"Lovely," said Kerris.

"Move the earth."

"What?"

"Move the earth under the Khan of Khans, under the dark magic."

"I…"

"Do it!" snapped the Major.

"I don't know how!" snapped the lion.

And with eyes still closed, the Seer reached out a hand across the horses to grab a grey wrist. Kerris yelped and Quiz bucked beneath him.

"Move…the earth…"

Their horses stopped as the Seer slid from his, pulled the lion from the pony's back. Fallon, Ursa and Bo halted as well, creating a protective wall with their mounts as Bo waved the Army of Blood around them. The Seer slipped his hands into Kerris' hair as if crushing his head with his palms and together they sank to their knees.

Fujihara pulled the pipe out from between his teeth and stared.

"Amnishakra," grunted Ursa to the *Chi'Chen* ambassador. "He is a powerful man."

"Move the earth," benAramis repeated. "Move it."

Clutching the baby, Fallon swung off her horse to hover over her husband, watching with large emerald eyes as he grimaced and groaned.

"Do you see it? Do you feel it?"

"Yes..."

"Do you feel the monster on top of the earth? By the fire?"

"It's like the bear," and he shuddered, eyes clenched tight. "The hairless bear in the Compound, only bigger..."

"Sink into the earth beneath the monster, become one with the earth, become it."

Kerris moaned, growled, lashed his own grey tipped tail.

"Move the earth beneath the monster or the girl will die. Move it now."

"But that's so far away."

"Just feel it. Do you feel it?"

"I feel it."

"Then move it."

Kerris clenched his fists and a small stone shot up from beneath the snow and they all stepped back. Soon, more stones – pebbles and dust and sand and grit, like a grey-brown cloud leapt from the road and began to circle around his hands. Soon, the earth beneath their feet began to move.

***

The Eye of the Needle was shrieking in its skin pocket and the Storm released a breath that sounded like the rumble of thunder.

"The Magic falls like a star from the heavens," they said, the Storm still a half beat behind his hairless companion. *"One by one they fall to*

their deaths."

The rumble of thunder was growing louder.

"They have seen us, we are known to him. He will not look away unscathed."

The fire began to pop and spit as the rumble of thunder shook the ground beneath them all.

"Geomancer! Geomancer sharpens his claws on the Khan's Ten Thousand!"

Those closest began to back away from the feast fire but the Khargan rose to his feet.

"Hold your ground!" he commanded, his voice booming over the roaring of the earth.

"Lord," cried Long-Swift. "It is Geomancery. The Oracle is calling Dark Forces!"

"No coward will stand in the Ten Thousand of the Khan!" he shouted. "Hold your ground or die by my sword!"

The Oracles were wailing now and the ground was shaking when suddenly, in the center of the feast fire, the earth began to rise.

Even the Khargan staggered back now as rock and black earth heaved from the ground, followed by huge clouds of dust. Next, stones as large as men burst from the pit, flew high into the air before crashing like rain onto the army. But no one moved, even as those beside and before and behind them were crushed, even as the gars of Jia'Khan collapsed in on themselves and the poles cracked and splintered, the army held its ground. The Storm was thrown from his place by the fire, crushing two other men beneath his weight and even the Bear was sent to his knees.

The earth coughed rocks and spat stones and it seemed to last hours but finally, the rumbling faded until all that was left was the choking black dust, settling like mist to the ground and the shrieking of the Needle in his pocket of flesh.

Long-Swift rose to his feet, swept his eyes around at the devastation, the village of Jia'Khan flattened, the many dead beneath huge stones. He looked as the Bear peered into the pit where the feast fire had been and raised his hands to the sky.

In a sound as disturbing as the voice of the Oracles, the Khan of Khans began to laugh.

***

Sireth opened his eyes just in time to catch the grey lion before he hit the ground.

***

Abruptly, Setse came awake.

She was under a lean-to, a makeshift gar fashioned from fallen trees and blankets and an old woman stared at her as she rolled to her knees.

"Is that a blue eye, child?" asked the woman.

"Where is Shar Ma'uul?"

"Who?"

"The yellow cat."

The old woman spat pine tar into a snowdrift and turned her face outside the gar.

"Tell the lieutenant the girl's awake and she's an Oracle."

It was like a ripple on a lake how the word carried through the villagers of Lon'Gaar and Setse peered out from under the blanket to see people moving, fires burning, weapons being sharpened. Children darted close, hoping to catch a glimpse of the mysterious girl who rode horses with the Enemy and but they quickly disappeared once they caught her eye. Soon, there was the crunching of boots as men approached and Setse rose to her feet.

It was a troop of ten moving like an arrow and at the point was a slim man with shaved head, cropped ears and sharp features. He had a scar along his jaw, carried a curved dagger and he scowled at her.

"I am Temujiin Altan, Lieutenant and Alpha of the 110th Legion of Khan Baitsukhan."

"Jalair Naransetseg, Granddaughter of the Blue Wolf."

"The Oracle of Karan Uurt. We've been searching for you, little rabbit. You are a long way from home."

"Where is Shar Ma'uul?"

"We have skinned him. The tanner is making me a spotted coat."

The men snickered and the lieutenant stepped forward, running his eyes over her slight frame.

"I have commissioned spotted boots as well. My betas have cooked the rest. Would you like to taste him? Or have you already?"

The snickering grew and the men pressed into her from all sides. She raised her chin so that her blue eye caught the light.

"You lie to an Oracle?" She looked at all the faces of the men around her. "Shall I tell you how the wife and children of Temujiin Altan have died?"

"They are not dead," Altan growled.

"They are. Hacked to pieces in their beds or burned as they fled. Karan Uurt is no more, razed to the ground by the 2nd Legion of Khan Baitsukhan because of the failure of the 110th."

Murmurs were heard throughout the camp as even the villagers pressed in to hear.

"The Khanmaker is coming," she said. "The Khanmaker and the Army of Blood. Help me or I will tell you in detail how you and your men will die."

There was silence in the camp and he studied her for a moment.

"You are a clever girl. And dangerous."

"You are the one choosing to laugh in the face of an Oracle."

"Feline pelts are remarkable things, are they not?" And he moved in closer, his eyes roaming over her face, her lithe young body. "His back had rings on it, with a spot in the center of each. They made perfect bullseyes for my archers."

"Your wife died calling your name."

"So you say."

"It is true."

"Then…" He raised a hand to stroke her throat, ran his fingers down to her chest. "I suppose I need a new one."

"Fire!" came a shout from the camp.

"Riders!" came a shout from the bridge and the Legion snapped to attention, including Temujiin Altan. He looked away for only a heartbeat, when Setse drove the heel of her palm up and under his chin. He staggered and like a dancer, she dropped her head down and swung her leg behind her, high over her back to crack his forehead with her foot. She whirled, struck him again with her fist and he dropped into the snow.

"Just like monkeys," she said, grabbing his dagger and bolting into the crowd.

***

The fires in the camp had roared to life, catching on anything and everything that would catch. Blankets, cedars, scraps of clothing and the villagers of Lon'Gaar tried in vain to put them out, scooping handfuls of snow and hard earth over the flames. The bridge was clattering with the sound of hooves but the Legion had been out of position and now they scrambled for any sort of cover. The bridge itself could not be seen as a wall of flame rippled and danced at its mouth, making targeting impossible. Arrows loosed either caught fire before they flew or were snatched out of the sky by an owl and dropped back over the camp.

Three Imperial horses leapt through the wall of flame, running down and stomping any dog foolish enough or sluggish enough to stay in their path. They were followed by warriors moving so swiftly that they were difficult to see. A lion in armour the colour of blood, swinging the fabled double swords and lashing a tail that could take down trees. A woman wrapped in smoke and shadow, leaping and striking and leaving a trail of soldiers in her wake. And finally, a dog sending arrow after arrow into legs, shoulders, arms and feet, wounding many, killing none.

It was over in a very short time as villagers and soldiers were corralled in the heart of the camp, circled by walls of crackling fire. Children wailed and women moaned while tending the wounded. Outside, the horses snorted and pawed at the rocky ground and the dog perched high on a rock, arrows leveled, making sure no one would leave the protective circle of the flames.

Kirin stood, hands on hips, both Blood and Jade Fang sheathed at the moment and he surveyed the people inside the circle of flame.

"Who is your Alpha?" he asked. The Alchemist translated and many heads turned to a small, slim man with a scar on his chin. "What is your name, *sidi?"*

The man spit on the ground. Kirin ignored it.

"We are here on a mission of peace but we will kill all of you if you do not cooperate. Do you understand?"

Again, the Alchemist translated and again, the Alpha spat.

"Ancestors are rising in the west. We must present a united front against them or all our Kingdoms will fall."

Like an echo, Sherah translated every word and at the word for Ancestors, there was a murmur from the group.

The Alpha growled.

"He says there are no Ancestors," said Sherah.

"But there are. Surely you saw their star last year."

Anther translation, another murmur.

"This is a trick of war," said the Alpha through the Alchemist. "You are invading our land to take more for yourselves. Your Wall is not enough for you."

"If we were trying to take your land, we would not be having this conversation."

There was nothing said for several long moments.

"Two of our team are missing. A yellow cat and a blue-eyed wolf. Where are they?"

Sherah translated once more but the Alpha said nothing.

There was a rush of wings and an owl dropped from the dark sky to settle onto the snow.

Kirin looked at the Alchemist before stepping over to the bird.

"Where is your Seer?" he asked.

The bird blinked one eye.

"Take us to Yahn Nevye."

The bird blinked the next.

He sighed, remembering that it was not words the falcons of *Sha'Hadin* understood and responded to. It stood to reason that it was the same with owls.

He closed his eyes and formed a picture of the jaguar in his mind.

The bird spread its wings and left the snow, disappearing into the blackness of the winter trees. Kirin looked at the Alchemist and followed.

***

They found the jaguar suspended by arms and legs between two twisted trees. He was high in the air and stripped to the waist. He had been used for target practice, as many arrows stuck out of the rosettes on his back like the spines of some great dragon. Blood ran down his sides, dark stripes along his spotted pelt.

Setse sat on her knees beneath him, blood dripping onto her head and freezing as it matted on her face. She was a terrifying sight.

"Shar Ma'uul dead," she said in a hollow voice.

Kirin moved forward, sliding the Blood Fang from its sheath. He sliced first the bindings at the ankles, then the wrists, taking the body as it slumped across his shoulders. He laid it, face down, onto the snowy rocks and Sherah knelt to examine the wounds. There were more than a dozen arrows embedded within the rings of his pelt and she removed them swiftly, dropping them into a pile by her knees. She studied the punctures, the pelt and the skin, the depth of the entries and the organs they had pierced.

"This one first," she said softly. "To the kidney. Then here liver, here lung and here spine. He felt them all until the last arrow to the heart here."

Kirin watched with detachment as she rolled the body over. The arrows were shallow and did not go through. Like most patterned cats, his chest and belly were white and as he lay like this on the rocks, he looked like he was sleeping if one did not look at the blood at his mouth. If one did not look at his eyes. The Alchemist quietly closed them.

He glanced over at the Oracle covered in blood. She had not moved. He sighed, knelt down next to the Alchemist.

"Is there nothing you can do?"

She turned her great golden eyes on him. *"Sidi?"*

"I know what you did for the Seer back in the forest of *Turakhee*.

Can you do the same for this man?"

"Necromancy is a dark art, *sidi.* It requires the bartering of souls. As you can see, I no longer carry a soul purse…"

He nodded. He remembered it well, the strange, unearthly, red pouch that had floated on spider silk and haunted her every step.

"But," she said. "There might be a way…"

She bit her lip and he felt himself being pulled into her once again, back into her world of riddles and mystery and wonder.

"Tell me."

"It is dangerous. And costly."

"I owe them," he said. "It was my pride that chased both of them into this trap. Tell me what I need do and I will pay it."

"Just say you wish it, *sidi,* and it will be done."

He could have sworn there were tears gathering behind her lashes. His clawless hands ached to brush them away.

"I wish it, *sidala.*"

She nodded, dropped her eyes to the body at her knees and suddenly, there were candles where there were none before.

"Return the girl to her brother. I will do what I can."

"Thank you. I am in your debt."

"Of course."

But she did not look up, and for that he was grateful.

He lingered a moment longer before rising to his feet and gathering the Oracle in his arms.

***

Kerris sat against the metal wall, arms draped across his knees, the tip of his tail tapping in time with his breathing. Another creature had tried its luck, charging him from the shadows but again, this attack was met with claws and the smell of blood was heavy on the sand. Everyone in the cell was giving him a wide berth but the silhouettes of Ancestors had completely blocked out the sun.

He was very tired but he didn't dare sleep. Not with the level of frustration and anger in this cell. The metal was whispering to him. It was very old and rather strong but there were places where the air had rendered it fragile and thin. It was good to know, for he was a-wanting out of this place. He needed to wait until the Ancestors grew bored and stopped peering down on him from above. It was like living in a cage.

He looked around. His eyes had adjusted to the darkness and he could see eight others in this particular cell. Three were simian but of races he did not recognize from his time spent in the Eastern Kingdom. Four were rat-like but again, unlike any type of rat he had ever seen and the last was simply like an Ancestor, only small and very hairy. He wondered why they were all in here and what they had done with his wife.

There was a scraping sound, and then voices. He did not rise to his feet.

Three Ancestors entered the cell, dressed in dark green fabric and face masks, carrying sticks and shields for protection. One Ancestor made his way to him, pointed something that looked like a bronze bo or staff.

"Where's my wife?" Kerris snarled. He was far too tired for diplomacy.

They locked eyes for a brief moment before the man turned, spoke to his companions. They nodded.

"Where is my wife?" Kerris repeated.

The stick coughed and there was a stinging in the pelt of his chest. He looked down, pulled out what appeared to be a tiny needle, much smaller than those used by his mother for the beading of cushions. He rose to his feet, but his legs had become the roots of gum trees and he staggered to his knees. The cell erupted in hollering and he knew the prisoners had rushed but everything began to spin as the masked face of the Ancestor bent down over him with a strip of metal, growing wider and wider until there was nothing else in the whole world.

***

The dog abandoned his post the moment he saw his sister. It was expected, Kirin thought. The boy wasn't a cat, wasn't even a soldier and

Kirin forgave him the breach of protocol as he handed the girl over. From the corner of his eye, he could see movement within the circle and he turned, drawing both Fangs and snarling. The Legion backed down, wary but waiting.

Kirin removed the saddle from Shenan, freed him and aSiffh to hunt. There was a flurry of wings and a rabbit dropped to the snow near the fire circle. He looked up to see the owl, staring at him from a rock.

"Thank you," he said, not knowing if owls could understand normal speech or if their communications were restricted to the thoughts of their Seers. With Nevye dead, there would be little for the creature to do and he wondered if it would remain with the company. The rabbits were a pleasant provision and he remembered the falcon Path. She had been a fierce hunter. They would have starved on many occasions had it not been for her skill.

"En yu wei?" growled the brother. He was dabbing the girl's face with a rag. For her part, Setse merely sat, arms folded around her knees, seeing nothing. The dog looked up at him. *"Shar haan baidag wei?"*

Kirin shook his head. "I don't understand."

"Shar?"

"Dead." He resisted the urge to add, 'murdered by your people.' He was quite certain it would not have helped.

The dog looked at his sister, stroked the bloody pelt on her cheek.

"Can dog cat love?"

Kirin stared at him a moment. It was a good question, as good as whether a lion and a sacred could love. Or a lion and a cheetah.

"I don't know anything anymore, *sidi.*" He sighed. "I suppose it is possible."

The owl stretched its wings, left the rock and disappeared into the darkness.

It was a long, cold night as they waited, the dog and his sister on the ground, Kirin and the Alchemist's horse standing guard by the fire. There was no wind and Kirin was grateful. He wasn't convinced that neither the Legion nor the villagers would remain imprisoned if not for the flames.

At some point, Setse took a long shuddering breath, whispered to herself.

"Setse, yu?" asked the dog.

"Eye of the Needle," she said.

Kirin turned around to look at her.

"Eye of the Needle, Eye of the Storm."

Slowly, as if in a dream, she rose to her feet.

"Eye of the Needle, Eye of the Storm."

Her brother seemed quite undone, for he merely watched her from his place on the ground.

"Eye of the Needle, Eye of the Storm, Eye of the Needle, Eye of the Storm."

She moved to stand beside Kirin at the circle of flame, stared through to the remnants of the Legion within. They stood and the Alpha approached on the opposite side. He raised his arms as if shooting an arrow and grinned wickedly.

She stared at him, her lips moving but no sound coming, and finally after a very long moment, she stepped through the flames.

In a movement as fluid and graceful as a dance, Setse pulled a dagger from her boot and plunged it into the man's throat.

Kirin lunged but the fire leapt higher, keeping him out. The villagers shrieked and the Legion attacked but it was all a dance as she whirled and spun, feet and hands and a flashing dagger. Naranbataar rushed the circle as well but the flames leapt higher still, roared louder and he was barred from entering. Throats, bellies, faces and arms, all was red as she moved, danced between them, evading their swords. The screams continued and the smell of blood rose in the smoke until the soldiers in the circle were down.

Slowly, she turned her matted face. Blood dripped from her dagger and the villagers shrunk back.

"Ugayai, Setse," came a voice from the darkness. *"Zogsoogooroi."*

The Oracle cocked her head at the sound.

"Uuchlaarai, Setse," said the voice. *"Enh Taiwain."*

She turned. In fact, they all turned as Yahn Nevye stepped into the light of the fire, an owl on his shoulder and eyes as white as the moon.

LONG-SWIFT

"Two thousand sleepers all dead?"

"Yeah," said Solomon as he looked up at a very gaunt Tony Paolini of CanShield North, Pukaskwa, Marathon, formerly known as Sleep Lab 2. "The rats there are brutal. They move in swarms and the Upper Kingdom has huge walls to keep them out. There were no such walls in Kandersteg."

"And you were able to bring nothing with you?" came the voice of Crystal Claire. She had been the youngest of them all, a mere thirty year-old when she went under. Now, she looked as old as Cece. "Why did you take a Humlander? Why not a Griffen or a Chopper?"

"I took what I could get as fast as I could get it," he said. "Those rats swarmed nightly and the power was intermittent. The cells were drained and the hydraulics were busted. Hell, you had six of you and it still took you almost seven years to get things going. I had no one else but those cats that came into my head once in a blue moon and kept me going."

"The IAR experiments," grumbled Portillo. "They played God with the gene code. It was wrong."

"No more wrong that how you're lying to your own people. There's no contagions out there any more. There's no mutagenic viruses turning people into animals. It was a feat of complex genetic engineering and it

was a success."

"So were the Sandman projects," said Washington and Solomon grunted. Kade Washington had always been bald. "The Arks were goddamn miracles. I just don't want to see a return to what got it all started in the first place. We can't let that happen."

"Then don't," said Solomon. "That was fear and miscommunication on a global scale. These cats are a people of integrity and honour. We need to be, as well."

"The IAR turned people into animals," growled Portillo. "We don't know what other monsters are out there."

"The IAR is gone, Rico," said Solomon. "Let it go. There are civilizations in Asia, thriving complex civilizations. There are people over there, people and culture and music and architecture and painting and singing and love and life. They're proud and strong and funny and sweet and smart and neurotic and right and wrong. Dammit, they're just like us, Rico. They are just like us."

"They are not human, Jeff."

"Yeah, maybe they're better."

Solomon bit his tongue but it was too late. He had just crossed a line and an uncomfortable silence fell in the dark room.

"We will take it under advisement, Jeffrey," said Jorgenson, on the last of the five screens. He was thin, pale and grey, like the paper of a very old book. "But our first concern is for NorAm and the people of the EUS."

"There is no more EUS."

"Jeffery—"

"How about the people of the world, Tad?" said Solomon. "How about that?"

"We will take it under advisement."

"We're losing comm," said Celine and she leaned forward. "We'll try again once the towers have recharged."

And one by one, the five screens faded to black, leaving the room very dark and very quiet.

Jeffery Solomon sat back, ran a hand through his bushy hair.

"Please don't do that," said Celine.

"Sorry," he said. "Sorry. I, uh, I'm gonna call Damaris."

Celine raised a white brow. "You really care about these animals, don't you, Jeffery?"

"People, Cece, not animals. Friends. If you can try to remember that, I will try not to shake my fleas on you. How about that?"

"Sarcasm doesn't become you, Jeffery."

"And bureaucracy doesn't become you." He rose to his feet. "Hell, we were scientists, Cece. We were in it for the good of the planet. When did we fall victim to the same petty minded dogmas that started the goddamned wars in the first place?"

"I think..." She sighed, tapped on the console with her fingers. Her sharp eyes grew distant once again. "I think we stopped being scientists when we woke up. We were leaders then, Jeffery. We had to make sacrifices and that changes you. Shepherding people changes you. Who is going to go where, who is going to get the chance to make love and when, who is going to have children. Who is going to go out into the cold to defrost the comm tower and who is going to take the front line against a swarm of rats. Making decisions that affect hundreds, thousands of lives changes you."

She tightened her lips. "We went to sleep scientists and woke up politicians."

He grunted. "It is the way of things..."

"Yes. I suppose it is."

"I want to go outside."

"You can't."

"I want to and I can. Come outside with me, Cece."

"Jeffery, you're talking nonsense."

"Come outside. Is there a door? There has to be a door."

"Jeffery, sit down." She reached up to touch the back of her skull. "We have a guest unit on the property. I can have you escorted..."

"I want to go outside. Your doors are on pulleys and your windows are dead ArcEyes. You're cobbling a life together out of old tech, dead politics and pseudoscience. We wanted so much better, Cece. We deserve it. It's a beautiful wor—"

He paused, cocked his head at her.

"You just called security, didn't you?"

"Jeffery, please..."

"You know, maybe the Captain was right. He said we'd had our turn. He said we had lost the right to rule. That we had been gone for a very long time and that maybe there was a reason we were gone. A lion said that, Cece. King of the goddamn beasts."

"Jeffery, that's enough..."

"Yeah, Cece, it is enough."

And he strode toward the door, swung it open on two guards pointing Dazzlers at his chest.

***

It was two days before the Khargan's Ten Thousand came upon the first of the Deer Stones.

It was simply a rock, tall elongated and chiseled with symbols, but it towered out of the stony plain like a beacon. It was a remnant of an Ancient time, Long-Swift knew, a time of Ancestors and war and was the first of many stones that dotted the plateau. It was a good sign, for the Bear had run them hard since the earthstorm at Jia'Khan and they needed to rest their bodies before any battle with the cats. Historically, there were very few battles that had been won against the Enemy. It was largely attributed to their horses but Long-Swift wondered if it wasn't due to the fact that cats were very thorough in their organization of people. Dogs were autonomous and did not welcome rule of any kind. A khan had to prove himself repeatedly before any dog would accept him as Lord.

The Bear was spending much time with the Oracle. Long-Swift had been surprised that the creature had joined their ranks, as neither Needle nor Storm were built for running. But while they had lagged behind the army during the day, they always managed to drag their massive frame into the Khargan's tent each moonrise. It walked with the fingerstick now, using it like a cane and the muscle and sinew had hardened like bone. Their strange syncopated voice whispered, shrieked and groaned all night and smoke from the gar smelled like burning flesh. The soldiers were not pleased however, and the Irh-Khan was beginning to hear murmurs within the ranks.

There was a sweep of wings and he looked up at the Deer Stone. A raven had landed on the top of the Stone, stared at him with shiny black eyes. He sighed. A raven at moondown. It was a bad sign.

The Khargan had asked him to choose runners and he was debating whether or not to choose himself. There were no more songs inside his head and he was certain the Singer was weeping. He wondered at that, wondered what could make such a powerful, elusive, magical woman weep and he remembered the prophecy of the Oracle. *"Swift as swift, but one is swifter. Singer of Songs caught by the Lover of the Lover of Lions.*" The 'Singer of Songs' was an obvious reference but the 'Lover of the Lover of Lions?' Who was the Lover of Lions? Who was the Lover of the Lover and what did any of it have to do with him? It was a mystery. Long-Swift was certain the Oracle's brain was as distorted as its flesh.

He shook his head and turned back to the camp, leaving the Deer Stone and the raven behind.

***

Naranbataar didn't know what to think. It had been two days since the battle for the bridge and everything had changed. The next morning, the lion had released the villagers of Lon'Gaar, given them food and provisions and promises of peace and sent them on their way. He knew they would run straight to the next town to warn the people and that there would be another ambush waiting for them somewhere, sometime on this road into Tevd. It was a deathly, anxious feeling and Naranbataar realized that he himself was not cut out for war.

He didn't know much of cats but he could tell the witch was sick. Her eyes, normally the deepest gold, were shot with black and he wondered if her magic was finally consuming her. It would make sense. According to his grandmother, witches started off beautiful but always ended up ugly. A man would be a fool for loving one.

And his sister…

His heart ached at every thought of her, the memory of her with the dagger and the Legion falling at her feet. He'd always known it could happen. She was an Oracle, therefore unpredictable, but she had never, never ever killed before, let alone with such ruthlessness and skill. He blamed the cats for that. The cats and Shar Ma'uul.

Shar Ma'uul was a new man. They said that he had been killed by the Legion but the witch had brought him back. He was healthy and strong. His hands were healed and his eyes, which used to be the colour of dry grass, were now white as the moon. He spoke the Language of the People without accent and moved with certainty and ease. But he could not take his white eyes off Setse and she was drawn even more to him, a ghostly moth to an unearthly flame.

They rode together now, Setse and Shar, sharing the lion's wild young horse, her arms wrapped around his waist. They slept together, their bodies curled against each other for warmth. His sister was a virgin, had never taken nor been taken as a lover but now, with this pairing, Naranbataar didn't know how long that would last.

Perhaps Shar, not the lion, was the one who deserved an arrow to the throat.

They were riding out onto the Plateau of Tevd. It was a good land for running, low hills instead of mountains, much sunshine and very little snow. The air was thin however and it took much breathing to fill one's chest. It was easy to believe this was a holy land. It was as if even the stones were holding their breath.

He looked up as the sky was filled with sharp cries and the falcon swept into view. The owl sprang from Shar's shoulder and the two birds circled each other, wings beating, talons extended. Naranbataar shook his head. Birds fought birds while cats and dogs worked as allies. The world was a strange and unpredictable place.

The falcon settled on the Shogun-General's gloved hand. She hissed and jabbed as he pulled a small scrap of parchment from her thin leg. Naranbataar watched in fascination. He couldn't read, few dogs had the skill. He could see how it would be an advantage, especially in times of war.

"They have made the bridge," the lion said and he looked up. "It takes a long time for such a force to move through the high passes. You cannot stop and start as easily as with a small party. The logistics are far too complex."

They all stared at him so he read on.

"The Seer is working with my brother and he would like to try something. We will stop now."

The Alchemist translated but it seemed to take everything out of her to do so.

Naranbataar shook his head.

"Not good," he said, using their complicated words. "Dangerous. Land good for archers."

The lion nodded.

"You and I will be eyes and ears while they meditate."

He understood, didn't like it.

The cats slid from their horses and Shar Ma'uul reached up to swing Setse down from the saddle. The man never wore his gloves now and Naranbataar growled at the sight of the spotted hands on his sister's waist. Worse when the cat led her to a stony spot, turned in circles before dropping to his knees and pulling her down next to him.

He looked at the lion again, certain they shared the same revulsion. He wondered if the cat would let him go free if he did kill the yellow one. Worse, he wondered if Setse would go with him or stay with the cats. Somehow he knew that if he killed Shar Ma'uul, Setse would take a dagger to him next.

And he did not know what to think of that.

***

"You?" said the Khargan, and he lowered the khava from his mouth. "You are Irh-Khan, not some common runner. Why would you want to do this?"

Long-Swift breathed slowly, measuring his words. The Storm sat by the fire, all but holding up the ceiling of the gar with his shoulders. The Needle was out of its pocket for once, placing and replacing the five eyes in various patterns on the rocky floor. Three eyes now were puckered and burnt, one was oozing, and they were shot through with a variety of colours, two blue, one brown, one gold but the fifth was in perfect form as if freshly plucked from its socket. The colour of that eye was white. Long-Swift was certain there had not been a white eye back in Jia'Khan.

"These are dangerous days, Lord," said Long-Swift. "We have had runners from Lon-Gaar and runners from the mining town of Cohdhun. We have had runners from the trading post of Gaar'Uurt and runners all the way from Lake Zhu. It is hearsay, Lord, all rumour and riddle. I cannot properly advise you without facts."

"I have the Oracle to advise me, Long-Swift."

"Then you will not miss me."

The Needle cackled like a crow.

He fears the Storm and hates the Needle, echoed their voices inside his head. *He will be Khan when you are dead.*

The Bear eyed him over the mug of khava.

"Long-Swift?"

"I live to serve the Khan of Khans, who is and always has been, closer than my brother."

Lover of the Lover of Lions, whispered the voice. *But the Lover of Lions is ours.*

And the Needle held up the golden eye. He cackled again.

The Bear released a long breath, adjusted his position on the ground.

"We will be at the Field of One Hundred Stones in two days. I will expect you there with facts. To advise me."

"Lord."

"And Long-Swift?"

"Lord?"

"Do not kill the lion. I do not wish you to be my rival just yet."

"I will only run, Lord."

"Then run now."

And Swift Sumalbayar slipped out of the gar of the Khan of Khans, turned his face to the south and began to run.

***

It smelled bad in here, Kerris thought as he debated the necessity of waking. Very bad, as if someone had both eaten and defecated in the same room. Repeatedly. Honestly, he thought. People were worse than animals when it came to this. Horses wouldn't do that even if stabled for days, but then again, horses were strong-willed and fierce. Not even Kirin could touch the discipline of a horse.

But he was hungry and usually friendly, so on the urgings of his belly, he pushed himself up to his hands and knees and opened his eyes.

It was another compound.

He sighed as it all came back. His memory had never been the best and he realized it was often a blessing. Probably as close to NirVannah as he would ever come, that sweet blissful state of nothingness and peace. He only ever found that in a bottle of sakeh or his wife's arms. This foul-smelling, filthy, beast-ridden compound, this was neither.

But it was different. Above him, was the sky, blue as blue could be. Odd, he thought. It didn't smell like blue sky but there it was for his eyes to see. There was rock under his palms, not sand and he could see trees, ferns, even mountains in the distance and it was very beautiful but wrong. Clouds moved overhead but there was no breeze. He wished he had the stones from his pocket. They would tell him what was wrong. They would speak.

Nothing in this compound was speaking.

He rose to his feet, stretched and yawned, wincing as the fresh scrape across his chest tugged with the motion. Still naked but something odd at his neck. He reached up with a hand, ran his fingers along a thin strip of metal around his throat, like a pendant or a collar. He tugged at it, found a clasp and tried to remove it but it buzzed with heat so he decided to leave it alone. He shook his head. At least, there weren't other prisoners here and once again, he thought of his wife, wondered where she could be and if she was well. He hoped so. The thought of a life without her voice was empty and sad.

Something was whispering.

He looked down to see a large rock at his feet. It was an odd shape, this rock and possibly not natural but it was talking, whimpering, pleading for him to pick up.

He glanced around. There was no one here. Nothing. Usually, stones did not speak to him. He and earth were mortal enemies.

Still it whispered so he reached down and the moment his fingertips touched its hard surface, he saw blood, heard screams in his mind. He snatched his hand away, took several steps back. No, this place was unnaturally still and he looked up at the sky again. Blue and white. Happy clouds, without a trace of water, wind or lightning.

He looked now to the trees, their branches waving in the breeze that was not there, to the ferns nestled at their trunks. He began to move towards them, walking at first but quickly breaking into a run when he realized that they were not coming any closer. They stayed the same size and shape on the near horizon and he broke into a sweat now and he ran as fast as he could, and suddenly, he struck metal and bronze and the faces of Ancestors pressed up against a wall as he hit. He was thrown onto his back and lay there, dazed and staring up at blue skies and fluffy white clouds sailing by on a breeze that was not there.

He could have sworn he heard laughter but his face was throbbing and his ears ringing and the smell of blood and rotting meat was overpowering. A large shape was moving in the corner of his vision.

He wanted his sword.

He wanted the katanah.

He closed his eyes and called.

***

"You are sure?" asked the Seer.

"Yes, yes, why not," grumbled the grey lion.

"You don't sound sure," said Fallon.

"Well, I'm not, am I?" said Kerris. "But there's no going back and this might be helpful in the future if I can learn to control the earth the way I control the lightning."

"You *can* control it," said the Seer. "You simply need the will."

"Oh, you sound like Kirin. I'm always lacking something."

"Kerris…" said Fallon.

"Right. Sorry. Instruct away, *sidalord* Seer."

"I told you I could train you," said the Seer. "There could be worse places to live than *Sha'Hadin.*"

"You *are* a persistent old bugger, aren't you?" Kerris grinned. "Will there be room enough for our kittens?"

"Six grey striped kittens," sang Fallon, and she raised Kylan high into the air. "Two down, four to go. All your little cousins! Wheee!"

"More than enough room," said Sireth with a smile. "The brothers would find it a delight to hear the voices of children."

They were sitting in a circle, facing each other and surrounded by the Army of Blood. It was mid-morning, the sky was bright blue, the air very cold and both monkeys and cats lay curled up with their horses. They had halted soon after crossing a bridge of Ancestral stone and the army needed a rest. The trail through the mountains had been very narrow and it had taken the better part of two days simply to cross the bridge. There was a campsite on the other side and a firepit with burnt skeletons of a horse and ten dogs and they knew something terrible had happened. But there was no room for six thousand soldiers and seven thousand horses, so they had continued on past the campsite up, up and up to a vast hilly plateau beyond.

Fallon lowered the baby onto a skin by the fire. He rolled and cooed and she stroked his dark wavy head.

"I think I have a plan," she said. "For the army. For when we meet the Khan."

"You are so clever," said Kerris. "Have I ever told you that?"

"Never," she grinned. "But you're stalling."

"Too clever."

The Seer presented his hands. "Shall we?"

The Geomancer sighed and took them. "We shall."

And they closed their eyes as small stones began to rise from the ground.

***

"Wait," said Jeffery Solomon and he paused, raising a hand up to the wire at the back of his skull. He was in yet another long, featureless

corridor, being accompanied to a 'guest unit' at the direction of Celine Carr. When he stopped, the two guards with him stopped as well, hoisting their Dazzler weapons a little higher in their arms.

"Right, got it," said Solomon, and he turned to the guards.

"Damaris Ward has asked me to look at your MAIDEN field," he lied. "It's full of holes and not working properly. We had the same problem in Switzerland but there's an easy way to compensate for it. Where's the generator?"

They looked at him.

"Guys," he said. "I'm Supervisor 7 of SleepLab 1. If anyone can fix it, I can."

They looked at each other.

"Call Jiān Ward, then. She'll tell you."

One of the guards shook his head.

"Unnecessary. This way, Super7."

And they set off along the featureless corridor in the direction of the MAIDEN field generator.

***

Bo Fujihara lifted his pipe to his lips, took a few good long puffs. Of all the items he had packed, he had been certain to bring enough tobacco. The way the cats felt about tea, he felt about tobacco. It helped him think, calmed him and brought him balance. And life was all about balance.

He looked over the wide plateau. To the south, the peaks were dark and imposing, but grew distant and blue to the east and west. They waivered in the thin morning light like a mirage and he wondered if this was the plateau of *Chi'bett.* If so, they would likely be close to *Lha'Lhasa*, the very westernmost reach of the Eastern Kingdom. He wondered if he were able to send some of the Snow through this territory for reinforcements. It would be a good strategy to catch the Khan's massive army between two smaller forces.

He shook his head. He was thinking like a soldier, not a diplomat. This was a mission of peace.

The cats were meditating and pebbles were circling around their joined hands. They were a miraculous people, he realized, a beautiful people, and he was glad he was on this journey with them.

He slid his eyes to the woman standing at his side. Her long marbled tail was lashing and he could hear a quiet growl from deep in her throat. Of all the cats, Major Ursa Laenskaya confused him the most. Apparently she was married to the Seer but Bo couldn't see it. She rarely spent time with him and when she did, the tension was raw, the hostility evident. Perhaps they needed another wife. *Chi'Chen* households frequently had two wives, sometimes three if the man could afford it. Emperor Hiro Watanabe had four. It seemed to work well for his people but then again, marriage to one wife seemed to work well for Kaidan.

"You do not approve, Major?" he asked.

"This is wrong," she growled.

"What is? Meditation?"

"Peace with dogs."

"You do not believe we should unite?"

"I do not believe all the stories. Even if Ancestors are rising, they can be beaten by feline steel and feline will. Peace with dogs is not worth the price."

"Your husband does not agree."

"My husband is the most powerful man in the Upper Kingdom. He could destroy the army of the Khan with a thought and yet he restrains his power to teach the grey coat and he restrains *me* to save the jaguar."

"But if he teaches the grey coat and saves the jaguar, then there will be three very powerful men in the Upper Kingdom."

"You know nothing of dogs," she growled.

The ambassador smiled.

"It is easier for a khamel to go through the eye of a needle than a proud man to enter the gates of NirVannah," he said, repeating her husband's line from days ago. "But I wonder, are there any proverbs about a proud woman?"

She snorted but said nothing.

He smiled again and slipped the pipe between his teeth.

***

The ground beneath their boots began to rumble and Kirin looked over at the Magic, sitting in a circle, eyes closed, hands clasped together. Yahn Nevye, student of Jet barraDunne, betrayed them into the hands of Sherah al Shiva, *ninjah* and *kunoi'chi*. Gave them over to the 112th Legion, the people of Jalair Naransetseg. It was an unholy trinity sitting there, causing the earth to shake beneath his boots and it suddenly occurred to him that his only other companion was a dog.

The rumble became a roar and the horses began to stomp and suddenly, a mound appeared by the Magic and a massive pillar of stone began to emerge from the earth. His hand slid to the hilt of the Blood Fang as he staggered back and back again, watching with disbelief as the pillar rose out of the earth like a massive cobra from a basket. The ground was shaking and the roar was accompanied by a grinding sound, like great wheels moving together. At its base, the Magic still sat, heads down as small stones rained down upon them and a cloud of dust rose up, choking their breath but they did not move from their place and the tower grew higher and higher. Finally, it ground to a stop, casting a long shadow and towering over the plain like a beacon

The Magic struggled to stand and they all shaded their eyes to study the massive structure they had helped produce. It was smooth and grey with rounded corners and was easily the height of ten men.

"Eye of the Needle," said Yahn Nevye.

The Alchemist looked at him.

"Eye of the Needle, Eye of the Storm," he repeated and he stepped forward, slapping his palm on the face of the pillar. The touch was like the force of an explosion, producing a boom that flung them to the ground once again and a second cloud of dust and pebbles fell like rain.

Kirin staggered to his feet.

"Why did you do that?" he shouted. "Why?"

"I don't know!" coughed the jaguar. "Honestly, I don't..."

"Yu?" asked Naranbataar as he studied the pillar. *"En yu wei?"*

"Oh," said Setse and they all studied the pillar now. "Shar, look. Deer Stone..."

Running up and down the entire length were etchings. Runes, carvings, symbols that hadn't been there before Nevye's touch. And without exception, all the markings were those of eyes.

"Eye of the Needle, Eye of the Storm," said Setse.

"What does that mean?" growled Kirin.

"We have a very powerful enemy," said the Alchemist as she turned and headed for her horse.

***

There was a boom that shook the earth, causing seven thousand horses to snort and stamp, creating a thunder all their own. Kerris arced his back and despite the clear blue morning, lightning flashed across the sky. Kylan was sleeping now on a skin and Fallon swung over to her husband.

"Kerris, be still. Shssshh," and she wrapped her arms around him. "You're fine now. Shsshhh..."

"Eye of the Needle," he gasped, blinking in the bright light of morning.

"Eye of the Storm," the Seer finished. "I understand now."

"Wait," said Fallon and she cupped his face, peered into the blue eyes. "What's this?"

"What?" groaned Kerris. "I just want to go to sleep now..."

She peered closer, then glanced over at the Seer.

"Look at his eyes..."

benAramis leaned forward.

"Damn," he growled. "Check mine as well, if you please."

The tigress released her husband and peered into the unnatural brown eyes of the Seer.

"Yep," she sighed. "Same."

Like a drop of ink spreading in a pot of clear water, the eyes of both Seer and Geomancer were turning black.

"In the words of the Ancestors," Kerris propped himself on his elbows. "What the *hell* is going on?"

"We have a very dangerous enemy," growled the Seer and he lashed his tufted tail. "There is indeed a Necromancer in the camp of the dogs."

"Wonderful."

"Can you beat him?" asked Fallon.

"I'm not sure. Can you pull the sticks, please?"

The grey lion did as he was asked, reaching into his pocket and pulling out a pair of short sticks.

"Five and *Two."* He shook his head. "The sticks are completely unreadable lately. I can't make any sense of them. First all colours, then all numbers."

"Five is death," said Sireth.

"Or five is just five."

"I think the numbers are significant," the Seer said.

"The Magic is five," said Fallon. "But two?"

"Woman," said Kerris. "Or just two."

"Two," said the Seer. "Two. I wonder…"

And he closed his eyes and said nothing for some time.

There was only the wind on the Plateau of Tevd, the wind and the sound of seven thousand horses, four thousand cats and two thousand monkeys resting, watching, playing dice by small fires. Other than those sounds, there was only the wind.

Kerris gazed up at his wife. "You are so very beautiful, you know that?"

"Well, I've been told I have nice markings."

"Don't ever leave me."

"I won't. I promise."

"Because the Ancestors are coming and the earth is hungry and I can't face any of them without you."

She grinned. "You can't do anything without me."

He reached a hand and drew her down, not caring that they were surrounded by seven thousand horses, four thousand cats and two thousand monkeys resting, chatting, playing dice by small fires. For other than those, they were completely alone with only the wind as their music.

***

She narrowed her eyes as she watched her husband deep in meditation and her chest tightened within her. He was so alone, a mongrel among men. So powerful but foolish in the use of that power. He could destroy the army of the Khan with a thought, she had told the monkey, and yet he restrained his power to teach the useless grey coat. To teach the Shogun-General. To teach her.

Sometimes she hated him.

And yet she missed him.

She felt her eyes begin to sting and chased it back. She was steel. Steel. The only thing that mattered in this small useless life was honour and steel. She had known this before she'd met him. She needed to remember it now.

She had been steel.

Find it in yourself, ***for*** *yourself,* he had said.

She had been his steel.

It is easier for a khamel to go through the eye of a needle than a proud man to enter the gates of NirVannah.

Yes, she was a very proud woman.

Sometimes she hated him. She never understood him. Always, she missed him.

She wondered how she could slip back into his bed and if he would let her.

***

It is said that all the mountains and the rivers of the world are born in *Shibeth.*

Kirin could believe it. This Plateau of Tevd spread forever, or so it seemed. In the very far distance, mountains gleamed blue and hazy in the thin air, and he wondered if it was a trick of the light. *Shibeth* was a magical place, a sacred place. He could believe even the sun and the moon were born here.

"Cradle of the Moon," said the Oracle, her head resting on Yahn Nevye's back.

From the back of his blood bay stallion, Kirin looked down at her. "Can you read thoughts, *sidala?*"

"Not all," she said. "Some. I hear them, not read. I not read."

And she smiled at him.

He sighed. They were inseparable now, the Oracle and the Monk and he wondered how long it would be before they were lovers. No different, he reminded himself, than lions and sacreds and cheetahs and tigers and mongrels. Love seemed to defy caste, defy Race, even defy Kingdoms. aSiffh had taken to them like the final piece of a puzzle, had no problems with either of them on his back. Cat, dog, desert horse. Life was entirely too strange to wonder anymore.

"There are scouts coming," said the jaguar. "Three runners from the Khan's army."

"How far out?"

"The Field of One Hundred Stones. A half-day at most."

"Have you been here before, *sidi?*"

"What? Me?" and Nevye looked at him. It was difficult seeing him with such eyes. "No. Never. Why?"

"You speak as if you know."

"Oh, I don't know anything," he said. "But I see so much more than I did before. Everything changes when you die, I guess."

Kirin grunted, knowing the Seer would say the same.

He narrowed his eyes, spying Naranbataar far ahead on the hazy plain and felt grateful for his vigilance. For the very first time, he began to allow himself to think that Unification might be possible. It was a hard road however, he realized. First the Year of the Tiger spent polishing the glass, next the Year of the Cat traveling through the Eye of the Needle. Not many men walked this road. Not many men could.

But women, it seemed, were born on this road.

He turned to look at the Alchemist. Her head was held high as she rode. She was a proud woman, more skilled than he could fathom, as mysterious as the moon at midday. But she was not right, not herself. There was an inky blackness growing across her golden eyes. He wondered what spells she had needed to cast to bring the jaguar back from the dead, what toll the Necromancy would take on her. *Just say you wish it,* she had said. Would she risk such a thing for him? And if so, why?

He looked back to the jaguar.

"Just runners you see?"

"Yes, three runners. But the Ten Thousand is close behind."

"You see them too?"

"No. Not really. Would you like us to try?"

"Us?"

"Setse and I." And he turned in the saddle to look at her. "She helps me focus. Like a star lens."

She beamed at him but Kirin thought he saw the same inky blackness beginning to spread across her one blue eye as well. Nevye's, however, were as white as moons.

"Yes," he said. "I would like you to try. See what you can of their actual numbers, their weapons, anything at all of their strategy."

"Eye of the Needle," said Setse.

"Eye of the Storm," said Nevye.

"And tell me please what that means, when you find it."

Kirin watched the man sit back, place his hands over the Oracle's hands at his waist. They both closed their eyes. On her horse beside them, the Alchemist watched, blinked slowly, smiled.

He shook his head, certain he could trust no one on this road through the Eye of the Needle.

***

She could feel him approach even before she heard the crunch of his split-toed sandals on the cold hard ground.

"Ursa," came his voice, rich with the accent of a lion, wrong for coming out of such a mouth.

She did not turn. She would not.

He smelled of woodsmoke and leather as he stood beside her to study the horizon.

"I need your help," he said.

"I am on watch," she said. "I cannot help."

"I need to go to the Shogun-General and the others."

"Why?"

"There are two Necromancers in the army of the Khan."

"Two?"

"One is sharp, the other is strong. I cannot beat them from a distance. I need to go to them, to wrestle their minds face to face."

"If they are strong, they will kill you."

"They might," he said. "Unless you were my steel."

Her jaw tightened.

"We could fight them together," he continued. "I destroy the mind. You destroy the body."

She thought for a long moment.

"Where are these pathetic dog Necromancers?"

"In the tent of the Khan."

"The Khan of Khans?"

"Yes."

"The Khargan?"

"Yes."

She thought for another moment.

"You want us to ride like the wind on our little desert horses to the battle front of Ten Thousand Dog Soldiers with their shrieking arrows, make our way into the tent of the Khan of Khans, and do battle with two Necromancers who are more powerful than you?"

He thought for a moment.

"Yes."

Finally, she turned.

"Now I remember why I married you."

"Oh please…" His eyes were shining at her. "It was the beard all along. Admit it."

"Idiot."

But she was smiling as she turned.

***

For some reason, the Field of One Hundred Stones made him feel sad.

There were hundreds of stones on a wide earthen mound, more stones than he cared count, most just taller than a man. But they were old and tipping and worn by wind and time. It reminded him somehow of death and he wondered if the stones were placed for the Khans of his people. The Plateau of Tevd. The place where the world was born and old men came to die.

He had selected two runners to accompany him, a red dog with a thick coat and a long-nosed cur with legs like a gazelle. They had made the Stones in good time, less than half a day but he knew it would take the Ten Thousand two. Moving such a force was problematic. The men were nearing exhaustion and the Khargan was running them hard. It would not serve them well once they met the Enemy and their bloodthirsty horses. He did not need to be an Oracle to see how such a meeting would end.

The sun was beginning his daily retreat under the blankets of his consort, the goddess moon, and he could see his breath against the colours of the sky. He looked down as his betas sat with their backs against the stones, wrapped in yak hide and drinking from their horns of wotchka. He wondered if the cats sent out runners and if they did, what they would be doing at night on a starry plain.

He had to admit he missed the Singer.

Missed the songs in her strange, elegant language, missed her golden eyes and unnatural profile. Missed the dreams of her and her long, strong hands. He knew the cats valued their Races, and so he wondered what race she was. He knew none other than lions and tigers. He had seen few cats in his lifetime, even running with the Bear.

The moon was waxing, rising above the distant mountains like the white eye in the Khargan's tent. He shook his head. The army was suspicious and muttering and that was a dangerous thing in an army. This would not end well for any of them if the Needle and Storm swayed the Khargan's mind.

He turned to the men.

"I will take first watch," he said. "I will wake you when the moon is smiling."

"Lord," they said in unison and he could smell the wotchka from their breath.

He cast his eyes across the Plateau of Tevd, wishing he could hear the Singer just one more time.

***

Someone was touching his knee.

The Blood Fang awoke, singing out of its sheath to stop at the throat of the dog before the Shogun-General even opened his eyes.

"Forgive me," he growled, blinking and sliding the blade back home. He was still astride Shenan and it was dark on the hilly plain. "What is it?"

"Runners," said the dog. "Three runners by a Field of One Hundred Stones."

"Deer Stones?"

He jerked his chin sharply in the direction of the plain where the tall chiseled stones rose out of the earth. They had been seeing them now for hours since they had created the pillar of their own but now there were hundreds, darker than dark, a forest of petrified trees.

"Ah yes," he said. "Deer Stones. Have the runners seen us?"

The dog shrugged.

Kirin reined Shenan to a halt and the others followed suit.

"The runners are ahead," he said, keeping his voice low. "We want to make contact and keep them alive. No bloodshed if we can avoid it. Is this understood?"

He looked at the jaguar. "This is not some kind of trap? The dogs are well-known for their strategic advances and retreats."

"I only see the runners," said Nevye. "The Ten Thousand are two days away."

Kirin turned to the Alchemist. *"Sidala?"*

"It is strategic, *sidi,"* she purred. "But not the way you think."

He shook his head. Riddles, always riddles.

"Release the horses. The dogs will have seven warriors to contend with."

"But *I'm* not a warrior," said the jaguar. "And neither is Setse. She can't fight."

Setse said nothing.

"She fights, *sidi,*" Kirin said. "Like the Snow."

The powerful smell of incense and suddenly, a wraith appeared at his side. He had not seen her move but she was *kunoi'chi*. There was nothing new in that.

"There is something that may help, *sidi,*" she purred.

"What is it?"

"Hmm." She smiled. "Strategy."

She turned away but she was humming to herself in strange, exotic keys.

***

Damaris Ward did not need to show her security badges to get into the labs. She was Jiān de Seguridad, Security Supervisor for the entire district. Everyone knew her on sight. Columbia District Shenandoah was small compared to Rocky Mountain or Marathon, more relaxed. She was able to run it well, tightly but without too many complaints. All in all, she was glad she worked here.

The labs were deep underground in case of a containment breach. Above them were the compounds and exhibits and she never had much use for those. Animals were animals, all dangerous, but she knew they were visited by many of the residents of CD as often as the comm labs, maybe more. They loved to watch them play, eat, mate. And more than anything, they loved to watch them fight.

This new Super called them friends.

She trotted down the spiral stair, her boots echoing on the grey metal and she nodded to the guard outside the door. It squeaked as he pushed it open for her and the smell of food paste struck her nostrils. It had to be difficult for the scientists who worked here. It smelled bad and sounded worse, as birds squawked and rodents threw themselves against the walls of their pens. She looked around, surprised at the lack of staff.

"In Screens," said the guard from the door. "Persis has gone down

to the new pen. Everyone wants to watch."

She nodded again and made her way to the room called Screens. Twelve people were crowded around three screens and they moved aside as she strode in. A man she knew only as 6 looked up at her.

"I've never seen anything like this before," he said. "Persis is talking to it. In Chinese."

She could see the linguist in contagion suit inside the quarantine cell, flanked by two guards with Dazzlers, talking to the most beautiful animal she had ever seen. It did, in fact, resemble a slim young woman with wavy hair and she was talking in a very animated, sing-song voice. Her hands moved with expression over her obviously pregnant belly. But she had a tail that moved like an animal's tail and orange fur that was covered in black stripes. In fact, the closer she looked, the more the young woman reminded her of the images of tigers in the crystal archives. She had never seen a living one. They had been extinct for centuries, even before the originals went under.

"Where is it from?" Ward asked. "Has Sengupta asked her where it is from?"

"Some place called the Upper Kingdom," said 6. "They came over in a sailing ship. Just the three of them."

"Yuh, the STS took it out. I wish it hadn't but it's automated." She leaned forward. "Are they from the IAR?"

"That's what Persis thinks," said another man. Her eyes flicked to his jumpsuit and the name Dell. "The woman speaks Chinese, Hindi, English, Mandarin, Urdu, Farsi—"

"Persis Sengupta is a linguist. Of course she speaks—"

"Not Persis," said Dell. "The tiger. Woman. Tiger woman."

Ward sighed, thinking.

"She came with clothes, correct?"

Dell nodded.

"And you weren't suspicious about an animal that wears clothes?"

"I was," said Dell. "Ask 6. I thought it was strange but he said it was a hunting adaptation, like a magpie."

"Magpies don't carry swords."

For his part, 6 said nothing.

"So, the other one?" she asked. "The male? Where is he?"

Dell looked down again as 6 pushed back in his chair.

"Hey, I'm not Jiānkeeper."

Dell shook his head.

"The Compound crowds are crazy to see him. They're putting him in with the leather-back."

"What? He just got here."

"I know! But comms have been cancelled and people want to watch—"

"Mā de!" she swore. "Get Compound on the feed. I need that grey out now."

And on a table in a corner of a lab ignored by a staff watching a linguist speak to an animal, a sword began to move.

***

He stood on the mound under the tallest of the stones, sifting the air for scent but the wind was blowing from the north, taking all traces with it. The plain was dark, the stones darker and the laughing moon hid her face behind her blankets of cloud. It was a very cold night, but still there was no snow. Indeed, the Plateau of Tevd was a strange and holy place.

There was a sound on the wind, a pulse, a heartbeat growing louder and he turned to wake the others when the song entered his head once again.

He smiled, welcoming her back as her voice slid up and down in her strange, exotic keys, musical and mysterious and so very other. The second voice joined in, young and sweet and inexperienced and he wished of all things to add his voice to the mix but he was a soldier and he did not sing. Still, he could listen and enjoy and imagine and he leaned back against the stone and closed his eyes when suddenly, there were horses thundering up onto the mound, shattering the music of the night.

He staggered backwards, pulling his sword and swinging but the horses struck him with their bodies, sending him reeling to the ground. He could hear the others shout and bark and he scrambled to his feet, snatching the sword from the cold hard earth. There was a figure, darker than the dark stones and he could see dual glints in the moonlight, swung his sword up and the night rang with the song of steel. He struck the long sword, ducked and swung again, deflected this time by the short. He scrambled down the mound, spun and swung, hearing the scrape of blades and seeing sparks leap from the clash of iron. To his right, his beta was fighting hand to hand with a very small warrior and he could tell it was a woman. She moved like a dancer, her hands and feet everywhere at once but he could not watch for the swords were upon him once again.

He snarled and lunged forward, bringing his sword up in an arc that disemboweled most opponents but the steel was jerked aside by silk, lengths and lengths of night black silk, looping and wrapping around his blade and he fought it but there was another woman and she moved like the night, like smoke and shadow and he wasn't certain of where she was or where *he* was, and he snarled and rushed forward but a boot sent him backwards, thrashing but trapped in length after length of black silk. He wrested himself to his knees but froze as a flare of light erupted before his face.

The barb of an arrow was pointed between his eyes, and he could see a dog at the end of the bow. Behind him, a lion holding two swords, one at his throat, the other at his beta. Another dog, a little slip of a girl, stood over the third who lay unmoving on the stone, but next to him, so close he could see the gold in her eyes, was the Singer of the Songs inside his head. She smiled at him.

Another cat came, bent down to his level. Long-Swift recognized the eyes of the moon in an instant, wondered how such a thing could have happened in a man.

"Enx tajvan," said the cat. *Peace.* He spoke the Language perfectly, without accent. *"Dajgui. Namaig Yahn Nevye gedeg. Che oilgoj bainuu?"*

Long-Swift snarled, lunged forward but the bowstring squeaked as the dog pulled it taut. The cat held up a spotted hand.

"Ugui, ènx tajvan, eregtai. Peace, brother. We come in peace."

The cat stood, gestured for him to do likewise and slowly, warily, the Irh-Khan rose to his feet, arms and torso still tightly bound in silk. He threw a glance at his men and the girl straightened.

"I did not kill them," she pouted and he noticed in the moonlight that one of her eyes was blue.

"Who are you?" he growled.

"Jalair Naransetseg, Granddaughter of the Blue Wolf."

The Oracle, the little girl who had evaded the 110th for months. He had so many questions for her.

"This is my brother, Jalair Naranbataar, Master of the Bow. And Sherah al Shiva, Magic and Shadow. Shar Ma'Uul, Powerful Seer and…" She looked to the figure towering over them all in the darkness. "Kuren Ulaan Baator, Shogun-General of the Upper Kingdom."

He narrowed his eyes. The girl noticed.

"The Khanmaker," she added proudly.

He swallowed as the words of the Eyes echoed in his mind.

"Come, Swift," said the Singer in fluid Language. "I will make tea."

***

They sat in a circle of candles. Both betas were bound at the wrists and knees with bolts of black silk and the archer had his arrows fixed on them lest they move. They would not take tea and growled such vulgar obscenities that Long-Swift was beginning to wish they had bound their mouths instead. For his part, only his wrists were bound and he stared at the tiny cup with horror.

"Drink," said the Singer and she raised a similar cup to her lips.

"You seek to poison me."

"No." She sipped her tea and he noticed her eyes, ringed with inky blackness, remembered the eye in the tent guilt with gold. "Just tea."

The lion was speaking and Long-Swift could not help but stare. Lions were icons to his people, totems of great importance. Killing one made you a Khan. Seeing one changed you forever.

"So, I hope you understand," the yellow cat was saying in the Language. "This is not a mission of war. The Upper and Eastern Kingdoms wish Unification with the Kingdom to the North."

"Never," he spat.

"Stranger things are happening, Lord," said the cat.

"I am not Lord," growled Long-Swift.

"Irh-Khan," said Oracle and the other dog, her brother, glanced at her.

"Irh-Khan of the Khan of Khans?"

"This is treason against the *Chanyu.*" Long-Swift laid back his ears. "You will both be disemboweled and left to die on a field of ravens."

"We will disembowel them and paint them with honey and bury them in an ant hill," snarled the red dog.

"We will rape the women and disembowel the men and paint them all with honey and bury them in an ant hill in a field of ravens," snarled the long-nosed one.

"Shut your mouths!" snarled Long-Swift. "You dishonor the Khargan with your talk."

"The Khargan dishonours himself with the Eyes of Jia'Khan!"

"Silence!"

"The Eyes of Jia'Khan?" asked the yellow cat. "Eye of the Needle…"

"Eye of the Storm," finished the Oracle.

Long-Swift growled but said nothing.

The cat turned and spoke to the lion. The lion spoke to the Singer who nodded. She reached to slip a blade, thin and sharp, from with the crush of her night-black hair, and Long-Swift knew she was *renzeg.* Killer, Hassassin, Ninjaah.

She sliced the silks at his wrist and sat back.

"Stay calm, Lord, or the Khanmaker will remove your feet," she said, her voice smooth as the silks on his pelt and she smiled. "*Only* your feet."

The lion began to talk when suddenly, the yellow cat rose to his feet. The Oracle did the same and they stood together, looking out over the Field of One Hundred Stones.

"Horses," they said at the same time. "Red and Blue Desert Horses cross the Holy Plateau of Tevd."

The cat spoke a heartbeat behind the girl and Long-Swift shuddered. It reminded him of the Eyes and he wondered if this was how such a thing began.

They sat for several hours until moondown when horses thundered up to the Deer Stones on the Holy Plateau of Tevd.

***

"Two Necromancers?" Kirin growled, lashed his tail and the Scales of the Dragon struck against a Deer Stone, chipping it. "Are you certain?"

"Eye of the Needle," said Sireth.

"Eye of the Storm," finished Kirin. "Yes. I understand now."

"I didn't ask for that," said Yahn Nevye as he sat facing the sunrise, arms wrapped around his knees.

"Be grateful," said Kirin. "You would be dead."

"But Setse would be alive and that was what mattered. Now, I owe my life to a Necromancer."

"You owe your life to many people, *sidi.* You owe your life to the Seer and to the Major and to me and Sherah al Shiva and Kerris Wynegarde-Grey and ultimately to the Empress of the Upper Kingdom. It is not your life. Not anymore. Not once you crossed the border into the Kingdom of the Dogs."

"Still, she shouldn't have done that," he said, shaking his head. "She, she shouldn't have done that."

"We all do things we shouldn't, *sidi,*" said Kirin.

The jaguar fell silent.

"Necromancy is a dark art," said Sireth. "It involves the trading of souls. Yahn, you said Setse would live if you died. What do you mean by that?"

The jaguar sighed. "We were crossing the bridge and the attack came. It was going to kill her, to crush her soul and take her life. I felt it so clearly…"

Sitting next to him, Setse laid her head on his shoulder.

"So I asked it to crush mine instead. It was a good trade."

"Not good trade," the Oracle grumbled.

Nevye sighed.

"You should kill me now," he said. "My life has been given to the Eyes. They control my destiny."

"Maybe not," said the Seer.

"You know they do. How did I make those markings on the stone? Why?"

No one had an answer for him, save the one he already knew.

"What if I take a sword, try to kill any of you?" He shook his head, sighed. "You should kill me now."

The Oracle slipped herself under his arm. Ursa growled at them, her long marbled tail lashing behind her back.

"And you, *sidala?*" the Seer asked, turning to the Alchemist. "Whose soul did you trade for his?"

Sherah said nothing.

The jaguar looked over at her.

"Whose soul did you trade for mine?"

"My own," she said quietly.

"No, no, no," Setse moaned.

"Therefore, I will trade for hers," said Kirin. "It was my wish, after all."

"I'm quite certain that was the point," said the Seer. "They make Khans out of the body of a lion, imagine what an Oracle like this could do with the soul of one."

The Irh-Khan growled, turned to Sherah, spoke quickly. She looked up.

"The eyes," she said. "The Oracle wants the Shogun-General's eyes."

Kirin grunted.

"If it's an eye he wants, he is welcome to one. I know two leopards who would be delighted to make me a patch." He grinned at the thought. "One made of *Kamachada* iron with daggers or blades or barbs of some nefarious sort."

And he flexed the Teeth of the Dragon. Claws of steel shone in the moonlight.

Sireth benAramis smiled at his friend.

"We may be able to avoid such things. Our clever Scholar has a plan."

They all looked at him.

"It will require sacrifice on all our parts, dedication and will and honour and perhaps even blood…"

Ursa spat on the ground but they were all silent as his words sunk in.

"We have three days," Kirin said quietly.

They looked at him.

"Three days until the New Year. The Year of the Dragon is almost upon us and a Dragon year is one of fire. There will be no peace in a Dragon year."

The claws slipped back into his gloves and he set his jaw. It had been broken so long ago.

"Three days, then, to follow the Rabbit and make peace with our enemies."

"Cat," purred the Alchemist. "In Namyanese, it is the Year of the Cat."

Kirin grunted.

"It is fitting, then. We have three days left in the Year of the Cat to make peace with the Dogs."

***

"Well, I just want to thank you for getting me my clothes. Not that it was cold in there or anything but, well, I'm just used to wearing clothes. Animals, now they don't have a problem not wearing clothes, but people, well there's just something about people that makes them want to wear clothes. My name is Fallon Waterford-Grey by the way, Scholar in the Court of Empress Thothloryn Parillaud Markova Wu, Twelfth Empress of the Fangxieng Dynasty, Matriarch of Pol'Lhasa and Most Blessed Ruler of the Upper Kingdom. I am honoured to meet you."

And she bowed, fist to cupped palm.

Damaris Ward blinked slowly, tried to bow but it felt strange, bowing to an animal. But once she had uploaded the translation algorithm for IAR Chinese into her feed, she had to admit the animal could not in fact be called an animal, for she was speaking—communicating at a level as high, if not higher than many of the residents of CD Shendoh.

"Damaris Ward, Head of Security. I am…honoured to meet you too."

"Damaris. That's a pretty name. It means gentle, I think. You don't really look gentle, though. You look strong." The young woman rubbed her round belly. "Ooh, I'm hungry. Is there any food and by food, I mean fruit? Like an orange or a pear? Not a pineapple and certainly not those disgusting blood-infused paste slices which might be fine for animals, but even then, not really. And maybe tea? A big cup of Hindayan tea? I do like it with milk and honey but if you don't have any that's fine. Milk and honey, that is, 'cause it's not fine if you don't have tea. Tea is really important, even if it's clear. My mother would drink clear tea but not me. Nope, I like my milk and honey! Have you seen my husband?"

They were in the main lab, out of the quarantine cell, and she was surrounded by the staff. They had brought her clothing and she had dressed quickly, the many layers of silk, linen and wool and silk a colourful contrast to the drab jumpsuits of residential living. It was a good thing the creature was friendly for it seemed the staff couldn't help but touch her. Her pelt was indeed like a tiger's, thick and warm and very soft.

"Your husband is in another compound," Ward said, hoping the grey was still alive. "He'll be here soon."

"And Solomon? Is he in a compound too?" She blinked eagerly and Ward could not help but look away.

"He is with our Supervisors. Debriefing." Ward turned to the staff. "Find some fruit and get the Compound on the Feed now. Go!"

They scattered, leaving the Security chief with Dell, Persis and the young 'tiger woman' who called herself Fallon.

"De-bree-fing," said the woman. "That's a word I've never heard. What does it mean?"

"One moment," said Ward, and she raised a hand to the back of her skull. "Where are you? Why? No, don't. Don't you dare! Jeff7? Jeff, no!" She stamped her foot. "Gāisǐ!"

The three looked up at her. She didn't know what to say.

"There is about to be an incident," she said quickly. "I have to go—"

A labkeeper peered in the room.

"Jiān Ward?"

"What?!"

"The sword is moving..."

"A sword? What sword?"

"Ooh," said Fallon. "My husband's sword? The katanah?"

"Yuh, señorita. *It's banging against the ceiling in the next lab..."*

The tiger woman blinked again.

"He must be calling it and if he's calling it, then it's important. Are you sure he's alright?"

The screens above them, which provided the yellow light, flickered.

Damaris Ward swung on Dell and Sengupta.

"Find her husband. Get him out of that compound now!"

If Jeffery Solomon was in fact doing what he said he was doing, all hell was about to break loose, unleashing all manner of wild on CD Shenandoah.

THE ARMY OF BLOOD

Ten Thousand Dog Soldiers running at dawn is an impressive, awe-inspiring thing. In fact, it is a terrifying thing, as they move like a sandstorm or thunderclouds or hail. They are unstoppable and they trample everything in their path. From horizon to horizon, they cover the Plateau of Tevd, heading south and rippling like the shadows of night. They move around the Deer Stones that interrupt their path, flow around them the way swift-moving water flows around rocks.

For hour upon hour, the Plateau echoes with their footfall, rumbles like the strongest earthstorm, raising clouds of yellow dust that carry on up to the skies. To witness such a sight is holy, for it speaks well of the power and might of the *Chanyu,* the Kingdom of the People of the Wolf.

One day apart and to the south, it is the same story.

Seven thousand horses trotting at dawn is an impressive, awe-inspiring thing. In fact, it is a terrifying thing, as they move like a sandstorm or thunderclouds or hail. They are unstoppable and they trample everything in their path. From horizon to horizon, they cover the Plateau of Tevd heading north and rippling like the shadows of night. They move around the Deer Stones that interrupt their path, flow around them the way swift-moving water flows around rocks.

The Army of Blood is no longer a dragon but a tsunami perhaps seventy across and thousands deep. At the head, a Grey Ghost on a mountain pony, a monkey to one side of him, a tigress to the other. For hour upon hour, the Plateau echoes with their hoofbeats, rumbles like the strongest earthstorm, raising clouds of yellow dust that carry on up to the skies. To witness such a sight is holy, for it speaks well of the might of the Upper and Eastern Kingdoms and the power of the dream of Unity.

Between these two armies, at a large mound of One Hundred Stones, a man stands alone on a plain. He is practicing *Chai'Chi'Chuan*, a dance with swords. He is *Shah'tyriah*, the highest warrior caste of the Upper Kingdom and he dances with both *katanah* and *kodai'chi.* The Blood Fang and the Jade Fang are his brothers. The only music that of his breathing and it is controlled and disciplined and counted. His mind is free as his body moves through the stances in the thin hazy air of Tevd. He is wearing no armour, only linen and wool and a tattered golden sash. His hands are bare, the clawless tips shine white in the bright morning sun. His tail is free of Scales, free of brace or gold or silken thread. From his head, a cue of golden mane ripples like a banner in the wind and the swords flash and sing like music.

A dog sits on the mound of Deer Stones, watching, and knows, in his heart of hearts, that everything has changed. Behind him high on the mound, hidden and private, a cat and a dog are lovers. It is quiet and sad, for they know they will likely not live to see the next morning and he wonders at the road that led them together. Three cats and a dog have gone north toward the Army of the Khan to kill the Eyes of Jia'Khan and he is left here, with the lion that moves like poetry. He wonders if he could ever move like the lion, where steel and bone are one. Swift knows that for him, for the Irh-Khan of the Bear, he is a changed man and nothing will ever be the same again.

His sword lies at the lion's feet. It is long and curved like a creek. They have not given it to him because he is their enemy and they are right in not trusting him. He looks over his shoulder at the runners, tied to the stones with cords of black silk and remembers the Singer, leaning into them as if in a kiss, as if drawing the breaths from their very mouths. Her eyes look very black after that but the runners no longer strain or curse. In fact, it is as if they are dazed and they remain slumped against the stones like dead men.

He feels the lion's eyes upon him, bluer than the moondown sky and he holds the gaze, allowing himself to be measured. He is a warrior still—Irh-Khan of the Khan of Khans and he knows that, like the lovers, he too will not likely live to see the next morning. It has been a good life, but he wonders at the people over the years, regrets not knowing the lives of those he has killed. He wonders now if he is the one who is captured. His sword is at the feet of a lion, after all.

The lion moves his foot and the curved sword flies through the air. Swift catches it by the grip, holds it in his hand. He has never named it. It is just a sword, taken from a fallen rival years ago. It is not beautiful but it is effective. He would name it Blood River, or just River, if he were that kind of man.

The lion gestures and Swift rises to his feet. And so dog joins lion on the early morning plain of Tevd as the lion teaches the dog to dance.

***

There was a small circle of seven Deer Stones in the middle of the north plateau and for the better part of the day, the Ten Thousand flowed past. There were no stragglers. Stragglers were not permitted in the Khargan's Ten Thousand. The last soldier in the pack would be beaten severely with sticks on the soles of his feet. He would never be slow again, no matter how his feet might bleed. Life as one of the Legions of the Khan was as brutal as it was glorious. Only the hardest and the best found homes there.

The seven Deer Stones waited for the last wave of the Ten Thousand to pass, waited for the better part of the day until the last of them disappeared on the horizon. Then, they moved, stepping out and stretching to the skies. Horses rose and shook the dust from their manes, snorted and stretched and yawned. They began to amble away in search of dried grass, snow or mice.

Naranbataar flopped onto his back.

"How possible?" he muttered in halting Imperial. "I live with Setse my life but never believe I could people so hide."

The Last Seer of *Sha'Hadin* smiled, understanding the sentiment as he stretched his long arms to the sun.

"Our Alchemist," he said. "She is a mistress of many skills."

"Kunoi'chi," growled the Major but she too stretched like the *Chai'Chi* mistress that she was. "*Ninjhustu* boasts a deadly skill set."

"Merely illusion. A common skill set for a woman," purred Sherah al Shiva and she arched her long, strong body like a bow. "Men see what they wish to see. They are easily deceived."

Ursa snorted but did not disagree.

"You ice powder hide us," said the dog and he pushed up on his elbows. "In mountains below Wall. Ice powder, silk, magic."

"Of course." She turned her proud face to the Seer. "Swift said the Oracles cannot run like the Army. They move as they move and make camp at night with the Khargan."

"He will be dead before tonight," said Ursa and she pulled her dual swords, flashed them in the thin air of Tevd.

Sherah's eyes were almost black. "The Oracles will know we are here."

"But the Khargan won't," said Sireth. The blackness had only ringed one of his. "He will be expecting the Oracle to help him defeat the Captain—"

"Shogun-General," corrected Ursa.

"Shogun-General, my mistake, but the Oracle will be dead."

"We stop Oracle so lion stop Khan," said Naranbataar. "But lion not kill Khan."

"That," said the Seer. "Is up to the Khan."

"Khargan not join," said the dog. "Khargan fight to death."

"Let him," growled Ursa. "The Shogun-General and the Army of Blood will crush him."

"Perhaps," said the Seer. "But that is not our battle. We have only one task."

She snorted again, but lifted her swords to the sun and one by one, they turned to the north to wait for the Eyes of Jia'Khan.

***

An eerie yellow dust rose from the earth as the Ten Thousand made the Field of One Hundred Stones. It was early evening, the air was unnaturally still and the sky was golden with the dying of the sun and very hazy with yellow dust. They had slowed to a walk once the Stones had come into view because visibility was limited and the Stones were everywhere. It had been a long run and they were tired but the scent of cats and horses was overpowering and all thoughts of bedrolls or khava or horns of wotcha were forgotten.

ala Asalan in hand, the Khargan moved onto the mound, sending several betas ahead to secure the Stones. He could hear the sliding of his army's steel, could hear the creak of bowstrings being drawn but there was no sound louder than the rush of his blood in his veins.

"Lord!"

He whirled, spied a beta between the massive stones and marched over to his side. Two runners lay slumped against a stone and the smell of wotchka was thick on their breaths. He nudged them with his boot. They did not respond.

"They were insubordinate," came a familiar voice and he turned to see Long-Swift sitting at the edge of the mound, sword across his knees. "I corrected them."

"Long-Swift? What are you saying?"

"They wanted to kill the lion, Lord. I would not let them."

And he nodded with his chin into the south plain where a figure was barely visible in the yellow haze.

The Bear grunted and stepped forward, narrowing his eyes against the thickness of the dust. It was an Enemy in blood-red armour astride a blood-red horse. The animal was dancing on the spot, tossing its head and champing its bit and the Khan felt a rush in the pit of his stomach.

"You are certain it is a lion?"

"It is a lion."

The Khargan looked to his left then to his right. A wall was formed as the Ten Thousand lined up to flank him. They seemed to go from horizon to horizon but he knew they were perhaps five hundred wide, twenty deep and he could see the bows and swords drawn, halah'bards and spears and axes gripped in powerful double-handed fashion. Beyond them, the Plateau of Tevd extended even farther, meeting dark mountains and Enemy walls but even the mountains were impossible to see for the clouds of yellow dust.

"Is there an army?"

"You can smell it."

"The dust is too thick. It is their Magic."

"Yes."

"We have Magic of our own."

"Where are the Eyes?"

"They come." The Bear snorted, unclipped the *kushagamak* from his hip. "They always come."

***

It was twilight when the lurching form of the Eyes of Jia'Khan came into view on the Plateau of Tevd. He was surrounded by a Legion, sixty soldiers walking as slowly as he. In fact, Mi-Hahn had spied them early on and Sireth had seen them a long way off. He knew the Oracles felt him too and they skirted the edges of each other's minds like shadows of night. He could hear their voices try to enter, kept them out but it was like stopping oil with the hands. Everything was blackened in time.

"That was unexpected," growled Ursa and she hiked her swords high. "They will have archers."

"We have an archer," said Sireth and he looked at the dog. Naranbataar bit his lip.

"Not enough arrows," he said.

"We have enough," purred Sherah and she wrapped black silk around her face.

The Legion was a wall but the Oracles towered above them all, a massive silhouette in the yellow dusk. Sireth was amazed at its size, bigger even than a bear, and he wondered if it was a natural race of dog or whether the Dark Arts enabled such an unnatural thing. Shouting went up as the Legion spied them and weapons glinted in the distance.

"Xiao," said Ursa to her horse. "Forever, you are Brave."

Together, they drove their heels and three cats, three horses and one dog bolted toward the Eyes of Jia'Khan.

***

Out of the yellow haze, three more shapes emerged on either side of the lion.

They were little more than golden silhouettes holding banners high over their heads. There was no wind and the dust hovered like a blanket, making breathing difficult in the thin air. The Khargan narrowed his eyes, cursed this dust, knew it was unnatural and wondered which of the Magic he was seeing before him. There were three horses. One carried a cat, one carried a monkey and the third…

He growled and looked at Long-Swift.

"Is that a dog?"

The Irh-Khan was on his feet next to him.

"The Oracle of Karan Uurt."

"The little girl?" He grinned. "She is riding with a cat?"

"A yellow cat. Yes, Lord."

"Perfect. We will use one spear to kill them both."

"Can Magic die at the end of a spear?"

"We shall find that out."

There was a ripple from the Ten Thousand as the blood red horse danced forward. The Lion raised a fist and his voice, the girl translating a heartbeat behind.

"People of the Wolf," their voices echoed across the Plateau. "We come on behalf of Thothloryn Parillaud Markova Wu, Twelfth Empress of the Fangxieng Dynasty, Matriarch of *Pol'Lhasa* and Most Blessed Ruler of the Upper Kingdom. We come on behalf of Amiratsu, Ojin, Nihon and Wa, Rising Suns of the Capuchin Council, and His Most Revered Excellency Emperor Hiro Watanabe of the Forbidden City, Eastern Kingdom."

"May the Sun always rise," said the monkey.

"We wish peace with Khan Baitsuhkhan, First Khan of Khans. Son of the White Wolf, Father of the Jackal. Ruler of all the *Chanyu* in the North."

There was no sound but the rush of blood in his veins.

"Ancestors are rising in the West. We have seen them. *You* have seen their star in the Year of the Tiger. The star that woke all Kingdoms and announced the Ancestors' return to the world of men."

"There are no Ancestors," shouted the Khargan into the dust. "You seek to invade our land and subdue the *Chanyu!* We are a free people! We will not be subdued!"

The Ten Thousand roared approval.

The dust began to settle and they could see a wall of soldiers, lower than those on horseback.

Another cat urged his horse forward. It was a small horse and a strange cat. The Bear had never seen a grey cat before and he wondered if it was Magic as well.

"There are Ancestors!" the cat shouted and again, the Oracle of Karan Uurt translated. "I have been in the West. They have weapons that make our swords look like spoons for sipping broth!

"Lies from the mouth of a cat!"

It was an army of cats and monkeys, banners and armour. But something was missing, something was wrong.

"I am Kaidan, Ambassador of *Pol'Lhasa,"* called the grey cat and this time, he was translated by the yellow. "I am here with Bo Fujihara of the Gate of Five Hands. We wish to discuss peace and mutual defense against the Ancestors. If you say no, then we will go in peace but be warned, the Ancestors will subdue us all unless we unite."

The Bear narrowed his eyes again.

"There are no horses," he growled and he looked at Long-Swift. "Where are their horses?"

The Irh-Khan shook his head.

"Where are your horses!" the Khargan shouted over the thudding of his blood.

"Proof of our intentions," called the lion. "We come as men, to men."

"Where are their horses?" he growled. "This is a ruse."

"They speak of the Star of Five Tails," said the Irh-Khan. "You sent the 112th Legion last summer. Perhaps we should hear them?"

"The Star of Five Tails…"

The Bear swung on him.

"You," he snarled.

"Lord—"

"You have already made a pact with them!"

"I have spoken with them. They are not here for war."

"I knew I could not trust you. The Eyes were right."

"The Eyes have turned your mind, Bear! They—"

"Lord!" he barked. "I am your Lord…"

He raised *ala Asalan* as Long-Swift, a friend since his youth, raised his own in defense. It was useless. No amount of hammered steel or canine bone could stand against *ala Asalan* and he swung, hearing the clank of iron as the Irh-Khan staggered back, dropping to one knee.

"The Fall of Ulaan Baator at the steel of Ulaan Baator!" cried a voice but he could hear nothing over the rush of his own blood.

In the other hand, he began to spin the *kushagamak.*

"I will cut off your legs and drag you behind the Oracle until you are nothing more than a tattered pelt on the plain."

"The Fall of Ulaan Baator," cried the voice again. *"At the steel of Ulaan Baator!"*

It was the girl, shouting from the back of her horse, the cat's yellow hands against her temples. The Bear turned to one of his betas.

"Shoot her," he snarled.

Like a snapping string, an arrow was loosed, the whistle piercing all hearts and he watched it rush in on her pretty face, her one blue eye that announced her as Oracle, waited for the crunch and snap of her skull but there was a swoop of wings and an owl snatched it out of the sky.

He snarled again, kicked out his boot and Long-Swift hit the earth, rolled down the side of the mound and the Khargan followed, the deadly *kushagamak* hook swinging at the end of its chain. He put his boot onto to Irh-Khan's shoulder, pushing him down to the ground.

"Will you hear us?" cried the grey cat. "Let it not be said that the Khan of Khans was not a man of reason!"

The yellow cat translated and the Khargan growled again.

"Shoot those on horseback. The owl can't catch five arrows at once."

The shriek of nightmares as arrows went up into the sky, hurtling toward the riders but before they reached their marks, they struck an invisible wall and shattered into a rain of splinters and tips.

The Khargan snarled.

"Magic," said the Irh-Khan from his place on the ground. "We must listen. We must find a way."

"Your death will be my glory."

"There are Ancestors," shouted the grey cat once again. "And so we must unite. We must form an Alliance with all the Kingdoms. The Kingdom of the Cats, the Kingdom of the Monkeys, the Kingdom of the Dogs and the Kingdom of the Horses. If you don't believe me, perhaps you might wish to ask the horses…"

A ripple went through the Ten Thousand of the Khan. It turned quickly into a roar as all attention was diverted to the flanks. The Khan growled as he finally saw the reason for the plains of dust.

Far to the east and far to the west of the Ten Thousand of the Khan, flanking them on both sides were horses, rider-less horses. Seven thousand fearless warriors in the Army of Blood.

***

Fallon Waterford-Grey swallowed, took a deep cleansing breath as she moved her half of seven thousand horses into position.

"Well," she said to the baby on her back. "It *was* my idea, after all. And boy oh boy, do I have big ideas."

The baby blinked his bi-coloured eyes but he was bundled tightly in a sling and had no means to move.

She studied the Ten Thousand from her position on the south flank. A good quarter turned where they stood, brought their weapons to bear on the new armies east and west. Perhaps five hundred abreast, perhaps twenty rows. Yep, ten thousand dogs on foot, at least half with the whistling arrows of death. She shuddered, remembering that sound. It would stay with her now for the rest of her life.

She cast her emerald eyes over her equine army. Ten riders per flank, two flanks with thirty-five hundred horses each. Each a formidable army in itself. The horses snorted and stomped, shook their heads to the jingling of metal and snapping of leather. They would charge in a heartbeat, they would trample the dogs into sand.

The dogs didn't stand a chance, even with the whistling arrows.

She ran her hand along the horse's painted neck, hopeful it wouldn't come to that. She'd lost far too many horses over the last two years. She was beginning to get a reputation.

She took a deep breath and looked back at the Stones.

***

The rock was weeping. The strange rock was whispering a warning and Kerris rolled forward as the rock came down where his head had been.

A shadow twice his size fell across him and he looked up. It had no pelt and its leathery skin swung like canvas, like black canvas sails across its massive frame. There were tufts around its face and a thin strip of metal around its neck and it rose above him, bellowing in the guttural language of the Gowrain at the miss.

It looked like a bear, a leathery, hairless bear. Kerris thought it was almost the most fearsome thing he had ever seen.

"Can you speak?" he asked, bouncing up onto the balls of his feet. "I'm sure you can. You just need to try..."

The leathery arm swung and the grey lion ducked back, noticing the hand and the lethal claws at the end of each finger. He marveled at them, so thick and curved and dagger-like and once again, he called for the sword. He could feel it trying, could feel the metal all around it, cursed the metal and the earth and the lack of sky.

The bear swung again and again he ducked, but the animal charged and it was unexpected and the two of them crashed backwards onto the rocks. Kerris kicked up with his feet and he raked the creature's chest and belly with his pedal claws. It roared and hammered its leathery elbow down onto the grey chest. Stars popped behind Kerris' eyes and he struggled to draw breath. He could have sworn he heard cheering but it could have been the stars.

He heard the rock whisper once again, reached out his hand and suddenly, it was there. He swung it into the leathery head, once, twice, three times before the bear rolled away and Kerris scrambled to his feet, one hand on his ribs, the other gripping the rock. He shook his head, wincing as a sharp pain stabbed from his chest. Something was bad, something was broken but honestly, all he could hear was cheering. He was hearing cheering and he looked around at the false tree line, the unnatural sky. It made no sense.

Slowly, the bear rose to his feet and studied him, the skin sliced along his chest and belly, dripping blood onto the ground. Kerris dropped the rock, held one hand out in front of him to pacify and calm. His head was spinning and he could taste blood on his tongue.

"Peace, brother," he panted in Imperial, then in Hanyin. He didn't know Gowrain. Didn't think most Gowrain knew Gowrain, but little was known of their culture in the Upper Kingdom. And, being a world away, this creature likely would not speak it anyway. It made no sense.

The bear opened its mouth, raised its upper lip as if trying to speak. It swung its head back and forth, back and forth and dropped its arms to pound the rocky ground.

Kerris shook his head.

"I don't know what you want," he said. "But we don't have to fight. That's really not a good idea..."

It stared at him a long moment and Kerris thought its eyes were rather sad. It swung its head again, looking over its shoulder before looking back at him. And then it did a rather strange thing.

It sighed.

It was as if all the air left its body when it did so, but it sighed, the sound of thunder and earthstorms and a lifetime of sadness.

Kerris sheathed his claws, dropped his arms to his side, took a long deep breath but winced again as the pain stabbed up from his ribs. There was a new smell now, a yellow one running along the clouds and suddenly, a light began to flash red and the sky split with the sound of shrieking metal. He clapped his hands over his ears while jolts from the metal at his throat threatened to send him to his knees. The bear bellowed at the sky, pounded the ground once again. The yellow eased up so Kerris could breathe and suddenly, it all made sense.

"No!" he shouted to the walls of trees and sky. "We will not— "

Yellow again, turning white with waves of heat from the metal at his throat.

It was over in moments, and he stood with hands on knees, panting for breath.

Lightning, *the yellow whispered in his mind.* I am your lightning. Call me.

"We will not fight," he gasped and he raised his eyes to the bear, could see the creature swinging its head, mouth open as if wailing but in silence. With all his senses, he could feel the yellow buzz from the bear's collar and this time when it turned back to him, there was no sadness, only fury.

And Kerris understood the weeping of the rocks.

***

They could hear the whistling arrows and Sireth prayed the Shield would hold. There were only two of them gifted and the Alchemist's eyes were as black as the night. He did not know how much longer she would stand against the Oracle's attacks or how he would stand if she fell.

Arrows shattered and dropped away, heads and shafts and splintered wood raining down on them as they thundered past. The wall of dogs was growing larger as they neared— spears, swords and deadly halah'bards raised to impale. He glanced over at his wife riding without reins, saw the fierce light in her eyes, her dual swords clutched in each hand. She was a warrior, glorious in battle and his heart swelled at the sight.

Naranbataar dropped to his knees, skidding along the rocky ground and he released arrow after arrow as he slid. The foremost dogs fell, their weapons hitting the ground and the horses leapt into the heart of the Legion.

***

"This is a bad idea," mumbled Kerris to the monkey at his side.

"Does your wife *have* bad ideas?" asked Bo.

"The Khan is proud and short-sighted," said Kerris. "He won't back down from a challenge like this."

"If it is war he wants," growled Kirin. "We can give him one."

"You have the heart of a diplomat, brother."

Kirin grunted, glanced over at the Oracle, at Yahn Nevye sitting behind her in the saddle. The man looked strained, his odd white eyes unfocused and he recognized the look from years of riding with Sireth benAramis.

"They've made a Shield," he said. "benAramis and the others. They've engaged the Necromancer."

"You will be fine," said Kirin. "You are stronger than you think."

"I can feel his teeth closing in. I don't know how to fight him."

"Can you make the Shield for us again?"

The man released a long breath, and then another.

"For as long as I can, I will," he said quietly. "Blue Wolf."

"Yellow Cat," answered the Oracle.

"If they can't make the Shield," said Bo. "Then I would rather die by an arrow than face one of their swords."

"I would rather not die at all," muttered Kerris.

"You pulled the sticks?"

"Five."

"Ah, well. Life is like the dew of morning."

"Frozen?" asked Kerris but he grinned.

Kirin turned his eyes back to the dogs, ten thousand soldiers on the Field of One Hundred Stones.

***

ala Asalan in one hand, the swinging *kushagamak* in the other and one boot on the back of his Irh-Khan, the Bear was a fearsome sight.

"Proof of your intentions?" he snarled over the thunder of hoofs and the roar of the Ten Thousand. "Proof of your intentions, indeed! We will kill you and feast on your horses for weeks!"

He raised *ala Asalan* to the sky.

"Shoot them all!"

The sky was ripped apart by the shrieking of arrows.

***

She leapt from her horse, rolling across their backs until her feet found solid ground. She swung the *katanah,* taking off an arm, cut up with the *kohai'chi,* opening a belly. She moved and pivoted, swung and struck. She was lightning, she was music, she was steel.

A thud to her shoulder, heat. Still holding the short sword, she yanked the bolt out of the flesh and leather of her uniform, sent both arrow and blade into the throat of the nearest dog. Sparing nothing, she leapt into the air, her high bootheel cracking the jaw of another even as she swung her other leg to snap the neck of a third. She landed in a crouch, blades crossed like scissors and she swept her arms wide, taking out any number of legs and hips and waists as she moved. She could not think of her husband, could not spare a glance. She was his steel and she would pave his way in blood or die in the attempt.

Next to her, a wave of black, a shroud, a shadow. Leaping and striking with palms and daggers and whisper-thin blades. Untouchable, unstoppable, the *kunoi'chi* moved like the wind, slipped like the ice, ducking arrows and bending steel and men fell at her feet as she sprang from shoulder to back, dropping to the ground with soldiers caught in her crossed ankles, swinging their torsos overhead to crash against their fellow soldiers. Her foot would lash, take down another, spring backwards onto her hands, cracking teeth and jaws with her heels. Ninjah with eyes as black as her cloth.

Naranbataar rushed the Legion, snatching bolts from fallen dogs, firing them before they found a home in his bow. Heat along his ribs but he whirled, snatched the sword and nocked it, sending it into the chest of its owner like a mighty arrow, its tip appearing out the other side as the soldier went down.

The priest merely walked through them all, robes whipping like banners, mane flying like wind. His arms were stretched out at his sides, and dogs were flung to their backs as if struck by invisible fists. He moved with deadly purpose and the Needle shrieked its glee, perched high on the shoulder of the Storm, slapping the inky pelt with one hand, holding on to the hood with the other.

The Storm swung a withered stick, the Seer ducked easily. The Storm stomped the ground and everything shook, yellow dust rose high into the air as if from a thousand horses. An arrow thudded into its chest, disappearing into the folds as if it were never there. A second arrow and Sireth could see the young dog racing through the battle, his hands filled with soldiers but knowing their target was the Storm.

"Give me the eyes," snarled the Seer. "And we will leave you to your fate."

"The eyes of the Magic for the eyes of the Khanmaker!" boomed the Oracles, the Storm a heartbeat behind the Needle, creating an echo like lightning followed by thunder. And the Needle disappeared into the pouch of skin, reappeared with five orbs, swinging at the ends of white tendon.

"Come get them, Seer!"

The Needle cackled like a crow.

"Higher! Reach higher!"

"I will have them!" and Sireth lunged forward, his long arms reaching for and grabbing the stick from his hand. It was an arm, he knew it the moment he touched it and the current of Necromancy ran through his body like the bite of a scorpion. He dropped it to the ground, his own arm useless now and reached again with the other, as if meaning to climb the mountain of dog but the Needle shrieked and held the eyes high above them all. The Storm's massive hand clasped the Seer's throat, drawing him close.

"Last Seer of Sha'Hadin," wailed the voices inside his head as a second massive hand fell across his vision. *"You see nothing!"*

"I see more than you, monster!"

"We take your eyes for our pleasure!"

"You take mine and I'll take yours!" barked the Seer. "Mi-Hahn!

Now!"

Suddenly, the Needle shrieked as a falcon swept down from the sky, grasping the eyes in its razor talons. The tiny Oracle wailed and batted but refused to let go but Mi-Hahn beat with furious wings, lifting both eyes and Needle upwards.

The Storm roared and released the cat, raising his arms to the skies but bird and dog were high up now. The Needle was swinging with his free hand, grabbing at wings, grabbing at tail feathers and it managed to pull itself up to Mi-Hahn's thin legs, closed on them with its toothless mouth.

Mi-Hahn cried out and swung her lethal beak down and into the remaining eye of the Needle and the wail could be heard inside all their heads. In fact, Sireth dropped to the ground, hands clutched against his temples and the shrieking went on and on. He could see it as if with his own eyes as the struggle was waged in the air and here on the ground, the Storm howled in agony as Naranbataar put arrow after arrow into his back.

Releasing its hold, the Needle plummeted to the rocky earth and hit the ground with a crunch. It lay for a moment, twitching and convulsing, before pushing itself up onto shattered arms and over onto a broken back. Blood bubbled on its tongue but there was also an eye, as white as the moon. It cackled and closed its toothless mouth, bursting the orb and spilling jelly out through the gums.

It did not move after that.

There was silence for a moment on the Plateau of Tevd before the Storm opened his mouth and at the sound, the mountains fell into the sea.

***

Kirin held his breath as the sky was blackened by the arrows of the Enemy, the whistling drowning out all thought, filling his heart with dread and the desire to flee. That was the intent, after all. But he knew his people, knew they waited for the shattering of the arrows upon the Shield.

They shattered.

In a hailstorm of splinters, the Shield held and he silently gave thanks to the gods, to Dharma and fate and the Empress, that he had not killed Yahn Nevye when he'd had the chance.

A second wave came, brought with it the nightmare howls of banshees, the screams of dying rats, steel claws dragged across stone. Again they shattered but there was motion to his left and he turned to see the Oracle and the jaguar struggling on the back of the horse. Together, they pitched from the saddle and Kirin knew the Eyes of Jia'Khan were working their dark magic. Heart in his throat, he glanced over at his brother but Kerris shook his head and Kirin knew beyond a doubt when the third wave came, there would be no Shield to stop it.

***

"Shar!" cried the Oracle as Shar Ma'uul arched his back in the rocks. It was growing dark but his robes were darker and she tried to find blood with her hands. There was none. "No Shar. You fight. Shar strong fighter!"

"The arrows," he cried. "I feel them all…"

His white eyes were wide, seeing nothing and his breathing was coming in quick, shallow gasps.

"There's twelve. Twelve! That's not a holy number. Why?"

"Shar, no. You fight."

"I'm falling! Falling from the Mouth of God…"

"No, Sherah save you. Silence save you."

"Don't look at my hands. Please, don't look."

She gathered his hands into hers. They were not scarred. He was not bleeding. It was Necromancy and it was killing him.

"Eye of the Needle," he whispered. "Eye of the Storm."

She squeezed his knuckles. "*I* save you, Shar."

"Eye of the Needle, Eye of the Storm, Eye of the Needle, Eye of the Storm."

"Blue Wolf, Yellow Cat."

"Eye of the Needle, Eye of the Storm."

"Blue Wolf, Yellow Cat. Say it. Blue Wolf, Yellow Cat!"

He gasped for breath, smiled quickly.

"Say it, Shar!"

"Blue Wolf."

"Say it!"

"Blue Wolf."

"Again!"

"Blue…"

Gasped, then was still.

"Blue Wolf, Yellow Cat," she said to herself. "Blue Wolf, Yellow Cat. Blue Wolf, Yellow Cat."

She rose to her feet, pulled the dagger that she had taken from the Lieutenant of the 110th Legion of the Khan. Turned to look over her shoulder at the Ten Thousand at the Field of One Hundred Stones.

"Blue Wolf, Yellow Cat."

And she sprinted across the yellow plains as the third wave of arrows was released.

***

The whistles of nightmare started once again.

"We fight!" shouted Kirin and he spurred his heels into Shenan's blood-red sides. "Now!"

Kerris turned on Quiz's back, shouted to a *Chi'Chen* guard in the rear and men began to move in the Army of Blood as a third wave split the darkening sky. The ground shook to as sixteen thousand soldiers rushed together across the plain and from the sides, seven thousand horses thundered into the battle, with nineteen leopards and one terrified tigress at the helm.

***

Fallon heard the shriek of the arrows, saw the rush of the Army and she dug her heels into her painted horse. It rose up on its hind legs, pawed the sky with its front then leapt forward, began to churn up the ground toward the dogs. Three thousand five hundred others followed.

***

Arrows rained down on them, killing many, wounding more. Feline and *Chi'Chen* armour took even more but as the Army of Blood charged, most arrows struck dirt and rock and emptiness.

One little mountain pony did not move.

As thousands rushed past, Kerris stared at the One Hundred Stones towering above them on the mound. Dust and pebbles began to circle around his fists as the tallest of the Deer Stones began to move.

It began to rise out of the ground with a noise like the grinding of great wheels before tipping and crashing down onto another, which shattered into pieces and rained to the ground, crushing several dogs beneath the weights of stone. Another pushed up from its bed, tipped and fell, crashing into a second and third until soon, the entire Field of One Hundred Stones were falling and the Legions scattered like rice at a wedding.

He gasped as an arrow thudded into his thigh. A second and third struck the pony. Quiz squealed and bolted and for the first time in living memory, Kerris fell off and onto the stone.

Forgotten by the Khan, Swift scrambled out of the way and unnoticed by anyone, Jalair Naransetseg raced into it as the armies collided with a sound like thunder.

***

Sireth leapt to his feet and back into the reach of the Storm, slapping his palms against the sides of the creature's head. And suddenly, there were two other hands added to his, long and strong and spotted with the pelt of a cheetah and Sherah al Shiva scaled the arrows to climb up the back of the mountain, wrapping her long legs around its neck. She began to spin black silk cords around the massive throat, over the jowls, under the jowls, across the eyes and pushed-in nose and mouth. Saliva swung in strands from its lips.

She brought her face down next to its ear.

"You are beaten, *sidi,*" she purred. "Release your claim on the Magic and the Eye of the Needle will be spared."

It wailed but no words came.

"Release the Magic."

Sireth closed his eyes and leaned into her hands.

"Release the Magic or my falcon will *eat* the eye of the Eye of the Needle."

"Nooo..." moaned the voice inside their heads.

"You may have his eye, *sidiStorm,*" hissed the cheetah in the tiny twisted ear. "But only if you release the Magic."

"We never release the Magic," it gurgled. *"We ARE the Magic..."*

And it dropped a massive hand to the bonestick and swung it up like a spear into the neck of the cheetah.

***

The Blood Fang swung, the Jade Fang sang, and he moved through them all like a wheat field. Arrows whipped past his face, thudded into the yori but still he moved. It was a dance, the dance of war, the *Chai'Chi'Chuan* with other dancers struggling for the footing but he would give none. Take the legs out from under one, take the arm off of another, he moved slowly but steadily through them all in his inexorable search for the Khargan. He could hear the screams as the horses ran men down, their hoofs lethal, their fangs deadly, their bodies alone unrivaled weapons on the battlefield. Once again, he missed alMassay, his best friend for so many years. He prayed the stallion was fighting battles wherever horses went when they died.

It was dark and lightning flashed down from the skies. Kerris, he knew, using whatever he had to take these enemies down. And truth be told, the dogs were enemies. There was nothing that could change that simple fact. Step, swing, slice and block. There was no road, there was no glass, there was no eye of the needle. There was only life and death and how the Bushido played out in between.

He would kill every last dog on this field as he danced this dance toward the Khan.

***

The eyes of the Khargan. She wanted the eyes of the Khargan.

The Oracle slipped through them like a weaver, her dagger leaving holes in flesh the way a needle leaves holes in fabric. Dogs, cats, monkeys, she did not discriminate, all were victim to her borrowed blade. From the corner of her eye, she watched the lion, watched how beautifully he killed. It was like a dance, she realized, a dance of blood, so she set her mind to do the same, to kill as many as he did, if not more.

She wanted the eyes of the Khargan. She would kill everyone in her path until she got them.

***

The claws would have sliced him open had he not been quicker but it stomped with one heavy foot and caught the tip of his tail, likely breaking a bone or two under the weight. He swung round with the rock again, connecting on the side of the bear's jaw, sending a tooth flying out but he managed to scramble away before the creature could recover. The yellow was buzzing up the walls of the sky and the red light over the sun was shrieking like a dying rat and the collars that were around their necks were to make them fight or endure the pain. It was a spectacle, a Show of One Hundred Tricks, and they were the acrobats.

Metal

"NO!" he shouted to the arena. "Are you not our Ancestors? Is this—"

He gagged as the yellow buzzed through his jaw, threatening to push his eyes out of their sockets and the bear struck him again, sending him reeling onto the rocks. Its weight fell on him, forcing the air from his lungs and sending pain anew rushing up from his ribs. He could smell its foul breath, feel the heat as its large teeth sank into the flesh between his shoulder and neck. The rocks were calling him now as he pulled up his feet, clawed at the thighs but the strength was draining from his limbs. He raked the hairless face, spraying blood onto his cheeks but the bear tugged away, strips of grey pelt and pink flesh in its teeth.

Metal *and* ***Earth***

The bear bellowed, pushed down with its arms and Kerris felt his ribs splinter under the weight. A strange lightness filled Kerris then but the metal was speaking and the rocks were speaking and there was nothing stopping him from understanding their language so he reached up and grabbed the bear's metal collar with both hands and closed his eyes and called.

The yellow filled the entire world and the bear howled in silence, arching its hairless back, mouth wide, tongue stiff and Kerris could see blood vessels burst in the brown eyes. The yellow flowed through him and he channeled it through the muscles deep into the organs until blood burst from the nostrils and the ears and claws began to smoke. He rolled over on top of it now, forcing the yellow deep into every fibre and the creature convulsed and spasmed and its eyes burst out from their sockets and the hair on its neck sizzled and burned. Finally, there was nothing, the body as hard and dry as the rocks beneath it.

He released it then, rising to his feet and scanning the compound with eyes of lightning.

He looked down. Sparks were circling around his fists, something that only happened when his lover called, so he raised them, sending the yellow up to the shrieking red light. It exploded like fireworks, with sparks and bits of glass raining down onto the rock of the compound floor.

There was a buzz at his throat but he welcomed it, wrapped his fingers around it, calling it, embracing and doubling the energy of it and it fell away, blackened by the heat. He closed his eyes and flung his arms wide, following the metal back to the very walls themselves, sending the yellow back through its path and causing the walls of sky and trees to shatter into a thousand thousand shards of glass and metal and fire and the faces of the Ancestors now, pressed up against a compound without walls to keep them safe.

The Show of One Hundred Tricks over, a mob of five thousand turned and fled.

Then there were Bones, a trio of white Bones, marching in from one side, weapons held in their hands but he sent the yellow into them, the weapons flying from their hands, Bones flying from their feet. The rocks were laughing so he called them too, willed them to rise beneath the Bones and he felt more than watched rocks as large as men heaved up from the ground. The Ancestors were fleeing from the compound, screaming as stones burst from the earth to fly like the birds, to rise up and sail high before crashing down on the shattered remains of the wall of sky and trees. Alarms were still wailing in the distance but finally he was alone in a compound with no walls and sparks circling around his fists.

He stood for a long time, feeling the wind on his face, breathing deep the fresh air of twilight. It was twilight. He hadn't known. He couldn't tell.

He could see buildings, low square buildings with the crowds of Ancestors still fleeing toward them. He could see towers and fences and grass and trees and sky and clouds and rocks everywhere. He looked down to see the bear at his feet, dead as if by lightning and he felt sad, wondered how long it had been here as a prisoner and how many people he had killed, but then, he heard voices and he saw Ancestors and Solomon and his wife, his beautiful wife and he wanted to leave, wanted to go home, wanted to crawl back into his bed of skins and blankets and furs and sleep for a hundred, thousand years.

The sparks dissipated into the night sky and his wife caught him as he sank to his knees.

***

The Snow is a remarkable thing to watch. On the battlefield, they move so swiftly they can barely be seen. Hands, feet, tails, swords, they move like cobras, they move like water and the sheer art of them is poetry to behold. But dogs are bigger, dogs are stronger and soon, even the Snow was falling under the iron of the *Chanyu.*

Bo Fujihara's face was streaked with blood as he rode his horse through the chaos to Kerris' side behind one of the fallen Deer Stones. He was wearing the kabuto of his people, tall and colourful with a red tassel from the crown, but in his hands was a long cylindrical shape wrapped in black fabric and gold cording. He sprang from his horse and passed it into Kerris' waiting hands.

"Solomon would kill me," the grey lion growled. "My wife will most certainly."

"If any of us live because of this, then a death at their hands would be a welcome thing." The ambassador sagged against the stone, looked down at the arrow sticking out of the grey lion's thigh. "You have been hit."

"So was Quiz. I can't find him anywhere."

"Quiz is a clever pony. He will find high ground and snow."

Kerris grunted, threw the fabric to the earth to reveal the weapon of the Ancestors, the strange instrument of tarnished metal and interlocking parts. The Breath of the Maiden. It looked so simple, could kill them all with a single pass. He shook his head.

"I can't."

"You must."

"This was a mistake, Bo. I should have just," he breathed out. "I should have just done this on my own. I mean, my wife is out there! Alone, Bo! Alone with the horses! What were we thinking?"

Bo laid a hand on his shoulder. "There is a proverb of my people: Both the victor and the vanquished are but drops of dew or bolts of lightning. Thus should we view the world."

Kerris sighed.

"Kaidan," said Fujihara. "Look at them. They love this, every one of them. They are soldiers. Nothing will stop the fighting until they believe that the Ancestors are worse."

Kerris let his eyes sweep over the field of battle, the cats dancing with their swords, the dogs hacking with their halah'bards, the Snow moving like water through them all. The sky was dark but the red was winning.

"They must believe that the Ancestors are worse," repeated Bo.

"The Ancestors *are* worse."

"I know this too. So take it. But I am a diplomat. If I must fight, I will fight like one."

And the ambassador put his pipe between his teeth and smiled at him and Kerris loved how smiles found their homes on *Chi'Chen* faces when an arrow struck him in the forehead and he went down.

Kerris staggered backwards, watched with horror as the body crumpled to the ground and lay twitching, smile still attached to the pink face. The pipe was on the rocks next to him, wisps of smoke curling from the bowl. He turned to watch the chaos, cat against dog, dog against monkey, horses running mad in the field of stones. The sky was black but the ground was blood red.

He scanned the battlefield for Fallon, knew it would be impossible with the sheer numbers of bodies on the plain, but he did see a painted horse, stumbling with empty saddle and swinging reins. It looked like hers and his heart lurched as he saw the arrows sticking out from its neck, flank, chest and spine. The saddle itself was littered with barbs.

The Ancestors were worse, he told himself as he fought the stinging of his eyes. *The Ancestors were worse.*

"Bolts of lightning," he muttered. "Welcome to the Show of One Hundred Tricks."

He hiked the weapon onto his shoulder and moved his finger across the plate.

***

Sherah screamed but did not release her grip on the Oracle of Jia'Khan. In fact, Sireth was certain she hung on faster, tightening her grip on the silk cords at his throat. As the Oracle began to weaken, the Seer steeled his will and reached up to the single eye of the Eye of the Storm. He could see it focus, the dark pupil grow sharp as it realized what he was about to do. The creature strained against their hold but the Alchemist held fast and the Seer was the husband of a warrior and so he extended his claws, shiny and black in the yellow moonlight and plunged them into the eye of the Eye of the Storm.

The creature thrashed its head, effectively pulling the orb out from its socket and leaving a string of tendon and vein. The Seer held the eye out, turned it toward its home.

"Do you see yourself, Storm? I don't know who or what you were in the beginning but this is what you have become. It is obscene and will be destroyed by flesh and by will. It only remains to be seen how you go, and if you manage to restore any honour you may have had in your youth."

The thrashings stilled and the breaths shuddered. The massive tongue protruded from its mouth.

"I know you hear me," said the Seer. "Release the Magic and use the last of your powers to heal this woman and I will place your eye next to the eye of the Eye of the Needle when we burn you. You will stare at each other until the next life, if you are granted one."

The Alchemist twisted the cord and finally, after what seemed like a lifetime, the ground thundered as the Oracle sank to its knees. Sireth pulled the dagger from his robes, the one given to him from his warrior wife and slit the cords that led from the eye. He dropped the eye and the creature sagged onto the stone, his breaths coming in long shuddering sighs.

Slowly, Sherah removed herself from the Oracle's back. The arm of bone was still embedded above her collarbone and Sireth moved around to help her. He grasped it with both hands, hissed as the dark chi burned his pelt, but he pulled it out swiftly, tossed it to the ground where it turned to ash and blew away on the breeze.

She fell forward and he caught her in his arms.

He smiled down at her, stroked her night-black hair.

"An eye for an eye, a life for a life."

She smiled at him.

"Of course."

And closed her kohl-rimmed lids under his tender hand.

***

There was a hum, then a thick beam of light that flashed across the night sky and every soldier—Imperial, Dog and Snow—stopped, utterly breaching their instincts and their training. Circles glowed for a long moment in several of the Deer Stones, before crumbling entirely, leaving large holes open to the night sky, crackling edges of charcoal and smoke.

Every man on the Plateau of Tevd stopped to stare as Kerris leapt onto a fallen Stone, sweeping his eyes across the plain. Far in the distance, a group of cats, dogs and monkeys were still fighting under one of the few Deer Stones left standing. He looked down at the body of Bo Fujihara, smile frozen beneath the arrow. He snarled and looked up, hiked the weapon and moved his finger across the plate once again.

The beam sought out the Stone and it glowed for several moments, its shape a sharp contrast against the darkness of the night. The fighters bolted, dropping their weapons as the Stone crumbled into dust, leaving only the sharp smell of blue in the air.

There was a blackness pressing down on him, the stench of death, the weight of shadows. He fought it off.

"Next?" he shouted. "Who would like to taste the Breath of the Maiden? Come on, people? Cats? Dogs? Monkeys? Who?"

There was silence on the holy Plateau of Tevd.

"I know. The Khargan! Where's the bloody Khargan?" He swung the weapon around in a large circle. "He can breathe the Breath of the Maiden, then tell us that we still need to fight."

His tail lashed and he swung the weapon around, fighting the heaviness to stay on his feet.

"Come on? Where is the Khan, the bravest of the brave? Is it too dark?" Sparks began to appear like fireflies out of the dark sky around his fist. "How about a little lightning, then? Drops of dew, bolts of lightning? Makes things so much easier when you can see who you're killing..."

"Be gaz'uul, saaral ma'uul," snarled a voice and a large dog stepped out of the darkness and up to the Stone. Kerris could see the golden manes of lions woven through his iron hair, the rings and rings of claws around his neck.

"Finally," said Kerris. "My name is Kerris Wynegarde-Grey, Kaidan of *Pol'Lhasa.* It is an honour to meet you, oh great Khan."

But he did not lower the weapon, nor did he bow.

The Kharagan grunted, gestured with *ala Asalan*.

"No," said Kerris. "You can't have it. You have no idea—"

The massive sword swung and the grey lion staggered back as the Khargan leapt onto the stone. Kerris swung the weapon up but the air shrieked with the sound of arrows and one after the other, three bolts slammed into the flesh of his upper arm and shoulder. He spun and dropped to one knee, the weapon clattering to the Stone at his feet.

Small eyes flicked down, large hands gripped the Lion Killer sword.

"Saaral ma'uul," growled the Khargan. *"Kudal oroj? Urgah dokai?"*

Kerris' head was spinning but stepped over the weapon, shielding it with his body. Using his left hand, he slid the katanah from the sheath at his hip.

"This is not the way, Lord Khan."

"Ugui gui, Saaral," and the dog shook his head. "*Minii te saingui bain.*"

And he began to spin the *kushagamak.*

Kerris was so very tired. He missed his wife, he missed his kittens, he missed Bo Fujihara, dead for less than a heartbeat. Truth be told, he missed Jeffery Solomon, his Ancestor and friend. But the crushing weight was bearing down on him, a blanket of stone falling across his vision and he realized it was the Necromancer, pressing his life into the dust. He took a deep breath, raised the *katanah* when another arrow whistled, striking him in the left shoulder and sending the *katanah* sailing across the stone and to the ground. Sparks showered up like fireworks as he staggered back again and high above their heads, clouds lit up as lightning leapt from black to black. Thunder rumbled across the sky and soldiers began to murmur.

"Five arrows," he muttered under his breath. "Maybe that's what it means."

Bleeding and spent, Kerris sank to his knees. Snow began to fall on the Plateau of Tevd.

"Khan Baitsuhkhan, First Khan of Khans. Son of the White Wolf, Father of the Jackal, Ruler of the *Chanyu...*" He sighed, shook his head. "Why can't you see that the world is so much bigger than the North?"

"Teneg khuur," grinned the Khan and he raised the Lion Killer high above his head.

Suddenly, there was motion and a red-clad figure leaped onto the Stone, stopping the blade with a red sword in a clang of steel. Sparks showered down across the stone. Kerris looked up, tried to smile.

"Hello, Kirin."

His brother snarled and the dog stepped back, grinning.

"Asalan."

"I am Kuren Ulaan Baator," growled Kirin, lowering the Fangs and he rose high on the Stone. "First Shogun-General of the Fangxieng Dynasty, Consort of the Empress and Lion of the Noble Houses of *Pol'Lhasa*."

He raised the Blood Fang once again.

"I am the Khanmaker. Fight me, Bear. If you dare."

And he leapt off the stone and walked slowly out to the center of the plains, deliberately turned his back to the Khan of Khans.

The Bear laughed under his breath and followed.

ULAAN BAATOR

The sky was black, there were no stars, only a thin yellow moon but snow was falling like ash across the plain. Fires had been lit and men of all races crowded against each other as the fate of the known world circled each other on the Field of One Hundred Stones.

They said nothing as they circled, Kirin sliding first the Blood then the Jade from their homes at his hip, the Khargan dragging the *kushagamak* along the ground. They did not look as they moved but they were aware, even down to the last hair, for it was a dance of sword and blood and steel. They were warriors born. It was, and had always been, the way of things.

Like music to the dance, the *kushagamak* began to spin.

It was a cruel weapon, a terrible weapon, the hook and chain of the Khan of Khans, and the Bear spun the lethal hook around and around until it was a blur but Kirin was not watching the hook. Kirin was not watching the Bear. Kirin had gone deep inside himself, where the heart of Bushido beat, strong and noble and whole.

Without warning, they both lunged and the clang of steel echoed across the Plateau of Tevd. *ala Asalan* was heavy but Kirin was skilled and he rolled with the force, bringing the Jade around to slice leather at the Khargan's belly. The hook slammed into the earth, the chains snapping like angry dogs, and the Bear drew it back, the hook swinging a wide arc toward Kirin's head. He ducked it easily but then again, the

Khan hadn't really tried.

They circled again, a low growl coming from the throat of the Khargan and Kirin lashed the Scales of the Dragon. They sent sparks up from the stones of the plain. The Lion Killer swung again, the Blood Fang parried but Kirin felt the impact up the length of his arm. He would not shake it out. Another lunge and both Blood and Jade caught *ala Asalan* between them like scissors and the sound made by steel on iron was the grating of dragon teeth. Again, sparks flew up into the night sky as they withdrew their blades and circled once more.

It was a dance, the heart of Bushido his drum, the sliding of steel his song.

The *kushagamak* spun again, even as *ala Asalan* sliced the space between them. It was a long blade, heavy and fashioned in such a way that Kirin knew a stab was the least of his worries. He pivoted as the blade moved through the air but the *kushagamak* whipped, its lethal hook no more than a blur, and Kirin stumbled as it caught the leather brace of the *soteh*, yanked him off balance and toward the Khan. He went with it though, rushing in and leaping from the ground as the Lion Killer sliced the air where his legs had been. As he leapt, he snapped his wrists and the Teeth of the Dragon sprang from the braces, raking the man's face with steel.

The Khargan staggered and Kirin landed lightly, still attached to the *kushagamak* by the braces of the *soteh* that covered his upper arm. He swung the *kodai'chi* up then, in a smooth motion, down and the leather plates and metal buckles fell away, leaving the arm bare of protection but free of the hook. The Jade's green iron gleamed in the firelight.

Five long slivers of red glistened on the face of the Khargan. He wiped the blood with his arm.

"Seken," he growled and raised the Lion Killer.

"Ulaan Baator," said Kirin.

The Khargan rushed and steel clashed once again.

***

It was snowing harder now as Ursa stormed through the last of the

Legion, slaying any left standing, beheading all that lay on the ground. Her uniform, once silver, was as red as the Shogun-General's and she picked up as many swords, arrows and bows as she could carry. Naranbataar was staring at the Eye of the Storm, still gasping its last under the yellow moon. He shook his head.

"What?" growled Ursa as she pressed bloody arrows into his hands.

"Could be Setse," he moaned. "Oracles go mad. None live. Unless like that…"

She looked at it.

"That is a monster," she said, spitting blood from her tongue. "Your sister has you."

"And Shar Ma'uul."

"You're bleeding."

He looked down to see fabric torn across his ribs. Beneath, the pelt was separated, the pink flesh exposed to yellow bone. He glanced at her, frowned.

"You also."

She grunted. Her arm was beginning to throb. She rotated it in its socket, shook her arm out.

"Keep moving," she said. "If you stop, you won't move ever again."

She looked over to where her husband was dragging the body of the Needle toward the Storm. Mi-Hahn was perched on the inky shoulder, four eyes in her talons, one in her hooked beak. The Alchemist lay pushed up on one hip, head down and bleeding out of an ugly wound in her neck. Ursa shook her head. Better to kill the woman now. One swift stroke of the *katanah* and she would feel pain no more.

"Get the horses."

And she left the dog to help her husband with the bodies of the Oracles.

***

He was skilled and powerful and Kirin knew he had met a formidable fighter in Khan Baitsuhkhan. The man swung the iron sword like a club sometimes, like a spear at others but not at all like a feline sword or even a *Chi'Chen* one. It was barbed like an arrow—it would do more damage coming out than going in. He wondered how many men it had slain and of those men, how many lions. Even more deadly was the hook and chain, but it was less wieldy than a sword. It struck with force but required much time to recover.

All these thoughts floated like wind chimes through his mind, like the snow falling from the black sky. There was little blood, not yet, save for the stripes across the Khargan's face.

The dog was standing now with his back turned, spinning the *kushagamak* but little else and Kirin counted the beats of his heart as he waited. He did not want to kill this man but he knew there would never be peace if he didn't. Retreat was not an option. Not now, certainly not after Kerris' demonstration on the plain. Everyone knew the Ancestors were back. Everyone knew their power.

He looked up at the sky, seeing the yellow moon through the snow clouds. He remembered another night like this, so very different, on a hilly plain in Turakhee. Beaten and strung between poles, he had lost so much that night. He was a different man and he realized that right here, right now, he did not fear this Khan of Khans. After riding with the Oracle, running with the brother, even dancing the *Chai'Chi'Chuan* with the Irh-Khan, he knew with certainty that he would never return to that gar in his dreams again.

At least one cat had found peace with the dogs.

The Khargan roared and swung the hook and Kirin moved but suddenly, the iron sword was there where he had moved and time seemed to slow as he slid backwards to avoid both weapons. The Lion Killer clanged against the Jade and again, the impact sent shock waves down the length of his arm. The Khargan jerked his arm back, yanking the *kushagamak* and it sailed toward his face. Kirin twisted his body, desperate to get his feet beneath him. The hook scraped the bronze of the kabuto with a clang, sending sparks up into the snow and bouncing away. His knee, the one damaged so long ago, sent daggers up his thigh and he cursed the rats of *Roar'Pundih.* It was a weakness. He hoped the Khargan hadn't seen.

He rolled on the ground, feeling the snow crunch beneath him and *ala Asalan* thudded onto the stones just a hands breath from his face. He flipped onto his feet, bringing the Blood up as the hook hurtled toward him. The chain caught the red *Kamachada* iron, wrapping around and around until all weapons were stilled. They locked eyes for a brief moment, a moment that lasted a lifetime, until the Khargan yanked the chain back and Kirin dipped the sword, allowing it to go. The hook sailed back toward its wielder, and the lion chased it home.

Both weapons out of position, the Bear bellowed and turned his body as the lion leapt up, bringing both swords down, tearing great seams in the Khargan's cuirass. Kirin continued up and over once again, the Teeth of the Dragon raking across the neck and jaw but this time, the Khargan rolled with it, closing his own teeth on the wrist of leather and the two warriors went down.

They rolled together, Kirin pulling his feet underneath to boot at the chest of the heavier foe, but the Khargan had the advantage, forcing lengths of chain across the lion's throat and using his weight to hold him down. Kirin brought both Fangs up to cross the back of the grizzled neck. He drew the blades, slicing much of the iron locks, freeing some of the gold and sliding deep into the surface of the pelt. They did not move for a long moment.

"Enx tajvan," said Kirin.

"Te sha," said the Bear but he released him. Both dog and cat staggered to their feet and once again, took their places on the circle.

***

From his place on the fallen Deer Stone, Kerris watched his brother move. It was like poetry, he thought, like music and lyrics they way steel and bone worked to become one. He could never fight like that, never had the grace in him nor the strength. His had always been the words, the charm, the luck. First was luck. And now, even that had fled him under the Necromancer's crushing hand.

He was kneeling in a black pool because of the arrows. Five arrows. Five, the number of death. They were all but drops of dew, and he had no will to call the lightning. The Breath of the Maiden lay at his knees. He couldn't even pick it up, so useless his arms. He wondered where Quiz was, if he was alive or in pain and his eyes stung at the thought.

And his wife…

He had failed. He had failed her, he had failed his children, he had failed his people. Fabled Kaidan, legend Kaidan, left to die on a fallen Deer Stone while others looked elsewhere. He deserved no better but he was quite certain he deserved no less.

Like a black cloak, he could feel the weight of the Necromancer on him, the pressure and lightness of blood-loss and fatigue and the earth, ever his nemesis, called to him, wooing him to lay himself down and let her cover him. He could sink into her arms, he knew it, sink deep into her and never be found again. She would take care of him forever and ever and he would slowly turn to stone inside her. It was a morbid thought, he realized, but somehow appealing. The Necromancer would like that.

He fumbled with numb fingers, managed to reach into his pocket for the sticks. They would help him decide. They always did.

They all stuck on the blood but he pulled two, squinted in the darkness to read them.

Two and *Wood.*

Two. Feminine, warm, encouraging, peace-loving, shiny.

Wood. Optimistic, life-giving, curious, steadfast.

He looked up now, his heart lurching within him, eyes scanning the sea of bodies even as the pressure from the black cloak was pushing him lower and lower on the rock. He felt his shoulders grow too heavy and he slumped forward into the black pool, hoping now that the earth would just swallow him up. He didn't want her to find him this way.

He closed his eyes, seeing his kittens, his mother, his brother fighting for his life, for all their lives and for peace on the plain. He didn't even feel his wife when she turned him over on the rock.

***

The lion advanced this time, swinging both swords so that they sounded like arrows in the wind. The Khargan leapt into the air, a feat Kirin had not thought possible from such an enemy, sent the hook sailing backwards toward him. It struck him in the chest, forcing all breath from his body and sending him staggering back. He looked down. The hook had snagged one of the links of the doh and he quickly brought the Jade up to shear the mail but the Khargan yanked him off his feet, yanked again and swung out with a savage kick to the injured knee. It buckled as Kirin dropped to the ground.

Pressing the advantage, the Khargan kept coming, swinging his booted foot toward Kirin's other knee but the Fangs sliced downward, keeping him back. The hook yanked again and Kirin rolled, knowing he was vulnerable now to the Lion Killer sword but his feet hit the ground and he sprang up, throwing himself headfirst at the Khargan and praying the lion-maned kabuto would take the hit. It did, and the Bear staggered back, almost losing his grip on *ala Asalan.* Kirin landed with both feet on the chain and unleashed the hook with a swipe of the Jade. He swung both blades down at his sides. They sang like falling sparrows.

"Enx tajvan," he said again.

"Tsus," sneered the Khargan.

The dog tugged at the chain but it was held fast by the weight of the lion. Kirin stepped forward onto the chain, and forward again. The Khargan yanked with all his strength as Kirin sprang to one side and the hook was released, hurling back to lance the belly of its wielder. Blood seeped out from beneath the tears in his cuirass.

Snarling, the Bear began to swing the *kushagamak* high above his head now, making wider and wider arcs with the chain and soldiers from all races stepped back to avoid being struck. The sound was like that of great fans and he began to spin *ala Asalan* as well and Kirin grew still, breathing the snow and feeling for the beat, the pulse, waiting for the rhythm of the dance to decide his next move.

***

The fire was visible for miles across the Holy Plateau of Tevd as the bodies of sixty dog soldiers were fed to the flames, and the heat of it melted the falling snow long before it hit the ground.

Sherah al Shiva was dying. She lay in the arms of Jalair

Naranbataar, silent and proud, her breathing as soft as a summer night. Her wounds were bound in lengths of black silk but the fingerstick of the Necromancer had started a bleeding that was unstoppable and the pelt of her neck and collarbone – normally a milk and butter cream – was shot through with the green-black ooze of rapid decay. Ursa felt nothing for her, this *kunoi'chi* and traitor, but she wished no one a bad death. This, Ursa knew, was a very bad death.

The Eye of the Storm knelt very close to the fire and Ursa watched as the inky pelt puckered and boiled. It had no eyes now, the Storm, and it rocked slowly back and forth on its knees. Even in such a position, he was still larger than the shoulders of most men. She could hear the deep rumble of his breathing and his breath rose up from his jowls as frost, for the night was very cold. Her katanah was poised and ready in the double-handed stance but she knew it would take more than one blow to remove his head even though her tang was sharp. She waited on her husband now, watched him with her ice-blue eyes.

Sireth benAramis knelt beside him, the body of the Needle laid out in front. Two puckered eyes, both brown, sat on the blade of his dagger, pupil to pupil. With a deep breath, he looked up.

"Eye of the Storm," he began. "I don't know the road you have walked to end here on the Plateau of Tevd, but it is a magical place, a holy place. You are a powerful Oracle, blessed with a gift that is rare and precious. You could have served your people with this gift but you chose a different road and it has led you here. Necromancy has consumed you, Storm. It has killed you and your companion and you are being given a death far more honourable than you deserve."

She glanced at him. Her husband was Brahmin. He did not believe in honour, only Kharma, her sister Dharma and the powerful, unrelenting wheel of life. It was the influence of the Captain – now Shogun-General – and the Way of the Warrior. Bushido, she knew, was a good master.

Her husband might be changed yet.

"You may find redemption, however, before you are given to the sword and the flames. Trade your soul, Storm. Trade your power and free the Magic. Heal their bodies and release them from your dark corruptions. You may yet find rest for your weary soul and that of the

Needle. Do it now and we will make your death swift and clean and honourable."

The Eye of the Storm, now eyeless, sighed, a sound like the dying of distant thunder.

We release them, came his voice inside their heads.

"Go, then, to your Ancestors, to the Ancient People of the Wolf and the Moon."

He nodded at his wife.

And her sword came down.

***

There was a scream to end all screams and the sea of soldiers parted to reveal a slip of blood in the shape of a girl, clutching her belly on the Plateau of One Hundred Stones.

The snow was falling harder now, and the red on the battlefield was a sharp contrast under the dark sky. She was a wraith, a shadow, a dagger of blood and when she straightened, all who saw her stepped back.

"Too late," she snarled and stepped toward the circle of flames. "Too late!"

He heard the Khargan snarl next, saw him turn his face to her, saw the hatred in his eye.

"You kill him!" she bellowed, louder than he would have thought possible from such a young girl. "Not even your eyes can save him now!"

The Khan pointed his iron blade at her heart.

"Jinqir," he growled.

"The Fall of Ulaan Baator at the steel of Ulaan Baator."

Kirin gripped the Blood, spun the Jade.

"The Fall of Ulaan Baator at the steel of Ulaan Baator."

And the Khargan lunged, sending the *kushagamak* like a stone toward her and Kirin bolted, praying his knee would not give out as he threw himself toward the man, leaping like a bird of prey. He twisted in the air, slicing with the red blade, slashing with the green and Khargan pivoted, jerking the chain and causing the hook to fall short, its lethal spike leaving only a drop of red in the middle of her forehead.

Kirin landed on his shoulder, rolled into a crouch, both swords swinging wide in his hands. He grunted as he watched the damaged cuirass fall away in two thick pieces from the Khargan's chest with a spray of blood. The dog bellowed and yanked the *kushagamak* back, hooking the kabuto under the rim and pulling Kirin out of position.

With a move like a wave on the ocean, he swung his gloved hand to roll the helm just as the Khargan yanked again and the kabuto flew into the air to land at his feet. With a grunt, the dog brought the Lion Killer down to pierce the helm. He raised it to his eyes.

"Gedereg yamar, Asalan," and he snapped the sword over his shoulder, sending the kabuto flying over the sea of soldiers. It disappeared in the night sky and the crowd.

The Khargan charged.

Kirin felt the cold air bite his scalp as he scrambled to his feet but the dog was there with a savage kick, his boot connecting with his bad knee and the lion staggered back. A second kick, this time to the other knee and he was forced to pivot on his weak leg, hissing at the lights that flashed behind his eyes. The Blood swung low and would have removed the man's legs but he was gone, once again leaping high into the air and pulling his knees to his chest before sending both feet into the ribs of the lion, sending Kirin arcing backwards. He twisted in mid-air, tucking the blades and angling his body so that the Scales of the Dragon lashed upwards, lethal daggers striking the Khargan's throat and jaw, leaving dragon lines once more across his face.

The necklace of lion claws, however, split and flew into the snow.

Kirin hit the ground on his shoulder once again, rolled over onto one knee, cursed his weakness as it buckled beneath him. He heard the hiss of the chain, ducked as it sailed past his head but the Khargan yanked and the hook doubled back, thudding into the plates that covered his shoulder. There was heat, there was pressure and he knew this would be bad. Swiftly, he swung his elbow, catching the chain to minimize the damage but the Khargan yanked again, pulling it tight and embedding the hook deep into the hollow beneath his shoulder blade. The dog yanked again and Kirin went with it, allowing the force to roll him forward and onto his feet. Both blades swung, were blocked by the Lion Killer, and they faced each other, foreheads almost touching and there was only the sound of their breathing on the plain.

***

They tossed the body of the Needle into the flames. Soon after, it was followed by the head of the Necromancer but his body was rolled onto the fire as it was too large to lift and dissecting his limbs in order to do so was abomination, lacking the honour they had promised. After a very long struggle, both corpses were engulfed in the fire and the flames leapt higher, burned hotter because of them.

Sireth sighed, looked down at his blade where both eyes sat. He lifted it carefully, closed his own eyes and slid them onto the pyre.

"Witch dead," said Naranbataar and they looked at him, holding the unmoving body of the cheetah in his arms. Her eyes were open and they were as black as cauldrons. "She save Setse from arrows. She save me."

"We're not finished," said Sireth. "We still have these."

And he looked at the five eyes taken from the Needle. One blue, one brown, one gold and one half brown, half blue. But the white…

"We're not finished."

And he lifted the eyes of the Magic by the long yellow tendons and dropped them, one by one, into the flames.

***

They pressed their blades together, the scraping low, the steel sending sparks into the night sky. Their breathing frosted the air but they themselves were slick with sweat and their boots dug into the snow on the ground.

"The Fall of Ulaan Baator at the steel of Ulaan Baator!" cried the Oracle again.

"Teneg jinqir," snarled the Khargan and he tugged the chain. Kirin hissed through his teeth and lights flashed again behind his eyes. He pushed them away.

"Killer of Oracles," she shouted and out of the corner of his eye, Kirin could see her step into the circle. She was a slip of blood, her dagger dripping in the yellow moonlight. "You kill the Oracles of the *Chanyu!*"

There was a murmur from the crowd. Kirin could have sworn she was speaking Imperial but the dogs were understanding every word.

"The other Kingdoms respect their Magic and the Magic serves the people. Not the *Chanyu!* We torture and kill our Magic. It is a disgrace to the name of the People!"

"Qarbo jinqir!"

"You are cursed, Muunokhoi Gansorigar of Gobay. All the Oracles you have killed curse you!"

Another ripple through the crowd.

"The Eyes of Jia'Khan have killed Shar Ma'uul, the yellow cat of many lives! Under a yellow moon! He was killed under a yellow moon!"

The Khargan snarled, shook his arms as if to push the Shogun-General away but with the hook still burning in his shoulder, Kirin snagged the man's leather coat with the Teeth of the Dragon, keeping him close.

"Shar sara, Shar Ma'uul," she moaned and sank to her knees. "Yellow moon, yellow cat. Bad omen for the *Chanyu.* Bad sign for Muunokhoi Gansorigar of Gobay. His reign as Khan of Khans ends tonight."

"Qarbo jinqir uu!"

A soldier pulled his bow, loosed an arrow that whistled toward the Oracle but, as before, an owl snatched it out of the sky. It flew over the crowd, dropping into a hand and people moved aside as a yellow cat stepped into the light of the fires.

***

Fallon Waterford-Grey lay quietly beside her husband on the Deer Stone, holding the baby in her arms. She had pulled the arrows from his body, tossed them into a pile on the ground. The snow was covering them now, like a white blanket. She had been trying to keep him warm but it was very cold and he had stopped shivering and she wondered how they would bury him when he died. Maybe they would burn him. Burn all the dead and she remembered a time, so long ago but only a year, when they had piled a Legion of dead soldiers and made a pyre that reached to the skies.

She had sung a sad song then but now, her throat was so tight she feared she would never sing again.

She hoped her kittens would have a good life in *Pol'Lhasa* and that the Empress would tell them stories about their mother and father and uncle and their journey in the Year of the Tiger and maybe the Year of the Cat because she was quite certain that they would all die here and no one would ever know.

"Metal," said her husband.

She opened her eyes.

"Metal," he said again and pushed up onto his elbows. "Metal dragons in the sky."

Her throat grew tighter still as he saw her and his eyes, which had been growing black as ink, were blue once more. He smiled at her, sun, moon and stars all rolled into one.

"Hello, luv," he said. "Are you an angel?"

She kissed him and squished between them, the baby cooed with delight.

***

People of all the races gave him a wide berth as he stepped toward the circle. He was an otherworldly sight – in fact, it seemed his feet did not touch the ground as he walked and his hair, loosed from the tight knot at his neck, was as white as his eyes. He looked around the circle, saw the Shogun-General and the Khargan with their locked swords, saw his lover kneeling covered in blood. The owl swept over them all before settling on his shoulder, home.

"The dragons are coming," his voice echoed and like the Oracle, Kirin heard him in Imperial, but the dogs seemed to hear something entirely different. "Three metal dragons, cutting open the sky."

"The Army of Bones," said Setse.

"Soon," said Shar and he held out his hand. She rose, taking it. "The Ancestors are here."

Kirin shook the Khargan's coat.

"Enx tajvan," he growled, one last time. "Peace between us. Yes or no?"

"Never!" the Khargan roared and shoved Kirin away, the Teeth of the Dragon tearing the leather to ribbons under their steel.

Both Fangs sliced up as Kirin stepped back. He could feel the heat of the hook in his shoulder. The chain was wrapped around his arm between palm and elbow and he stepped further into it, began to loop it in great lengths from his hand. He pulled it tight and the Khargan snarled. Began to spin the loose chain now, looping it around *ala Asalan*, whipping it in great circles around the Bear who ducked first left then right to avoid the coils but to no avail. Soon, both lion and dog were bound in links of metal and the Khargan bellowed in fury, straining at the *kushagamak* with arms and chest until the chain shattered, the links flying into the crowd. With hook still embedded, Kirin stepped back holding the Blood in one hand, and the Jade and the chain in the other. He raised both swords to his eyes. They gleamed in the firelight.

"Te sha," the Bear growled and lunged with *ala Asalan*, swinging it like a cleaver. The Jade met it and sparks flew up into the night. But the Jade was poetry and she danced like a leaf on the wind, slipping under and over the iron sword, wrapping it in length upon length of chain and the Khargan slammed a fist forward, into the chest of the lion, only the lion was not there and the Blood met his wrist with the song of steel. The fist dropped to the ground and blood sprayed across the rocks.

The lion roared and plunged the red iron blade into the belly of the dog until the hilt of the Fang pushed against the leather of the coat. He felt his hand grow warm, could hear the rush of the crowd, saw the glint of the tip out the Khargan's back. He twisted the blade until the Lion Killer clattered to the stone and slowly, he helped the man sink to his knees.

The sky was beginning to break. Pink, orange and red, blood red. *Dawnglow red, stay in bed.* He slid the Fang out and blood splattered onto the snow. The Kamachada iron was redder than red.

He breathed slowly, deeply. Crossed his arms, slid the blades up to the Khargan's throat.

"Jalair Naransetseg," he called but his eyes did not leave the Khargan's. "Ask him one last time if there can be peace."

She translated as she stood, hand in hand with Shar Ma'uul—Kirin could no longer think of him as Yahn Nevye—and the Khargan growled, even as blood appeared on his tongue, between his white, white teeth.

"Never," he said in Imperial.

Kirin sighed, and swung wide his arms.

The head flew from the neck. It took a lifetime as it flew up into the dawn sky, iron hair and lion's mane, before it hit the snow and rolled, stopping at the feet of Swift Sumalbayar.

The Shogun-General reached overhead, grabbed the hook still lodged under his shoulder blade, yanked it swiftly out and braced against the waves of heat and pain that burned through his flesh. He stood tall on the plain, swept his eyes across the sea of faces. Cat, dog, monkey. An ocean of many drops. They were spellbound. He looked for and found, the face of his brother, supported by the tigress, both bloody but standing. There were tears streaking Kerris' grey face but he managed a smile. Kirin did not return it.

"Who is beta?" he bellowed. "Who is Irh-Khan to the Khan of Khans?"

And both Blue Wolf and Yellow Cat translated, his voice a heartbeat behind hers.

Swift stepped forward.

"I am Swift Sumalbayar, Irh-Khan to the Khan of Khans."

"I am the Khanmaker," said Kirin. "Swift Sumalbayar, you are now Khan Sumalbaykhan, First Khan of Khans. Son of the White Wolf, Father of the Jackal, now Ruler of the *Chanyu,* made by the Khanmaker without the death of a lion."

He took a deep breath, gripped the Blood Brothers in both hands.

"Will you accept peace with the Upper and Eastern Kingdoms? Will you unite with us in defense of our lands and our ways in the face of the Ancestors?"

Dog and Cat translated and the new Khan met his gaze, held it for a long while.

"Enx tajvan," he said finally. "Peace between us."

Kirin sheathed both Fangs and, fist to cupped palm, he bowed.

The dog stared at him before stepping forward and grasping his elbow. Kirin frowned, remembering something similar between Sireth benAramis and Jeffrey Solomon.

"Do same," said Setse. "Do same."

Kirin stared. He had been fighting since sunset and every fibre of his body ached. He had been riding for over a month with monkeys and dogs. His brother back from the west, his lover back from the dead. His glass had been polished, shattered, rebuilt into something completely different than anything he could have ever imagined. But here he was in the Lower Kingdom surrounded by people of all races, conferring ultimate power to a dog because he was, in fact, the Khanmaker.

His life, he realized, was a strange and unexpected thing.

He stretched his stiff, bloody fingers and gripped the man's elbow, their arms side by side and there was a murmur that rippled across the sea of faces like a wave.

The sky began to whine.

All the people on the Field of One Hundred Stones looked up as the shrieking grew louder and deeper and the earth rattled beneath their feet. Suddenly, three arrows shot across the sky, bright and shining in the morning light, leaving trails of white cloud behind them. The sky echoed with the sound of their passing.

"Dragons," said Setse and Shar, his voice a heartbeat behind.

"Jets," said Kerris. "The Ancestors have found us."

"Bones next," said Setse.

"The Army of Bones."

Kirin sighed, realizing that the war had only just begun.

***

And so, the Year of the Cat ended with the death of a dog and the Year of the Dragon commenced with a trio of dragons racing across a new morning sky. It was fitting, it was poetic and most of all, it was epic, but cats are, after all, an epic people.

By noon that day, the Seer, the Major, the Archer and the Alchemist returned to the Field of One Hundred Stones. All soldiers, the Ten Thousand of the Khan and the Army of Blood, were given the task of clearing the Field of bodies, reclaiming the weapons and burning the rest. While the dogs stayed on the north plateau, and the Army of Blood stayed on the south plateau, there were few skirmishes and most of the time was spent quietly. There were no songs of celebration, there were no campfires or drinking or tales. This was a somber time, as peace had come at a very high cost and knowledge that the Ancestors were a reality in our land filled us all with dread.

The horses wandered freely and only a few dogs were trampled in their passings.

Bo Fujihara was dead and we all grieved his loss. I had known him for years as a fine statesman and an embodiment of the spirit of peace. All the Kingdoms of the World are lesser since his passing. He will be much missed.

The Magic was healed. Kerris had taken five arrows but he was as fit as ever I remember him. He spent his time either conferring with the new Khan and the Chi'Chen *soldiers or making love to his wife. I wished he was more discreet but then again, that is Kerris. He will always be a free spirit and I was glad that he was there, with me during that time. It was, and always will be, important.*

We are taking the combined army to Lha'Lhasa, *historic seat of the Rising Suns of the Capuchin Council. We should be there in little more than one month, for the roads into* Lha'Lhasa *are narrow and treacherous and an army of this size will meet some difficulty. There, we will discuss our new roles as three distinct but unified Kingdoms. The falcon, Mi-Hahn, has been sent to* Pol'Lhasa *with the news and I expect to be met by some resistance but the Empress will see the wisdom of this action. I have yet to read her letter. For some reason, I am afraid. Dogs, weapons, wars, magic. These things I can accept but this woman has the power to slay me with a word. Still and ever, I suppose.*

It is harder for a khamel to go through the Eye of a Needle than a proud man to enter the gates of NirVannah.

I am still, and will likely always be, a proud man. But I have been in the Prayer Room of the Empress. Perhaps that is my NirVannah. I hope I will find myself there again one day.

- *an excerpt from the journal of Kirin Wynegarde-Grey*

***

He watched her as she sat on the snowy ground, surrounded by candles that flickered with unnatural light. They were Alchemy candles, not dampened by the snow or put out by the wind. Her hair was loosed, rising and falling around her face, calling like come hither fingers. It was dawn and they were leaving but here she sat, playing with candles and stones and the baby.

She turned her face, her profile long and elegant and proud and he could see her lips quirk at the thought of him watching her from the shadow of the Deer Stones.

"Will you join us, *sidi?"* she purred, her voice rich and smoky like incense.

"Yes," he said. "If I may."

And he waited for he knew it was coming.

"Of course."

He moved around to stand in front of her, hands behind his back, let his eyes fall to the baby on its hands and knees between the candles. He took a deep breath, a cleansing breath. Life was too short for any other kind.

"May I," he began. "May I see him?"

She looked up quickly, her eyes as golden as an evening sun. It was good to see them gold.

"Your son? You wish to meet your son?"

For some reason, his eyes began to sting. He chased it away.

"Yes."

And she smiled in such a way that he thought he would die right there as he stood, but he did not and she reached up and took his hand and lowered him down to sitting. Learner's Pose, for his knee was weak, but still.

She leaned forward, lifted the baby and swung him to face the lion.

"Shogun-sama," she said. "This—"

"Kirin," he said. "You may use my name."

"Names are powerful things."

"Yes, Sherhanna-chan. They are."

She smiled again and he could have sworn it was she who was blinking back the tears. She took a deep breath.

"Kirin-san," she said. "This is your son, Kylan."

From his place on the ground, he bowed at the waist. Just a little bow, fist to cupped palm.

"Kylan," she said. "This is your father."

The baby looked at him with his large bi-coloured eyes. It did not move, merely hung there, staring.

"Here," she said. "Hold him."

And without waiting for his response, she passed the baby into his reluctant hands.

His heart was thudding in his chest. He didn't know what to think, even less what to do. It wasn't a sword, it wasn't a horse, it wasn't even a scroll. It didn't hiss at him the way his niece, Solodad, had. It didn't squirm, it didn't fuss, it merely hung there from his gloved hands and he realized that perhaps the Teeth of the Dragon might frighten it but then, in a most unexpected reaction, it smiled at him.

"Oh," he said, surprised.

"He likes you," she said. "You may speak to him. I would like him to know the sound of your voice."

"I am honoured to meet you, Kylan," he said and he looked up. "He looks like a lion."

"Yes," she purred. "No spots."

"But the eyes, is he—"

"An Oracle?" and she grinned, a grin both wicked and wise. "Of course."

He removed one glove, flexed his clawless fingers and with great care, as one would touch an eggshell, he touched his son's night black hair. It was soft and wavy like his mother's, shone blue in the early morning light. He ran one finger along the kitten's cheek and smiled as it grabbed it with one tiny fist.

"He is strong."

"Like his father."

He took a deep breath.

"I will arrange an escort for you both back to *DharamShallah.* One thousand warriors will accompany you and the Scholar. You both will stay in the House Wynegarde-Grey. There are many rooms and our mother is blind."

She laughed, lowered her golden eyes.

"I am not returning to *Pol'Lhasa, Kirin-san."*

He stared at her.

"But, where?"

She looked down, took a long breath, then looked back up, chin high and proud.

"Swift Sumalbayar has asked me to be his wife."

"Swift?"

"Yes."

"Khan Sumalbaykhan? You are to be his wife?"

"It is an advantageous position, good for both our Kingdoms. It will unite us."

"But he's a, he's …" He let his words trail off as he wrestled with the thought of this.

"He is a good man, Kirin-san," she said. "Almost as good as you."

He nodded, setting and resetting his jaw.

"And the baby?"

"Will be with me."

"Does Swift know I am the father?"

"I have not told him. But he knows."

She lowered her eyes and smiled. It played about on her lips a moment and he wondered at that.

"He calls me the Lover of Lions."

He breathed out again.

"You may tell him that you are not only the Lover of a Lion, but the beLoved."

He did see the tears now and she looked down at her son. He passed the baby back.

"That is a good plan," he said finally. "I am happy for you. Both of you."

And he made a move to leave but she laid a hand on his glove.

"You are happy with her?"

"Her?"

She said nothing. She didn't need to.

He lowered his eyes now.

"I have loved her since I was in my fourth summer." He shrugged. "It is the way of things."

"It is a good way."

He sat back, for the first time finding comfort in her presence.

"You will be the wife of a Khan."

"Khanil."

"Khanil Sherhannah."

"Rah," she said. "He calls me Rah. The sun-god of the Aegypshans. They worship the moon."

"Khanil Rah," and he smiled. "It suits you."

And he leaned forward and kissed her forehead, allowing his lips to linger a moment on her pelt, breathing in one last time the scent of her, the incense in her hair, the smoke, the magic.

He rose to his feet.

"When he is old enough, send our son to *Pol'Lhasa*. I will train him myself."

"Of course."

And he left her to the candles and the baby to take his place at the head of the army.

***

It was a strange ship that they were given, not a sailing ship but a different kind of ship. A Griffen, Solomon had said, some sort of flying helship, but Kerris thought it looked like a dragon. It would take Kerris and Fallon to the Eastern Kingdom and then continue on to take Solomon and three others on to SleepLab 3 in Kalgoolie, Australia. Damaris Ward was accompanying him as Head of Security, along with zoologist Armand Dell and linguist Persis Sengupta. They had been asked to leave CD Shenandoah as they were all deemed a threat to security of the base. The cats for obvious reasons, Solomon for his irreparable dismantling of the MAIDEN fence and the other three for removing the young tigress from quarantine and thwarting Medicore's plans for the twins. It seemed to be an acceptable solution to all of them.

The inside of the flying ship was old and smelled of mildew and rust but it did fly under the skillful hand of Damaris Ward. And so they sat as stars glittered outside the small windows, drinking tea and studying maps.

"The Capuchin Council meets twice a year," said Fallon. "They are from all over the Eastern Kingdom and they journey to and from Lha'Lhasa, *gathering the thoughts and wishes of the people."*

"The Council won't be strong enough," said Kerris. "We'll need to speak to the Emperor himself and he's in Bai'Zhin. *They won't give us troops unless we speak directly to him."*

"But will he listen?" asked Solomon. "I mean, it's a good plan but it falls apart if he doesn't listen."

"He'll listen," grinned Kerris. "He loves me. I spent many months in his Forbidden City. It's a perfect place for Fallon to have the kittens. Chi'Chen *women are marvelous midwives."*

His wife beamed at him.

Solomon shook his head. "That's great, but don't believe for a minute that Cece will leave it alone, not if there's any chance that there are more 'monsters' who can do what you did in such a short span of time. You trashed the entire Compound."

"CanShield North is furious," said Persis. Her hair was beginning to grow back and it looked like the fuzz of a new peach. "My director said Paolini wanted all animals in the compounds exterminated."

Dell shook his fuzzy head. "I'm glad I'm not there for that."

"Well, if you meet the dogs, you might reconsider," grumbled

Kerris. "That will be the trickiest bit of diplomacy ever. I'm not sure even Kaidan can do that."

A lean shape in black fatigues crossed into the cabin and Jeffery Solomon brightened at the sight of her.

"Hey, want some tea?" asked Fallon.

She shook her head. Like the others, her hair was growing back under her goggled cap, but the tattooed eyebrows were still remarkable. She had given up the most by helping them and her conflict was evident. Still, she was there and had piloted the Griffen without complaint and Solomon realized he owed his life to her as well as the cats.

"The Forbidden City is a walled city," she said. "With a courtyard wide enough for an army. We can land the Griffen in the middle, no problem."

Solomon looked at all the faces.

"We're making history, people. These Empires have never seen a human. We *are the creatures here, creatures of myth and legend and they might not want us back. Any thoughts before we take 'er down? Yes? No?"*

He smiled at Kerris and Fallon, before looking up at Ward.

"Take 'er down."

***

The snow had not stopped since the night of the battle and the Field of One Hundred Stones was thick and white. They filled the plain and Kirin wished the Ancestors could see this dragon of a very different kind. They spread out from horizon to horizon, as far as the eyes could see. Of the Khargan's Ten Thousand and the Army of Blood's six thousand men, only nine thousand survived. Of the seven thousand horses, six thousand survived. Six thousand horses, and one mountain pony.

He looked at the sight, Kerris on Quiz, Fallon on yet another horse, a grey this time. He shook his head. He'd given up counting. She was carrying a wrap of linen and a banner pole, smiled at him once she'd caught him looking.

"So, um, I was thinking..."

"Yes, sister?"

"I was thinking that we really can't use the same banners and flags we did before, right? I mean, not if we're one big united army riding under three Allied Kingdoms. It doesn't really speak 'Alliance' if one guy carries a dragon banner and another guy carries a sun banner and the other guy, well, he doesn't carry a banner at all 'cause he and his people don't really have banners, right? I mean, most of them can't even read or write but they certainly could paint if they had the inkling…"

He opened his mouth, realized his mistake, closed it again.

"So anyway, I took the liberty – oh I do love that word, Liberty. It just rolls off your tongue. Liibbeeeerrtteeee… Liberty, Liberrrttee…"

"Luv?" said Kerris, looking up at her. "The banner?"

"Oh, yes, right! Well, so I took the…*Liberty,"* and she winked at him. "To design a new one, one with all symbols of the Three Kingdoms combined. I mean, it's just an idea and I've shown it to the new Khan and he likes it and I showed it to a bunch of *Chi'Chen* soldiers and they liked it and well, I'm certainly no artisan but I hear the monkeys are really good at that. If Bo were here, he could do it but he's not and well, we're weeks away from *Lha'Lhasa* so I thought, well, until we get there, we could use this new banner. So, what do you think?"

And she blinked at him, the tip of her tongue poking out of the side of her mouth.

"May I see it?"

"Oh! Oh, hah hah! Yes, yes of course! Um, here…" It was a long sheet of linen and she unfurled it for him to see.

"See? The sun is the symbol for the Eastern Kingdom and the Moon is sort of, kind of the symbol for the Lower Kingdom so I sort of combined them here, like this…"

And she made motions with her hands.

"It looks like a Tao wheel," he said quietly.

"Yes, that's what I thought too. The red is the Yang, the white is the Yin, and here…are the twin dragons of *Pol'Lhasa*, wrapped around them both…"

She swallowed, looked up at him, emerald eyes earnest.

"So? What do you think?"

"It's exquisite," he said.

"What? Really? You mean that? You like it?"

"Yes, sister. I like it."

She sat back on her horse. "Wow."

Kerris grinned at him.

"That looks like the scribblings of the Alchemist's baby," growled Major Ursa Laenskaya as she and her husband rode up on their desert horses. Shar Ma'uul and Jalair Naransetseg followed, riding together on aSiffh's sturdy young back.

Kirin grinned.

"So?" he said. "Back to *Sha'Hadin?"*

"I'm afraid so," said Sireth. "As much as I would love to see *Lha'Lhasa* and the artistry of the *Chi'Chen*, I believe we need, now more than ever, to be training our people in the Gifts and the Arts."

"People are stupid," said Ursa. "They need to be trained."

"And Ursa will train them," added the Seer.

"With a stick."

"When we've returned, we will send a falcon," said Kirin. "You will make it to *Pol'Lhasa* one day."

"Promises," grunted the Major.

Kirin looked over at the yellow cat with the white hair and eyes like the moon and the blue wolf riding behind him, hands wrapped around his waist. The owl rode on his shoulder, head turned almost upside down. Kirin shook his head.

"And you, *sidi?* Are you taking your Oracle back to *Sha'Hadin* as well for training?"

"No," he said. It was difficult to know where he was looking because of his eyes. "But we are leaving."

"Leaving? Where? Why?"

"Ulaan Baator, you have saved my people," said Setse. "But my people must learn to save themselves. The *Chanyu* do not train Oracles. They fear them, they shun them, they make them live apart as beasts. This must change if we are to help defeat the Ancestors."

"Defeat the Ancestors," repeated Shar, his voice a heartbeat behind hers.

"With the blessing of the Khan, we are going to cross the Land of the People, searching out Oracles and those with the Gifts to help make us strong. Then we will find a good place, a safe place, a place high in the mountains and we will call on the Last Seer of *Sha'Hadin* and he will come and train us all."

He looked at Sireth. The mongrel shrugged.

"It's a good plan," the Seer said.

Kirin looked back at the jaguar, sighed.

"Then I wish you success, *sidi, sidala.* I look forward to working with you soon."

"I'm sorry," said Shar.

"No, *sidi.* You must do what your Khan asks and your heart demands."

"No, I'm sorry for, for what I did."

Kirin said nothing.

"Actually, I didn't do anything and that was the problem. I didn't *do* anything. I knew what they were doing and I didn't stop them. I didn't say anything. It was Jet barraDunne and Chancellor Ho, two of the most powerful men in the Kingdom and I was afraid. I hated myself but I was a coward. And for that, I am terribly, terribly sorry."

Kirin looked down, released a cleansing breath.

"In Shaharabic, aSiffh means forgiveness."

Shar stared at him.

"You are riding a horse named Forgiveness."

The jaguar smiled as tears spilled from his white eyes.

"*Bayartai,* Rani," said Setse and she gazed down at her brother. "You protect me all my life. I love you so much."

He smiled up at her and Kirin could see tears there as well.

"*Bi camd khairtai,* Setse." And to Shar Ma'uul. "Take care Setse. She my life."

Shar grinned. "Have you seen her fight?"

Naranbataar laughed. Setse looked up at the Shogun-General.

"*Bayartai, Ulaan Baator. Il bayarliaa.*"

The owl lit from his shoulder as the desert horse wheeled and loped out of the crowd, her dark hair and his white flowing together like the tao wheel. Soon, they were little more than specks on the horizon.

Strange, he thought to himself. Yin and Yang were in all things. Perhaps, in a small way, so were Blue Wolf and Yellow Cat.

"A wife and a noble purpose," said the Seer, watching them. "Now, he can be happy."

Kirin smiled.

"And so, we go," said Sireth. "Have you read your letter from the Empress?"

"I have not. No. Why?"

"No reason," but he grinned and turned his horse, digging his heels into its side and flying like the wind. Cats, dogs and monkeys bolted out of his way.

"He thinks he can beat me," Ursa snorted. "He is an idiot."

And she bowed, fist to cupped palm. He returned it and she spun Xiao on his back legs, leapt off in pursuit. They two were little more than specks in no time, the party of Imperial escorts struggling to catch up.

Khan Swift Sumalbaykhan strode up to the fore. He was wearing nothing to set him apart from any other dog, no mane of lions, no skulls for armour nor claws around his neck. But he was a tall man and he walked with authority and Kirin was glad this was not the man he had to fight on the Field of One Hundred Stones.

"We go now?" he asked as Khanil Rah glided forward on a night-black mare, the baby in a sling across her back. She smiled at him and Kirin waited for his heart to lurch, for his chest to tighten.

It did not.

High on the back of Shenan, the blood-red stallion, he looked out over the army. There was hardly room. They seemed to fill the entire Plateau of Tevd

There was a ripple of movement and soon, a runner broke from the crowd, ran up toward them. Naranbataar pulled his bow, aimed an arrow at the man's head but the Shogun-General held up a hand as the runner dropped to one knee.

"Asalan Zhu!"

"Tiim?" said Kirin. He needed to begin to speak the language. Of all the things he had needed these last years, he knew this would be the hardest.

The dog held up an object, scraped and dented but recognizable and Kirin smiled as Naranbataar took it from the man, passed it up. It was the kabuto, the hammered bronze helm in the shape of a lion's mane. The pheasant feather was bent but the tiny hook remained. He took it, tucked it under his arm, looked down at the man, and bowed at the waist, fist to cupped palm.

The dog did likewise and a roar went up from the nine thousand on the plain. He looked over them all.

"Tell them," he said to Naranbataar. "That from now on, they are to be known as the Army of Nine Thousand Dragons."

And he placed the helm on his head, pulling the queue out through the hole at the crown.

The young dog shouted his translation and the Plateau of Tevd thundered with the voices of cats, dogs and monkeys. Kirin looked down at his brother on the mountain pony.

"This is only the beginning, Kirin," said Kerris. "We have a hell of a lot of work to do."

"I am beginning to see that," said Kirin as he nudged Shenan in the side.

"I mean, the monkeys might not even want us in *Lha'Lhasa.* It's a pretty bold move."

"It was my idea," said Fallon and she grinned to herself. "Boy oh boy, do I have big ideas."

And as the Nine Thousand Dragons set off into the early morning light of the East, Kirin reached beneath the plates of the doh and into his sash, slid out the tiny slip of parchment. It smelled of orange and lotus and Ling.

He unfolded it, read it once and then again.

His heart skipped a beat and a rush of cold swept from his head down to his toes. He swallowed, slipped the parchment back into his sash.

"I am with child," was all it said.

***

It was said that a dragon had landed in the central courtyard of the Emperor's Forbidden City in Bai'Zhin.

The noise itself first awakened the sentries, then the servants then the Royal Family themselves, and it was early morning as Emperor Hiro Watanabe and his four wives and seven children watched from the balcony as the magical creature lowered itself to the ground in a rush of wind and flying leaves. It was immediately surrounded by five thousand of the Emperor's elite Snow Guard for it was a metal dragon and no one knew if metal dragons were peaceful and good, or capricious and nasty. In fact, no one knew anything at all about metal dragons, for such a thing had never existed. Dragons were fire, water, air and stone but never metal.

It is also said that Kaidan, fabled Kaidan of the Upper Kingdom and his lover the Lightning came out of the dragon, bringing weapons for the Emperor and gifts for his children, and bringing with him Ancestors from the Star of Five Tails. It is also said that while the guards pointed swords and spears and arrows at Kaidan and his friends, the Emperor himself ran on slippered feet from the balcony and through the Hall of Celestial Purity down the steps and many corridors of the residence until he himself raced out into the courtyard. It is also said that the Snow Guard were confused whether to drop to their knees in the presence of their Emperor or to redouble their weapons in order to secure his safety. Regardless, one thing is agreed on and that is the fact that Emperor Hiro Watanabe raced through those soldiers to embrace Kaidan like a brother and for weeks afterwards, all of them dined and danced and discussed matters of great importance. Only then did the dragon take the Ancestors to a new land, leaving Kaidan and his wife the Lightning in the Forbidden City, for she was with child and Chi'Chen *midwives are known throughout the world for their skill.*

It is said that eight months later, Kaidan returned to the Eastern Kingdom with the Lightning and an army of Nine Thousand warriors of all races—cat, dog and monkey. It was led by a Shogun-General in blood-red armour and a new Khan from the Lower Kingdom with his feline wife. They met in Lha'Lhasa *where all life begins to talk with the*

Rising Suns about the coming of Ancestors and what that might mean for the Kingdoms of the World.

These are the things that are said and more than this, these are the stories that are sung for they were written in the Year of peace and tranquility. They were written in the Year of the Cat. Other stories were written, other songs sung, but those belong in another book, ***The Art of War: A Book of Blood and Bones*** *written, naturally, in the Year of the Dragon.*

To be continued in

Snow in the Year of the Dragon

An Excerpt from

Snow in the Year of the Dragon

By H. Leighton Dickson

First Light at the Borderlands

Australian Eastern Seaboard
The Year of the Cat

According to Kerris Wynegarde-Grey, there are dragons in the world.

Divine protectors of the Upper Kingdom and Supreme Beings over all creatures, dragons are the ultimate symbol of Good Fortune and Life. Their celestial breath, or *sheng chi,* wards off evil spirits, protects the innocent and bestows safety to all that hold high the dragon banner. They are the greatest force on Earth and show their power in the form of the seasons, bringing water from rain, warmth from the sunshine, wind from the seas and soil from the Earth.

Kerris Wynegarde-Grey knows this. Like him, dragons are elemental.

There are nine different races of dragons, according to Kerris. There is the Horned Dragon, the Winged Dragon, the Celestial Dragon (which protects the mansions of the gods), the Spirit Dragon (also called the Wind Dragon), the Dragon of Hidden Treasures (which keeps guard over concealed wealth), the Coiling Dragon (which lives under the oceans), and the Great Golden Dragon (which once presented the Sacred Empress Mei Lin Rosario Tang with the elements of writing.)

The last of the nine is the Dragon King, which actually consists of four separate dragons, each of which rules over one of the four seas. He can summon his separate selves to become one large, four-headed dragon and the Empires of the World tremble at his step.

Within those nine races, there are wind dragons and water dragons, dragons of fire and dragons of ice. There are dragons that live deep in the earth, crush stone with their teeth and breathe sand like incense. According to Kerris, there are even metal dragons, although those are considerably more rare and are usually closely tied to Ancestors. That makes them dangerous, best avoided at all costs.

Perhaps the most dangerous however is not really a dragon at all. The Year of the Dragon is one of fire, said the Shogun-General in a previous life. There would be no peace in a Dragon year. They are violent and unpredictable, with incessant waves of calamity, upheaval and change. They are also filled with luck. Men may make their fortunes in the Year of the Dragon, then just as quickly lose them. And for those born in the Year of the Dragon (called the Dragonborn) Dragon years are just bad luck.

Not many have seen a dragon. They have never been killed nor skinned nor have they been sighted by large groups of people to confirm their existence. Dragons are elusive and mysterious, understanding the ways of cats far better than cats do themselves. But Kerris has seen them, he has assured me. He knows where they live and how to find them and many have learned much from Kerris' understanding of dragons, including Jeffery Solomon.

"Well, he says they're real," said Solomon, nose pressed against the Griffen's dirty glass. "And I believe him."

"There are no such things as dragons, Seven," said Damaris Ward from the helijet's console. "Kerris has an active imagination."

"Kerris is a talking lion who controls lightning and trashed the entire CD compound with his mind." Solomon grinned. "That's one hell of an imagination."

She grunted, turning back to her controls and he let his eyes linger for a moment. Long of limb and elegant of profile, Damaris Ward was a security chief, not given to flights of fancy. She was rarely without her goggled cap but now, wisps of dark hair flipped out from beneath it. She hated every lock and would shave it all in a heartbeat if given the chance. So very different than Pilar.

Odd. He hadn't thought of Pilar in ages. A lifetime.

He sighed, turning his attention to the windows.

It had been weeks since they had dropped Kerris and his very pregnant wife off at the Forbidden City of *Bai'Zhin* and since then, they had been piloting the Griffen southward, keeping low to search for any sign of humanity. They had seen *Chi'Chen* fishing boats along the eastern coastline and feline villages scattered across the Vietnam peninsula but once they'd reached the New China Sea, it was like people of any sort had disappeared. Malaysia, the Philippines, Indonesia and New Guinea, all were lush, tropical and empty of civilization. Clearly, the earth had flourished in their absence.

Now along the beaches and rugged shores of eastern Australia, the Griffen soared low over the water, spray rising beneath the helijet's curved wings.

"It's beautiful," said Persis Sengupta. "The way the water moves against the land like that. I've never seen anything like that before."

"The waves," said Solomon.

"Yes, waves," she said and flashed him a tentative smile. She was a beauty herself, with great dark eyes, expressive lips and short hair slicked elegantly off her forehead as it grew in from the pre-flight stubble. She was strapped into her jumpseat, body straining against the belts but hands pushing her back into her chair. Conflicted, Solomon knew. A cultured woman in a raw land. She stared out at the water. "Waves…"

"It's caused by the pull of the moon on the oceans," said Armand Dell in the seat behind her. He wasn't wearing belts and he hadn't taken his eyes off the coastline in hours. "And it's actually eroding the shore with each wave."

"Well if there are dragons in the water," she muttered. "I hope the waves erode them."

"There aren't any dragons," said Ward from the console.

"But Seven is right," said Sengupta. "Kerris wasn't a normal lion."

"Person," said Solomon.

"He wasn't a normal person either," said Solomon. "What if there *are* dragons now?"

"There aren't," said Ward.

"This is a new world," said Dell. "The animals we had in the compound were either natural mutations or genetic manipulations. Who knows what's out here now."

"Not dragons," said Ward.

"Either way, the gene pool's a very different place than when we went under."

"It's beautiful," Sengupta said. "But I hate it. It's too wild."

"Life without people should be wild," said Dell. "It's only people who try to change things to suit themselves."

"I want to go back."

"You should have thought of that before you started talking to the animals," said Ward.

"People," said Solomon. "Not animals."

"I stand corrected."

"I was doing my job," Sengupta grumbled. "It wasn't my fault we found an animal that could talk and it wasn't my fault that I could communicate with it."

"Her," said Solomon.

The linguist raised her chin.

"It certainly wasn't my fault that the grey trashed the compound. We could have still been there if it hadn't trashed the compound. See? Wild."

"Kerris and *he*. But Dell," said Solomon. "How did he do that anyway?"

Dell looked up.

"Who? Kerris?"

"Yeah," and he turned to look at the zoologist. Dell was beginning to grow scruff that might one day be called a beard but he was still young. It might take months for him to grow what Jeffery Solomon could grow overnight. "I mean, animals can't control lightning. People can't control lightning. How is it that you splice a few genes and voila, someone can control lightning?"

"I…" Dell blinked at him.

"And Sireth – the one who saved me – I can still hear him in my head sometimes. You're the zoologist. How can they do that?"

Dell shrugged.

"Maybe they didn't just splice genes," he offered. "Maybe they augmented them."

"But how?"

"The IAR had no controls," said Ward from the pilot's seat. "No regulatory commissions, no governing bodies. I suspect the scientists overseeing each project could pretty much do what they wanted."

Solomon shook his head, looked back out the window.

"Nah," he said. "That doesn't make sense. There's got to be a better answer."

"We may never know, Seven," said Ward.

"Oh look," said Sengupta. "Pelicans."

They all pressed their noses to the glass.

Pelicans, flying low to the water in a perfect V, and they watched these birds that had changed so little even with the wars, the plagues and the mutations. They were familiar, they were natural and to these scientists, they were a comforting sight.

"I'll get closer," said Ward. She angled the stick and the Griffen dipped a wing. It was a quiet, solar-powered Helijet, making little noise and soon, they were alongside the flock. Solomon could almost feel the ocean spray on his face.

"These are nice," said Sengupta. "Pelicans are not terribly wild birds."

"I love to watch their wings," said Dell. "Pure biomechanics in motion."

Solomon grinned again, remembering the time a young tigress drove a Humlander. That, he had to admit, was not so much biomechanics in motion as an accident waiting to happen.

"Is that our shadow?" asked Sengupta and she pointed to a dark shape under the water. It was moving as fast as they were, mirroring the trajectory of the flock.

"I don't think so," said Solomon.

"A whale!" Sengupta shouted. "They still have whales!"

"Then it's all worth it," Dell breathed. "Some of us believed that the whales should have survived, even if we didn't."

The shape grew darker as if rising to the surface. Solomon frowned.

"Damaris…"

"Yuh, I'm going to get some altitude," she said. "I don't want to be knocked out of the sky by a breaching whale."

"Wait, I want to see the whale," said Dell.

"I don't," said Sengupta. "He can stay in the water where he belongs."

Solomon pressed his forehead against the glass as the Griffen began to rise when suddenly, the creature burst upwards with a great spray of water. Ward threw her weight onto the stick and the Helijet banked steeply, sending both men out of their seats to the cabin deck. Solomon scrambled to his feet and through the window caught a glimpse of blue water and grey skin, a huge gaping mouth and rows of dagger teeth. The body of a pelican struck the glass and the Griffen bucked again, before the great creature crashed back to the water and disappeared beneath the waves.

"What the hell was that!" cried Sengupta.

"That was no whale," muttered Ward.

"*Physeter macrocephalus?*" cried Dell. "*Carcharodon carcharias?* Both? Neither? An entirely new species? New Genus? New Family? New Order? I have no clue, *Jian.* It's blown all my training out the door."

Solomon peered at the skies above, the water below.

"So…where are the pelicans?" he asked.

"Where are the pelicans?" repeated Ward.

Only a few feathers floating on the surface.

"It swallowed an entire flock of pelicans," said Solomon. "I can't believe it."

"Don't talk about it," said Sengupta. "I hate this place."

"It was like nothing I've seen in any of the archives," said Dell. "Like a *Physeter macrocephalus* crossed with a *Carcharodon carcharias,* only bigger. Much bigger."

Sengupta stared at him, her dark eyes flashing.

"What are you saying, Dell?"

"*You're* the linguist," grinned Ward from the stick.

"Sperm whale and Great White Shark," Sengupta snorted. "I know the terminology, *Jian.* But one's a mammal and one's a fish. You can't splice those."

"Of course you can't," Dell said. "But you saw that! It's just, well, it's just..."

"It's been a long time," said Ward. "Who knows what else the IAR was playing with?"

"Dragons?" said Solomon with a grin.

"Shut it, Seven."

"Kalgoorlie isn't on the water, right?" asked Sengupta.

"In the middle of the desert."

"Good." And she wrapped her arms around her chest.

"Right," said Ward. "Executive decision. No scanning Sydney or any of the other coastal cities. On to Kalgoorlie."

"On to Kalgoorlie," echoed Solomon.

But the Griffen did fly a little higher after that.

***

to be continued

Books by H. Leighton Dickson

TO JOURNEY IN THE YEAR OF THE TIGER
TO WALK IN THE WAY OF LIONS
SONGS IN THE YEAR OF THE CAT
SWALLOWTAIL & SWORD

Available April 2016
COLD STONE & IVY

June 2016
DRAGON OF ASH & STARS

ABOUT THE AUTHOR

H. Leighton Dickson grew up in the wilds of the Canadian Shield, where her neighbours were wolves, moose, perennial-eating deer and the occasional lynx. She studied Zoology at the University of Guelph and worked in the Edinburgh Zoological Gardens in Scotland, where she was chased by lions, wrestled deaf tigers and fed antibiotics to Polar Bears by baby bottle! She has been writing since she was thirteen, has three dogs, two cats, one horse, three kids and one husband. She has managed to keep all of them alive so far.

Please visit us at http://www.hleightondickson.com
Or on Facebook at:
http://www.facebook.com/HLeightonDickson

Made in the USA
Charleston, SC
24 September 2016